Everything We Lose

A Civil War Novel of Hope, Courage and Redemption

ANNETTE OPPENLANDER

First published by Oppenlander Enterprises LLC, 2018
First Edition
www.annetteoppenlander.com
Text copyright: Annette Oppenlander 2018
ISBN: 978-0-9977800-7-9
Library of Congress Control Number: 2018930268
Design: http://www.fiverr.com/akira007
Editing: Yellow Bird Editors

"The story of the American Civil War is essentially one of human beings—Northerners, Southerners, Blacks, Whites, men, women—holding themselves accountable for the future of a nation."
—Aberjhani, Journey through the Power of the Rainbow: Quotations from a Life Made Out of Poetry

"I never, in my life, felt more certain that I was doing right, than I do in signing this paper [Emancipation Proclamation]. If my name ever goes into history it will be for this act, and my whole soul is in it."
—President Abraham Lincoln

ALSO BY ANNETTE OPPENLANDER

A Different Truth
Escape from the Past: The Duke's Wrath (Book One)
Escape from the Past: The Kid (Book Two)
Escape from the Past: At Witches' End (Book Three)
47 Days: How Two Teen Boys Defied the Third Reich
(Novelette)
Surviving the Fatherland: A True Coming-of-age Love
Story Set in WWII Germany

DEDICATION

To the many who fight daily for survival and basic
human rights.
To those who fight against human injustice and
oppression.

ACKNOWLEDGMENTS

A huge thank you to my husband, Ben, for being my best friend and sounding board. My writing group buddies, Susan and Dave, provided invaluable feedback—so did Sara Kocek from Yellow Bird Editors.

CHAPTER ONE

August 5, 1861

The robin in Adam's hand trembled, its left wing fanned uselessly across his palm.

It's all right," he murmured softly. "Be still."

His mother's voice floated into the barn. "Cows need milking. Don't forget the eggs."

"In a minute." Adam's forefinger slid along the bird's radius, the equivalent of a human's upper arm. A shudder went through the feathered body as the robin made a feeble attempt to inch away.

Fashioning a splint from a wood shaving, Adam realigned the wing, tied a few knots, and placed the robin inside a wooden cage hanging from the rafter and out of reach of the cat. He'd lost patients before and wasn't about to let that happen again. For good measure he caught a cricket and fed it to the bird.

He nodded at the beady eyes watching him attentively. "I'll get you worms later." He always sensed the animals understood him.

"Adam, did you hear me?" His mother sounded equally tired and irritated. "Where are you?"

"Right here, Ma." Adam hurried from the barn. "Found a robin and fixed its wing. I'll get to the cows now."

"You and your animals," his mother said, but he could tell she was pleased by the way her mouth twitched. With a shrug he went to work milking and then feeding the cows, cleaning the chicken coop, and collecting eggs.

The sun stood high and promised another searing day by the time Adam entered the cabin. It was no more than a single square room with a tiny alcove in the back where he slept. Pa had built it ten years ago, each board sawn and notched, each gap filled with a mixture of straw and mud. The fieldstone chimney had taken months to complete.

Adam's stomach lurched with hunger as he placed sixteen eggs and a full milk bucket on the table.

"Wash up," his mother said, placing biscuits and a small chunk of butter on the table. "I'll fix your eggs." It took all his will not to grab the bread and wolf it down. Ma wouldn't approve. Not even now while his father was away.

Swallowing saliva and a groan, Adam hurried back outside. The pump stood in the front yard—if you could call it a yard. Except for the rough-hewn fence, it was nothing but a patch of grassland like the rest of the rolling foothills with the Appalachian Mountains as a backdrop. He kept his lids half closed against the glare and hesitated. He felt pinched today, as if his energy were carried away by the wind. To his left the corn swayed, its leaves so brown and dry, it produced a noisy rustle. Crickets chirped, unperturbed by the gritty air.

With a sigh, he dipped his hands in the pail and cooled his burning forehead. It was early August and he'd soon be roasting like one of the chickens his mother occasionally baked in a clay pot over the fire.

By the time he sat down to eat, he felt lightheaded. His sister, Sara, a year younger than he and already at the table, smirked and pointed a forefinger at his cheek. "You missed a spot."

Ignoring her, Adam filled a bowl with oatmeal when he caught a warning look from his mother. With a sigh he lowered his head. As his mother prayed, his mind drifted to his sister.

Most of the time Sara was all right, but ever since she'd turned fourteen she was acting prissy, washing her hands and face between every single chore, even after doing laundry, and sneaking glimpses in the tiny looking glass above the kitchen sink. Not to mention piling her hair in all sorts of strange ways as if she were one of the fancy ladies in town.

"Amen."

Ma's voice jolted him back to present, and he began to shovel.

"I'm sorry the two of you have to work so much." His mother

tugged a strand of blondish hair behind her ear and attempted a smile. "Pa thought the war would be over quickly. He'll return home soon, hopefully. His ninety-day enlistment should be finished and he promised me."

Sara patted her mother's arm. "Don't fret. It'll be all right."

Adam nodded between mouthfuls of biscuit and egg. It wasn't Ma's fault. Though Pa had only been gone since April, it felt like a year as most of the additional work had fallen on him.

Union soldiers were paid thirteen dollars a month. With the harvest short two years in a row, they'd needed the extra money. Adam didn't really understand the other reason his father had joined. He'd said it was the right thing to do and that President Lincoln knew what was good for the country.

If he was honest, he didn't care one hair's breadth about the reasons. All he wanted was for Pa to return so he could get back to a normal life. At least one that left him a bit of time to hunt and visit his friend, Tip, at the neighboring plantation.

Tip lived a mile and a half down the road on the Billings estate, a thousand times the size of Adam's homestead, sharing one of the shacks in the slave quarter with his mother, Mama Rose. The Billings were famous for their fruit orchards and high-end tobacco plants they grew on hundreds of groomed acres.

He'd met Tip a few years ago at the Greeneville market where Tip had accompanied his mother, the Billings's main cook. Tip's coffee brown eyes had locked with Adam's green ones as Adam stood behind the makeshift table selling eggs and homemade butter. A dimple appeared in Tip's right cheek and his white teeth flashed a smile. There was something curious in Tip's face— something that said, hey, I'm here to learn about the world—that Adam had never seen in other people, let alone slaves.

An easy friendship developed, their visits to each other's homes as frequent as they could manage. In truth, it was mostly Adam going to see Tip, since Tip was rarely allowed to leave the plantation. One of these days, when neither of them had to work, they'd go fishing all day or hunt squirrels. Adam had taught Tip how to shoot a rifle, a secret they kept from both their families.

Adam swallowed the last of the egg and straightened.

"I'm going to the field," he said, turning a reluctant eye away from the fresh bread loaf on the counter.

They were growing corn, wheat and a tiny patch of tobacco.

That was in addition to the vegetable garden his mother tended. They also had a handful of apple trees, now loaded with unripe fruit. Adam could already taste the pies Ma would bake in the fall and winter.

He sighed again, squinting as he stepped into the blazing sun, too hot for this early in the day. The air, dry and filled with the scent of butterfly weed and the honeysuckle hedge his mother had planted along the garden fence, quivered, the sky a bit hazy near the mountaintops.

By the time his mother called for dinner, Adam's body ached, his back a mess of knots and his neck tight with sunburn. He'd plowed a section of turf, chopped wood, and repaired part of the split rail fence surrounding the vegetable garden. Still, there were a hundred more things to do. Making a stop at the barn, he'd pulled a handful of earthworms from his pocket and fed them to the robin, who swallowed them whole.

"I'm going to visit Tip after dinner," he was saying between bites of corn and potato when he heard a horse galloping. They never had guests—Tip was always quiet and barefoot unless snow covered the ground, and their other neighbors were too busy and worn to make the trek.

Sara and Ma had heard it too and rushed to the front door. Adam was faster. He yanked it open, expecting to see his father, Pa's face lined with a rare smile.

The man on the horse wore a uniform, but it wasn't Pa. He looked vaguely familiar, perhaps somebody from Greeneville who'd volunteered for the war just like Pa. Except this one wore the broad-brimmed hat of a cavalry captain.

Yanking the horse's reins and coming to a stop in a dust cloud, he yelled, "Mrs. Brown."

"Mr. Pritchard." Ma's voice trembled. "What brings you out?"

Pritchard's face looked pinched as he dismounted and began to fumble inside his jacket.

"I'm sorry, Mrs. Brown. I wanted to deliver this myself…after all, I've known Vincent for a long time…and with the furlough, I thought…" Clearing his throat he held out a wrinkled letter. "I was coming home anyway."

Adam stared at the stilted script and the words WAR DEPARTMENT on the letterhead, his heart already knowing what his mind refused to acknowledge.

"It happened so fast," Pritchard said. "One minute Vincent was fine, the next he was…we were cut off at the Battle of Bull Run, total carnage. A terrible waste…" Pritchard's voice faltered.

Somewhere in the recesses of Adam's consciousness he heard his sister whimper, but his gaze was on his mother who'd taken the paper, her blue eyes wide as pools.

"Ma?" Adam said, trying to catch a glimpse of the writing. But Ma didn't seem to hear. Her arm with the crumpled letter fell to her side and she stood there swaying, neither crying nor speaking.

"Mrs. Brown, if there's anything I can do…" Pritchard glanced at his horse, clearly wishing to be somewhere else.

At last, his mother found her voice. "That's very kind. We'll be fine." She placed a hand on Adam's forearm, clamping down as if to draw strength from his body. Pritchard had one foot in the stirrup, eager to leave.

"Mr. Pritchard," Adam's mother called with a thin voice. "Where is he…?"

"Near Manassas, Virginia. We made sure he was properly buried." Pritchard tipped his hat and gave his horse the spurs.

"What was he doing in Manassas?" his mother mumbled. Then she sagged to the ground, her fingers sliding off Adam's arm.

"Ma?" Adam said again, his voice foreign and tinny in his ears. With the other he tugged at Ma's arm, but she sat in the dust, staring at the distant mountains, her eyes glazed with unshed tears.

"Come on, Ma, I'll take you inside," Sara sobbed. As their mother slowly rose, Adam took the letter from her hand, his eyes racing across the scribbled lines… to the inevitable.

"…*we regret to inform you that your husband, Vincent Addison Brown, was killed in battle. He died a hero…*"

Pa was dead.

Adam had wanted to continue school, wanted to become a veterinary surgeon. No more. Not that chances had been great before, but now they had died. Like his father.

He wanted to collapse then—to bury his head in the earth, to fill his eyes and ears with the rich soil Pa had loved, to stop thinking and feeling.

But he couldn't. He stood rooted and stiff as the black oak shading the house, his throat strangled with an invisible rope.

CHAPTER TWO

"So sorry about your Pa." Tip leaned on a bale of straw in Adam's barn, his cheeks damp with sweat. He kept shaking his head. Word about Mr. Brown's death had gotten around quickly, and by the next evening he'd raced to Adam's house, afraid what he'd find—and afraid for Adam, his only friend.

Adam remained mute, his eyes seemingly glued to a leather harness he was repairing.

"Supposed to work on Master Billings new porch," Tip continued, his eyes achy from dust and the effort not to cry. "This more important. Mama Rose send her wishes."

Tonight Adam seemed more like a child, small and fragile like Missus Billings, whose middle looked like a wasp's ready to snap in two. He awkwardly patted Adam on the back and glanced around for something to do or say. Nothing came to mind as Adam kept staring into space.

"You all right?" Tip asked after a while, swallowing away the lump in his own throat. His friend's sadness hung around him like a heavy black cloth, making his shoulders sag. He'd always been able to tell when people felt happy or bad. He could sense their mood long before they opened their mouths.

Adam reminded him of his own mama's sorrow. Before Tip was born, his father had been bludgeoned to death by a slave trader in Africa. Mama Rose's eyes carried that same dimness. And as with her, he felt powerless to help. Relief swept through him, followed by shame. Relief he hadn't known what he was missing, ashamed he felt glad about it.

He smashed a fly that had landed on his thigh and fed the robin, his fingertips stinging from the impact. "What you going to do?"

Adam shrugged. "Help Ma, I guess. What else can I do?"

"How you going to manage the farm without your Pa?"

Adam inspected his palms, where calluses and blisters competed. "Work harder and longer."

Tip glanced around the modest barn, the air stifling even now. He'd be happy to have a place like this. It was tiny compared to the Billings's plantation where he'd grown up, but it belonged to Adam's family. He possessed nothing, not even the rags he wore. No, he was nothing but property, a concept he hadn't understood for a long time.

Clearing his throat, he said, "I help when I get away."

"Hah," Adam spat. "Billings will keep you busy forever. He *owns* you."

Adam was right. Jack Billings would never let him and Mama Rose go. He sighed, racking his brain for something good to say, something to distract Adam. "Master says the war is going to get worse."

It was well known the Billings were staunch supporters of the Confederates. Ever since April, when Tennessee had seceded to the south, Jack Billings had praised the South's new president, Jefferson Davis. Each night, the Billings's living room was filled with guests who discussed in no uncertain terms how the South was going to defeat Lincoln.

"Old Billings won't let you join?" Adam kicked up dust with his boot.

Tip chuckled. "Negroes ain't allowed to be soldiers. Don't want to anyway. I have my own farm one day."

"Where I'll fix your horses," Adam said darkly.

"That right." Tip straightened, his chest bulging under the faded bib jeans. He liked to think he'd be free one day, even if Mama Rose said it was foolish and to keep quiet. "I better go before Master find out and get his whip." Suppressing a shudder, Tip made two strides to the barn door. "Come soon. Mama Rose fix you chicken soup. She say it mend things."

Adam nodded, but Tip could tell he wasn't really listening.

Falling into an easy run, Tip headed across the meadow and

woods toward the Billings estate. He'd been born here shortly after his mama had come to America. And though the slave quarters were at best hovels with drafty walls and ramshackle beds, this was his home.

Mama Rose had told him about her village in Africa. She'd been a young girl of twenty, newly married and pregnant when they'd taken her away.

Quit thinking about freedom. It never happen. Most of the slaves he knew at the plantation seemed to accept their fate, so why couldn't he stop thinking about a different life? He'd been born a slave just like they had, and yet he was restless. If he were honest, he didn't understand how Mama Rose could be so resigned. She'd been free and happy in Africa.

He'd be fuming mad. Actually he was fuming mad. If not for himself, then for her. He grimaced. Maybe one day he'd own a house where his mama could live in peace.

His attention returned to the path winding its way through the patch of woods. Just like Adam, he loved the quiet, the rustling of birds and squirrels, and the coolness of the trees. The shadows were long and he knew he was late—later than he'd wanted to be. His stomach hitched with worry as he pushed his legs to go faster. He'd skipped the dinner hour to be with his friend and make it less obvious that he'd left. He was supposed to ask permission, but when Mama Rose had come running into the vegetable garden with the news about Adam's Pa, he'd not thought twice.

At last he slowed down. In the dusk, the lights of the kitchen glowed softly, reminding him that he hadn't eaten. This was his mama's domain where she ruled and created her famous dishes. He was proud of what she'd accomplished and wanted to do just as well.

No, better. He pressed his lips together. For now he'd stay quiet. No point in talking about it with his mama and downright dangerous to mention it anywhere else.

"Where have you been, boy?"

Tip froze. Master Billings had an uncanny way of appearing out of nowhere. Despite his massive frame, he walked silently, reminding Tip of a stalking cat, ready to pounce and devour.

Billings senior twirled his cane, ready to spear a beast. "I was looking for you earlier. About that porch…"

"Yessir," Tip said, bowing low. "I see Adam, just for an hour.

He lost his Pa in the war and—"

"You left without permission? Wilkes said he didn't know where you were."

"Yessir. Sorry, Sir," Tip stammered. "I meant to ask but Adam my friend and…" He cringed, knowing what was going to be next.

"And though you are clearly not allowed to leave the plantation, you left anyway?" Billings came to a stop next to Tip. "Bend over."

His gaze on the kitchen window, Tip crouched low, hurrying to cover his head with his arms and hoping his mama wouldn't glance outside as the walking stick crashed on his shoulder blades.

CHAPTER THREE

Adam worked his body hard, as if he could labor away the pain. Because as soon as he stopped he noticed things. Things that made it impossible to forget. Things like the cabin, or Ma, or the carriage Pa had built. His father's memories were everywhere.

That's when the pain gnawed at him from the inside, sharp teeth that scraped at his heart. In those moments he had to slow down, his breath as ragged as if he'd run a sprint, his back wanting to curl itself under an unbearable load.

The mountains in the distance appeared solid yet uncaring, blurred.

When at last he grew aware of his boots standing in the soil, the wind sending puffs of dry dust to attack his skin, he resumed his chores. He thought of the letter under his mattress, tattered and stained from the hundreds of times he'd read it. Not so long ago he'd dreamed of going to New York, where the first school of veterinary surgery had opened. It had always been a long shot. Now it was impossible. His life was over. He'd always work on the farm, from sun up to sun down until he'd wake up one morning to discover he had turned into an old man, his skin as leathery and shriveled as Mr. Porter's, their neighbor to the west.

Dinner was silent. Adam's mother had baked a mince pie from the nuts they'd collected last fall, a treat he'd always loved and associated with special days. But a heavy stillness that neither of them had the strength to break descended like a smothering curtain as soon as they sat down. Ma struggled to keep the farm going, and the blue of her eyes was dull as if all the energy had drained out of her. Sara's formerly fancied-up hair hung in wild tangles, covering her tear-reddened cheeks. Adam rushed outside as soon as he swallowed the last bite.

Tip was harvesting lettuce when Adam arrived at the Billings plantation. In the distance, the main house rose two stories tall. White columns shaded the enormous front porch, where, on nice days, Mrs. Janet Billings and her assorted female guests sat fanning themselves and sipping lemonade. Adam had never been inside the main house. Tip spoke of plush carpets the size of Adam's vegetable garden, chestnut furniture oiled to perfection, and a dining table that easily seated fifty people.

"See Mama Rose." Tip wiped the rich soil from his fingers. "Take these with you. I be there soon." He held up a basket of salad greens, onions and tomatoes.

Adam headed for the kitchen, a room jutting out from the back of the main house where Tip's mother reigned.

Mama Rose looked up from the half dozen pots bubbling on the double stove and smiled. "Adam, my boy."

Adam always marveled how a voice could be like sweet molasses, but that was exactly how it sounded to him. Next thing he knew he was swallowed by a huge bosom as Tip's mother hugged him tight—suffocating was more like it. Before he could utter a word, she released him and gripped his shoulders, her eyes studying him.

She was short, nearly as wide as tall and her red-and-yellow-checkered dress billowed around her. But being short didn't stop her from running a tight household. Except now she was all soft and yielding. "How you doing?"

Adam swallowed and nodded, unable to pull away his gaze. She was looking right at his soul, a cesspool of anger and grief.

She shook her head. "Tsk, tsk. It will pass," she said quietly. "You find your way. I see it in your face."

Adam blinked. All he saw was a lousy life shoveling dung.

"Eat some of my pie. Tipper pick blackberries this morning." Mama Rose turned to her ovens where half a dozen baking tins were cooling. "Tell me how you like it." She handed him a humungous piece on a wooden board.

Adam nodded, his throat too dry to talk, yet his mouth watering from the rich fruit aroma. He knew that Tip's mother had worked her way from a common slave to a house girl, then kitchen assistant and later main cook. After memorizing every recipe, she'd invented many new ones.

He carried his pie to the table and slumped on the bench.

"Good," he managed after a bit.

Mama Rose set a mug of milk in front of him. Skirts swishing, she returned to her stove to stir a pot. "How is your Ma?"

"She cries a lot at night," Adam said between bites. The butter crust was melting on his tongue, the blackberries juicy explosions.

"A dreadful fate for a woman." Mama Rose gripped the wooden ladle tighter. "A shame."

Adam remained mute. Ma would be alone for the rest of her life and no amount of pie would remove the bitterness from his mouth.

Three young servant girls appeared, dressed in black skirts, white blouses and aprons. They looked as fresh as if they'd stepped from a cool pond despite the fact it had to be a hundred degrees in the kitchen. Even their caps were the spotless white of cream puffs. Tip's mother gave orders, and one-by-one the pies disappeared toward the Billings's dining room.

"Where is that boy?" Mama Rose cast a worried look toward the back door.

Adam noticed a frown between Tip's mother's eyebrows. It was the only wrinkle on her face, so unlike his own Ma's gaunt features. "He said he'd be right in."

"Better go find him," she said. "I have to do something with this mess." She nodded at the vegetables and a half side of butchered sheep hanging from a ceiling hook. "Guests tonight. Master want a second meal at midnight."

Shaking his head, Adam hurried outside. How could these people eat all the time? But more importantly, how could Tip's mother work nearly around the clock fixing a hundred dishes a day?

Adam was just about to yell a playful insult at Tip when he noticed his friend standing rigid at the edge of the salad patch, a shadow looming over him.

"You are a big boy." Nathan Billings's voice was venomous. By the way he slurred Adam knew he was drunk. "Flex your arms."

"Mr. Billings, please." Tip stepped backwards to put distance between him and the Billings's only son.

"Please what?" Nathan said. "It's Master Billings to you. And as your master I order you to show me your muscles."

Tip looked down, and Adam knew he was trying to hide his anger. He could've easily squashed Nathan Billings, who was short and blond and so unlike his dark-featured father that people whispered he wasn't a Billings at all. Even in the late sunlight he looked pale, as if color had a hard time sticking to him.

His face glistening with sweat, Tip lifted one arm and flexed his bicep.

"Aw, look at that. Where do they find people like you, boy? You look like you escaped from hell, all black and burned."

Adam held his breath, but Tip just stood silently, his eyes downcast.

Nathan scrutinized Tip's chest, his lips curled into a sardonic smile. "I think they got you from the bottom of the earth."

Tip didn't move.

Adam hurried forward. "Mama Rose needs your help, Tip," he shouted.

Without a word, Nathan Billings stalked off down the path. Adam noticed how a shiver of relief ran through Tip.

"Next time, I'll have a whip," Nathan yelled from the edge of the garden. Ignoring Adam, he marched toward the main house.

Adam rushed over as Tip silently grabbed his produce basket. "What was that all about?"

Tip shrugged. "Young Master drink."

"He's harassing you for no reason. Have you told Mama Rose?"

"She got enough worries. Besides, she can't do nothing about it."

They'd reached the backdoor to the kitchen. Tip's eyes met Adam's. They said to keep quiet—they said *I'll deal with it*.

How, Adam wanted to ask as Mama Rose yanked open the door. "What is taking you so long, Tipper?"

"Nothing. I wash now and go with Adam for a bit." Tip hurried back outside.

"What has gotten into that boy?" Mama Rose mumbled. But then her eyes wandered to the newly arrived piles of leeks and potatoes and she bustled off to organize her helpers and cook another meal.

Adam scurried after Tip, who seemed to want to drown

himself under the pump. Water splashed as a puddle formed beneath his feet.

"Easy, Tip," Adam said quietly. "How long has this been going on?"

Tip, finally satisfied with his bath, wiped himself off. "What?"

"You know, Nathan picking on you?"

At first it seemed Tip was going to dismiss Adam's question, but then he shrugged. "It start when he come home from school last summer. Now that he eighteen he drink all the time. His father busy buying up land and his mama worship him. So he chase the young misses and come after me for entertainment."

"Has he...hit you?"

"A couple of times when old Master away."

Absentmindedly, Adam held a hand under the dribbling pump. "You need to tell somebody."

"Who I tell?" Tip's voice was thick with frustration. "I just wish Master send me to help with the war. I don't care. I rather dig trenches than stay here."

"You may get your wish. I heard President Lincoln has asked for 500,000 volunteers. If the north grows their military, the south will follow."

"I don't understand what it all mean," Tip said. "Your Pa, he fought for the Union. And Master here and all the other rich families are for the south."

"All I know is that Lincoln wants to abolish slavery. And the south, like the Billings, loves slaves." Adam squinted against the setting sun, which tinted everything orange. "Let's walk down to the creek. It's cooler there."

"Can't imagine Master ever letting me go free."

Adam shrugged. It was about as hard to imagine as half a million men fighting in the war.

"You going to join like your Pa?" Tip asked as they settled next to the water, a tributary of the Nolichucky River that drained the Blue Ridge Mountains of eastern Tennessee.

Adam unlaced his boots and dunked his toes in the water. "Not planning on it. They took Pa's life. Ma received a letter from the government with fifty-two dollars. That's all that Pa was worth to them." Fresh anger seized him and he spit into the water nearly black in the vanishing light. "Besides, Ma needs me to work the fields."

Tip waded into the shallows to harvest cattails. "Maybe you get a few slaves to help on the farm."

Adam fervently shook his head. "A good slave costs hundreds of dollars. Besides, Pa always was against it."

"Against what?" Tip said.

"Keeping slaves. Pa said it was immoral."

"You be good Master." Tip began to nibble the stalk of a cattail. "Want some? Taste like corn."

Adam shook his head. For a moment only the trickling of the creek could be heard. Somewhere above them a bird settled in to roost.

"How can a person own another?" Adam said.

"It's the way things are."

"How can you be so accepting after what Nathan just did?" New fury tightened Adam's throat. "He's an arrogant bastard."

Tip shrugged.

"Come on," Adam said, "I saw you were stinking mad. You said you'll be free one day and own your own farm."

"I want to," Tip said simply. He spit the remains of the cattail into the water. "You know it impossible. Master never let me go. I still be here when I'm an old Negro like Jonas."

Nearly sixty-five years of age, Jonas was the oldest Billings slave. He'd been on the same ship as Mama Rose and quickly worn out with hard labor. Now all he could do was keep the two-dozen fireplaces stocked and run simple errands. On the side he arranged bouquets of flowers in such a way that every visitor took time to admire them.

"Nonsense," Adam said. "Things will get better." *You don't believe it yourself. Why would Tip?*

It was late by the time Adam returned home. To his surprise, a light shone in the window.

"Guess what?" Sara said as soon as he entered the cabin. She was in her nightdress, her long blonde hair tied into a thick braid.

"What?" In no mood for conversation, Adam stalked toward his alcove.

"There is a dance in town next weekend. Allister has asked me to go with him."

"So what." Adam yanked his sweat-soaked shirt over his head. All he wanted to do was sleep. It was almost midnight, and he knew he'd pay for it tomorrow.

Sara hurried to his side, her voice low and humming with excitement. "I think he wants to marry me."

"You're just a baby. Go to bed," Adam hissed, suddenly aware that he didn't want to take his pants off in front of his sister.

"You're such a bore." Sara's voice rose as it always did when she was angry.

To his relief she blew out the candle and climbed into bed next to their mother who was lying motionless.

Most nights when Adam lay awake and wondered if she was still breathing, he'd wanted to get up and check. But he never did, himself unable to move in the constant knowledge that Pa would never return.

CHAPTER FOUR

Tip crawled into bed, which consisted of a corn shucks mattress that rustled with every move and a quilt his mother had stitched together from scraps of cotton. It was soft and smelled a little like her. He'd waited until Mama Rose was asleep before coming inside—not only to keep her from seeing his raw shoulder blades, but because he needed to think.

Adam was right. Young Master Nathan was getting worse by the day. He was used to regular beatings and had learned how rage showed in a man's eyes, how the pupils shrank and the skin around the cheekbones retracted. It was different with Nathan. There was something cold and sick about it, like some monster was ready to burst from his soul. He wanted blood for the fun of it.

Unable to find a comfortable position, Tip rolled on his side. The skin on his back had broken apart, the old scars seeping and sticking to his shirt. Next time would be worse. And the time after that...

What could he do? He was trapped—a slave with no rights. Always working, always afraid, nothing but property to be treated like dirt. He also had to look out for Mama Rose. He'd break her heart if he tried to escape. And there was Elda, the girl he loved, a young housemaid, no older than fourteen. He'd managed to walk with her a few times on Sundays, her smile shy, her eyes so dark and her lashes so long, he wanted to spend all day looking at them.

What he really wanted was to go north where Negroes were rumored to be freemen. A preacher had stopped by in May, telling

17

them about the northern states where he could volunteer for the war or work in a factory, make something of himself.

A ragged sigh escaped him. He'd never do it.

"Get up, Tipper." Mama Rose's voice was soft yet firm. "Time to pick peaches. Young Master ask for peaches with his grits."

Tip squinted to keep out the light though it was hardly necessary. Dawn was breaking, the candle just bright enough to light the wobbly table. Remembering his back, he quickly changed his shirt and hurried to the pump.

His stomach growled by the time he headed to the kitchen, a bushel of peaches, skin fuzzy and soft, under one arm. He'd wolfed one down earlier before Wilkes, the overseer, a small man with cruel eyes got out watching their every move.

Now Tip was ravenous. He hoped Mama Rose had oats or grits ready. He was supposed to eat with the other slaves in the slave quarter cookhouse, but if the kitchen was empty, his mother usually let him eat at the corner table near the backdoor.

When he was little, she had cooked often for the other slaves in the quarters. She'd made porridge from couscous, the traditional breakfast she'd grown up with. Now she had time only for Master's family and their never-ending stream of visitors.

"...it better be done by the time our guests arrive," Jack Billings said as Tip opened the backdoor.

"Yessir." Mama Rose attempted a curtsy. "All be ready."

Tip bit his lip. Everyone knew his mother was the best cook in Greeneville, making meals at the Billings's plantation a sought-after event. Why was Master pushing her to do more all the time? He worried about her, especially lately. Even the smallest walks wore her out, her breath labored, her face damp with sweat.

"Peaches." He abruptly plunked the basket on the table, hoping Master would leave—especially since the air was rich with the flavor of porridge and brown sugar.

Jack Billings's thumb rubbed across the silver horse head adorning his walking stick. "Ready to work on the porch, boy?"

"Yessir." Tip bowed his head, swallowing saliva and a nasty comment. There wouldn't be any porridge for him this morning. Instead he trembled, despising himself for the fear that had crept into his heart. It was always this way—the anger, the frustration of having to follow orders, the certainty of punishment at the slightest mishap.

"Come with me."

Tip nodded at his mother, his mouth dry. Why hadn't he stopped by the pump before coming inside?

The stack of milled boards next to the barn seemed a mile high, each log sawn square and twelve feet long.

"You can manage, I'm sure," Billings said before turning toward the main house. Tip stared after him for a moment as his stomach clenched with a mixture of hunger and fury. But then he noticed Wilkes cross the path, fingertips drumming the handle of the whip on his belt.

Taking hold of a log, Tip bit back a groan. His shoulders screamed from the weight on his bruised skin. Forcing his legs forward, he strode toward the mansion.

By evening, he was soaked in sweat. He'd lugged most of the lumber to the construction site. Numb with pain he was so tired, he barely had energy to eat, let alone think about plans for a new life far away from the Billings.

CHAPTER FIVE

When Adam entered the cabin the following Saturday afternoon, Sara was standing on a chair as Ma adjusted the seams of a cream-colored gown, Adam had never seen.

"I loved this dress...wore it the first night your daddy took me out." Ma tugged at the lace as if she'd heard Adam's silent question. "You'll look beautiful." She smiled at Sara, her eyes shiny.

Adam ignored both women and began to rummage for a piece of bread. Unable to find any, he picked up a cucumber and took a bite. The women whispered, his sister striking poses while Ma worked on Sara's hair. With a disgusted look at both of them, Adam headed for the door.

"You better go along tonight," Ma called after him.

Adam's hand with the half-eaten cucumber froze in midair. He couldn't believe his ears. "What do you mean?"

"I mean it will do you good to socialize with young people for a change." Ma attempted a smile and he noticed new lines around her eyes and mouth.

"I don't care to jump around like a dandy."

"That won't happen if you try," Sara said with an appraising look. To her mother she added, "I don't see why Adam has to go. Allister is perfectly capable of watching over me."

"That's what I'm afraid of," their mother said.

"So I'm the chaperone?" Adam inspected his grimy fingernails. "You heard Sara. Allister is the perfect gentleman."

"You'll go with them, Adam." Ma's mouth was set, and Adam

knew arguing would be fruitless.

"Hurry up then," Sara yelled as he slammed the door behind him.

Allister Porter arrived with a wagon. He looked like an idiot, Adam thought, his auburn hair tamed by loads of pomade, probably stolen from his grandfather, old Dallas Porter. His face was covered in freckles so numerous he looked blotchy. What did Sara see in him anyway?

Allister couldn't quite hide his disappointment when Adam mounted his horse to follow them into town. Adam had put on his Sunday pants, the only spare pair he owned. To top it off, his mother had given him one of Pa's shirts, blue and white cotton. It wasn't as big on him as he'd expected. His body was making odd changes, his shoulders now as broad as his father's while his waist remained small. In addition to the ridiculous dress-up he wore his favorite hat, a brownish-gray felt contraption that blended in perfectly with the wheat and oat fields they traveled through.

Sara was ignoring him. So was Allister. Once in a while she giggled, and Adam noticed with disgust how Allister kept touching his sister's shoulders and forearms. Of course, he made it look like it was accidental, but Adam knew better. He wanted to smack the lecherous sap in the nose. Marrying Sara. Hah! What would Pa say? Surely, he'd never approve of the sod. Which meant it now fell to him, Adam, to keep an eye on the silly girl.

Adam loitered near the entrance to the Greeneville dancehall when Sara showed up and sagged on a bench.

"It sure is nice to catch the breeze," she said, fanning her reddened cheeks. "The air inside is just too stuffy." Adam made a face, ignoring the soft sounds of fiddles and guitars that drifted through the open windows.

The clip clop of a horse approached. Adam rolled his eyes as Nathan Billings tipped his hat.

"Now, Miss Sara, don't you look mighty pretty?" From the top of his stallion he looked almost normal, had there not been the watery blue eyes glued to Sara's face. Pale as ever he wore an evening suit with an embroidered vest and calf-leather riding boots that probably cost more than Adam's family earned in a year.

Even Adam had to admit Sara looked a hundred times prettier

than any of the girls inside. No matter that some of them wore fancy gowns, Sara's thick blonde hair and smooth skin, not to mention her striking blue eyes set off by a matching satin ribbon, were hard to forget.

Sara nodded, throwing nervous glances toward the door where Allister had disappeared earlier to get punch. Adam, bored yet irritated with watching the halfwits inside dance themselves into a frenzy, stepped next to Sara.

"Isn't it a bit below your standards to show up at a farmer's dance?" he said coolly, looking up at Nathan.

Nathan's mouth quivered the slightest bit before he resumed his smile. "What business is it of yours?"

"It is my business. Sara is my sister, so you better stay away?"

"Adam, please." Sara placed a hand on Adam's forearm. "Don't…"

"Don't what?"

"I'm sure Mr. Billings has no ill intentions."

The smile on Nathan's face deepened. "That's right, Miss Sara. I'm only admiring your beauty as any gentleman would."

"You've admired enough, so get going," Adam huffed. *You're no gentleman*, he thought squinting back at Nathan. "I'm sure there are plenty of rich ladies you can visit."

"You should teach your brother some manners." Nathan tipped his hat a second time. "I wish you a pleasant evening." He kicked his horse so hard that it jumped, its front hooves nearly striking Adam in the chest.

"Why do you have to be such a nasty?" Sara cried as soon as Nathan had disappeared. She furiously fanned her face. "Mr. Billings was perfectly polite."

"Right." Adam pulled off his hat and scratched his forehead. He wasn't about to share Tip's plight or the rumor that one of the Billings's house slaves was pregnant with Nathan's child.

Just then Allister appeared with two glasses.

"They had to make more punch with so many people," he said, oblivious to the tension between brother and sister.

Sara shot him a crooked smile and took his elbow. "Let's go inside and dance some more."

"Oh, absolutely," Allister hurried, though Adam was sure he'd hoped for a walk in the dark street for some private time.

"Make it quick," Adam called after them. "It's time to go

soon."

With a sigh, he ambled off down the wooden sidewalk. Sitting here and watching the merriment of Greeneville's youth was almost too much to bear. All along Main Street Confederate flags dangled above walkways and shop entrances. Many businesses had posters in the window.

FREEMEN!
Of
TENNESSEE!

The Yankee War is now being waged for "beauty and booty." They have driven us from them, and now say OUR TRADE they must and will have. To excite their hired and ruffian soldiers, they promise them our lands and tell them our women are beautiful...that beauty is the reward of the brave. Tennesseans! Your country calls! Shall we wait until our homes are laid desolate; until sword and rape shall have visited them?

NEVER! Then

TO ARMS!

And let us meet the enemy on the borders. Who so vile, so craven as not to strike for his native land?

The undersigned propose to immediately raise as infantry company to be offered to the Governor as part of the defense of the State and of the Confederate States. All those who desire to join with us in serving our common country, will report themselves immediately.

J.B. Murray.
H.C. Witt

May 17th, 1861

Neal and Roberts, Printers, Morristown, Tenn.

How had his father decided to fight for the north when most of the town was pro south? What difference did it make anyway?

Even if tomorrow was Sunday, in the morning he'd go back to farm work and that would be all he'd do.

.

CHAPTER SIX

Adam was inspecting a sore on their only hog, a two-hundred pound boar Sara had named Fred, when he heard horse hooves. Fred was supposed to have been butchered months ago, but none of them could muster the strength to do it. Fred had been in the family for years.

"Looks like we're having visitors," he mumbled as he smeared a paste of ground sage on the hog's hindquarter.

Straightening his aching back, he walked outside where a dust cloud grew steadily larger. He craned his neck back toward the house and called, "Ma, come quick!"

By the time, the two riders stopped at the gate, Sara and Ma were by his side.

"Mr. Billings, to what do I owe the honor of your visit?" Ma said with a cool smile.

Adam admired her self-control.

"Mrs. Brown, I wanted to tell you in person how sorry I am for your loss." Billings senior bowed from his saddle. But Adam's gaze was drawn to his son, Nathan, who wore a ruffled white shirt with a leather vest. To Adam he looked pompous and girlish. Nathan's pale eyes, shaded beneath a broad-brimmed black hat, were on Sara.

"Thank you," his mother said.

"It must be difficult for you." Jack Billings's voice dripped with concern. "Taking care of a farm without your...Vincent...with just your children."

24

"What's that supposed to mean?" Adam huffed, but Ma put a calming hand on his shoulder.

"We manage," Ma said.

"I wonder if we could talk for a minute." Without waiting for a reply, the old Billings dismounted and moved toward Adam's mother.

"Of course," she hurried, "will you come in for refreshment?"

Adam was going to follow, but as their eyes met, Ma shook her head. Biting back a comment, Adam decided to visit the vegetable garden in the back of the house where a window was always open during the summer to allow for a breeze.

Before he made it into the garden, he noticed Nathan taking Sara's elbow and leading her away from the house. Adam wanted to smack away his possessive hand, but the draw of the secret conversation was stronger.

"...I can only imagine how you must struggle," Billings senior said as Adam crouched beneath the window.

"We manage just fine," his mother said again.

"Mrs. Brown, wouldn't it be easier and safer...with the war and all...if you moved into town?"

He heard his mother clear her throat before answering, "Sure, but what would I do? My children are nearly grown and—"

"That's exactly why I'm here," the old Billings said. "I'd like to make you an offer for your land."

"Why would you want to buy my land?"

Billings's low chuckle filled the air as if Adam's mother were too stupid to see the obvious. "It isn't anything special, but if I can help a poor widow and in exchange raise a few more head of cattle..."

"Well, it is special to us. I'm certain Vincent wouldn't want us to sell," Adam's mother said.

"All I'm asking is for you to think about it, Mrs. Brown. Just imagine," Billings's voice grew quieter and Adam squeezed closer to the window, "you'll be free from all the hardship of working through bad harvests and cruel weather. You can live in town close to other people and the conveniences of refinement."

"What would I live on?"

"Ah, that."

Adam sensed that Billings had waited for this... his bait reeling in the prize.

25

"Let's see, how many acres do you own?"

"Around two-hundred."

"Which are worth, what? Seven or eight dollars an acre? I'd be willing to give you ten. With two-thousand dollars you can do a lot, Mrs. Brown. Just to help you out."

Adam wanted to jump through the window and take the man by the throat. What were they supposed to do without land? Pa had been so proud of their farm.

He raced around the house, but by the time he arrived at the door, Ma pushed it open from the inside, followed by Jack Billings.

"Where's Nathan?" the old Billings asked, heading toward the two lone horses tied to the post.

Ma's eyes flashed at Adam. "And your sister?"

Adam shrugged and, turning away from Ma's thunderous expression, broke into a run. "Sara?" he called.

The barn was empty.

He continued to the cowshed, then the chicken coop. Neither Sara nor Nathan were anywhere in sight. A feeling of unease crept up his spine. He'd seen Nathan stare at Sara. Even a blind man understood what that look meant.

Adam's cheeks grew hot as visions of Nathan Billings pushing himself on a helpless Sara unfolded. He was a farm kid and no idiot. He'd once kissed a girl on the cheek, but Nathan Billings wouldn't mess with a harmless kiss. He'd go for Sara's virtue.

With a pang, Adam remembered the pond a quarter mile away. Spring fed, it offered fresh water even during the hottest summers. A ring of willows offered shade. It had been one of the reasons his father had chosen the land. No other farm in the area had a spring and when the creeks ran low in the summer, many couldn't water their crops.

In the distance, his mother was calling Sara's name. Even from here he heard the irritation and worry in her voice. He sprinted over the low-rising hill. From here the land fell slightly toward the pond.

Sure enough, he could make out Nathan's hat and Sara's blonde braid as they circled around the water's edge.

"Sara, what are you doing?" he yelled catching up to them. He knew he was red-faced and probably looked like a fool, but he had trouble breathing from the fury constricting his chest.

"Walking," Sara said dryly. "What is it to you?"

"Ma wants you," Adam said, ignoring Nathan's insolent stare.

"It sure was a pleasure, Miss Sara," Nathan said, reclaiming Sara's arm for the walk uphill.

Adam marched behind them, suppressing the urge to kick Nathan in his fancy riding breeches.

As soon as their guests had ridden off, he wheeled around to face his mother, who was dusting off the back of Sara's wrinkled shirt. "Why would Billings want to buy our land?"

"I see that *private conversation* means nothing to you," Ma said.

"Sorry, but I—"

"What are you talking about?" Sara asked, wriggling away from Ma and sitting down at the rough-hewn kitchen table, where two coffee mugs still stood. Billings senior had not touched his.

"He says our land is not worth much, that I'd be happier and safer in town."

"What are we supposed to do there?" Adam shouted. *What about Sara and me,* he wanted to add.

"Lower your voice," Ma said. "I didn't say I was going to agree. I may be a widow, but that doesn't mean I can't think for myself."

"What are you going to do then?" Adam said.

His mother smiled. "Absolutely nothing. We'll continue as before. Mr. Billings can find his land somewhere else."

A slow grin spread across Adam's face. To his surprise, Sara's eyes filled with tears..

"Mr. Billings will be mad," she said. "He may hurt you."

"So what?" Adam said, jumping from his chair. "Let him come back. I'll tell him what I think of him." For emphasis he punched the air.

Sara's cheeks glowed pink. "Please don't."

Adam spun around to face his sister. "Just promise me to stay away from Nathan Billings. Even Allister is better than that creep."

"Why do you always pick on me?" Sara cried and stormed outside.

"Leave her be," his mother said. "I'll talk to her later. Ever since your father died..." She sighed. "Better pick us some beans for dinner."

"Yes, Ma," Adam grumbled as he headed into the garden.

Adam dreamed his father had returned. A hammer in his right

hand, he kept pounding at the walls of the barn. Stop that, Adam yelled, but his father continued beating the wood. Slowly, he drifted into consciousness.

Somebody was knocking at the tiny window above his bed.

Adam jumped on top of his straw mattress to peek outside. "Who is it?"

"Tip. Can you come outside?" Tip's voice sounded muffled, as if he were speaking through cloth.

Adam sprinted to the front door, yanked it open, and almost collided with his friend. "What time is it?"

"Don't know."

"What happened?"

"Master Nathan hit me again. Bad this time."

"I'll get the lamp. Meet me in the barn."

As Tip stumbled off, Adam went back inside to grab their largest oil lamp. Ma would be mad because it was made of crystal, a gift from Pa for her birthday, but he didn't care. He needed to see what was wrong with Tip.

Tip sat leaning against a straw bale. Adam cringed when he raised the light. Tip's face glistened with blood. One eye was swollen shut, his upper lip split. There were bruises on his right cheek and welts on his bare shoulders.

"We better call a doctor."

"No doctor," Tip stammered. "You help me. I seen you with the animals."

"But you may be busted up inside." Adam moved the lamp above Tip's head to investigate a gouge in the skull. "Your shoulders look like raw meat."

"I almost fight back," Tip said. "But if I had, they hang me. Despite what young Master do to me."

Adam swallowed bile as he thought about what to do. Blood had never bothered him, but what if Tip died just because they didn't get the doctor? He'd heard of head injuries that showed much later. What if Tip blacked out, never to wake up again?

"Did you tell Mama Rose?" he asked, trying to hide his shock.

"Not Mama Rose. She worry as it is." Tip shivered and slumped sideways.

Adam carefully draped a horse blanket across Tip's legs and rushed to the house. He'd have to wake his mother. There was no way he could do this alone and in the dark.

"Ma?"

"I'm awake. What is it?"

"Tip's all broken up. Nathan Billings beat him."

"Stoke the fire. I'll be there soon."

They spread a sheet on top of clean straw and placed Tip on top. For the next two hours they worked on him. Ma instructed Adam to boil water and fetch her stash of lavender and rosemary. Together, they washed Tip's sores and bandaged them with strips of an old cotton underskirt. They fed him a brew of tea laced with the last of Pa's whiskey. To the best of Adam's knowledge, Tip didn't have any broken bones, but the head injury could be severe. If he made it through the night, he wouldn't be able to work for days if not weeks.

After his mother went back to bed, Adam remained by Tip's side, watching his still form and listening to his labored breath. No way he'd sleep now. What if Tip died? He had to decide what to do. In an hour or two Mama Rose would be up, looking for her only son. She'd go crazy if she couldn't find him. He had to go and tell her.

Fighting his mounting fatigue, Adam hurried to the Billings estate. In the east, the first light of dawn crawled across the horizon. His mind whirled, thinking about how best to tell Mama Rose about the injuries evil Nathan Billings had bestowed on Tip.

As he expected, Tip's mother was already in the kitchen. The aroma of coffee and grits filled the air and Adam realized that he was starving.

The spoon in Mama Rose's hand halted in midair. "You hurt," she cried.

"Not me," Adam stammered, realizing that his shirt was covered with Tip's blood. "Tip came to us last night. He's injured."

The wooden spoon plopped into the kettle as Mama Rose moved toward Adam.

"What happen? Tell me!"

"Nathan got him with the whip. I did the best I could, but he's terribly sore."

"My boy," Mama Rose said, her soft voice filled with such sadness that Adam wanted to hug her. "Now I understand what been biting him. I wish he come to me." She placed a forefinger on her layered chin. Then she turned and shouted orders at the two sleepy girls who were placing dishes on a tray.

To his surprise, she grabbed her shawl. "Let's go." And after an appraising look at Adam's middle, she quickly grabbed four freshly baked rolls and a pastry sprinkled with walnuts and stuffed them in Adam's hands. "Boys need to eat."

All morning, Mama Rose fussed over her son as he dozed in and out of pain-induced sleep.

Sleep was a great healer, Adam's mother said when she brought tea and biscuits into the barn. Adam reluctantly resumed his duties in the fields and with the animals, but stole back several times.

By early afternoon, the barn felt as hot as a coal stove and Tip's face was shiny with sweat. Despite the heat he shivered, his eyes rolling as he mumbled in his sleep.

When Adam snuck inside, he found Ma embracing Mama Rose.

"Don't you worry." Ma grabbed Mama Rose's hands. "We'll stay with him. He's strong and will heal."

Mama Rose straightened with a sigh, her dress wrinkled and dusty from the straw bale she'd rested on. "I better return to my kitchen. Thank you for taking care of my boy. He all I have." A single tear rolled down her cheek. "I come back as soon as I can, once I speak with Master."

She bowed her head and slowly ambled outside.

Adam spent the night next to Tip in the straw.

Mama Rose didn't return the following morning. Tip was awake, eating fried eggs and a precious strip of bacon. His left eye was still shut, but his wounds were crusting over. Adam, who had changed the bandages, had instructed Tip to keep away any flies that wanted to land on the open sores.

By evening there was still no sign of Mama Rose. Adam was contemplating whether he should run over to report on Tip's progress when he heard horses. By the thunder of hooves, it was a large group. He shot up from his resting spot on a pile of straw and rushed outside. Ma hurried to his side, Sara in tow. He watched his mother set her jaw, that gesture setting off warning bells.

Sara took his hand. "What do the Billings want now?"

Before Adam could express satisfaction that Sara had obviously changed her mind about Nathan, a glint of metal caught his attention.

The riders, who had already passed the gate and halted near the cabin in a cloud of dust, carried rifles now pointed at him, Ma and his sister.

"You're harboring a run-away slave." Jack Billings's former smile had been replaced with cool detachment. "As you know, this is a grave crime. I've brought witnesses and the sheriff."

Adam gasped as something cold gripped his insides.

"Mr. Billings, we're harboring no slaves," Ma said in a calm voice. "Just the opposite, Tip was beaten within an inch of his life by your son." She squinted at Nathan Billings, whose horse was next to his father's. "Had we not helped him, he could've died, which would've surely been a huge loss to you."

Billings senior shook his head. "You should've sent for me, Mrs. Brown."

Adam watched him closely. He was enjoying himself, his jaw relaxed, his dark eyes bright with excitement. It made Adam's stomach turn. Next to him, Nathan smirked as if what he'd done had no more significance than squashing a gnat.

"Why, we were too busy keeping *your property* alive." His mother's voice was sharp. Adam felt intensely proud of her.

"Mrs. Brown, we're here to pick up the runaway." Sheriff Tate's voice boomed across the still sweltering front yard. He was a portly man with a grayish beard and matching side burns, his eyes rheumy from too much food and drink. "Will you tell us where he is?"

Adam's gaze met his mother's. She nodded. "In the barn. He's quite weak."

Four men, including Wilkes and two other overseers with whips on their belts, headed into the barn, emerging seconds later with Tip between them. They'd tied a rope around his hands in back, shoving and kicking him toward the waiting group.

"Boy," Billings Senior yelled, "next time you won't be so lucky. We'll hang you on the spot."

"Master Billings," Tip mumbled. But then he lowered his head.

A whip cracked and sliced across Tip's back, nearly sending him to the ground. Wilkes grinned. The whip sang again. By the third time, Tip sagged to his knees, only to be dragged to a cart with a low wooden bed.

Adam wanted to scream at Jack Billings and Nathan, their faces as indifferent as if they were sipping cups of tea. They were ready to kill just to make a point. He tried to get Tip's attention and assure him somehow that things would be okay. Their eyes met for the briefest moment. Had he imagined Tip giving the tiniest nod?

"Mrs. Brown, you shall hear from me soon," the old Billings said. "I've already spoken with Judge Dowell."

Adam noticed how a shiver ran through Ma's body. "I'm not afraid to explain our actions," she said, her voice strong as ever.

But as soon as they were inside the cabin, she sank on the bench by the fireplace.

Sara placed a protective arm around her mother. "What is he going to do, Ma?"

"I don't know. I'm afraid he won't let it go."

"But we did nothing wrong," Adam said. "Tip could've died." His stomach twisted. *Still could.*

Ma shook her head. "It doesn't matter. Tip is a slave and therefore the property of the Billings. If they want to beat him, they can. If they want to kill him, they can. To them he's nothing but property, not a human being."

"Blazing idiots," Adam yelled. He wrenched open the door and ran outside, mumbling curses into the direction the Billings had left.

The moon, nearly full, looked cool and distant, casting deep shadows across the land.

CHAPTER SEVEN

The wagon rumbled along the trail, each turn of the wheels sending darts of pain through Tip's spine. His head wound throbbed. A crust covered his cheek, his right eye large as a goose egg and too swollen to open. Despite getting plenty of water at Adam's house, his throat burned with thirst.

The men on horseback spoke quietly, sometimes laughing and whistling as if all this were great entertainment. How he hated them. He ground his teeth to keep himself from shaking. He pulled up his knees, but the unyielding wooden sideboard dug into his hips and shoulder blades. The pain kept him in check, kept him from throwing himself off the wagon.

Despair replaced rage. Until now, he'd at least felt strong. Other than an occasional beating, he'd never been sore for very long. This was different. He felt broken, tossed aside like a useless tool. All he wanted was to run away or better yet kill Nathan Billings.

He worried about Mama Rose and what they'd do to her. He could deal with anything as long as they left her alone. The squeak of the wagon grew monotonous and he dozed off.

"Get up," Wilkes said. The overseer's fingers clamped down on Tip's arm like an iron cuff.

Tip scrambled from the wagon platform, his back so raw, he had trouble standing. Wilkes shackled him, a chain connecting his feet and hands, making every step a chore.

As if he could run away. Or would.

They dragged him to a field behind the slave quarters the coloreds used as a meeting place, nothing but an open area with a fire pit and a few planks for seating.

To Tip's horror, thirty or so slaves were assembled. He was placed into their midst, reading fear and pain in their expressions. He wanted to call to them, tell them he was going to be all right. Instead he stood frozen, only his eyes searching for Mama Rose.

"See what happens when you run away?" Jack Billings said, cutting off the murmurs. "Tip here thought he could *escape*." He turned to face Tip. "Obviously I've been too easy until now. Giving you more freedom than you deserve. Letting you roam about our land."

New murmurs erupted as Billings paused for effect. "That's over. From now on you stay within your quarters unless you're on the job. Anyone found wandering about receives a lashing. Wilkes here will take care of it. That goes for all of you."

Wilkes grinned, tapping the whip attached to his belt. But Tip only watched Mama Rose who sat in the front row, her eyes black with tears and worry. Elda held her hand, her gaze flitting between Tip and the men surrounding him. No more than five feet tall, she had a slight figure, her scrawny legs hidden by a bulky housedress. It'd take nothing but a whiff of wind to blow her down.

A fierce longing took hold of him. He wanted to protect Mama Rose—to take her and Elda away. He felt as if they could hear his heart pound. How he wanted to be near them.

Look at yourself. You useless to them.

"Not to worry, I'll decide on proper punishment," Billings continued with a smile. "In the meantime I expect your best work. No talking, no gossip. Now go and get busy."

Tip watched everyone scatter, his mama ambling toward the house, Elda supporting her elbow. Mama Rose's shoulders trembled. Even from a distance, he knew she was crying.

New despair gripped him as he realized he could do nothing at all.

Billings hadn't wasted any time—the summons arrived the next afternoon.

Judge Dowell's long face looked stony when Adam and his mother walked into the courtroom. Sara had been told to stay home, and while she'd protested, she seemed to be secretly glad to remain behind.

A group of Greeneville's citizens had assembled in the back: The barber and grocer, a few of Jack Billings's friends, bankers, solicitors, and other plantation owners, old Mr. Porter, and his grandson Allister.

Adam sat next to his mother behind a table. The Billings clan, including the frail Mrs. Billings, was assembled across the aisle.

"Mr. Billings, why don't you begin and state your case?" Judge Dowell said as he leaned back in his chair.

Jack Billings got up, carefully clearing his throat as the low mumble of voices died down.

"Your Honor, three days ago I was alerted that my slave, Tipper, had gone missing. He'd been there at night and was gone the next morning. Naturally, I assumed he'd run away. Imagine my surprise when Mama Rose, Tipper's mother, came to me the next day and told me that Tipper was staying at the Brown's farm." Billings scanned the room, his eyes dancing. "As you know, aiding a run-away slave is a grievous crime."

"No need to cite the law for me," Judge Dowell said. Adam suppressed a smile. Maybe the judge would see reason after all.

"Of course. My apologies." Jack Billings bowed toward the Judge's raised bench. "What I meant to say was that I went to investigate, taking witnesses and the Sheriff with me." He paused again as if he expected applause. Adam dug his fingernails into his palms. "As expected, we found Tipper hiding in the barn at the Brown's farm. We immediately escorted him back, and he is now locked up."

Adam's mind raced. What was that supposed to mean? Had they thrown Tip into a cell? He was much too sick to be alone without care.

"...I thought it most prudent to alert your Honor of what happened," Billings was saying. "After all, we can't set a precedent. Where would we be if our slaves could move about and visit others at their free will?"

"You may sit down, Mr. Billings," Judge Dowell said. His face unmoving, he addressed Adam's mother. "Mrs. Brown, tell us what happened with the slave, Tipper."

Adam's mother stood up, smoothing her Sunday skirt. Except for the trembling in her hands, she looked calm. "Your Honor, my son Adam is a friend of Tip...Tipper. On the night in question, let's see that was three days ago, Tip appeared at our farm around two in the morning." She threw a glance at Adam. "Adam alerted me to come to the barn, where Tip had collapsed. He was covered in blood with multiple bruises and open cuts. He had a serious head wound. His right eye was swollen shut and there was open flesh on his shoulders."

A sigh went through the audience, but faded away when the Judge raised his eyebrows.

"Adam and I spent several hours cleaning Tip's wounds and feeding him. It is my belief he could've died or been permanently injured, had he not come to us. Since Tip is Mama Rose's only son, he would never run away. He cares about her too much. He simply didn't want to tell his mother what had happened—that Nathan Billings had beaten him to near death without provocation."

The courtroom erupted in shouts and mumbles.

"Silence." Judge Dowell smacked his gavel. To Adam's mother, he added, "Why wouldn't he have asked for help at the Billings plantation?"

Adam's mother narrowed her eyes. "He'd been beaten by the son of the master. Would you go to the father to accuse the son?"

Several people hooted but quit as soon as the Judge threw them a dark glance. "I can hardly comment, Mrs. Brown, as I'm not a slave nor slave owner, but I do believe I'm following your reasoning."

Adam's mother smiled for the first time. "Tip is devoted to the Billings, his loyalty unmatched. It is unfortunate that cruelty is used to exert authority over the already powerless." Here she looked over at Nathan and then Jack Billings who sat stone-faced. "That's all I have to say."

"Thank you, Mrs. Brown. I'm calling a fifteen-minute recess." The gavel swung anew.

As he straightened and disappeared in his chambers behind the bench, the courtroom erupted in loud discussions.

Adam patted his mother's forearm while he watched the Billings clan whisper to each other. He would've loved to know what they were talking about. Even more so, he wanted to be gone from here. The place was giving him the creeps. From what he'd heard, things were looking up for them and Tip. Surely, the judge would order Jack Billings to set his son straight.

Much sooner than Adam expected, the door to chambers

opened.

Judge Dowell shuffled to his seat. "I've reached a decision."

The courtroom sank into silence as Adam leaned forward. "It appears that Tip was injured from a beating and sought shelter and medical attention at the Brown farm. Mrs. Brown, the Christian woman that she is, let her heart and compassion dictate her actions. As such we cannot fault her." Judge Dowell paused, looking gravely around the room. "However, the slave laws are clear in that the owner of a slave has the right to discipline his possession anyway he sees fit. Even if it seems excessive in this case, that is the law."

In the back of Adam's mind, warning bells went off. The judge was turning full swing. Feeling his fingers tremble, he gripped his mother's hand. Judge Dowell leaned forward and addressed Adam's mother directly.

"While compassion is a noble trait, Mrs. Brown, the right course of action would've been to send a messenger to Jack Billings and alert him of Tipper's whereabouts. I'm sure if Mr. Brown had been alive, he would've set you straight. By taking matters into your own hands and even asking Tipper's mother to visit, you violated the most sacred law of the slave owner. As such, I have no choice but to pass judgment in favor of Jack Billings."

Cheers and boos erupted behind them. Adam sank back in his seat, struggling to breathe. The room was closing in on him, a terrible foreboding that settled like darkness over him.

"Mrs. Brown, I sentence you to a fine of one-thousand dollars, nine-hundred-fifty dollars payable within one month to Mr. Jack Billings as imbursement for the violation of slave law, and fifty dollars to the court."

As the gavel struck the desk with a thud, Adam tried to comprehend what the judge had said. All he'd heard was one-thousand, the number reverberating in his brain over and over.

To his right, Nathan sneered while Jack Billings got up and shook hands with supporters. To his left, his mother sat rigid as a statue, reminding Adam of the time when they'd gotten the news about Pa.

CHAPTER EIGHT

"Ma, where are we going to get the money?" Adam asked when they arrived home. The entire drive back, his mother had been quiet, gazing into the hills. When she didn't answer, Adam gripped her shoulders. She'd lost more weight and under his strong hands felt frail as the robin he'd rescued. "Ma, please?"

At last she looked at him. "Jack Billings will take the farm," she said, her voice thin. "He found a way to steal it from us."

"The bastard," Adam yelled, his fingernails accidentally clawing his mother. "I'll kill him."

His mother caught his arm. "Listen to me. You stay away from them. They're powerful and dangerous. Maybe I can get a loan…"

"You know the banker is one of Billings's friends," Adam said. "He'll never go against them."

"We'll have to find a way," his mother said as they headed toward the cabin. "Let's not tell Sara yet," she whispered. "Not until we have to."

Adam nodded, trying to force his face into neutral as the door flew open.

"What happened?" Sara's blue eyes flashed with excitement and worry.

"We'll have to pay a fine. I'll visit the bank tomorrow," Ma said.

"But they beat him half dead," Sara said. "Why do we have to pay?"

"Good question," Adam mumbled. "It's the slave law and we *helped* Tip. So Billings made it sound as if we'd hidden Tip away…helped him escape."

"Tip would never run away."

"We know that," Adam said. "Everyone knows that." New anger roiled. He wanted to break something. "Why did Pa have to join the war? None of this would've happened if he hadn't gotten himself killed."

His mother smacked the cast iron pot on the table. "Adam Brown, you apologize this instant."

Adam clamped both hands around the edge of the seat so they wouldn't fly up in a rage. "Why should I? He's gone anyway."

"But I'm here, and so is your sister." She tried to catch Adam's gaze, but Adam turned to stare out the window. "Let me tell you something about your Pa. He was an honorable man—"

"Who needed money."

"Who believed Negroes should be free. He wanted to do the right thing by the President. He didn't do it for the money. We all expected it to be…quick."

"Quick to be killed." Adam stood abruptly and hurried outside.

Stupid war, stupid Pa, stupid Billings.

All afternoon, he fumed. Cleaning stalls and spreading manure on the fields, he tried to find a solution. None came to mind. Not then, not that night or the next day when his mother took the wagon into town. After breakfast he let the robin go, but even its cautious flight into the brush didn't make him feel better.

He still hadn't apologized. Ma expected it, but all he could think of was Billings stealing their land. They'd be left with nothing. He'd work for pennies as a farmhand, his sister would marry freckled Allister, but where did that leave Ma? She'd have to rent a room in town, take in laundry or become a seamstress.

Worst of all, it was his fault. What did Pa have to do with it?

He'd been the one to see Mama Rose. If he'd only gone to Jack Billings instead. His vision became hazy with tears as he marched toward the cabin for lunch.

No, he couldn't go in like that. Sara would pester him. He'd have to pull himself together first.

He broke into a run, his mind occupied with visions of his mother in a torn dress, peddling cheap whiskey. It felt good to move, and soon he was doing nothing but breathing hard, enjoying his muscles moving like one of those fancy threshing machines the rich estates owned. Only when the Billings plantation came into view did he realize he'd come to see Tip.

"Mama Rose," he yelled as he entered the kitchen. To his relief she was there, bent over the stove, ladling chicken soup into a tureen.

"Adam, what you doing here?"

Adam suppressed a groan when Mama Rose turned to face him. Dark lines edged her gentle brown eyes. Her shoulders stooped low in defeat.

"I…need to see Tip," he managed.

"You can't," she said, wiping a tear from her cheek with her apron. "He locked up." A deep sob escaped her. "Master think of selling him. Master says Tipper trouble." She hugged Adam.

"He can't do that," he mumbled. Numbness spread through his limbs until he felt as empty as a leaky pail. He couldn't move, Mama Rose's words repeating in his mind. Surely, Billings would come to his senses. Tip was too good a worker to send him away.

Sniffing, Mama Rose stepped back and pulled a giant white handkerchief from her pocket. She blew her nose loudly before patting Adam on the shoulder. "Master can do whatever he wants."

"I've *got* to see Tip," Adam said.

Mama Rose nodded. She took two meat pies from a tray, wrapped them in a cotton napkin and handed them to Adam. "Give these to him, but don't let anybody see you. If you get caught, say the pies are yours. They starve him. Come back here and tell me. I pack you a basket to take home." She paused and took hold of his arm. "How your mama? I hear bad things. Is it true?"

Adam bit his lip and squinted for good measure. Word had gotten around fast that his family would soon be homeless. Without a word, he stuffed the meat pies into his pant pocket and headed for the door before he remembered that he didn't know where they kept Tip.

"Where is he?" he asked.

"In the grain shack behind the stables."

Adam hurried down the lawn, past the servants' quarters, to the other side of the main house where a two-storied horse barn held the Billings's prized stallions. A slave a bit younger than he was lugging straw bales inside and gave a weak nod.

Adam scanned the area but didn't see anyone else. When the boy disappeared inside the barn, Adam stole past the stable's main gate around the corner.

The *grain shack* was twice the size of his cabin, and stored hay and oats for the horses, wheat and rye for cooking. It had no real windows but a number of slots for ventilation. The door was closed, a chain and open padlock attached to the handle.

Adam tiptoed around the building and was just about to call through one of the gaps when he heard voices.

Without making a sound, he peeked through the slot closest to him. In the gloom of the shack, Nathan Billings was standing over a cot and what appeared to be Tip lying on his side.

"How do you like it now, boy?" Nathan was saying. "I'll send you right back to that hell you came from."

Adam cringed when he saw something flash in Nathan's hand—a knife with a long serrated blade. *He is going to kill Tip.*

Adam broke into a run and threw open the door yelling, "Leave him alone."

Surprise showed on Nathan's face, but only for a moment.

"If it isn't the farm boy. You going to rescue your friend?" His pale eyes flashed mockingly. "Soon we'll get your land and your mama will become a whore."

"You filthy bastard," Adam said, his voice choking with fury.

"You want a piece of that?" Nathan's knife flashed, slicing into Adam's shirt, nicking him in the chest. Adam didn't feel it.

With a grunt, Adam lunged forward, wrapped an arm around Nathan's neck, and pulled him to the ground. As Nathan slashed back and forth with the knife, Adam, an easy thirty pounds heavier, kept away until he was able to roll on top. Nathan's scrawny body was no match for his work-toughened muscles. Then he began squeezing Nathan's neck, pushing his knees into his shoulders. Under the pressure, the knife fell from Nathan's hand.

"Adam, stop." Tip's voice reached through the haze. "You kill him."

"He deserves it," Adam said, trying to get his breath under control. Realizing what he was doing, he relaxed his hand.

"You bastard," Nathan croaked. Adam looked back and forth between Nathan and Tip, who nodded, imploring him with his eyes. He wasn't entirely sure what had just happened, but the terrible anger he'd felt moments ago had ebbed. He jumped up as Nathan got to his knees and then stood heavily.

Rubbing his throat, he coughed. "You're going to jail for that." His eyes were full of hatred, his voice cold. "Maybe I'll even get your head."

"He don't mean nothing by it," Tip said from the cot. He'd spoken quietly, the chains around his arms clinking softly.

"You shut your hole or you won't live another day." Nathan picked up his knife. Wiping off the dirt with his sleeve, he half turned toward Adam. "I could say Adam got angry and killed his former slave friend," he cackled.

"Liar," shouted Adam.

This time he jumped at Nathan with such force that they both flew several feet against the opposite wall. Adam felt something crunch in his shoulder. Sharp pain shot up his neck and along his arm. He looked down, expecting Nathan to slash at him, but Nathan had gone limp. His eyes were closed, his lids bluish. Alarmed, Adam stumbled backwards.

"Stop." Tip frantically yanked on his cot, dragging it to reach Adam.

Adam felt dazed and his shoulder throbbed as if poked with a red-hot blade.

"Leave before they see you," Tip whispered.

Having trouble standing, Adam's gaze wandered to the wall where Nathan Billings lay crumpled like a colorless rag doll.

"I killed him," Adam murmured as the realization settled in.

"Hurry. Get out." Tip picked up the knife and stuffed it under the blanket on his cot. "I say I did it."

"No!" Adam rubbed his injured arm. "They'll hang you." He hurried to close the door and returned, anxiously scanning the room where boxes and burlap sacks were stacked to the ceiling. "He can't be found here."

Tip hung his head. "My life over anyway."

Adam hurried to his friend's side and slumped on the cot. "Now you listen. Promise me to take care of yourself. Mama Rose needs you. I don't think you'll get sold. I don't think Billings will do it.

"You'll be free one day, you'll see. President Lincoln said so. Once they win the war. And you'll get your farm. Pa always said you can do anything if you work at it all the time."

Adam grimaced. Just a few days ago they'd sat together dreaming about a free life. Now Tip was in shackles and he...*what had he done?* Panic rose in him, sending bile to his throat. He jumped up and grabbed Nathan's legs.

"What you doing?" Tip's eyes were as soft as his mother's. And something else was there: a glimmer of hope.

"I'm going to put him somewhere outside so it's absolutely clear you didn't do it."

"Nathan, where are you?" Janet Billings's voice floated in through the vents. "You promised me a ride, honey."

Adam rushed to the opening that was closest to the stables and peeked out. Nathan's mother, wearing a gown of crisp cotton with a soft pattern of cornflowers, its blue reminding Adam of his own mother's eyes, stood waiting outside. She held a dainty umbrella of cream-white lace to shade out the sun and a pair of riding gloves. "If you don't come soon, I must go back inside," she said, her voice almost too quiet to hear. "It is dreadfully hot today."

"You think she look in *here*?" Tip whispered.

Adam shook his head and kept watching the yard. His mind screamed *leave*. Yet he stood with indecision. He couldn't go outside while Janet Billings was near. Thoughts of what he'd done roiled inside his head, panic drying his mouth.

To his relief, Janet Billings slowly wandered back toward the main house when Wilkes crossed her path. She was too far for Adam to hear, but Wilkes's voice boomed easily across the lawn. "Sure, M'am, I'll be happy to search for him. Give me a few minutes...I'll be right back."

To Adam's horror, Wilkes headed straight toward the stables and then made a sudden turn toward the grain shack. Obviously it was well known that Nathan Billings liked to torture Tip.

Adam leaped from the window, grabbed Nathan's feet and pulled him toward a stack of burlap sacks. He had mere seconds to hide them both. From the corner of his eye he saw Tip turn on his side, pretending to be asleep. Desperately yanking at the sacks to make space, he pushed Nathan, who felt soft as a bag of flour, and himself into the opening and cowered low.

The door flew open. "Mr. Billings, are you in here?" Wilkes rushed to Tip's cot. "You awake, Boy?"

Tip grumbled and rubbed his eyes. "Something wrong?"

"Have you seen Master Nathan?"

Tip shook his head, his brown eyes wide. "No, Sir."

"I wonder why the shack was unlocked," Wilkes mumbled as he turned and walked back out.

"They pick up wheat for the kitchen earlier," Tip offered, but the overseer was already gone, the chain rattling on the outside.

Adam slowly rose as Tip sat up on his cot. Their eyes met.

They'd both be hanged come morning..

CHAPTER NINE

"What is that?" Tip asked as Adam sagged next to him on the cot.

"What?"

"That smell?"

"Oh, I forgot." Adam pulled the half-crushed meat pies from his pocket. "From Mama Rose. We might as well eat." How could he feel ravenous and nauseated at the same time? He'd missed lunch at home, and who knew what time it was now. Ma had surely returned from town and probably wondered where he was. The list of chores materialized in his head, getting longer by the minute.

"This *is* good," Tip mumbled between bites. Adam nodded, too busy to chew. The buttery crust was filled with beef, carrots, leeks and onions in some kind of secret recipe gravy. He could've eaten ten.

"Sorry I got you into this mess," Adam said quietly. "I don't know what possessed me."

"You look out for your Ma and...for me." The cot creaked under Tip's weight as he turned toward Adam. "You never know how much it mean to me that you come to protect me."

"Nice protection." Adam grimaced, his heart heavy with unknown consequences.

"People talk about you visiting."

"What do you mean?"

"Jonas say, whites never friends with slaves. But you my friend for a long time."

Adam glanced at Tip, sitting hunched over on his cot. "People

45

are stupid. I just wish I'd have some way to help—"

"Tip?" Mama Rose's voice drifted through the opening behind them.

"In here," Tip called as Adam jumped up and rushed to the wall. Through the air vent, he could see Mama Rose carefully ambling toward the shack.

"Can you unlock the door?" Adam whispered.

Mama Rose took a step back. "Adam? What you still doing here? I thought you forget your basket."

"Hurry, unloop the chain."

Adam heard her mumble, skirts swishing along the outer wall. He wanted to scream *hurry or we'll be dead*. Any moment they'd be found out. In his panic, he stumbled to the door just as something rattled outside. Within seconds he was once again swallowed by Mama Rose's hug.

"Why you in here?" she asked.

"It bad, Mama," Tip said from the cot. "Adam need to leave. You too."

Adam wasn't really listening. He'd gone behind the burlap sacks to inspect his deed. Nathan was half lying, half sitting against the sacks, his face white as flour, his eyelids purple. He looked like a ghost.

A cry escaped Mama Rose as she clapped a hand against her mouth. "What happen?"

"It was an accident," Tip explained. "They fought after Nathan say Adam's Ma a whore and the Billings take their land."

Adam dragged Nathan from the stacks and hoisted him on his shoulder. He nearly fainted, fiery darts shooting down his back. At the door he stopped, his gaze returning to his friend.

"Don't worry. I'll come back soon."

Tip's eyes looked huge in the gloom. "You be careful."

Adam turned abruptly, the air squeezing from his lungs. "Let's go," he gasped. Mama Rose rushed outside looking in both directions before waving Adam through. He could only see to his right because Nathan's body was blocking the view. If anyone noticed him now he was done for.

"To the stables," Adam heaved. "You go back now. No need to be involved." Mama Rose quietly nodded and locked the shack, but not before tossing Tip another meat pie.

Adam stumbled forward. *If I could just be lucky for once.* Nathan seemed to gain weight with every step. Somehow fear kept Adam going. Twenty more feet... ten... five.

He sighed as he entered the horse barn's alley. Stretching the length of the building, it was deserted. In the nice weather most horses were on pastures or ridden. On either side, partitions showed each horse's name written in wooden letters. Adam clambered farther in, the gloomy light not gloomy enough to hide. He'd decided to put Nathan into one of the empty stalls when he heard a neigh to his left.

Adam shifted his weight to turn and there, two feet above him, towered a magnificent horse. Its skin was chestnut, smooth as silk with a black mane and dark brown ears. It whinnied again and Adam recognized the name: *Magnus Alvariss*, a thoroughbred Tip had mentioned a few months ago. Mr. Billings had bought him from a famous breeder, but the stallion had proven unmanageable, throwing off countless riders, kicking and biting everyone who came near.

Serves them right, Tip had said at the time. *Master isn't nice to animals.*

"You going to bite me?" Adam puffed as he approached the box. The horse eyed him curiously as if to decide whether to attack. To his surprise, it whinnied softly and nodded its great big head. "Is that a yes?"

Adam scanned the box. He had to get rid of Nathan's body and take off before anyone saw him. Still he was drawn to the animal. He propped Nathan's body on top of the stall's door, well aware that the horse could easily take a chunk out of his neck.

"You're a good boy," Adam said as he shoved and let go, Nathan gradually slipping and then disappearing behind the door.

"Our secret," Adam whispered, absentmindedly patting the horse's head. It didn't seem to mind and nuzzled closer. "You poor thing, all locked up in here with these idiots. Maybe one day I'll come and get you."

The stallion's brown eyes followed him as Adam reluctantly turned away.

Sprinting to the barn gate, he quickly scanned the outside, coming eye-to-eye with the stall boy from earlier. The boy, both arms heavy with water pails, nodded, sweat running down his temples.

Adam's stomach cramped painfully, his throat so dry, the

greeting he'd intended to express came out as a wheeze. The stall boy had seen him twice now and would tell the Billings as soon as they found Nathan.

Turning abruptly, Adam raced off, using the cover of the slave quarters and flowering hibiscus hedges. A mile down the road, he came to a sudden stop.

A terrible thought was grabbing hold.

He couldn't go home.

He'd just killed Nathan Billings, the son of one of the richest landowners in Tennessee. Even if he'd stashed Nathan in the barn, suspicion would surely fall on him. The slave boy had seen him, maybe Wilkes or Mrs. Billings. He had motive. Not only had Nathan tortured Adam's best friend, Jack Billings was going to take his farm.

They'd hang him and his mother would be shamed. Sara, too.

Adam froze. What if they blamed the horse, thinking that Nathan had tried to ride him? They'd shoot the stallion. He might as well have pulled the trigger when he placed Nathan inside. Why hadn't he just thrown him in an empty stall?

Adam's legs buckled and he slumped to the ground. The spot used to be one of his favorites, a small stand of hickory and oaks, filled with the earthy smell of last year's rotten leaves and the songs of Whip-poor-wills and Cuckoos. He'd felt at peace here, a quiet hideout from Sara's nosy questions.

Now all he felt was loneliness. He flinched when a Blue Jay squawked above him, followed by the shriek of a Cooper's Hawk zigzagging through the trees.

He'd never known a heart could actually ache as he realized that he longed for the farm life he'd despised only hours ago. He'd thrown it away, never to see his mother and sister again. From now on he'd be alone.

Forever.

As exhaustion set in, the ache from his shoulder mixed with the ache of his heart until he wanted to scream.

Adam awoke with a start. He was freezing. The gentle patter of rain filled the air, soaking the ground and his clothes. He straightened slowly, his body old as the earth.

The memory of Nathan lying white and ghostly on the floor pierced him like a knife. He saw Tip shackled to the cot, and his mother pacing the floor, tugging at her hair with weary eyes.

Everything had been his fault. Ever since his father had died he'd made one wrong decision after another and destroyed the lives of all the people he held dear. Why hadn't he informed old Billings when Tip showed up? Why hadn't he kept his temper with evil Nathan? A sob escaped him, a sound so desolate, he stuck his forefingers into his ears to drown it out.

Had the earth opened up at that moment, he would've gladly jumped into the hole. There was only one thing he could do.

He had to disappear.

CHAPTER TEN

Tip awoke. By the screams outside he knew they had found young Master. There were the sharp voice of Wilkes, the furious shouts of Jack Billings, mingled with the calming sound of another voice, probably the doctor. He wondered how much time had passed.

He straightened, the chain that connected his legs to the cot rattling. The skin on his ankles was raw and bleeding. He'd gone from slave to prisoner. Why had he thought being a slave was so bad? At least he'd had a place to sleep and much better food than most people in his position could dream of. Now he had nothing. He was going to be sent away. Without Mama Rose.

Not only that. He'd gone to ask Adam for help and caused them to lose their farm. It was his fault, and he was powerless to do anything about it. He sniffed, his vision fuzzy with tears.

After a while, he took a drink from the bucket next to him and sat back down. Despite the heat, he felt cold inside, as if somebody had tossed his soul into an icy pond.

There was nothing to do but wait. He gingerly touched his cheek. The bruise around his eye was healing, but his shoulder blades burned with every move.

Pulling hard, he dragged the cot toward the wall and peered outside. In the dusk men dashed back and forth. Shouts rang out. Torches blazed. Through the opening Tip watched Missus Billings scream and drop to the ground, her puffy skirts rising up around her.

Elda ran over to fan her face as several men left the barn, a makeshift stretcher between them. Tip recognized Doc Schwartz walking alongside, his square bag dangling from his long arms. He'd come to see Mama Rose once when she'd taken with fever, and Tip was forever grateful for his help.

Missus Billings came to and was put on her feet by Elda and old Jonas. Just then Elda looked straight at Tip, her eyes glistening as if she were ready to cry. He wanted to call to her, assure her that everything was going to be all right, but the words stuck in his throat.

Too late anyway.

Elda took Missus Billings's elbow to lead her back inside.

With a sigh, Tip rearranged his cot and lay back down. Nathan Billings would never beat him again, but old Master wasn't finished yet.

When the door rattled open, Tip expected one of the slave boys.

It was Wilkes.

"Get up," he said, a nasty grin on his face.

"What going to happen to me?" Tip asked as Wilkes bent low to unlock him.

Instead of an answer, Wilkes shoved him in the back. Tip stumbled outside, glad for the fresh evening air. He envied the mocking bird singing high above on the barn, untouched by human cruelty and free to fly wherever it wanted.

"Climb in." Wilkes pointed at the same cart Tip had ridden on from Adam's farm. A spare horse was tied to the back.

No sooner had Tip slumped against the hard side of the wagon they took off. Nobody was around. By the smells of baked cornbread and meat roasting, it had to be dinnertime. They were all inside eating. He should've been hungry, but all he felt was numb.

He caught a glimpse of the big kitchen and the shadows moving within. He wanted to shout to his Mama, to stop Wilkes, but he knew it was of no use. His home and the world he'd known were slipping from his grasp like a rowboat tossed into a hurricane.

The wagon picked up speed as they left the Billings plantation. Tip kept his gaze low. He knew it would've been smart to look around, watch the road to learn his way. But he couldn't make his head rise. In fact, his skull was so heavy, it felt like breaking off his neck. He'd never see Mama Rose again. In his haste and surprise, he'd forgotten to take the knife. He couldn't even cut his own throat if he had to.

By the time they stopped, Tip's back throbbed anew. He still couldn't see well, his one good eye doing the work for two. In the shadow of the half-moon he saw a farmhouse, bigger than Adam's farm, but nothing as grand as the Billings place.

"Out!" Wilkes said, his fingers twitching on the whip.

Tip scrambled from the wagon as the front door of the farmhouse opened. A man of perhaps forty with small eyes and a cruel smile appeared, wiping a greasy hand on his protruding belly and carrying an oil lamp.

"Here's your merchandise, Rawley. You'll want to keep a keen eye on this one," Wilkes said. "If you know what I mean."

"What about the horse?"

"A gift from Mr. Billings."

"Fine, fine," the fat man said, slapping the overseer on the back.

Tip looked around in terror, uncaring about his tears. He stumbled toward the new Master who eagerly grabbed the chain behind Tip's back.

"Walk, boy."

The man led him around the house where a couple of huts squatted in the dark.

"Get in here." He unhooked the chain as Tip made his way inside the smaller one. It was pitch black inside and he tripped, catching himself against the opposite wall.

"Watch out," a deep voice moaned from the ground. "Who there?"

Tip slowly sank to the floor as the door was locked from the outside. "Tip," he managed. "Tipper…from the Billings plantation."

The voice in the darkness came to life. "That fancy place in Greeneville? Master talk of eating there once."

Tip swallowed, forcing back tears. "My mama, Mama Rose, their cook. Her cooking famous."

"Oh, what I give for some pie," the voice said. And after a pause. "My name Balder."

"How long you been here, Balder?" Tip asked.

"Long time, maybe two years or three."

"You don't know if two or three?"

"Not keep track, Master always make me work, even Sundays.

Too tired to count days."

Tip wanted the man to shut up. "Is there a bed in here?"

"No bed, sleep on ground."

Tip let himself crumple to the floor. The place smelled horrible, like an outhouse. And things were going to get much, much worse—he could feel it in his bones.

For the first time in his life he considered running away.

CHAPTER ELEVEN

It was dusk when Adam entered a dirt road that led northwest to Morrisville. He'd made the thirty-mile journey once with his father two years ago to pick up a plow with a cast-iron moldboard. They'd driven the wagon, and Pa had talked the entire way about growing the farm and buying more land every few years until they could one day build a larger home.

Adam's sight blurred. His father's dreams were dead. So were his own.

After dark he found a brook to drink and wipe himself down. Then he crawled into a thicket, dug into a pile of leaves and slept.

The sun stood high when he awoke, his stomach growling angrily. He drank his fill and continued walking. A couple of times he heard horses.

Scared of the Sheriff or Billings's henchmen, he jumped off the road and waited until the riders passed. He'd have to change his name, just in case. Beards were perfect to hide a face, but at best he was feeling some stubble on his chin and a couple of hairs on his upper lip.

He picked blackberries and found a few wild blueberries. Still, his stomach continued to ache as he remembered Mama Rose's meat pies and Ma's stews. He thought of Ma's worried eyes, Sara's face, imagined them pacing the floor of their cabin—his home. He'd told Tip he'd be back soon... *Stop that.*

Morrisville's dirt roads were clogged with wagons, horses and delivery carts. Dust coated sidewalks and porches, Confederate flags decorated windows and poles. In the background, Adam heard the sounds of a steam locomotive leaving, the chug-chug gathering speed.

Men in business suits, farmers in coveralls and straw hats and women shading their faces with umbrellas bustled about. Everyone seemed to have a place to go and something to do except for him, a murderer who wandered the streets.

With every hour he felt more desperate. He had no money, not even a knife or a bite to eat. He wore his work shirt, sweat stained with a tear under his left arm. His shoulder ached with every step to remind him of what he'd done, and there was a bloodstain on his chest where Nathan Billings's knife had nicked him.

He had to look like a beggar, and Ma was surely frantic with worry. But to write a note he needed paper and pen, and he had neither.

The aroma of fried chicken drifted into his nose. He swallowed hard, trying to walk faster, but his eyes were drawn to the pub's black board advertising chicken, mashed potatoes and a beer for fifty cents. His stomach gurgled uncontrollably while his legs refused to carry him away from the enticing smells.

Unable to continue, he leaned against a post belonging to the veranda of a boarding house. Adam could see a man and a woman sitting at a table, its blue and white-checkered cloth matching the curtains.

"You need a room, young man?" A woman of perhaps sixty with a gray velvet cap and a matching gray dress appeared next to him.

"No Madam, I...don't have any money."

The woman wrinkled her skinny nose. "Then I suggest you move on before I call the sheriff and he arrests you for loitering. You scare away my customers." She kept standing there, her eyes squeezed together against the brilliant afternoon sun.

Adam shrugged and continued up the street. Voices drifted out of shops. "Good afternoon, Mr. Diggins...good day, Ms. Steel... isn't it a fine evening..."

He couldn't stay here. Everyone knew everyone else. Slowly he wandered toward the train depot, where a few passengers waited. But when he tried to enter the station's platform, a conductor stopped him.

"Where to?" the man said, his cap too tight on his broad skull.

Adam shrugged again. *Don't know,* he wanted to say but that sure looked even more suspicious. "You've got your ticket, I presume." The conductor held out a palm. "I can tell you how long you've got to wait. Trains are running awful late these days, tracks being torn up by the Yanks."

"Don't have one yet," Adam mumbled. Not waiting to be sent away again, he again dove into the bustle of Morristown. He was only thirty miles from home and already stumped. What would his father think of him? A pathetic failure with no money and no prospects.

"Join the Confederates. Preserve our way of life," somebody yelled behind him. "We need volunteers. Stop the Yankees. Don't wait till it's too late," the voice continued.

Adam slowly turned. Near the post office stood a man in a Confederate uniform, its grayish blue bright and clean in the evening sun.

"You ready to join, son?" he said as Adam sauntered near.

"What does it pay?" Adam asked.

The man glanced at him skeptically. "You fighting for the cause?" He hesitated, giving Adam another disapproving look. "Eleven dollars a month."

Adam nodded, but before he could say another word, his father's voice began to whisper. *A man must live a lifetime with his deeds, so make sure you do the right thing.* It was so clear that Adam jumped and turned around.

"Son, what's the matter with you?" The soldier glanced at him curiously. "Not enough for you? That's all you're going to get. Got to train all you young scoundrels first, so take it or leave it."

"I think I'll leave it," Adam said. Without waiting for a reply, he marched down a side street and was soon out of town.

The light was turning gray, the path deserted. Cornstalks grew eight feet high on both sides, creating a green tunnel. Looking quickly left and right, Adam picked two ears of corn and began to eat. The corn was juicy and sweet but did little to calm his stomach. It reminded him of Tip. Had it only been a few days since they'd sat at the creek dreaming about a future?

That was before he'd destroyed everything with his rash decisions.

What would become of his only friend? If Mama Rose was

right, Billings would sell Tip to some other plantation. He'd never see him again. Not him nor Ma and Sara. Their farm would be gone, all because of his actions.

His situation was hopeless. He thought how it would feel to die. Maybe he could just lie down and give up, fight no more.

But it wasn't that easy. Even now, his body demanded things while his legs kept walking. His stomach was a great big cramp while his mouth felt dry as sawdust. He needed water badly. Why hadn't he drunk from one of the troughs in town?

As the trail crested, he stopped. Before him the land rolled in soft hills, covered in corn and bean crops. He scanned the area in search of a place to sleep when he noticed a soft light about two hundred yards to his left, a path splitting away from the main road. Wiping the dust from his face, Adam swallowed and headed toward the light.

"Hello?" he called out. The last thing he needed was someone sticking a gun in his face. The path ended in the yard of a small farm similar to his own. *You don't have a farm anymore.*

He asked himself if he'd feed some stranger who showed up at bedtime.

"May I help you?"

Adam knew it was a woman's voice, though the person standing in the door of the tiny two-story house wore coveralls like a man and a battered straw hat.

"I'm looking for something to eat. I'm traveling north and..." He was out of ideas.

"To do what?"

Adam frantically looked around for any signs of a flag or weapon. If the woman was a Confederate supporter, she'd hate him on the spot.

"Visit my uncle."

"I see." The woman hesitated. "Come closer. I want to see your face. If that's possible under all that grime."

Adam hurried near. "I don't have any weapons."

"What's a boy like you doing wandering the countryside?"

Adam shrugged. Nathan Billings's lifeless face floated into his memory. "Nothing, just visiting my uncle."

"Where does he live?"

"Lexington." It was the only town Adam knew in Kentucky.

"Where's your Ma?"

Adam cringed. "She's dead." If he wanted to survive, he had to get used to lying.

The woman raised her lamp to his face. Hazel eyes met his. They were surrounded by crinkles and offset by a stern mouth as if the woman had talked herself out of laughing.

"Why do I have the feeling you're telling a ruse? You're not very good at it."

Adam lowered his gaze. "I'm going, then." He quickly turned, but the woman's hand shot out and gripped his forearm.

"Not so fast." She held on to him, apparently trying to make up her mind. "All right, come in. Actually, the well is over there. Wash up and then come in. I'll fix you something to eat and you can start over with your story."

Adam hurried toward the well, only half listening. He'd gladly tell any story for a full stomach.

The house consisted of a tiny living area with a cast-iron woodstove and table. Judging by the wide bed in the corner, more than one person was living here. In fact, he could've sworn he'd seen movement near the barn, but the light was fading and he no longer cared about anything but the mouthwatering baked bread sitting on the stove.

"You like eggs? I'm not much for killing my hens," the woman said, "but I can fix you a nice omelet."

Adam nodded, watching the woman crack eggs into a red clay bowl.

"There is water on the table. Sit down and drink your fill, I'll give you some milk later." Again Adam nodded. He was back in his own kitchen, Ma fixing dinner, familiar sounds of pots clanking— familiar sounds of home. The ewer grew heavy in his hand and he spilled a few drops. Abruptly, he leaned forward to wipe them away with his elbow.

He wanted to run then, run from this place of kindness that made his heart ache worse than when he'd been walking in the fields. Yet, his limbs remained in place, heavy as lead and just as unyielding.

He looked up in surprise when he heard the woman say, "Eat."

The room turned silent while Adam stuffed himself with eggs, green beans, and bread with rich creamy butter. He was chewing so hard, his sight turned blurry.

"You might want to slow down so you can breathe once in a while." The woman had settled across from him and was watching his every move. In the gloom of the single oil lamp it was hard to tell how old she was. "Now tell me again why you're on the road with nothing but the clothes on your back."

Adam swallowed. "I'm running away. They're taking our farm and I'll have to find work somewhere else."

"Hmmm, who's taken your farm?"

"Mr. Billi—" *No names.* "I mean, a plantation owner." Adam stuffed the remaining bread into his mouth. At last that part was true. When the woman didn't answer he continued. "My best friend is a slave at the plantation, but he got beaten so hard, he almost died. I took care of his wounds, but the owner said we helped my friend escape. Now they're taking our farm to pay for the fine." Saying it out loud made it even worse. To his embarrassment he felt tears stinging his eyes. "I'm going to Kentucky," he croaked.

"So it seems," the woman said dryly, though less gruff. "Where is your father?"

"Pa was killed…in the war." To Adam's surprise the woman sighed and jumped to her feet.

"Men and their wars." She sounded as if she were going to spit. "Which side did he choose?"

"Yankees," Adam said, draining the last of the milk. This was it. The woman would throw him out any second.

"Was he…in Virginia?"

Adam nodded. The woman's right hand fluttered to her hair which was braided and snaked around her head. "Your Pa and my husband were probably in the same place."

"Is your husband dead?"

"No!" the woman cried. "At least not that I know." She slumped back into her chair, her eyes far away.

"Can you tell me where I can join?" Adam said into the silence.

"I thought you were looking for work. Or was it visiting your uncle?"

"I didn't know… I thought you were for the Rebs."

The woman nodded gravely. "This country is being torn apart. Brother against brother, cousin against cousin. It's shameful." She threw him another look. "The Union established a camp near

Barboursville, Kentucky. That's all I know." She leaned forward, holding his gaze. "My advice is to go home. Don't get mixed up in the war. Work the land. It's the one thing you can rely on. It'll make you happier."

Adam looked away. Happiness was a thing of the past. The worst of it was that he'd not appreciated his life, not realized his happiness. Even after Pa died, he'd had Ma and Sara, Tip and…his home.

His sight grew blurry, and he became aware of the woman watching him.

"You can sleep in the barn tonight." She straightened to clear away the dishes. "I'll get you a blanket. Tomorrow I'll give you breakfast and something for the road. Just promise me you'll go home."

Adam grabbed the blanket and headed into the barn, his last thoughts about Ma sitting by the door waiting, and Sara's eyes dark with fear.

CHAPTER TWELVE

Tip froze when a key rattled in the door and a light danced toward him. He'd been lying awake for the last hour, listening to Balder snore, trying to decide what to do.

"Up. Hurry," Rawley shouted, noisily scratching his chest.

Before Tip had time to scramble to a stand, his face exploded in agony as the whip sliced across his cheek—the only good one he had left.

"Faster, lazy ass." The whip sliced through the air. "I heard you're no good. We'll teach you quick." Balder was already at the door standing at attention, staring straight ahead. He was probably glad Master beat up on somebody else.

Tip stumbled into the yard where a couple of torches flickered near a mud puddle and what looked like a well. An old colored man and woman were wiping themselves down, the man's gray hair matching his beard. As soon as Tip drew near, they scrambled out of the way, their faces furtive, eyes to the ground.

"Take a drink and follow me," Rawley barked, ignoring the old couple.

As the first light of dawn tinged the sky, they walked along a patch of bushes into a field. Above them, a Downy Woodpecker scrambled up a walnut tree and out of sight.

Tip shuddered when he saw an old mule strapped into a harness. Even in the twilight, he could tell the animal was on its last legs. Balder wordlessly grabbed a scythe while the Master motioned Tip to take hold of the plow behind the mule.

The whip made contact with Tip's shoulders, then across the mule, which lurched forward. Pain seared through Tip's back, nearly buckling his knees as he gripped the wooden handles. Good thing his palms were work-toughened.

His skin felt raw and stuck to his shirt as he followed the mule into the morning.

By the time he was signaled to stop, the sun stood high above the field. Some overseer, whose suspicious gaze followed Tip's every move, had replaced Rawley.

Heads low, Tip and Balder walked toward the shacks where the old slave woman had set out a couple of bowls with oat gruel and biscuits. Not looking left or right, Tip gobbled them down, drinking extra water to give his stomach the impression of fullness.

Within minutes, the whip cracked once more, Tip and Balder competing to be first back on the field. Tip had worked hard at the Billings farm. He hadn't really minded. But the unrelenting sun on his shredded flesh made him weak. His legs wanted to stagger and buckle, just like the mule.

Worse was that Master and his overseer were watching every move he made. At the Billings place he'd been left to do his work. He'd been trusted because of Mama Rose and had enjoyed respect among the slaves. Tip felt his eyes go wet. The three slaves at this place looked beaten up and beaten down.

That night Tip lay in the dark, too angry to sleep. His back was beyond sore and he had to lie on his side which brought his nose closer to the stinking floor. He'd been given a dirty blanket, which he'd rolled up beneath him to take some of the pressure away from his back.

He wished he'd stayed put when Nathan beat him, or maybe asked old Jonas for advice. Now Adam had killed Nathan Billings and would go to jail. Tip's throat grew tight. Adam would be hanged. The Billings were powerful and told others what to do. That included the sheriff and judge.

Stifling a sob, Tip rolled to his other side, numb to the screaming in his back.

Mama Rose had to be inconsolable. When he was little she'd told him over and over that he'd saved her life. He as a baby needing her, then growing into a toddler and finally a young man had been the only joy in her life. Why had he gone to Adam for help? Now he was stuck in this hellhole without any time to himself, without his mother, without Adam.

A sigh escaped him as he wondered what Adam was up to. Would he return to the Billings to look for Tip? Probably not, at least not officially. Would the Billings connect Nathan's death to Adam? Maybe he was already on his way to the gallows. Tip's chest squeezed together painfully. Everything was his fault. He'd as good as killed his best friend.

In the darkness, Adam's face floated in front of him. He remembered their walks along the river, Adam smiling as he talked about going to veterinary school one day, and Adam's sadness after he learned about his father's death.

Tip grimaced in the darkness. Maybe he could send a note to Mama Rose and Adam.

He could write a little, but in this place he was lucky to get food. He wasn't even sure this Master knew how to read or write. Before Mama Rose had gotten so busy as the Billings main cook, she'd taken him to another slave who had since died.

This slave had been an important man in his native Africa, a wise man who'd traveled and read many books. In the evenings and on Sunday afternoons when the slaves had a bit of free time, Mama Rose and Tip had studied with the wise man.

Tip stretched his raw shoulder as he tried to remember the letters he'd learned long ago. His mind seemed filled with cotton. He had to try harder. Eyes wide open he drew a capital A in the darkness. Adam's name began with A. He'd work on it from now on, try to remember each letter in the alphabet, even if it'd take him a year.

Feeling slightly better about his new goal, he drifted off to sleep.

CHAPTER THIRTEEN

"Do you have paper to send a letter to my family?" Adam asked while devouring a humungous breakfast of boiled oats, fried eggs and potatoes.

The woman nodded, producing a piece of yellowed scrap with a stain in one corner.

Adam had written a hundred letters in his head, but now that the paper lay in front of him, he didn't know how to start. *Dear Ma, I killed Nathan Billings and don't want to be hanged.* No way. The less he said, the better. Jack Billings and his friend, the sheriff, were probably searching the farm right now.

> *Dear Ma,*
> *Had to leave. Don't worry and don't look for me. I'm fine.*
> *Adam*

Remembering something, he tore a tiny piece from a corner and scribbled two numbers on top before sticking the scrap into his shoe. Then he folded the letter and stood up.

"I'd be obliged if you could mail this for me next time you're in town. I put the address on the outside."

The woman shot him a strange look but nodded. "Looks like you haven't changed your mind. You'll need to head further west until the end of the lake. Turn north the first road you get to. It's a good seventy miles." She pointed at a bundle on the table. "This will last for three days...if you're careful."

Adam's throat tightened again. He longed for a hug because for that instant he would be able to fool himself he was in Ma's arms. He steadied his trembling hands and tucked the food under his arm. "I…"

"Don't bother. Maybe someone will do the same for my husband."

"I hope you'll see him very soon."

Hiking the rolling hills of southern Kentucky, Adam felt almost cheerful. The land was green, the woods cool and refreshing. It helped to have a full stomach. But as he moved farther away from his mother and sister and all he'd known, he couldn't shake the sense of doom. Lead weights were attached to his limps, making him move ever slower.

So his father had joined because he'd believed Lincoln and wanted to do his part to help end slavery. Adam thought of Tip, and the way he had to endure endless beatings. How could you be somebody's property? It all didn't make sense except to make the southern landowners rich. But what could he do, a farm boy without a family?

Just get it over with. Do what Pa did and stop running. His insides churned with the thought that his life was almost over.

Here and there he hitched a ride on a farmer's cart. He slept in fields and hay barns. The weather continued to be hot and dry though the first signs of fall were fast approaching. Birch and maples were turning yellow and red, wheat fields, stalks heavy with fruit, swayed ready for harvest. On the third day he reached Barboursville, a small town in southern Kentucky.

He was chewing the last of the bread when he marched into town. The place was asleep except for Union flags moving in the afternoon breeze.

Adam stopped a man in the street. Wearing spectacles and broad sideburns, he looked like a solicitor.

"Sir, do you know where I can enlist?"

The man gave him an appraising look. "Camp Andrew Johnson is that way. You can't miss it."

Adam nodded. For the first time in days he felt a twinge of purpose. Pa had gone off to join the Union. He was simply following in his footsteps like thousands of other men.

Two miles east of town the area opened up into a broad field covered in rows and rows of canvas tents. Soldiers marched up and down paths. Dust clouds coated everything. A makeshift fence surrounded the fields and a couple of rough-hewn log houses and outbuildings that looked like a former farm.

As Adam approached, a man in a dark-blue jacket and black boots stepped into his way, rifle cradled at the ready. "Where to?" he shouted.

"I'd like to volunteer." Adam's voice sounded thin among the bellowing men assembling for parade.

"See that fellow over there." The soldier pointed toward a tent that stood slightly aside and was larger than the rest. In front of it sat a soldier behind a traveling desk. Trying to look confident, Adam headed for the tent where fifteen or so men stood waiting.

He struggled to relax while throwing uneasy glances at the recruits in front of him. They all seemed much older with full beards and broad shoulders. What if they sent him away because he was too young?

As the line snaked slowly toward the table where the recruiter wrote into a notebook, Adam's bowels began to rumble with anxiety. The strange farm woman had said he was a bad liar, and maybe she was right. He wouldn't know—he'd never had much need to lie before. But one thing was for sure; if they kicked him out now, he'd have no place to go.

"Name, age, where from?" the soldier drawled, his voice squeaky with a strange accent.

The man in front of Adam gave his name as Wilbert Drake, age twenty-seven from Corbin, Kentucky. "Stand over there." The recruiter pointed toward one of two loosely formed groups. "Next."

Adam stumbled forward.

"Name, age, where from?" The pen hovered over the list of fresh entries.

"Adam Br—" Watching the pen, Adam began to sweat. He couldn't use his real name. What if Billings was looking for him?

"Adam who?" The recruiter looked up from his paper. "Hurry, sonny, we've got a war to fight."

"Blythe...Adam Blythe."

"Age and state." The pen waited.

"I'm over eighteen and I stand on my word. I'm from Tennessee." Adam sucked air, wondering if he'd be called out, but the recruiter kept scribbling before pointing a finger toward the waiting crowd.

He thought of the paper in his shoe with the number eighteen on it. Except for his name, he hadn't lied. With a pang he realized that his 16th birthday had been yesterday. In the past they'd celebrated with cake and small gifts. A new lump formed in his throat. All that was over.

"Group on the right."

Adam nodded numbly and joined the men near the tent's entrance. There were ten or twelve of them, mostly older except for one boy with the red flaming hair of carrots. Freckles covered his cheeks, reminding Adam of Allister Porter, but that was where the similarities ended. The red-haired kid had bright blue eyes and a pug nose, with an expression of curiosity and good humor.

"Where you from in Tennessee?" the boy asked, his eyes dancing mischievously.

"Greeneville," Adam said, immediately regretting that he hadn't made up a different town. "You?" he hurried.

"Aw, you've never heard of it. My kin lives in Pigeon Forge, south of Knoxville. Nothing there but a few shacks, a mill and a church. I had to get away and find something more useful to do." The boy smiled, revealing a missing front tooth. "I'm Westfield, everyone calls me Wes. Now mind you, that's my *first* name. Who names their kid Westfield? I think Pop was drunk when I was born. Who knows what he thought at the time—"

"Adam...Blythe," Adam said, amazed how one could talk that much without being invited.

"You just got here?"

Adam nodded.

"Arrived here myself this afternoon." Wes flashed a smile, obviously uncaring about the gap among his teeth. "You think we'll get weapons today? I sure could use myself something to shoot. I got a bull's eye once, but Pop lost our rifle in a game of poker."

Adam shrugged. "No idea what they'll do—"

"I'm Corporal Ryker," somebody roared behind Adam's right ear. "Gather round and listen." Adam and his group scrambled for position. The man's face in front of them was covered under a full beard the color of coal, the rest of his skin ruddy as if he'd been dipped in freezing water. "I don't have much time, so here goes. You'll follow me, two at a time in a nice *straight* line to your quarters. You'll be four to a tent, so make it out amongst yourselves." Ryker squinted at them with barely disguised contempt.

"What a grump," Wes whispered as he stepped next to Adam.

"Private." Ryker marched straight to Wes. "You've got something to say?"

Wes fervently shook his head.

"That's *no, Sir,*" Ryker spit. "Now move your sorry asses so we get there before the war is over. You're going to be part of Col. James P. T. Carter's Second Regiment of Tennessee Volunteer Infantry. Don't forget that."

Adam tried to remember what the corporal had said, but the noise outside was deafening as hundreds of men shouted commands, fired practice shots, drums beat and pots clanged. He marched as best he could, trying to dodge the heels of the man in front of him while aligning his steps with Wes's. He thought he heard Wes sing a little tune about 'an old oaken bucket,' but he was afraid to look sideways.

His mind whirled with the realization that he was stuck. He hadn't really thought what it meant to be in the Army. He had, after all, volunteered. What he hadn't realized was that they'd all signed up for three years of service. Three years. The air closed in on him as he thought of his mother.

You wanted to die anyway, so what does it matter how long you signed up for?

They passed more tents and when the man in front of him stopped without warning, Adam kicked him in the heel. Before he could utter an excuse, he noticed the Corporal coming around.

"ABOUT FACE," Ryker yelled and when the group shoved to turn his way, he yelled even louder. "That means you swivel on your heels to look at me. Keep your distance from your neighbors." He shook his head. "I suppose you'll learn all that."

Nobody in Adam's group spoke, and Adam tried to keep a blank face. He'd be dead soon anyway, so who really cared if he stood perfectly straight with his heels pressed together?

"At four o'clock," Corporal Ryker scrutinized an elaborate gold pocket watch, "which is in thirty-three minutes, you'll report to the quartermaster. That's the last tent in this row." He pointed down the endless path. "Where you'll receive your uniform and assorted provisions.

"At exactly five o'clock you'll take position on the field behind us to meet the rest of your regiment. Now count to four and move into your tents."

Adam felt Wes's eyes on him, but before he could say anything, Wes was already tugging at his arm.

"Come on, let's take up house. This one looks pretty homey to me." He dragged Adam along, throwing open the flap of the nearest tent. "How about this side?"

"You two bunking on the left, then we'll take the right." The man who'd spoken was short as a girl, but the moustache he sported would've won any contest. It reached clear across his face, its two dark-brown handlebars cutting his cheeks in two. "I'm Marty Jackson and this here is Thomas Miller."

"This here struttin' fellow is Adam Blythe and I'm Westfield Jones," Wes said. "Everyone calls me Wes."

They shook hands all around and having nothing to do slumped to the ground. Now that he was calmer, Adam noticed how the air sweltered in here. "If you don't mind I'll open the flaps," he said, jumping back up.

"It's stinking hot in here," Wes said brightly. "Where you folks from?"

Adam didn't listen as he fastened the cloth to the tent's sides. It didn't help much, but it was an excuse to check the outside without the grouchy Corporal breathing down his neck. His throat felt like sandpaper, but he doubted he could wander around to find a water source. At least the wind felt good on his damp forehead. What he really wanted was a bath, but that was out of the question on this broiling dusty pasture.

Two hours later he stood on the parade field. Despite the evening hour, sweat ran down his arms and sides because the jacket he'd been issued was wool. He'd be glad for it once winter arrived, the quartermaster's assistant had said as he handed out uniforms— long dark-blue jackets with endless buttons, pants and boots, a spare set of drawers and socks. With that came a weird-looking hat they called a forage cap, a sheet of cotton canvas that could be attached to a second piece to form a tent roof, a wool blanket, a knapsack, a canteen, a sack of coffee beans, and a box of hardtack.

All the while Wes was talking up a storm, commenting on the clothes, the food and the men around them. The quartermaster himself handed them muskets, sixty rounds of ammunition in a leather cartridge box, a percussion cap box, a bayonet, a knife and flint. Don't waste it, he'd said.

By the time Adam had stumbled back to the tent his arms were falling off. How was he supposed to fight rebels if he was loaded like a donkey? *What does it matter*, he reminded himself, *you'll be shot pretty soon anyway.*

"Might as well throw that dog collar out," Marty said when Adam inspected the cravat that had been issued with the uniform.

With a shake of his head, he flung it in the corner. It'd be a wonder if he ever got the hang of being a soldier.

Now he stood among several hundred recruits to be part of the Second Regiment Tennessee Volunteer Infantry, soaking his brand-new outfit. He was glad to be a few rows back, away from the stern watch of their commander, Col. James Carter. Carter who had a full beard and dark hair, looked strong as a runaway bull as he addressed them.

"You've come here to help us stop the Rebs from poisoning this country with slavery, and to make us whole again. During the next few weeks we'll train you to become soldiers. You'll work hard and get to know your messmates. I expect every one of you to give your best. Nothing less will do."

Adam's mind drifted off. The collar of his jacket scratched his neck, the rifle's sling dug into his shoulder still sore from the fight with Nathan Billings.

"...you'll keep your eyes on the color guard and your ears tuned to the drums."

Adam cranked his neck to watch two men carrying the Union flag on a long pole and the boy, no older than himself, carrying a drum with an eagle painted on it.

"Now return to your quarters for dinner."

Adam thought of the mess of salt pork, sugar, beans, hardtack and potatoes he'd received. It had never occurred to him he'd have to cook his own food. Wes had tried a piece of hardtack earlier and complained of instant toothache. The stuff seemed to be solid as a fieldstone and just as tasty.

"We'll meet for evening drill at seven o'clock, first in your squad, then together," Carter was saying, his gaze sweeping across the crowd in such a way that Adam felt himself singled out. To his relief, the Colonel went on. "I don't need to tell you that you are the Union's feet on the ground. As our infantry, you are the most important soldiers of this war."

The drums beat and Carter smartly marched off. To Adam's left and right, men barked orders he didn't understand. From the corner of his eye he saw Corporal Ryker heading their way, face red, eyes squinting as if he were ready to kill someone.

"You and you, you two, line up here. And..." he shouted as his gaze fell on Adam. "You and your neighbor to the right."

"That'd be me," Wes said, cheerfully joining Adam's side.

"You eight here are my squad," Ryker yelled over the din of his fellow corporals. "Until we get ranks complete, that is. From now on you assemble like this, four in front, four in rear."

"Yes, Sir," several of the men answered before Adam could jump in.

"What was that?" Ryker said. "Louder."

"Yes, Sir," the eight shouted. Adam thought his voice sounded weak and throaty. He was parched.

"Now follow me to quarters. Remember your feet, left first. Repeat after me, one, two, one, two."

By the time Adam finally lay down it was dark. Watching Marty and Thomas, he'd fixed a less than dismal dinner of half-cooked beans, potato bits and salt pork, followed by sugared coffee. He'd never cared much for coffee, but it seemed the only drink available except for tepid water. At least it had given him a boost to make it through two more hours of drills.

His lower back ached from the unaccustomed standing, and his forehead pounded from too much sun. He was a private now, no longer his own man, but the property of the government.

Just as well, he thought before drifting off, pushing away the faces of his mother, Sara and Tip.

CHAPTER FOURTEEN

Tip quickly learned that Master Billings and this Master had little in common. It wasn't just the way he had to work harder and longer every day. Whatever this Master did seemed dumb. Neither the Master nor the overseer did any physical labor. Why would they wear out their only help, the two slaves who ensured there'd be food on the table? The old colored couple, Mary and John, stayed in the house to help the Missus and her six small children.

Master Rawley was a drinker. Like Nathan Billings, the alcohol made him mean. And where Nathan had been drinking every few days, Master Rawley never went anywhere without a flask. By early afternoon when he made the rounds across the field where Tip and Balder worked, he was slurring his speech, his gait uncertain as he watched them. Only one thing he got better at with drink: using his whip.

"Too slow, too slow," were his favorite words when he came to a stop behind Tip. After plowing the field, he and Balder were seeding fall crops of spinach and turnips. "Lousy rotten bastards. Paid a premium for you working like old women." The whip sliced the air and then their backs. Wherever the tender skin on Tip's back had just begun to heal, new welts appeared.

It was clear to Tip that it didn't matter how hard he worked. He'd be beaten for principle alone.

Consequently, he became angrier with every passing day, the constant soreness like a flame heating his fury. He knew he'd be dead within a year. He'd already lost weight from the little food they received, and the wounds on his back had no chance to heal. It was a wonder they weren't festering. Why had Master Rawley paid all the money when he was wasting his purchase?

And so, in the few minutes of respite, Tip began to think of escape. Where to was the big question. He couldn't return to his mother, nor anywhere nearby. Word would get around instantly. At the Billings farm they'd talked about freemen in the north, Negroes working like white people, going about as they pleased. It was hard to imagine nobody telling him what to do, being paid for his labor and sleeping in on Sundays.

Finding freedom was the one thing on his mind. He thought about it as he dug. He thought about it as he plowed. He thought about it cutting wood and feeding chickens. Yet, the idea seemed ludicrous, a shifting cloud of an image he couldn't pin down.

Which direction was north? He didn't even know where he was and how to avoid being caught.

Thinking back to his ride with Wilkes, he couldn't be more than twenty miles from the Billings. That meant he was still in Tennessee. He shook his head, knowing he'd have to take his chances—even if he died on the way.

He made a point of watching Smith, the overseer. Bent low over the soil, Tip turned his head this way and that to learn the man's habits. And knew soon that there was no chance he'd ever run during the day. Smith cradled his rifle like a precious child and even if he sat in the shade with his eyes momentarily closed, Tip could tell, the man noticed every sound.

There was also Balder.

Among the Billings's slaves, Tip had known camaraderie, a mutual respect for each other. His new fellow slave brother was either too dumb or too beaten up to care about anything. Tip noticed how he'd go for the biggest piece of corn, the largest chunk of bread. There seemed to be no consideration for anyone but himself.

So Tip stayed alone and kept his thoughts well hidden. He'd have to escape during the night when he'd have the longest possible time to get away before his absence would be discovered.

But every evening he was locked up in the hut and though it was filthy and looked ramshackle, its walls and roof were sturdy with a tiny barred window. The few times, usually on Sundays, when it was still light enough to see anything in the gloomy dankness, Tip investigated the ground. He'd fashioned himself a rough mattress from an old burlap sack and a pile of corn shucks. At least he wasn't on the soiled floor anymore.

One evening as he sat on his bed, his hand touched something hard. A rock was stuck in the corner, nearly buried in the dirt. Glancing casually at Balder, who lay unmoving on a pile of dirty straw on the other side, Tip tugged at the rock. He soon worked it lose enough to remove and stuff underneath his mattress.

Tiredness forgotten, he waited for Balder to go to sleep. Every time he felt himself nod off, he tore open his eyes. Darkness had fallen outside by the time Balder's snore filled the air. Leaning against the wall, Tip began scratching at the dirt. Hard and full of clay, it'd take months if not years.

Still, here was his ticket to freedom. He'd dig himself out, no matter how long it took.

CHAPTER FIFTEEN

It was still dark when the bugle announced reveille. Adam was used to getting up early, but he hadn't slept well for days. Marty and Thomas snored, and so did countless others, the sounds easily traveling through the thin canvas walls.

Wes seemed unperturbed as they stumbled to the latrine, but Adam was self-conscious about the lack of privacy. Somehow he'd never given much thought to what being a soldier meant. He'd imagined lying in ambush and shooting at rebels, not this swarming assembly of men stuck together every minute of the day, their sweat and grunts, their grimy faces inches away.

The only good thing was that it distracted him from the terrible guilt that kept creeping up in the early morning hours when he lay awake.

They assembled for roll call and breakfast call, marched and drilled, marched and drilled. They had shooting practice, faked bayonet attacks on straw bales, and practiced hand-to-hand combat. At night, they sat around camp, cleaning their rifles, writing journals and telling stories. Adam listened most of the time. He couldn't afford to give anything away.

"Hey Blythe, isn't it time to *acknowledge the corn*...tell us about yourself?" Marty Jackson's moustache looked wilted, but his greenish eyes sparkled as he searched Adam's face.

Adam had been drawing in the dirt and kept quiet. Let Marty pick on somebody else.

"Adam," Wes said, thumping Adam in the side. "You not

talking tonight?"

Adam flinched. "What?" When he looked up, his three tent comrades stared at him curiously. "Sorry, wasn't listening."

"That's abundantly clear," Marty said. "We all talk about our families and where we're from and you're keeping tight. You get in trouble or something?"

Trying to appear calm, Adam slowly shook his head. He could feel his cheeks burn. So much for lying convincingly.

"Looks like you're right, Marty," Thomas Miller chuckled. An easy six feet tall, he was skinny as a walking stick. "He blushes like a girl."

"Just leave him be," Wes said, giving Adam's shoulder a good-natured pound. Adam pulled away, irritated that they didn't leave him alone, and especially irritated that Wes seemed to always be in a good mood, no matter how bad things were. Most of all, he was irritated with himself. He wished he could let go of his former life and accept the men's easy camaraderie.

"Sorry, I didn't mean to be..." Adam tried. "Just got a lot on my mind."

"I don't understand why we don't get to move to Camp Robinson," Marty said. "I mean, everyone is going up there. But we have to stay around to be *home guard*."

"If that isn't the dumbest thing I ever heard. What's a home guard anyway?" Wes said.

"We protect the area instead of attacking Rebs." Marty thoughtfully massaged his moustache. "I'm afraid it'll be boresome."

Adam scraped his boot across the ground where he'd drawn the outline of a cabin and a horse. Why did he have to feel such a longing for what he couldn't have anymore? Now he couldn't even shoot rebels.

"Why did we volunteer if we can't even fight?" he said to no one in particular. They all nodded, apparently glad that their mostly mute companion was finally speaking.

"Especially when you're so good with the musket," Wes said with a grin. "Did you know, boys, that Adam here is an amazing shot? Even grumpy Ryker couldn't find much fault today."

"Where did you learn to shoot?" Marty asked.

"Pa taught me." A hundred years ago, he and Pa had spent every Saturday morning in the woods, using a tree stump for target practice. He'd learned to shoot squirrels and rabbits, even birds, but had soon lost interest. Killing an animal without real need felt wrong.

"He must be very proud of you," Thomas Miller said. He'd taken off his jacket and opened the top buttons of his shirt, drooping around his slender neck. Uniforms were made for average men, not tall and thin ones.

"He's dead," Adam said. "Rebs killed him in Virginia—"

"Boys," Ryker came to a stop in front of their tent and that of their neighbors. "You heard the orders. Tomorrow morning the majority of this camp will head north to Camp Robinson. Captain Isaac Black will take over the home guard. We'll be part of that. Keep on your toes. General Zollicoffer wants Kentucky. He's pushing north from Cumberland Gap." Ryker glanced at them, wiping his damp face with a handkerchief.

Somewhere in the distance the drums sounded taps.

"You heard it, boys," Ryker said. "Get yourselves inside."

When Adam lined up for afternoon parade the following day, the field had shrunk to less than two hundred men, the ground mud and dust where tents had stood and men had slept. What was he doing here standing around? He wanted to fight and forget.

"We're organizing a foraging party," Ryker said after the last round of practice marching. "Collect what you can without too much trouble."

Though Adam was glad to escape the monotony of the camp exercises, he wondered what Ryker meant by "without too much trouble."

Food had gotten worse over the last week, part of the reason why most of the men had been sent north to Camp Robinson. Rumor had it that soldiers there feasted on beef stew and fried potatoes, and that they received brand-new 1861 rifled Springfield muskets instead of the smoothbore muzzleloaders Adam and his buddies carried. The Springfields used Minié balls, conically shaped ammunition that was rumored to hit targets ten times farther and more accurately.

"Wonder what we'll find," Wes said as they headed toward the outskirts of Barboursville. Their foraging party consisted of four squads, each man equipped with sacks intent to fill. Since it was September, most crops had been harvested as they fanned across fields, entered farms and outlying homes.

Farmers donated with a weary expression on their faces, their wives and kids cowering in the back. They collected apples, potatoes, a few chickens, assorted greens, slabs of bacon, and a few ribs. Adam was in charge of carrying eggs, but no matter how carefully he moved, they kept breaking, soaking through the burlap, and leaving a gooey mess on the trail.

They had just crossed the bridge over Little Richland Creek when he heard something. Wes was several steps ahead and Adam caught up to him.

"Did you hear that?"

Wes stopped abruptly, placing his potato bag on the ground. "There." From the corner of his eye, Adam saw Marty turn his head. He'd heard it, too.

Somewhere in the distance beyond the stand of woods, horses neighed and voices called commands. Judging by the clatter, it had to be a large assembly.

"Everyone down," Marty said.

"Come on, let's go back to camp and deliver the goods," said one of the boys, a beefy man who was the farthest ahead. "I'm starving."

"What if they're Rebs," Marty whispered. "You wouldn't want them to march right into town and on top of us."

"Let's wait and see who it is," Wes said, slumping behind a clump of juniper bushes. "I could use a little break just about now." Half grumbling, half anxious, they took cover. Adam had a good view of the bridge. Past it, the road split the fields in two, on the left the last corn, on the right stubble. But Adam scrutinized the stand of oak trees seventy-five yards beyond.

There, he heard it again. Indistinct clatter like wagon wheels and chains clinking together, horses neighing and snorting. There were voices, too, but they were hard to make out. Someone was definitely coming.

Adam squinted, but the dusk was making it hard to see. His eyes were tearing as he strained to penetrate the softening lines. What if they were Union forces and he'd shoot at them by mistake? Or worse, if they were Rebs he might be dead in an hour. *That's what you wanted.* But somehow he wasn't quite ready to die—at least not today.

"You think they're Rebs?" Wes whispered. He was lying next to Adam, musket trimmed across the field.

"Possibly," Adam said and suddenly he was scared.

He'd not expected it, thinking he'd be indifferent once the fighting began. Now that he was close, he was losing his cool.

Behind him Marty was crawling closer. "They've got to be Rebs," he said. "Otherwise they'd have come out on the path by now. Didn't Ryker mention some Reb General wanting our skins?"

That's when Adam saw it: a movement near the edge of the trees where the road disappeared into the shadows. Somebody was standing there behind a tree, someone with light blue sleeves, the same light blue he'd seen on the Confederate's uniform in Morristown. Adam could just make out the corner of one shoulder and an arm before it took cover. His breath caught as he gripped the musket tighter.

"I saw something," he whispered. "Rebs are hiding in there. I reckon they've seen us."

A murmur traveled up the line of his group.

"Wonder how many there are," Wes said. "I'll send one of the boys to alert Ryker and Captain Black."

"Wonder if we should shoot?" Marty said. Just then, Adam noticed puffs of clouds erupting across the field, followed a split-second later by the sound of explosions. Splinters rose from the bridge's wooden planks as the earth around Adam got peppered with hundreds of bullets.

Remembering his training, he aimed high at the trees and fired. Everyone followed except that their shots were snuffed out by the roar of the return fire.

"Not good," Wes whispered as they reloaded. "There must be hundreds of Graybacks."

More shots thundered. Adam kept his head low as he peeked across the expanse. It was dark now, and he could only guess from memory where the road was or how high he had to aim. His nose stung from the gunpowder and his ears rang. Nobody had told him that war was loud and smelly. Adam suppressed a shiver as he realized this could be his last night alive.

"They're not going to make it across *this* bridge," Marty said grimly, shooting into the dark to prove his point. "Not as long as I'm here."

"We won't be able to hold them off," Adam whispered. "Not with a handful of boys. Hope Black is coming soon."

He hadn't quite finished when he heard movement behind

him. With Barboursville only a quarter mile away, a handful of townspeople had crawled closer to watch the spectacle.

Adam kept reloading and shooting, their volleys quiet compared to the massive blows from the other side. Time lost all meaning as they shot and reloaded.

Adam fingered his ammunition. Almost out. Luckily, the shots from across the field were slowing down. Then stopped. Quiet settled. The air grew cold and dampness seeped into Adam's skin.

Adam rolled on his back, staring into the night sky. His right shoulder ached from the constant recoil, inflaming the injury he'd sustained from the fight with Nathan Billings.

Nathan had been cruel, but he, Adam, was a killer. His thoughts wandered to Tip. Maybe Billings had allowed him to stay home for Mama Rose's sake. Deep down he knew it was unlikely. Jack Billings was not the forgiving type.

Surely Ma and Sara had received his letter by now. He'd already been gone for weeks. Maybe he'd write again if he got the chance.

"Anyone know what time it is?" he asked. There hadn't been a single shot fired from the Rebs in several minutes.

"I reckon between one and two in the morning." Marty had been a sailor in his former life and could read the stars like other people read clocks. Even when it was cloudy or raining like right now, he always could tell time.

"I wish we could go back to camp," Wes said. "I have a hankering for some hot coffee and grub. I'm all soft from this drizzle."

"They'd come after us," somebody said.

"We'll hear them. Either way we won't hold them off for long," Wes said.

Adam stiffly sat up. "We hardly have any bullets left." He felt naked, exposing himself to the enemy. Any second a shot could kill him. *So what*, his mind argued, but he felt anxious nonetheless. He was soaked to the bone, and his stomach was beyond growling.

"What if they come across while we're in camp? We're supposed to protect the town."

"Right, right," a few of them mumbled. "Some of us will accompany the townspeople to warn everyone."

"I'm staying," Adam heard himself say. What was that about

being miserable and wanting food and a tent?

"Me too," Wes said. "What's hot coffee when I can be with such fine spirited comrades?" To emphasize the point, he slapped Adam on the back. "Let'em rip. Let's give those Rebs a piece of our mind."

Adam grinned.

"Look at that," Wes chuckled. "Glad your face is cracking."

Adam's smile deepened. "Idiot." But secretly he was glad to have Wes next to him.

"I'm going to take care of that bridge," Marty said. "Come on boys, let's tear up the planks, make it harder for them stinking Rebs to cross."

They felt their way to the bridge, using their bayonets to pry up the wood. From the field behind them, a few Barboursville citizens quietly joined.

Adam awoke at dawn. He'd been dreaming about Tip, who'd smiled and laughed as he entered a tiny log cabin in the middle of a giant cornfield.

Next to him, Wes was whispering with Marty when the sound of horse clip-clop raised the hairs on Adam's neck. Shaking the cobwebs of sleep from his freezing damp body, Adam peeked past the hole where the bridge used to be. That was how far he could see. Heavy fog like milk covered them. Even now the approaching horses sounded muffled.

"Let's spread out," Marty whispered. "Some of you in the ravines and below the bridge. "They're coming."

That's when Adam noticed they'd lost another ten men. Apparently they'd left in the night to return to camp.

As Adam contemplated whether to shoot or find a better hiding place, the first riders came into view. They looked like ghosts floating in the gray light. The soft rattle of sabers and the reflection of the steel muskets said otherwise. The riders abruptly stopped, apparently realizing the bridge was missing its surface.

A second later, Marty fired. Adam and the others followed, their shots answered from across the ravine. More Rebs moved closer through the cornfield. Across the bridge, an officer fell over, his body sinking onto the horse of his neighbor before dropping to the ground.

Adam didn't wait to see what came next. He kept firing when

he noticed rebels spilling down the embankment into the ravine by the dozens. To his right and left, cavalry had already crossed the creek and climbed up the ravine, undoubtedly to close off their retreat. Somewhere nearby, a cry rang out. One of the boys had been hit. Before he could fire another shot, the cavalry's horses on the other side of the bridge moved left and right.

"Clear the way for the artillery," somebody yelled.

Adam looked at Wes, who'd stopped in his tracks. Adam shook his head. Wes nodded.

"Time to go," he whispered, the words traveling down the line. They crawled backwards, and one by one, retreated into the brush. The few onlookers from Barboursville scattered.

Marty moaned as they assembled a hundred yards away. A blackish hole showed in his coat near the shoulder, blood dripping from beneath onto his boot.

"Damn Rebs. I know we got at least one of the riders. Looked like a lieutenant." He grimaced. "Somebody is going to have to look at that."

Wes shook his head, for once looking grave. "I can't stand the sight of blood. You can have my whiskey ration, though."

"We can't stop here," Adam said, scanning the ground behind them. "Rebs are on horses. They'll be fast."

Several men helped Marty carry his gear. As they stumbled past the town toward their camp, a soldier in dark blue hurried to meet them.

"Camp has been abandoned," he said. "Stay together and head north." Without another word he turned and raced off.

"I say we hoof it north to Camp Robinson," Wes said. "Barboursville will have to fend for itself."

Adam threw a glance at Marty whose face shone with sweat. A few hours ago they'd complained of boredom. Now Marty needed a doctor and they were being chased by Rebs. Ignoring the gnawing in his middle and with one eye on Marty, Adam shouldered his gun.

CHAPTER SIXTEEN

Every night when they returned to the hut, Tip dug. His fingers ached, and he loathed the feel of dirt on his skin. He hardly ever had time to wash, and he never received new clothes. His overalls were shredded at the cuffs, the knees ripped. Mama Rose would have a fit if she could see him.

As winter neared, Rawley provided an old shirt and a pair of work boots that were too tight. Tip's heels and toes were sore every night, blistering his skin and making each step misery.

He hoped his feet would stop growing. He was as tall as Balder, the coveralls short around his ankles, but his muscular chest had thinned, and he could count his ribs.

He felt his body weaken every day, the dinners of watery soup and biscuits not nearly enough to replenish his starving muscles. With Mama Rose he'd never known hunger, and he found it almost unbearable to tolerate the constant gnawing. But worst was the crushing weight of loneliness. Neither Mama Rose nor Adam knew he was here, and even if they did, they wouldn't have been able to change one thing. He had nobody to rely on but himself.

One day when he'd delivered a basket of potatoes to Mary, who cooked for the family, he lifted a spoon. It lay on the stove and when Mary had turned away to slip him a piece of bread, he stuffed the spoon into his pocket. He felt bad for stealing, especially since Mary was probably going to get in trouble, but he was so miserable that he couldn't bring himself to care much.

At first he scraped the loosened dirt beneath his mattress, but after a while he knew he had to get rid of it or raise suspicion. So he carefully filled his overall pockets with the sticky mud, a complicated undertaking in the dark. Each pocket took an hour to fill, and his arms burned with fatigue, his mind repeating letters and wanting to give into sleep. Balder didn't always snore, and Tip worried about him noticing something at odds. If Balder found out, he might tell Master to gain an advantage.

Tip shuddered. There was no telling what Rawley would do to him.

Each morning when it was still nearly dark, Tip emptied his pockets on the way to the field. He was frustrated about his progress. He couldn't remember what a q looked like, nor did he have a chance to write anything down. He had neither paper nor a place to write. So he scratched letters into the ground to immediately erase them or wrote them in the air in the dark.

But what good did it do him to know anything? He'd never write a real letter. It was forbidden for slaves to read and write. Keeping slaves stupid and ignorant was a way to control them. Mama Rose had warned him never to tell.

"You got any family?" Tip said into the dark after they'd settled in for the night.

"Ain't remember my mother much," Balder said. "I think I have a sister, but not sure."

"You ever want to run?" *Why had he said that?* Tip felt the tension rise in the dank space.

"Not sure where I go," Balder said. "I see bloodhounds tear the flesh off men. I see them lashed to death."

Tip nodded even though Balder couldn't see him. Just last week Rawley had him go along to help with a delivery of timber. A colored man or what was left of him had been strapped to a post. His eyes were gone, his chest white ribs picked clean by crows and rats. A terrible stink had enveloped them as they drove past.

"Let that be a lesson to you," Rawley had said as if he knew Tip's thoughts. "See what they do with slaves who run."

Tip hadn't answered, too afraid to give away his thoughts.

"You ever run?" Balder said, bringing Tip back to present day.

"Didn't have to," Tip said. "Not with my Mama being the cook and all." He wanted to say a lot more but didn't dare.

"What about now?" Balder sounded casual enough.

"You say it right. I'm too tired."

Balder turned quiet and Tip soon heard a deep snore from the opposite side. Despite being exhausted, despite his pockets full of dirt, sleep refused to come.

Why had Balder asked about running? Had he noticed something? Seen the hole in the wall under his mattress? He couldn't wait much longer. The risks were too high.

He'd rather take his chances than stay and get caught anyway.

CHAPTER SEVENTEEN

Adam was soaked in sweat. Afraid to slow down and be slaughtered by the Rebs, they'd walked most of the day, nervously glancing over their shoulders. They'd split up in groups, each of them heading north. When they finally stopped, it was mid-afternoon.

They used a hedge along a field as a windbreak and cover. Adam was already tired of hardtack, but nobody felt like making a fire and what they'd saved from the raid needed cooking.

"You think they'll punish us for leaving the fight?" Marty said, resting his head against a boulder. He looked white as a summer cloud, and Adam worried he was losing too much blood. Adam had torn up part of Marty's shirt to make a bandage and slow the bleeding. But he was no surgeon and had no idea what damage the bullet had done.

"Don't see how," Wes said. "Unless the captain wants us dead." He slumped down next to Adam and pulled off his boots. "My feet hurt like something fierce."

"Stick'em in the creek over there." Adam pointed at the brackish water fifty yards away. His own legs felt wobbly from all the running and he wished for a nice stew from his mother.

"How much farther is it?"

"Four more days at least, if we make good time." Marty's moustache trembled as he took a sip from his canteen. "We'll need to find clean water tomorrow."

"You know where it is exactly?" Wes asked.

Marty shrugged. "Near Danville."

"What if there are Rebs in-between?" Thomas slumped next to them, inspecting his coffee tin.

"We'll hear them a mile away. They trample around like a damn herd of cattle," Marty said grinning. An unhealthy sheen covered his forehead. He was pretending, that much was clear.

Adam anxiously glanced across the field. "What if they're in a small group?" Horses were much quicker and Marty kept their pace slow.

Now that he thought about it, he was shaken up. He hadn't been in the Army more than a few weeks and already he'd been in a major skirmish when they'd told him he'd be some lousy boring home guard. They'd numbered a few men, and the Rebs were in the hundreds if not thousands with plenty of heavy artillery. It just showed how little his Union leaders knew. He'd obviously have to judge for himself.

Strange, just a few days ago he'd not cared to live another day and now he worried about the Rebs finding him. It's the boys, he thought. I don't want them to get hurt. He was growing used to Wes's cheerfulness and his constant chatting, even found himself craving his company. He also liked Marty whose shirt looked rust-colored and whose breath labored even when they sat still.

There. Something moved in the distance.

Adam clamped a hand over Wes's mouth. "Shhh."

He'd found he heard much better than the others, often alerting them to this sound or that. Of course, most of the time it was nothing: a squirrel digging for hickory nuts, a couple of deer grazing or a harmless farmer urging on his horse.

"Blythe here hears the grass grow," Marty would say, his moustache twitching with mirth. After which Adam would walk off fuming, suppressing a nasty comment, only to have Wes follow and slap him on the back.

"Come on, chap, Marty is as deaf as my grandfather," Wes would say. "He's secretly glad you tell us what's out there."

Adam would squeeze out a nod and finally join the boys once more. Still, they all stuck together as if they'd known each other for years. He knew he was acting all huffy, but he couldn't help resent the men. They'd joined because they wanted to, not because they'd had no other options. And they certainly weren't running from the law over a stupid rotten mistake of killing the son of a wealthy landowner.

Adam shuddered, thinking what would happen to him if he ever returned. They'd string him up by the neck within a day. He imagined his mother, her eyes wide with shame and sadness, watching as he marched to the gallows. Sara would stand next to her, tears streaming down her face. And there was Tip.

Now that Nathan Billings was gone, Tip would finally have peace. He'd be punished for running, of course, but he'd be able to stay with Mama Rose, tend his garden and maybe marry Elda one day. Adam knew all about Elda. Tip had only mentioned her once, but Adam had recognized the same dreamy expression on Tip's face as he'd seen on his sister's talking about Allister.

The fourth evening, they came across a farm. With provisions nearly gone, Thomas suggested asking for supplies rather than resort to stealing.

"You think they're supporting the Rebs?" Wes said as they settled a hundred yards from the homestead.

"Does it matter?" Marty, leaning heavily against a tree trunk, twirled his moustache. "If they don't cooperate we'll show'em our muskets."

"Who's going?" Thomas said.

"I think Blythe should go," Marty said. "He looks more innocent and younger than us."

Adam grimaced. If they only knew.

"But look at this face," Wes said. "He hasn't laughed in a year. Who's going to take pity on a grouch? I think I should go."

"Better yet," Marty's moustache trembled to hide a grin, "You go with him. I'm sure you won't have trouble explaining things in the right way. I mean just in case, Blythe here can't find the words."

The other men hollered as Wes and Adam headed toward the farmhouse. It was a simple two-story with a couple of rocking chairs on the front porch. The barn door stood open and Adam noticed a horse buggy inside.

Looking at Wes, Adam knocked at the door. Strange nobody had heard them.

Finally, Wes whistled, a high shrill sound drilling into Adam's ear.

"What did you do that for?" Adam said, rubbing his right ear. "You telling the Rebs we're here?"

"What Rebs? Can't see any—" Wes froze just as Adam turned around.

"You there." A man in manure-caked pants approached from the barn, a musket trimmed on them. "State your business."

Adam's finger twitched on the musket he was casually holding in his left hand. Why hadn't he paid attention? To his frustration, Wes wasn't doing any better. He'd clamped his gun under his armpit.

"We're looking for food," Wes said. "Whatever you can spare."

"Can't spare nothing," the man said. From his haggard features he looked like he was struggling. "Why you back? Them soldiers in Fort Robinson already robbed me clean." He hurled a brown splash of chewing tobacco their way.

Adam nodded. "Sorry, mister. It was a mistake. We're on our way then." He slowly moved down the porch, hoping that Wes would follow.

"Damn scoundrels stealing me blind," the man said as if he hadn't heard. Quick as a flash he aimed at Adam's chest. His rifle trembled, but he looked determined. "Maybe I should blow you away. Two less Yanks in the world won't make a lick of difference."

"I wouldn't do that, mister." Marty, his voice sharp as a razor, came into view around the house corner. "Drop your gun."

"You're surrounded." Thomas approached from the left.

The man's jaw began to quiver and he lowered his gun. Keeping their muskets pointed, Adam and the boys disappeared into the woods.

"I guess that went well," Wes said.

"You need to be more careful." Marty shook his head. "You may not always have backup. That codger looked as if he was ready to blow your heads straight to hell."

"Looks like we're within foraging distance of the camp," Adam said to change the subject. He'd been careless and almost got shot by some lowlife poor farmer. "I suppose we better keep going." His gaze fell on Marty's shirt, where a bright red stain was spreading.

Next thing he knew Marty was on the ground, his eyes closed and his lips pale.

"He's bleeding again." Thomas dropped to his knees to poke

at the bloodied cloth.

"Leave it," Adam said. "I'll take another look. Help me remove his shirt and jacket."

The bullet hole was inflamed, red splotches spreading toward his ribs and across the stomach.

Adam sniffed. He'd smelled the foul odor before on a goat they'd kept for milking. From what he could tell the hole was too far to the side to be near an organ, but the shot was still inside, causing the festering. "I've got to find the slug," he said aloud. He'd hoped the surgeon at the new camp would take care of things. But Marty was out of time.

"Make a fire. I need hot water," he ordered. "And somebody rip his shirt into strips and put some into the water."

Marty mumbled something, his head going back and forth beneath his great moustache. While the boys heated water, Adam inspected his tools. The knife he carried had a wide blade. He'd have to use the tip only or he'd do more damage.

"I need whiskey."

"I rightly understand you want a drink, but it may slow you down." Wes peeked at him, his eyes full of disgust, his pallor greenish.

"Not for me. Marty needs it."

"He's in no shape—"

"Just give me the damn whiskey." Adam felt sweat drip down his forehead. He was liable to kill Marty, too.

Wes rummaged through his bag and handed him a half empty bottle of white liquid. "Boys won't like it."

Ignoring him, Adam stuck his knife in the boiling water before poking at the bullet hole.

Marty screamed and began to thrash.

"Drink." Adam held the bottle to Marty's lips. Marty swallowed a bit and shook his head.

"More!"

Marty took another sip and slumped to the ground again.

"Hold him down," Adam yelled. Thomas, Wes and one of the other boys plunked down on Marty's arms and legs, pinning him to the ground.

The hole oozed as Adam began to dig. Bile entered his mouth as the oozing turned into a stream. In the bloody mess he couldn't see a thing, certainly not find a bullet. Marty would bleed to death.

Concentrate. Adam put all his attention into his hand, forcing his fingers to do the seeing. About an inch and a half in, he felt the slightest resistance. Something hard...the slug? He continued poking, blood now gushing from the opening.

A shiver ran through Marty as his eyes rolled. He'd passed out.

"He's bleeding like a pig," Wes said, letting go of Marty's right leg. "Better get to it before we have ourselves another dead soldier."

"Hush, let him work," Thomas said.

Adam ignored them. Ever so slowly he worked the knife behind the hard object and maneuvered it toward the surface. When he looked down all he could see was blood: on his hands, the ground, soaking into Marty's pants and running across his stomach. In the middle of the mess was his knife and on its tip lay a grayish Minié ball, deformed and deadly.

"You got it," Wes yelled jubilantly.

Adam didn't answer, worried about the terrible blood loss and festering wound. Even with the bullet gone, Marty could easily die just like their goat. Adam bit his upper lip until it hurt. He needed to keep it together.

"Find me dry cloth. We need to bandage him." After mopping away some of the blood, Adam pulled a strip of fabric from the steaming water with his knife and lowered the cloth into place as a compress. Was he imagining it or was there less blood flowing?

With the help of Thomas and Wes, they wound the remaining material around Marty's shoulder and upper arm until the compress was in place.

Adam leaned back exhausted. Marty looked as pale as ever. Time would tell if he lived.

"You did it, Blythe," Wes slapped him on the back. "Better take a drink yourself. You don't look so good."

"My name isn't Blythe," Adam said. "It's Brown, Adam Brown." He took a swig, the liquid burning its way into his innards and awaking the gnawing.

To his surprise Wes said nothing. Only his green eyes burned like a question mark and something like acknowledgment.

"Better clean yourself," Thomas said, arriving with an armful of firewood. "We'll fix us some taters."

Too exhausted to think about Wes's strange reaction, Adam

stumbled toward the brownish creek. His limbs were filled with rocks, his mind reliving the bloody surgery. He rinsed his hands and forearms, cooled his face, but the stains on his sleeves and pants remained.

What would the boys do if Marty died? He shuddered. He should've waited until they reached camp. Let a real surgeon do the work. Who knew what he'd done inside the wound.

Taking turns dragging Marty on a makeshift stretcher, they reached Camp Robinson the following evening.

They smelled it before they heard it, a potent mix of cook fires, latrines and gunpowder. Thomas, the oldest in the group, asked to speak to the commanding officer to report the attack in Barboursville.

"And you did what?" Captain Melton said as they lined up in front of a tent.

"Sir, we were attacked by the Rebs," Thomas said. "They swarmed across the ravines after we tore up the bridge. There were hundreds if not thousands. When they announced they'd get the cannons ready, we found it best...we decided to retreat and report up here."

Captain Melton waved an arm. "We've already got a report about the shooting. Some of you arrived yesterday."

Thomas shrugged, looking at Adam and Wes. "Sir, I don't understand, we came straight north. Well, as best we knew with Marty being shot—"

"Looks like we'll have ourselves a new target in Barboursville. Report to the quartermaster and get yourselves situated. Dismissed, soldier."

"Let's take Marty to the ambulance," Thomas said.

"No, no," Marty mumbled. None of them had noticed he was awake. "Not the dead place. Let me stay with you."

"But we've got to get you to the surgeon," Adam said.

Fingers clawed at Adam's leg. "You mustn't let them get me. You take care of me." Marty's eyes were filled with pleading. "I'll die in there."

Adam opened his mouth, but nothing came out. Who was he to tell Marty anything? Wouldn't he want the same thing?

"Let me at least get the doctor to take a look."

Marty nodded, his eyes closed again. Adam leaned in to take a whiff. He smelled nothing but faint whiskey and dried blood.

An hour later, Adam and the boys found a spot in one of the endless tent rows. Marty was settled inside. From what Adam could see, there were thousands of men. They'd drawn rations, his knapsack filled with potatoes, apples, salt pork and fresh allotments of coffee and hardtack.

Not long after they'd set down to fix a meal, the ruddy face of Corporal Ryker appeared in their midst. "If it isn't the home guard. You boys sure didn't see that coming," he chuckled. "Drill at six o'clock. If your mate isn't better by morning, he'll have to go to the field hospital." He glanced at Adam. "Look sharp, Blythe. You made it through one skirmish. Won't be the last."

"Jones and Miller report to picket duty at eight o'clock."

"Yes, sir," Wes and Thomas shouted.

Adam made a face as soon as Ryker left. For once, Wes remained mute. In fact he looked strangely serious, his eyes downcast as he unrolled his blanket.

"You all right?" Adam asked.

"Fine."

"Why don't I believe you?"

Wes shrugged, seemingly more interested in a piece of lint on his bedroll.

Adam met Thomas's gaze. Thomas shrugged as if to say leave him alone. "We all need a good meal and a good night's sleep."

All through dinner Wes sat hunched over, not uttering a word. Adam didn't pay much attention, his mind occupied with Marty. He was awake and chewed on a piece of potato, but Ryker wanted him on his feet tomorrow.

"You heard what Ryker said," Adam whispered as he changed the dressing on Marty's wound. So far he couldn't tell if anything was boiling inside. "You think you can get up."

Marty nodded. "I'll try my best."

Adam knew it wouldn't be good enough.

To Adam's surprise Wes was still unchanged by morning. When they assembled for parade, he kept his head down, his shoulders slumped as if he were wearing an iron knapsack on his back.

Right now Marty needed his attention. He and Thomas had

Marty between them. Marty swayed a few times as Adam gripped his arm. He had trouble holding his musket, which weighed well over ten pounds.

There were hundreds of recruits standing in neat rows, a sea of blue coats. Many of the men looked as if they were newly outfitted, their indigo jackets clean, brass buttons shiny.

"Sir, a word," Adam said when he saw Ryker stomping past.

"Make it quick, Blythe."

Adam lowered his voice. "Marty needs another day or two. He's getting better. I checked his injury." Adam spoke faster. "If he goes into the infirmary he may never come out. Please. You want extra men, and he's a good soldier."

"You an expert now?" Ryker squinted at Adam. "All right, take him to quarters and get back here on the double. Report to me in the morning. If he isn't better, he's going."

Adam breathed deeply. "Yes, Sir, thank you."

"You sick or something?" Adam said to Wes after he'd changed the dressing on Marty's wound during lunch.

Wes shook his head. He hadn't uttered a word all morning.

"Come on, Wes. You've been a talking machine since I met you four weeks ago."

But Wes remained mute and to Adam's surprise his eyes shone a bit too bright. He wanted to say something, but then he clamped his mouth shut. Who was he to ask somebody to speak? He, a murderer who'd lied his way into the Army.

Life in camp turned truly miserable when winter arrived. By December, the camp had grown to more than three-thousand men, acres of tents spread in all directions surrounded by hundreds of mules and horses grazing on pastures.

Adam had never been this cold in his life. He slept in his coat and pants, often wearing his boots, wrapped in a wool blanket, but the frigid air had a way to crawl into the tents, seep through his clothes and make him shiver.

Despite the cold, his nose was constantly bombarded by stink. The latrines—open holes with boards above them—spread their stench all over camp. He'd learned to do his business in the open next to dozens of others.

His own body reeked, and his hands were black from powder,

dirt, and other things he didn't want to remember.

Arguments broke out here and there, quickly snuffed out by the captains in charge. Adam had lost track how many captains there were. He only worried about Ryker, whose foul mood had not improved, and Wes who was a different man all together.

"You reckon we'll see any fighting soon?" Marty said one evening as they sat huddled around the fire. He'd recovered. His moustache drooped a little these days, but he was back to making jokes and often patted Adam on the back as if to say thank you. Still under Carter, they were now part of the 12th Brigade of the Army of the Ohio. It was Christmas day, and they had each received a helping of beef and applesauce for dessert.

It was the only concession that this was a special day. It was the first Christmas Adam was not spending with his family. Last year they'd been happy at home, Pa laughing as he carved a wild turkey he'd shot the day before, Ma dishing up yams and beans, followed by pumpkin pie. Then they'd unwrapped their gifts. Adam had received a pocketknife from his parents and a knitted scarf from Sara.

He wondered if Tip was having a Christmas dinner with Mama Rose and the other Negroes at the Billings plantation. They always celebrated with a huge meal, singing together and sometimes dancing. What he wouldn't give to stop by and chat with Tip.

"What're you sighing about?" Thomas scratched the back of his neck. "You missing your kin? I miss my wife something fierce."

Adam looked around. Marty and Thomas were watching him expectantly, even Wes temporarily snapping out of his gloom. This was his chance to share some long overdue history. He knew the boys wondered about him.

"Come on, Blythe, quit bellyaching. What can be so horrible you can't talk about it?" Marty stroked his moustache. "All of us have some dirt in our past."

Adam shook his head, his gaze on Wes. Obviously, Wes hadn't told what he knew about Adam's name. "Nothing to talk about. I left Ma and my sister on the farm. My father is dead."

"How are they managing without you?" Marty said. "If you don't mind me asking."

"We were about to lose the farm anyway. Had to pay a fine. I assume Ma lives in town now."

"You haven't written to them?" Thomas looked incredulous. "Boy, are you in serious trouble. My wife would have my hide if I didn't write every week. She always says it's the only thing that keeps her going."

Adam swallowed, his throat dry and achy. Maybe he was coming down with something.

"Thomas is right, Blythe," Marty said, throwing a curious glance at Wes, who sat quietly chewing a piece of leftover tack. "You've got to let her know you're all right. It's downright cruel not to."

"I figure she'll hear if something happens to me." It was out before Adam realized it. "I mean, what can I possibly talk about?" How had he gotten himself into such a discussion?

"Wes, help me," Adam said, trying to make his mouth curl into a smile. But Wes just shrugged and continued chewing.

"Here," Thomas said, handing Adam a piece of rough paper. "Marty has a nice pen and some ink. Write something good."

"Maybe he can't," Wes finally said, his right cheek bulged with tack.

"You mean he can't write?" Marty said.

"I mean he can't cause there are other reasons."

Adam threw Wes a thankful glance, but Wes didn't seem to notice. Wes was right, of course. How could he write now that he'd changed his name? He'd have to come clean with his mother, and if the military read his letter they'd soon find out his real story. His breath caught. If something happened to him, his mother would never find out. The Army would send a letter to the Blythe family in Greeneville.

"Sure makes me wonder what ails you, Wes," Marty said, his forefinger thoughtfully tapping his chin. "Ever since we arrived in camp you've been different. No more cutting up, just a big long face."

"Can't see it's any of our business," Thomas said.

Adam moved closer to Wes. "Thanks. Anytime you want to talk…"

But Wes turned away, curling into a ball beneath his blanket.

A week later they received orders to march south. Ryker had said that pesky General Zollicoffer who headed a huge Reb force still occupied Cumberland Gap and that it was time to see what was what.

Tired of camp life, Adam was glad to get away from the endless routines of marching in columns, dressing the line, drilling with the regiment, and lining up for parades.

That is, until the second day of marching, when it became apparent that camp was paradise compared to this. It rained buckets all day and all night. And the next day and the day after that. They kept marching, Adam's skin white and squishy beneath the uniform. They drew rations once, the supply wagons having trouble keeping up. Beneath the thousands of marching feet and horse hoofs, the roads had transformed into oceans of muck. At night the miserable cold crept into his bones until he felt his teeth chatter. Adam was sharing a dog tent with Wes, who hadn't spoken more than a few words since they left.

His boots were soaked, and so were his uniform and bedroll. He welcomed picket duty and building rifle pits, but what he really wanted was to see action and get it over with. No more thinking, just blowing up Rebs and maybe getting shot as well.

It had been raining steadily, the road covered under a foot of muck. Progress was slow, artillery often stuck for hours. They took turns digging out the wheels, the mules slick with filth and sweat, painfully slow work that left Adam breathless and weak in the legs.

"One of these days you're going to have to tell me what's ailing you," Adam whispered one evening as they crawled into the dampness beneath their canvas. If he were honest, Wes's strange behavior worried him. They hadn't seen that much fighting and he wasn't ill. "You playing possum as soon as we make camp. Isn't healthy the way you're acting."

As usual, Wes remained mute. Adam dug into his blanket, wondering if he'd ever be warm again. The fires they managed were barely enough to warm water, and most nights they weren't allowed to make any in case of enemy spies.

They'd hoofed it fifty miles south when they were ordered to stop and hunker down. Zollicoffer was rumored to be close. It was the middle of January and the rain continued. They'd been marching for eighteen days.

"You seen Wes?" Adam asked Marty as they lined up for breakfast.

"Thought I saw him earlier, probably picket duty or digging breastworks. The light was pretty dim. Seems my eyes aren't what they used to be." Marty tried a smile, but Adam thought he detected a glimpse of anxiety. The lousy food was giving them scurvy and causing night blindness.

After morning drills, Adam began to worry. Wes always waited next to him and for the first time this morning he wasn't there. What if he had deserted? Run off like a chicken? But that wasn't like Wes. He'd never shied away from danger. They were supposed to clean their muskets, but Adam decided to take a walk. If they stopped him he could always say he needed to use the latrine.

Their encampment was large—not as large as the one at Camp Robinson but spread out over half a mile. Adam carefully made his way through the woods, trying to memorize the path so he could find his way back. The brush here was thick in places, and men had crawled half way beneath bushes. Every few feet Adam was liable to step on someone or get tangled in gear.

At last he reached open ground, keeping his ears and eyes tuned for soldiers on picket. Some of them had nervous trigger fingers, and he wouldn't be the first one to be shot by his own men. Adam looked around, the trees heavy with rain drops, the ground slopping wet. Nobody had stopped him. Not yet. The Reb camp was supposed to be close and he'd run into pickets any second.

"...you little shit," a voice hissed. Even from a distance, Adam could hear its menace, a coldness that reminded him of Jack Billings.

"Let me go," someone else said.

Adam froze. Wes's voice was unmistaken. Adam took a few steps, careful to avoid any sound. When he peeked around the trunk of a large pine he couldn't believe his eyes.

Wes stood in front of a man with reddish hair streaked with gray. He'd grabbed Wes's collar and was choking him. Despite his thin build, the man looked strong and sinewy.

"This is where I find your scrawny butt, heh," he sneered. "You run all the way into the Army without telling me." He glanced up for a second, Adam ducking behind the tree. "Imagine my surprise when I see you line up in camp," the man continued. "Have been waiting for an opportunity to have a word." The forest grew silent. Adam didn't dare move for fear of making noise. When the skinny man spoke again, his voice was softer and a bit hoarse. "You be good, you hear. Not a sound."

To Adam's surprise Wes whimpered something unintelligible. When Adam looked again, the man was dragging Wes deeper into the woods. Adam followed.

"You be nice and still now," the man said, his breath coming in spurts. He was yanking at Wes's pants, pulling them down. "I've missed that white little ass."

Adam watched in horror as the man lifted Wes's long coat and pushed against him. Without thinking, he rushed forward, his eyes on the man's back and the musket leaning against a tree stump. Wes was still whimpering while the man had begun to grunt.

"Step back real slow, mister, or I'll blow your brains out." Adam dug the tip of his muzzleloader into the man's back and grabbed his musket. His hands shook, yet the anger was making him forget danger. "Wes, get dressed and head back to camp."

Wes turned, his cheeks wet with tears and snot. Head low, he moved past Adam and melted into the woods.

"You crazy, boy?" the man scoffed. He'd obviously recovered from his surprise and his eyes burned with hatred.

"Not as crazy as you," Adam said, keeping his barrel trimmed on the man. "Now walk real slow. Or I'll say I shot you by mistake cause I thought you were a Reb."

The man stumbled forward. "I'll get you for this. You'll need eyes on the back of your head."

"Fine with me," Adam managed. Inside, rage and worry competed. That man was evil, even worse than Nathan Billings. He'd kill for the fun of it. At least North and South played on an even field, each side having a chance to fight. Not this one. That man's eyes had glinted with malice. He'd lay in wait and slit your throat.

Men were staring as they marched back into camp. "I need a commander," Adam said when he saw Ryker charging his way through the men.

"Blythe, what is the matter with you? Why aren't you cleaning your musket? You confused, taking your own side prisoner?"

"Not confused, Sir," Adam said. "This man…" Adam had trouble getting the words out. What had the bible said about Sodom and Gomorra? "This man was forcing himself on a private like an animal," he spit.

"Is this true?" Ryker said, his eyes squinting at the man. "Your name?"

"Sir, Jonathan Westfield, everyone calls me Jon." He lowered his arms. "This boy here is delusional."

"We'll see about that. Right now you both come with me. Blythe, drop your weapon before you shoot somebody."

Adam reluctantly lowered his gun as he followed Westfield and Ryker. So Wes had lied about his name, too. His last name was Westfield and somehow he was related to Jon."

"Private, keep an eye on this man while I sort out their story." Ryker nodded at a guard, pointed at Westfield, and gestured for Adam to follow him into the tent. "From the beginning, Blythe."

"Sir, I was taking a walk when I came across this man hitting a private and then pulling his pants down."

"Who's the private?"

Adam shrugged. "I'd rather not say." He remembered Wes's face so full of shame. He had to have recognized Jon Westfield in camp after they arrived in September. That's why he'd been acting strange. Adam felt his own cheeks warm. Hard to imagine what Wes had gone through. Impossible to explain.

"So it's your word against Westfield's."

"Yes, Sir."

Ryker stepped closer to Adam and lowered his voice. "I realize you want to protect the other man. But this is the time to speak up."

"I can't."

"Fine then, dismissed."

"Sir, I…"

"Dismissed. Back to your campsite. I sure hope your musket is perfect. Will inspect it shortly."

Ignoring Jon Westfield, Adam hurried toward his tent.

Wes was sitting with Marty, polishing his belt buckle.

"Where've you been," Marty said. "Missed breakfast. We may have a bit of coffee left."

"Not hungry." Adam tried to get Wes's attention, but he refused to look up. His cheeks were dry but still glowing. Remembering Ryker, he slumped next to Wes and resumed polishing his gun.

"You make me the laughing stock of the whole regiment?" Wes hissed when Marty got up to go to the latrine. He threw down his buckle, his eyes spitting fire.

"I never—"

"Why didn't you leave me be?"

Adam was speechless. Here he'd thought Wes would be thankful for being rescued. "He's abusing—"

"He won't stop anyway," Wes said, slumping back down. "Now he has a reason to kill me...and you. Why don't you mind your own beeswax?"

"I didn't tell them it was you," Adam said quietly. When Wes didn't answer he looked over. Fresh tears shone in Wes's eyes. "Surely Ryker will kick him out."

"Doubt it," Wes mumbled, wiping a sleeve across his face.

"Is that why you left...you volunteered?"

Wes gave the tiniest nod.

"Who is he?"

"My uncle."

How long has he been doing this, Adam wanted to ask but one look at Wes told him it was the wrong time. Wes looked as if a breeze would mow him over. Most of all he wanted to ask why Wes had seemed acquiescent, why he hadn't fought back. "Why don't you take a rest?" he said aloud. "I've heard rumors we're going to see action soon."

Without a word, Wes disappeared inside the tent. Adam could've sworn he heard sobbing.

CHAPTER EIGHTEEN

Tip lay shivering on his cot. It had to be below freezing, and the single blanket didn't help to stave off the creeping cold. During the day it wasn't so bad, even if the shoes Rawley had given him were thin. The fields lying dormant, they'd moved on to the barn, fixing the ever-growing spaces in the roof, cutting firewood and tending chickens.

He had to leave soon. The hole behind his mattress was large enough now. He'd stuffed it with dirty straw, but it was only a matter of time before someone saw it on the outside. A couple of times, Tip had snuck to the backside of his hut where a broken-down plow rusted next to old buckets and assorted piles of rotting wood.

He was determined to run as soon as the snow melted not to give away his footprints. He'd willed himself to set aside a few pieces of bread, tucked into an old cloth. If he didn't hurry, the bread would mold and be eaten by rats and mice that swarmed Rawley's farm.

"Wait!" Rawley yelled as Tip was making his way to his hut after a measly dinner of grits and gravy. Tip's hands were chapped from the cold, and he longed to roll up in his blanket. His legs felt weak these days, his body giving slowly. His arm and leg muscles were thinner, and his eyes often matted in the morning.

Tip stopped, suppressing a shiver as Rawley ambled closer, his breath a cloud of whiskey. In one hand he carried an oil lamp, in the other hand, the whip. Tip watched longingly as Balder disappeared in their hut. What if Balder had discovered his hole and ratted him out?

"Let's go, boy. I've got a job for you." Rawley waved the lantern toward his house. Tip lowered his head to hide his relief. Other than the kitchen, he'd never been inside the main house. Mama Rose, he thought, trying to ignore the terrible ache that inhabited his stomach like a disease.

"Faster," Rawley slurred, the whip cracking next to Tip's ear. Tip stumbled forward, catching himself on the steps to the front porch.

The main house reeked of unwashed bodies and urine. Two of the smallest Rawley children sat on the floor, their faces grimy and their noses running. Though a fire burned in the hearth, the house was dank.

Obviously, Missus didn't know how to take care of things.

"Quit gawking," Rawley interrupted Tip's thoughts. "Over here."

In the corner leaned the former kitchen table, missing one of its legs. "Can you fix that?" Rawley slurred.

Tip nodded, trying to ignore the aroma wafting from the cast iron pot bubbling above the fireplace. He couldn't think straight, imagining the rich stew Rawley and his kin would soon eat.

For a moment he was taken back to his mother's kitchen, the immaculate counters, the ovens scrubbed clean every day and filled anew with amazing delicacies. Most of the time he managed to push the memory of Mama Rose away, hoping his feelings would fade a bit. Hoping the pain would lessen.

The opposite was true.

He nearly stumbled once more, realizing that the more he tried ignoring his feelings, the stronger they became.

"What's the matter with you, boy?" A poke to his kidneys brought Tip back to present day.

"Need a hammer and some nails," Tip said.

Rawley impatiently waved at the sideboard where an assortment of rusty tools lay scattered. One of the toddlers began to scream, and Rawley abruptly turned to pick up his son. The transformation was amazing, the ruthlessness in his eyes replaced with concern.

"Now, now, careful," Rawley soothed as Tip rummaged through the tools.

He found a few nails and a hammer and stuck them in his pockets. Then he picked up the table and reattached the leg.

It was dark when he entered his cabin, the air thick with impending snow. At the bottom of his pocket rested one of the nails.

CHAPTER NINETEEN

"Report to duty," a voice hissed. "No lights."

Adam shook himself awake. He sensed Wes in the dark next to him. Judging by the freezing temperature, it had to be early morning. They scrambled out of their tent, groping for muskets, ammunition, and caps. It was raining again.

"Listen here." Ryker's voice strained to remain low. "Looks like Johnny Reb is taking position half a mile south of here. From now on, not a sound. I don't want to hear any talk, no fires, no nothing. We're going to move out and form a line of fire."

Adam opened his eyes wider. How was he supposed to find his way in this blackness?

"Put your arm on the shoulder of the man in front of you," Ryker said as if he'd heard him.

Left hand stretched, right hand wrapped around his musket, Adam marched in painstaking slowness. All he could hear were the breaths of the men in front and back, rain dripping from branches above and the occasional crack of a broken tree limb.

As dawn crept across the sky, they took position along a line of brush. The land fell slightly toward a dark-colored stream. Dense trees covered the rise on the other side. Adam was lying on the soaked ground, his head behind a stump, musket trimmed on top. Supposedly, Rebs were hiding on the other side of Fishing Creek.

The assault started out of nowhere, thousands of mini-explosions volleying across the water, a high-pitched whine like clouds of hornets with lethal stings. Slugs splintered wood, splintered like shrapnel, the dull thud when they found a target, shells tearing flesh and bone. With every round the gunfire fog grew denser until Adam couldn't see a thing, the acrid air attacking his eyes and nose, the rain continuing unabated.

The moaning grew louder as more men got hit, their cries tearing at Adam's nerves. He wanted to go and see if he could help, but that was out of the question. Medics were supposed to do that. Of course, there were way fewer than needed.

Ryker had told them that General Thomas was expecting reinforcements from Somerset to surprise the Rebs. Why weren't they coming, Adam wondered. Judging by the increasing cries of his fellow men, they were being beaten thoroughly. He kept his head low, shooting across the gurgling creek, reloading, shooting, and reloading until he lost all sense of time. To his right, Wes was doing the same, his expression one of mechanical concentration.

The order to move forward and to the left came in the afternoon. Zollicoffer, wearing a white coat, had been shot and killed, but Union General Thomas wanted to keep up the pressure. Adam's stomach felt hollow, his nose and throat burning from the gun smoke. It was hard to see anything through the fog as they slowly made their way to the creek and across. He could feel Rebs lurking close.

It was a strange feeling, like running naked among a crowd of girls, exposed and helpless. His skin tingled with nerves, every step uncertain, his ears on high alert to pick up enemy sounds. But how were you supposed to hear anything if there were hundreds of men moving next to you and the air was filled with breaking twigs, suppressed coughs, and heavy breathing?

He'd just made it across the creek when searing heat tore at his right arm. He dropped the musket, his hand useless and limp as blood ran down his forearm and dripped into the mud as if somebody had turned on a faucet. The agony grew until he saw stars in the sky ahead, bright flashing lights that connected to the thumping in his arm, moved up his shoulder and into his legs. He dropped to his knees, clutching at his sleeve that looked ragged, a blackish stain spreading and soaking into the wool.

The battle noise that had erupted the moment Adam's arm exploded, faded into the background. All Adam heard was the pounding in his ears, and all he could feel was the fire in his arm—

a flame that burned hotter by the second until he thought he'd pass out.

"Adam?" Wes's face floated above. It looked detached, like a balloon.

Adam drifted, flying through the air in waves, up and down, up and down until the ache grew unbearable. Something clawed at his arm, sharp teeth tearing like a wild animal ready to maul him. He wanted to scream but his throat was tight and sore.

"Not much farther," somebody panted.

"He's hurt." Wes's voice was shrill. "Somebody help him."

Adam sagged to the ground and passed out. When he came to, it was hard to tell how long he'd been here. Dozens of men lay near him, some still, some moaning.

Adam propped himself on his good hand, the ache in his arm dull now, hammer pounding bone. He couldn't feel his hand or move his fingers. Somebody had wrapped a cloth around the wound to stem the flow, probably Wes.

Next to Adam, a man lay on his side, his coat shredded in front where his stomach used to be. He wheezed, blood oozing from the corner of his mouth.

He's going to die. Just then Adam felt himself lifted on a stretcher and carried into a tent. A man with sleeves rolled up, forearms and hands crimson, bent low to finger Adam's side.

"Take off his coat. Call me when you're done," he ordered. "Quick, looks like he's lost a lot of blood."

Adam felt his arm explode as two orderlies untied the bandage and yanked his arm free, cold air scorching with a thousand flaming tongues.

"He's ready now," one of them yelled, and Adam watched in horror as the man with the bloody hands returned, the knife blade in his fingers glistening. *I'm going to lose my arm.* Then he passed out.

Adam drifted in and out of consciousness. His body had turned into a desert, hot and dry and burning with every breath. He dreamed of his mother standing by his bedside, her dress red and low cut, her cheeks and lips painted pink. No, Adam wanted to yell when Sara appeared next to his mother, dressed in the same red, her breasts pushed high in the low-cut blouse. He wanted to scream, but his mouth was filled with cotton, unable to utter a sound.

After the horrible heat, Adam began to shake with cold. He

felt himself quiver beneath the blankets, his legs and feet trembling so violently that he thought he'd fall from his cot.

He couldn't be sure, but he imagined seeing Wes a few times, his eyes serious and shiny.

The light behind Adam's eyelids was bright. Maybe he'd gone up to heaven, God waiting for him in the brilliance of a summer sky.

"…think he's waking," a voice said.

"Shhh," someone else answered.

Adam raised his eyelids. They felt dry and gritty as if his eyeballs had been dipped in sand. Somewhere near him faces floated. Adam squinted, recognizing Marty's handlebar moustache and Wes's red hair.

He wasn't dead after all. The memory of being shot hit him. His arm. He tried looking to his right, but his neck felt as stiff as if he had a board attached to it. Concentrating on his arm, he felt a dull throb, a thrumming that stayed in tune with his heartbeat. Where was his hand? He couldn't feel his fingers.

Terror set in as he realized one of the sawbones had taken his arm. He'd be an invalid left with one hand. Why hadn't they just killed him? This entire time he'd expected to be shot dead. Not once had he considered the possibility of being maimed.

"Can you hear me?" Wes said.

Adam fought the stiffness in his neck and turned slightly. He nodded.

"Hey," he croaked.

"Looks like you're going to live," Wes said brightly. "Didn't look too good for a few days. You had a nasty fever."

"Lucky chap," Thomas chuckled. "With all them lead pills flying like hornets, you should've been dead."

"Can't wait to get you back with us," Marty said. "Not the same without a grump like you around."

Adam nodded again. "Sure thing." Though he wondered why they'd want him back with one arm. He'd not be able to shoot a thing with his left.

"Oh, we won," Wes said, looking smug. "Rebs ran like chickens all the way to Tennessee. Got ourselves some nice artillery, loads of horses."

"They call it the Battle of Mill Springs," Marty said. "Ryker was in a good mood for about five minutes."

"Okay boys, time to go," another voice said. "This private needs rest, and it's time to change the bandage."

As Wes and Marty turned away, not without patting Adam good-naturedly on the head, an orderly began to busy himself on Adam's side.

"You lie nice and still now," he said as Adam felt the throbbing in his arm spread to his shoulder and down his spine. He couldn't look over, couldn't bear the sight of a bloody stump.

He heard the orderly sniff as icy air hit his skin. It felt as if his entire arm had been dipped into a frozen lake. Strange how he felt things that weren't there.

"You were lucky the bullet didn't smash the bone. Doctor says you'll get some feeling back in your hand. May not be much, but better that—"

"What?" Adam's head whipped around. Next to his side laid his arm, white and slightly bluish, fingers half uncurled. He couldn't feel them, but the hand was there. All of it. He sighed, taking in the shredded wound on his upper arm.

"What is it, private?" the orderly said. "I'm just wrapping up your arm again. Doctor wants it nice and still for now."

"Fine," Adam said, finding his voice. All of a sudden he felt deliriously happy.

"Look at Blythe," Wes said as Adam marched back into camp a week later. His arm was in a sling, still sore, but he'd been able to move reasonably well. The camp had relocated south in pursuit of the Rebs who'd lost the Battle of Mill Springs decisively, leaving behind a thousand mules and a dozen pieces of artillery.

"Welcome back," Marty said.

"Good to see your face," Thomas chimed in, patting him on the back.

"If it isn't Blythe," Ryker hollered a while later, after Adam had settled by the fire. "Next time, don't get yourself shot so soon. You missed all the fun."

The boys laughed.

"Rebs were cowards." Wes's blue eyes danced like the old times. Adam thought of Jon Westfield and wondered what had become of him. The feeling of unease—icy fingers creeping up his spine—was back. Wes's uncle was more dangerous than the Rebs.

"If I may have a word, Blythe," Ryker said after dinner. Adam had struggled to clean his canteen, the feeling in his right hand so weak that he couldn't hold on to anything.

"Yes, Sir." Adam attempted to raise his arm to salute.

"Forget that," Ryker said. "Get your arm in shape before it snaps off, Private."

"Yes, Sir."

"Blythe, I've talked to the captain, and we're going to let you go on furlough for a few weeks. Your arm isn't any good yet, so you may as well go home. Isn't too far to Greeneville from here. May even catch a train. Report back to me in one month." Ryker turned away, leaving Adam standing in the field, mouth agape.

He was free to leave.

And he had no place to go.

CHAPTER TWENTY

Adam trudged through the muck—every step made a sucking noise as if the earth wanted to engulf him. Signs of battles were everywhere, the ground broken open with deep rifts like scars, trees shredded and burned, the air filled with the putrid smells of fire pits and latrine holes.

He'd been awake most of the night, thinking about what to do. He could tell Ryker that he'd rather stay here and get better. But that had to be suspicious? Why would a private on furlough want to stay around when he'd been offered a break? No, he had to leave.

Images of home appeared in his vision: Ma in her garden, picking beans, in the kitchen, washing dishes and stirring a pot. Tip sitting on a straw bale in the barn smiling, Sara scowling at him across Allister's head.

With each memory his longing grew, until the morning when he hastily rolled up his blanket and headed out. Making his way to the train station ten miles away, he went back and forth between elation and despair.

But with every mile he traveled closer to Greeneville, his hopelessness grew stronger. Going to the farm was useless because Ma and Sara wouldn't be there any longer. And he couldn't go to town where Jack Billings was surely having wanted posters attached to every pole and shop window. If just one person recognized him, he'd be done for.

He stopped in his tracks. As crazy as it sounded, the only

person he saw was Tip. He'd sneak in after dark and surprise him at slave quarters.

Adam got off the train at the station prior to Greeneville. It was another five miles, but he'd walk rather than risk to be noticed in town. Besides, what were a few miles when he'd traveled hundreds with the Yanks?

So much had happened since he'd left, yet only six months had passed, and the memory of Nathan Billing's lifeless body felt as fresh and raw as last August.

Icy sleet hit his face as he lumbered through the woods. His arm was on fire. No matter how he tried to keep it still, the constant walking jostled his shoulder until every step became agony. Not to lose his way, he stayed close to the tracks until the landscape grew familiar. Here were the woods he'd roamed as a boy, going hunting with his father, mushrooming with Sara and meeting Tip for an hour of relaxation.

He passed the trail that led to his farm, the temptation of following it as strong as the urge to run. Maybe he could just sneak closer. But it was early evening, an hour before dusk and anyone could see him cross the open fields. He couldn't risk it. His heart beat loudly, aching, asking why he couldn't just wait here until dark, wait to find out if his mother was still there.

What were the chances? Ma and Sara were probably long gone, and Jack Billings had gotten his greedy paws on their land—Pa's land.

A sob escaped him, rattled him awake. His right arm ached in the sling, his hand and fingers still nearly useless. *Move*, his mind told him. *Wait*, his heart said.

He walked on, the cold seeping into his clothes and the sling of his useless arm. He'd left his musket with the Army, but still wore his uniform, his civilian pants and shirt long gone. He wondered what would happen if he ran into Rebs.

Tennessee was one mixed bag, changing sides within miles of a town, Union to Confederate and back again. Families were split over the war, brothers fighting on opposite sides. Who knew what was going on in Greeneville these days? What a mess this war was. What good was it doing? *You know why Pa joined.* Lincoln had said they'd stop slavery in the south and give every colored person freedom.

Wasn't that a good enough reason? He thought of Tip and

Mama Rose who were forced to work for the Billings and had no life of their own. His Pa had died for the cause. Surely that was reason enough. But then what would happen if the Rebs won?

He stopped in his tracks, listening. Leaves rustled above. They were dry and brown and had never made it to the ground, the sky beyond laden with more snow and sleet. Something out there was moving. Boots trying to be quiet. Adam slipped off the path and took cover behind a fallen tree. The ground was slushy, a mix of half-frozen leaves and soggy moss.

The steps moved closer as somebody passed by not fifteen feet from him. Adam carefully removed his cap and glanced across the tree trunk. The man wore a Confederate uniform, long grayish jacket over light blue pants. He marched quietly with long strides as if he knew where he was going. Adam waited, envious of the man's purpose.

By the time Adam got up, he was shivering. It was dusk, and light was waning fast. He hastened his steps. His stomach reminded him that he hadn't eaten since breakfast. Maybe he could have dinner with Tip in his room. He was pretty certain the slaves weren't going to give him away. They stayed to themselves most of the time. And they had always liked Tip.

The Billings main house, windows brightly lit, loomed ahead as Adam snuck to the slave quarters. He knocked on Tip's hut, glad nobody was outside. After knocking again, he entered. The place was chilly and deserted. Adam hesitated. Waiting for Tip in the safety of the hut was best. But what if he was doing different work and wouldn't return for a while? There was one other place Tip could be. Adam sighed and stole back outside. Head low, he ran toward the kitchen at the back of the main house.

The backdoor stood ajar and Adam quietly stepped closer to listen. Mama Rose was giving orders to the serving girls. She sounded as if she had a cold, her voice scratchy and somehow slower, almost dragging.

Delicate aromas of beef stew, fresh-baked bread and something sugary drifted through the door, making Adam almost faint. He waited another minute, calculating what his chances were to be discovered by Jack Billings or his overseer Wilkes.

Adam tiptoed inside. "Mama Rose?"

The woman behind the stove turned. She wasn't the Mama Rose Adam remembered.

This woman's hair had gray streaks, and the skin around her mouth furrowed. Her eyes were dull and her back hunched. Tip's mother had aged twenty years.

"Adam?" Mama Rose whispered. "What happen to you?" She took in Adam's coat and drenched hair. Without another word she rushed forward, and Adam felt himself engulfed by her soft chest. "You a soldier now?" she stammered on. "You hungry? You must be hungry."

"What is going on, Mama Rose? Where's Tip?"

She let go abruptly and busied herself at the stove, filling a plate. Adam stood rooted to the floor, watching Tip's mother who seemed like a different person. Any moment somebody could come in and see him.

"Sit, boy, sit."

Adam slumped in the corner, the bench where Tip used to eat when he visited his mother. All energy had drained from his bones. His body soaked up the warmth and the orderly kitchen. This was what staying in a house felt like. Not filth and freezing cold, not flying bullets and death, but quiet and a clean table, scrubbed pots and a dry roof.

He wanted to ask about Tip again, yet his mouth watered. The beef stew with carrots, celery and onions melted in his mouth, the potatoes slathered in rich gravy exploded against his tongue. Not even his mother's cooking had tasted this good.

Mama Rose placed a plate with a slice of buttery crumb cake in front of him. "Peaches and apples are finished. Confederates claimed much of our stores." As she turned away, Adam placed his good hand on her forearm.

"Please tell me what's going on? Where's Tip?"

A terrible transformation took place in Mama Rose. Her shoulders began to quiver, her face an ocean of hurt.

"Master sold him," she managed as a tear dribbled down her cheek.

Adam stared. "What do you mean?"

"After he run to you, Master sold him."

"Where is he?" Adam straightened, the dinner forgotten as he remembered Tip's dreadful beating, Jack Billings locking him up in the grain shack, and Nathan's still face. He'd been so careful, hiding Nathan in the barn. "Billings didn't think Tip had anything to do with Nathan's death?" he managed.

Mama Rose shrugged. "Don't know where he is. I beg Master, ask him many times. He won't say." She paused and stared at him. "What you mean, Nathan's death?"

"You know," Adam said, glancing furtively around the deserted kitchen. Shrill laughter seeped through some door, followed by the tinkling of glasses and the plinking of piano music.

Mama Rose sank into the chair across from Adam. "You left, you never know about Nathan." She nodded to herself.

"What are you saying?"

"I say, Master Nathan is alive."

Adam jumped from the bench, the plate nearly toppling to the ground. "I've got to go," he said, his eyes wild. He'd never realized it, but he was a dead man whether Nathan lived or died. In a way this was worse because Nathan would want him hanged.

"You hurt, you stay a while."

"Can't." Adam hurried to the backdoor. "Do you know anything about Tip's new master? I want to find him." As soon as he'd said it out loud, he knew that that's what he had to do.

Mama Rose pulled herself up with effort. She reminded him of his grandma, Pa's mother, who'd moved with utmost slowness and never smiled. "Don't know, boy. Jonas says, Wilkes take him in the cart and return four hours later."

"I'll find him," Adam said, pulling the door shut behind him.

"Wait." Mama Rose labored around the kitchen, sticking things into an old tablecloth. "Here," she said, her breath loud and strained.

Adam nodded grimly and melted into the darkness. Now that he was outside he wasn't so sure he could find Tip. Not without Wilkes's help, and not without being seen by too many people. He rushed up the path that led back to the main road and collided with a dark figure.

"Watch your step, man," Nathan Billings said, raising a lantern to Adam's face.

CHAPTER TWENTY-ONE

Adam stiffened. He stared at Nathan whose face shone pale and otherworldly.

"What's a Union soldier doing at our plantation?" Nathan squinted as he took in Adam's uniform. "You lost or something?"

Adam managed a nod, the air in his lungs refusing to power his voice.

Nathan pointed to his right. "The path to Greeneville is that way. Don't come back here. I hate the North."

Adam nodded again and stumbled forward.

"Wait."

Adam stiffened, his back still turned to Nathan. Any moment, a knife would tear into his ribs.

"Don't I know you? You from around here?"

Adam slowly turned. His heart banged against his ribcage. This was it. Nathan would recognize him and call for help.

"You mute?" Nathan's voice was half impatient, half indifferent.

"Just visiting," Adam croaked. "I'm from Kentucky."

When Nathan didn't answer, Adam hurried off. Away from the man he'd attacked and who for some reason didn't recognize him—away into the safety of the woods.

Had he changed that much? Pa always said war had a way of changing men. Faces grew gaunt and eyes dark with untold horror—the horror of seeing your fellow man sliced open next to you, his blood leaking into the ground until none was left.

But then, Nathan surely had seen his face. Why had he not recognized him? They'd met many times before, fought hard with their noses inches apart. Something was odd. He shuddered, imagining Nathan rushing him. With his bad arm he'd be no match even for puny Nathan Billings.

And Mama Rose was a wreck. Tip had disappeared to some other farm and obviously wasn't able to contact his mother.

Adam's throat grew tight. It was hard to watch Mama Rose's suffering. He had to do something. Find out more about Nathan, search for Tip. When he looked up, the forest was ending. He'd been walking blindly, but now he recognized the fields surrounding his home. With a shrug, he clambered on. At least it was dark now and he could sneak up to the cabin.

A half-moon shone, clouds drifting, shadows black on the path in front of him. He hurried on. Any second he'd be able to see the house and barn.

He stopped abruptly. In the bluish light of the moon, he noticed that the fence that had once surrounded the cabin was torn down. But that wasn't what made him gasp. The cabin was gone, the remains of the chimney a finger pointing into the sky, the barn half collapsed. It couldn't be. His mother and sister had lost their home. He had lost his home.

Regret swept through him as he remembered their last talk. He'd accused Pa of causing all their issues when all Pa had done was gone to fight against slavery—against what they were doing to Tip and Mama Rose. He felt his face warm with shame. He wanted to take it back, go to that moment in time and start over.

But he couldn't. He'd messed up one thing after another, helped destroy their farm and handed it all to rich Jack Billings.

The old Billings had made good on his threat to take their land. Not only that, he'd destroyed the only home Adam had ever known. What if Ma and Sara had died in the flames? Dread choked him like the acrid smoke of gunfire, joined by hatred so intense, he let out a grunt.

He stumbled toward the remains of the barn, pieces of wall in back, broken beams half-smoldered and long cold. He sank to his knees and sifted through the rubble.

Everything was gone.

After attacking Nathan, he'd left, knowing his future was gone. Now his past had evaporated too. He felt numb. And bone tired. Somewhere in the back of his head and against the odds he'd hoped to see his mother and Sara. Now that was over.

They're dead, the voice in his head whispered. His vision turned inward as he crumpled to the ground. He realized that even while he'd been away, he'd somehow imagined Ma and Sara living in the cabin, the home Pa had built with his hands.

He cried, not caring what happened next.

But his body had other ideas. He began to tremble, the icy air chilling his bones.

When he finally rose, the moon stood low, throwing long shadows, its light fading quickly. Frost had settled around him, a white coating that crunched under his feet. He walked off slowly. The arm in the sling throbbed angrily. Not bothering to find the trail, he headed west across the fields. Dried corn stalks rustled, the loneliest sound ever.

A thin grayness appeared along the horizon, another day. In the distance, a farmhouse came into view. Lights shone from two windows upstairs. Shreds of memory returned, Sara riding with Allister on the buggy. Allister carrying lemonade to his sister. His own bad mood during the dance. What had he been so grumpy about? It was hard to fathom now.

He continued, his gaze low, his feet dragging. What was the point of it all?

"You there."

Adam looked up, half expecting he was dreaming. But the man with the rifle was real enough.

"What're you doing on my land?"

Adam blinked, trying to figure out what the man had said. "Just passing through. Sorry."

But the man didn't seem satisfied and rushed closer, gun at the ready and pointing at Adam's belly.

Go ahead. Shoot me.

"You with the Yanks?" the man said. "What're you doing out here then?" The man looked past him as if Adam were leading a troop and another attack imminent.

Adam stopped, his eyes downcast. Before him stood Allister's grandfather, old Dallas Porter.

"I'm on furlough." He half raised his injured arm, immediately regretting it as sharp stabs drilled into his shoulder and down his spine. Something warm trickled along his fingers. "I'm your neighbor, Adam Brown."

"What?" Dallas Porter rushed near, his eyes roaming as he looked Adam over. "I'll be darn." Without another word, he pawed Adam's good arm. "Better come inside, boy."

Adam's vision blurred, the edges of the house quivering as if it were alive. He had no strength left, his arm an inferno, demanding all his attention. Let the old man drag him into his house and call the sheriff for trespassing. At least he'd be warm for a bit.

"Look who I found wandering around outside," Dallas said as he closed the door behind them.

A scream rang out, shrill and high in Adam's ears. He stared uncomprehendingly while Ma and Sara rushed at him.

"Adam," his mother cried. Tears streamed down her cheeks. "Where've you been? I thought, you..."

Sarah clung to him as if she never wanted to let him go. "What happened to you?"

At that moment a terrible weight lifted off Adam. The lump in his throat and chest released into his eyes. He didn't bother wiping his face as he hugged his family. The only people he had left. The people he loved.

"You're living here?" he said in wonder. "I thought you were in town or.... What happened to the farm? It's all gone."

Ma stepped back and took in his bloody arm, the sling and whitish fingers beneath. "You're hurt," she cried. "Allister, get the hot water going. This soldier needs help."

Minutes later, Adam found himself sitting at the Porter's kitchen table, telling his story.

"What I don't understand is why Nathan didn't recognize me. I ran into him at Tip's place today." He looked around the table at the familiar faces—his mother, Sara, who looked a lot older than he remembered, Allister, and his grandpa.

"I heard Nathan has amnesia." Allister flashed a smile, his gaze lingering on Sara for the briefest moment. He'd grown a lot, his shoulders wide and his chest muscular. He no longer looked like a boy, but a man. And despite the freckles, Adam had to admit, he was pretty handsome, with a strong jaw and kind expression. Not only that, he seemed to carry no grudge from their earlier encounter at the dance when Adam had been less than friendly.

"The Billings's doctor says it's a matter of time before he regains his memory," Mr. Porter added.

"Why did you have to fight him?" his mother said, shaking her head slowly. Her face was thinner than he remembered, the lines around her mouth deep furrows.

"He threatened Tip with a knife. I had to stop him." He didn't add that Nathan had also called Ma a whore. What was he supposed to do, just let it go? "What happened to the farm?" he said to change the subject.

His mother's face fell and her upper lip quivered. "I'm not sure. Sara and I were in town. I must've left the wood too close to the fire. When we returned, everything was burning. Mr. Porter and Allister tried to help, but it was too late."

Adam glanced back and forth between his mother and the old man, who was shaking his head. "A terrible thing."

"You don't suppose somebody started it?" Adam said. He had a hard time believing his mother would be so careless. She'd always been systematic, so much so that it used to drive him crazy.

"Why would anybody do that?" Sara said, exasperated.

"Are you really that naïve?" Fresh anger rose in Adam. "Billings wanted our land. He knew he'd have to pay more with the house." He paused. "What happened? Did you sell it to him?"

His mother nodded at old Mr. Porter. "Mr. Porter here lent me the money. He agreed to help me work the farm. And with Allister's help we were sure we could survive. But now…" she looked around the room, for a moment forlorn.

"We can rebuild," Adam said. "We have that stand of pine and oak. Good wood. It'll take time, but—"

"How are *you* going to help?" Sara said, her cheeks still aflame from Adam's sharp words. "You made sure nobody could find you, and now you're a Union soldier."

Adam jumped up. He opened his mouth to shoot back an answer and froze.

Sara was right. He'd run away, and now he was the property of the government. Unless…

"What if I desert? I mean I used a different name and all…" His face fell. He couldn't risk it, not because he'd be found out by the government, but because Nathan Billings would regain his memory and recall how Adam had attacked and nearly killed him.

"You mustn't," his mother said, patting his hand. "It's wrong. You made an agreement."

Adam nodded. "So what are we going to do?" he said in a

small voice. His body felt heavy all of a sudden, his arm filled with knife blades. Allister's face was turning fuzzy as if he were swallowed by fog.

"Sara, take your brother—" was the last thing he heard before sliding off the bench.

CHAPTER TWENTY-TWO

Tip lay listening. It was hard to tell time, but he guessed it must be past midnight. Balder slept restlessly, undoubtedly freezing just like Tip. They had no fireplace, and the air was as chilled as outside, the single blanket making little difference.

Tip sat up quietly. All he heard was the wind howling across the roof shingles and Balder's snorts. Rawley was surely asleep by now. Tip rummaged beneath his mattress and grabbed the rag with his food ration, the spoon and nail he'd rescued last night. He couldn't bear the thought of spending another night.

He carefully pulled the mattress away from the corner where a hole of two by two feet gaped. Sliding onto his stomach, Tip shoved aside the old straw and pulled himself forward and through. Three more feet and he was free.

Crouching low, he swiped the dirt from his overalls. The wind rattled the huge black walnut tree near the main house. No lights shone, but Tip had memorized Rawley's farm well. He took a few steps and listened again. Nothing. To his left stood the cabin of Smith, the overseer. Considerably larger with several windows, he imagined Smith behind the glass, aiming his rifle.

He shuddered. The man had an uncanny habit of sniffing out trouble. It was as if he could look straight into Tip's brain and dig out what Tip was thinking.

Ignoring his fear, Tip continued past the main house until he felt gravel under his feet, his soles achy with cold. He sat down and put on his boots, his ears on high alert. Nothing.

At the end of the lane, he turned left, figuring that had to be north. Based on the sun, it was the correct way. His face was damp with sweat despite the cold, and his heart pounded in his neck. Every little crackle in the underbrush made him flinch.

He couldn't be caught, not now. He had no pass. Any white man could stop him and ask for the owner's pass, a scrap of paper that explained where a slave was headed and why. Without it, he was automatically a runaway, giving anybody the right to stop him, lash him or, if no owner could be found, sell him for a profit.

As he stumbled along, his heart filled with the longing for light and a fire. Mama Rose's face appeared in his vision, and with it her warm smile, the heat emanating from the ovens, and the hot food he'd shoveled carelessly. He stopped in his tracks, the draw to go south and find his mother as strong as if somebody had pulled his arm. Some part of him had always thought of returning home when he got free. But it was impossible. Rawley would check with Billings first, and if he were caught nearby, Mama Rose would suffer for it.

No, he'd never see her again—not now, not ever. Tears blurred his vision and he slowed.

The icy air brought him back. The wind had picked up speed, shaking the trees and piercing his skin. As the memory of the colored at the stake returned, his skin shredded and his eyes missing, Tip forced his feet forward.

By early morning he crawled into a thicket. *By now they know I'm missing* were his last thoughts before he passed out.

He woke in the afternoon, his limbs stiff with cold, his stomach ravenous. He pulled out a piece of bread, ignoring the greenish mold around the edges. Eating slowly, he retraced his steps to the road. He needed water but was afraid to lose his way. He continued down the path, stopping every so often to listen. His thighs burned with fatigue, and his toes chafed in the leaky boots.

At dusk he came to a cross in the road.

Which way was north? To his frustration, thick clouds covered the sky, threatening more snow. The road meandered constantly, and he had no idea which way to take. He decided to go straight.

A mile down the path he stopped. Ahead a light shone, but he couldn't tell what it was. His heart beating fast, he crept closer. His throat burned with thirst now, and a fresh wind whirled snow into his face. Ahead was a homestead, smaller than Rawley's, smaller even than Adam's cabin.

Behind the matted windows two men, three women and a handful of children cramped around a table. Candles threw a warm glow on the bowls filled with some kind of stew. One of the men's faces was nearly covered under a mass of matted curls and beard. Tip licked his lips, his hunger a fist in his stomach. He thought of Mama Rose and how he'd taken it for granted that he could see her any time he wanted.

The ache in his belly increased. She had to miss him worse.

He skidded across the yard until he found the pump, drinking his fill despite the freezing liquid chilling him to the core.

Then he saw the barn, the smell of hay like an invitation, a warm place he could burrow into until dawn. He'd leave before anyone was awake.

Bone tired, he crawled inside and slept.

"Tell Billy we caught ourselves a Negro. By the looks of it a runaway." A man in his thirties held a pitchfork to Tip's chest. "Not a move, boy."

Tip fought through the cobwebs of sleep, trying to remember where he was. The farm... the hay barn. He eyed the man in front of him who didn't look too strong. He gripped the nail in his pocked. He could take him.

A second voice chimed in. "What'd you find?"

"Runaway slave for sure."

"Where you from?" The second man spoke slowly as if Tip were dimwitted. He pointed a rifle at Tip's head.

Tip was dumbfounded. He couldn't make his brain work.

"The devil got your tongue?" the man with the rifle poked at Tip's cheekbone.

Tip shook his head. "No, Sirs."

"Wonder if there's a reward," the first man said. "Did you hear of anyone missing a slave?"

"Not yet." Let's ask Billy." The rifle dug deeper into Tip's cheek.

"Isn't far. You want to take him?"

"Where you from, boy?"

The barn door creaked. "Billy, over here," the man with the rifle shouted, his eyes glittering with excitement. His front upper teeth were missing, his mouth a black hole with foul breath.

Billy, who Tip recognized as the bearded man at the table last night, limped near, his pants and hands muddy as if he'd dug in the dirt on his knees. Snapping a whip, he said, "Good catch. Let's keep' em. Put' em in the root cellar. Will go to town tomorrow, ask 'round."

Tip began to tremble, his heart sick with foreboding. He'd seen Rawley angry before, but he knew that he'd seen nothing yet. Rawley would either kill him or beat him within an inch of his life.

The whip came down hard.

Mama Rose was the last thing he remembered before passing out.

CHAPTER TWENTY-THREE

Adam looked around Porter's dinner table where Ma, Sara, Mr. Porter and Allister were assembled.

"How am I going to find him? I've got less than two weeks before I must return to duty."

He'd slept for two days straight, only waking long enough to use the outhouse or sip a bit of soup Ma had brought him. Every time he woke, he felt the presence of Sara or Ma near his bed. Before he could muster the strength to speak, he was asleep again.

"I'll make inquiries," Mr. Porter said. "I know the woman who cooks for the Billings's overseer, Wilkes."

"I'd like to come," Adam said as he finished off a second helping of fried potatoes, beans and bacon. He was feeling much stronger. His arm was healing well—there was even some feeling in his fingers again. Not enough to hold a gun, he mused as he kneaded a piece of leather.

Every second was wasted. Waiting around in Mr. Porter's house was driving him mad. If he couldn't help Ma, maybe he could at least help Tip.

Mr. Porter nodded gravely. "We'll go in the morning."

They took the wagon into town. Mr. Porter stopped at the feed store to pick up spring seed and a new axe. Adam followed the old man into the store, wishing he could wear other clothes. But neither Allister nor Mr. Porter had extra coats, so Adam continued wearing his Union uniform, which Ma had cleaned and mended.

"Good morning, Selma," Mr. Porter addressed the portly old lady who stood behind the counter. She wore a long white apron with ruffles, her gray hair neatly swept into a bun.

"Dallas, what brings you out so early?" The lady's eyes glinted, apparently happy to see Mr. Porter, Adam noted with a smirk.

Dallas Porter stepped to the counter, his hat stuffed under his left armpit. "Say, you wouldn't happen to know where Tip went. You know, Mama Rose's only son. This here soldier is a friend." He cleared his throat. "With you cooking for Mr. Wilkes, I thought..."

Selma tipped a very clean forefinger on her chin, thinking. "I believe he's working for Mr. Rawley in Hawkins County."

Adam didn't hear the rest of the conversation as he tried to remember where Hawkins County was. At last he could do something useful. He rubbed his numb hand, willing it to work again. His thumb twitched as if it had a mind of its own.

Adam rode out the next morning. He'd borrowed Allister's mare, his leather bag filled with bread and cheese and a map Mr. Porter had drawn. He wished he had a gun, though it was useless anyway. He couldn't aim a pistol with his left hand, and his right arm wasn't strong enough to hold a musket.

He asked a few times along the way until he stumbled upon the Rawley farm. Something inside him recoiled as he took in the run-down farmhouse with its thin trail of smoke rising from a crumbling chimney. Farm equipment in various states of disrepair, rusted buckets, moldy straw bales and broken pieces of furniture lay strewn. Fifty yards away stood a shack with a tiny window that reminded Adam of a chicken coop.

"Hello, anybody home?" he yelled. Picking his steps through the littered yard, he knocked on the door.

A worn-down woman of indefinable age opened, a small child clinging to her right hip.

"Yes?"

"Are you Mrs. Rawley? I'm looking for Tip, a slave boy. I heard he is working for you—"

Something in the woman's expression made him stop.

"You better speak to my husband," she whispered, her dull eyes nodding toward a ramshackle barn.

Adam had taken a few steps when he stopped abruptly. Near

the barn entrance a horse stood tethered to a metal pole. Its head drooped low, but Adam's eyes were drawn to the skeletal body that was covered with festering sores. He carefully stepped closer not to startle the horse, but it didn't seem to hear, a frozen caricature welcoming death.

"What did they do to you?" he whispered, his fingers caressing an inch or two of undamaged skin on the horse's neck. The horse just stood. Adam's hand slid toward its ears, through the matted forelock toward its nose.

The horse whinnied weakly, its lips barely moving. Adam squinted. The marking on his forehead was shaped like an elongated heart. It reminded him of something.

The scene in the Billings's barn bubbled to the surface, Nathan sliding into the stall of *Magnus Alvariss,* the way the horse had looked at him, its magnificent head and walnut-colored mane. This stallion was broken and nearly dead, but it was the same horse.

Adam's insides twisted at the sight of the injuries and the memory of the once beautiful horse. He wanted to kill the bastard who'd done this.

"What are you doing on my land?" A man had appeared next to Adam, startling him.

Adam was so worked up that he had to remember why he'd come in the first place. "Excuse me, I was searching for a slave who I believe is working for you."

Rawley's crusty eyes narrowed, but Adam continued anyway. "His name is Tip. He's— "

"Nothing but trouble, that boy." Rawley spit on the ground and headed toward the house.

"I need to speak to Tip," Adam called after the man.

Rawley slowly turned. "Hard to do, boy ran off the day before yesterday. When I catch him, he'll be sorry he ever lived."

Adam stood staring. Tip had escaped. The Tip he knew would've never run. Things had to be terrible. His gaze fell on the animal next to him.

"I'd like to buy your stallion," he blurted. As soon as he said it, he knew it was the right thing.

"That sorry excuse of a horse? It'll be dead in a week."

"How much?"

Rawley's face lit up.

Greedy swine. He'd rather have the horse live one day with him than one hour in this godforsaken place.

"Fifty dollars."

"What?" Adam said. "You said yourself the horse is almost dead. Twenty."

"Forty-five."

"Thirty."

"Forty, that's my last offer." Rawley spit again, nearly hitting Adam's boot.

"Fine, forty." Adam cringed as he unpeeled four ten-dollar bills. After saving his money for six months, he'd felt reasonably well off. Now he was back to eleven dollars, most of which he'd need for the train fare and grub back to camp.

He'd wanted to give most of it to his mother. His gaze returned to the stallion. No, he couldn't leave him here. Not like this. Not as long as he had a dime in his pocket.

The return to Porter's farm was slow. Adam rode Allister's horse, pulling the reins of his new horse with his left hand. The stallion was so sick, he walked as if asleep. Off and on he stumbled, his hooves too heavy and low to maneuver a low rise in the road. Then he paused, a tremble starting along his neck and traveling down his rump to his hooves. Adam's heart ached. Rawley was cruel and stupid. He'd nearly killed the horse. What had he done to Tip?

"I'm going to take care of you," Adam whispered as he led the stallion into Porter's barn and installed him next to Allister's horse. "From now on you'll be Charlie."

Sara hurried to meet him. "Did you find him?" Then her eyes fell on the horse. "What is that?"

"This is Charlie…I bought him. Charlie, meet Sara."

"Why did you get him?" Sara looked at Adam incredulously. "He's nothing but leather and bones."

Adam's mother entered the barn. "Let your brother be."

"But Ma, he's wasting money on a half-dead animal."

"Charlie isn't dead yet," Adam said, collecting brushes, rags and water. "Until he is, I'm going to take care of him." Adam dunked a cloth into the water and began to carefully clean a sore on Charlie's shoulder.

"What did you find out?" Ma asked. "Did you see Tip?"

Adam shook his head. "Tip ran away." His arm sank. "You

should've seen the place, it was dreadful. Dirty and cruel. No wonder he escaped."

"You think he'll try to see his Mama?" Sara asked. She picked up a handful of oats and held them under Charlie's nose. Charlie sniffed, swiped a tongue across and began to chew noisily.

"Unlikely. Not if he thinks he'll endanger her," Ma said.

"Where would he go then?" Sara said.

"That's what I've been thinking about the entire way home." Adam looked at his mother and Sara. "I've got no idea."

His mother sighed. "I don't know if I should tell Mama Rose or not." She patted Adam's arm. "Take your time. I'll have dinner ready when you're finished."

Adam nodded. Ma's warmth made him want to crawl inside her arms. How could he ever have considered leaving without telling her first?

"I'll be in soon. Need to put liniment on him."

Two hours passed before Adam was satisfied, Charlie nibbling hay and carrots, his sores cleaned and treated.

CHAPTER TWENTY-FOUR

Tip awoke, his head on fire. The touch to his temple unleashed sharp pain as something sticky trickled down his cheek. His stomach revolted, and he dry-heaved.

The twisted face of Rawley hung above him like a terrible apparition. Except it wasn't an apparition, it was real. Tip had just enough strength to turn his head sideways before the whip came crashing down across his chest.

"You filthy bastard," Rawley hissed, taking a swig from his bottle. "I'll show you who is boss. You'll not walk another yard when I'm done with you."

Tip turned his mind inward as his body took the punishment. Mama Rose had told him about God and that things would be all right once he died. His heart ached with longing to see her one last time, and to visit Adam at his farm.

He remembered their meetings, the last time Adam had come to help him with Nathan. Nobody else had ever stood up for him. He shuddered as tears pooled behind his closed lids.

The pain was unbearable, his body broken. Blood sprayed as Rawley continued to beat his back and chest. Tip no longer felt it.

He was ready to die.

When Tip opened his eyes, the light shining so bright, it sent darts into his eyeballs. He'd gone to heaven. Somewhere in the distance shadows moved, but he couldn't focus. He was floating in fog, weightless even lighter than a feather. He was no longer afraid, nor did he feel any pain.

The shadows came closer but before they reached him, he was asleep again.

"Can he hear us?"

Tip heard a soft voice. Maybe it was God speaking to him, though he was sure it was a female voice. Who knew, maybe God was a woman. He wanted to grin then, but something was pressing against his face. He was being smothered. Alarmed he opened his eyes and… all he could see was white. As he stared, the white came into focus: whitewashed walls and, near his nose, bright-yellow woven fabric.

"Look, he move," the soft voice said. Tip twisted his head to the other side, unleashing a deep ache in his neck that travelled down his spine to his buttocks. He was lying on his stomach.

Not three feet away stood an angel. He blinked, trying to get a better look, when the angel bent closer, brown eyes meeting his.

"Glad to see you awake," the angel said. "I'm Giselle."

Tip wanted to speak, but all he could do was grunt. He licked his lips. His mouth was dry as the desert. "Water" he wanted to say, but the word wouldn't form. He tried to push upward to his elbows as an excruciating throbbing made him collapse.

"Lie still, your back is…" A hand floated closer to touch his forehead. "You must be patient."

"Water."

Giselle held up a red clay cup and supported his head. The cool liquid extinguished the flames in his throat. "What happen?" Tip managed, closing his eyes.

"You almost die," Giselle said. "But you healing now." He could hear a smile in her voice.

Where am I, he wanted to ask but his tongue didn't obey and he drifted off again.

The next time he awoke he was lying on his side, the room in front of him bare except for a nightstand and a thin rug on the dirt floor. He slid his feet off the bed to stand and collapsed on the mattress, the room spinning, his back shooting pain.

He straightened a second time, slower this time. When he touched his forehead, his fingers met a bandage. The movement made his head throb. Planting his feet firmly on the ground, he pushed off. For a moment he stood, swaying back and forth like the cattails he'd harvested a lifetime ago. He continued trying until he was able to stand for a minute, then two.

His breath came ragged as if he'd run across a field and he lay back down.

How long had he been here?

He vaguely remembered being hauled toward some town, Rawley showing up on a horse. He'd gotten off right then, swerving in drunken stupor, swinging his ...

"You're up." Giselle rushed to his side. She was a short woman of perhaps twenty, and her dark chiseled cheekbones reminded Tip of his mama.

"Where am I?" Tip asked, sitting back up.

"You at Master King's plantation."

"How long..."

"Two weeks. You in bad shape. We not know if you..."

Tip nodded. He knew what Giselle was saying. He'd almost gone to the other side. Almost. He'd seen the threshold, the place of no return where everything was light and simple. He'd wanted to go. Be done with this life. Leave behind the pain and the agony that squeezed his heart and made him leave his body.

Something had held him back. He couldn't explain it except that he had turned back from the edge to keep living.

What had Adam said? Someday you'll have your own farm. A grunt escaped him. He might as well become the prince of Africa.

"What is it?" Giselle's worried eyes focused on him.

"Nothing. Tell me about Master King." The room spun anew, and Tip collapsed on the cot. He'd never felt this helpless. It was embarrassing.

Giselle temporarily went out of focus, and he blinked. The cabin reminded him of the place he'd shared with Mama Rose. But the window let in glorious light and the place looked spotless despite the dirt floor.

Giselle quickly walked to the door and after a glance outside closed it. Despite the fact she was covered in a heavy wool jacket, she moved with the ease of a dancer. She returned to his side and sat down on the edge of the bed.

"Master good many times," she whispered. "He ain't use no whip unless..."

"Unless?"

She shook her head. "Master have near fifty slaves. Most are field hands, but we have five in the house, a new gardener. I'm

Master's daughter's personal slave. Her name Millie. Known her since she a babe." Giselle smiled.

"Why I here?"

"Master buy you for little. He...we all think you die. Miss Millie make him...she see you at the town square. Master always do what Miss Millie want."

"I want to go outside," Tip said, eying the new clothes neatly folded next to his bed.

Really he wanted to get away once and for all. Why were things always so complicated? He'd run off only to be captured. He was still a slave without rights and still just as far from his mama and   freedom.

"I help you dress."

Tip straightened as Giselle guided his legs into loose cotton pants, tied a pair of new boots and draped a cotton flannel shirt around his shoulders.

"Take my hand," Giselle said.

He wanted to swat at the arm. Here he was weak, just like the time he'd gone to seek help from Adam when he'd caused Adam's kin terrible hardship. The next moment he was back on the bed.

"You too stubborn. Lost a lot of blood, your wounds need time." Giselle extended her hand again. "Either you take it this minute or I leave."

With a sigh Tip gripped Giselle's forearm and stood. The room swayed and returned into focus. Slowly he hobbled forward, then outside, where a cool bright sun greeted him.

"Is that the new Negro?" A girl of about fifteen, her locks tamed with an assortment of colorful ribbons rushed up to them.

"This is Tip," Giselle said. "Tip meet Miss Millie."

Tip bowed his head.

Millie laughed, her voice like church bells, bright and soaring in the clear morning air. "He's very shy, isn't he?"

"Thank you for saving me," Tip said though he wasn't sure if it was Millie or Giselle who'd worked this wonder.

"You're quite welcome, Tip." Millie stepped closer. "It is a curious name."

"Short for Tipper."

There was the laugh again, high and glorious. Tip felt himself smile in return, only to be reminded by a sharp stinging that his cheek had been torn by Rawley's whip. That wasn't the only thing that hurt. He shivered and his legs grew softer with every step. He leaned heavily on the woman.

"I take you back inside," she said as if she'd heard his pain.

CHAPTER TWENTY-FIVE

Adam stared blindly across the passing wintry landscape. Ice and snow coated the fields. Nothing moved in the low light, a stillness that didn't match the train's vibrations or his insides. He'd waited hours in the ruin of his former cabin, hoping that Tip might stop by to find him. But he hadn't shown. Until the last day Adam had waited and tried to think of ways to get in touch. He knew Tip had learned to read a bit, but what were the chances Adam's would reach him. Paper would fall apart in the dampness, and it was obvious Tip hadn't planned to see him.

How could he fault his friend for staying away? He himself had hardly dared to come near. Tip was a runaway slave with no rights. Anybody could stop him.

Frustrated and worried, Adam had spent every night with Charlie. He slung his good arm across the horse's neck, sticking his nose into the coarse hair. It felt warm and comforting as he stroked the rough skin. The stallion was doing a bit better though his legs were still weak and he didn't have the strength to do more than softly neigh.

He talked to Charlie, telling him about Tip, Wes and the boys, Ryker and Jon Westfield.

"Just be glad you aren't a warhorse," he joked as he said good-bye the last morning. "You be a good boy."

The last morning, Sara stopped by with hot tea and one of Ma's treats, minced pie. "You were right about the Billings." Her gaze met his across Charlie's back. "I'm sorry for doubting you. I was...dumb."

"I'm sorry for being so hard on you. I didn't mean it. I didn't think it through." He laughed, his throat a bit raw. "I suppose I was the bigger fool."

Sara rushed around the horse to embrace him. "Oh, Adam, please be careful. I couldn't bear if something happened to you."

The train slowed, approaching another station. Outside, carts, horses, soldiers and vendors mulled, everyone in a hurry, their eyes wide and urgent as if they were frightened. A double line of men marched along the tracks, their uniforms a mix of blue and gray, some with short jackets, some long. Adam wondered how they'd tell each other apart on the battlefield. The air was heavy with odors of cooking, tobacco smoke, manure and unwashed skin.

Adam leaned back, grateful he had a few hours before joining his troop. Sara and Allister had promised to take care of Charlie, Adam leaving his last dollars. After paying for the train fare he was as broke as when he'd joined the Yankees.

Thanks to Ma's care, his right arm felt reasonably well. The bandage was small, the hole nearly scarred over. Strength was another matter. He curled his fingers, which felt thick and unyielding. He knew he was one of the lucky ones. Men were dying in large numbers now, many from injuries on the battlegrounds, and even more from disease.

Pa had gone into the war because he believed that stopping slavery was the right thing to do, but it had never been the reason why Adam joined. He'd wished to die then. He took in a sharp breath, realizing he no longer wanted to die. Not only that, he wanted to stop the Rebs. Because if he didn't, people like the Billings would continue enriching themselves with the labor of others, whipping and killing slaves at whim. For the first time since dreaming about becoming a veterinary surgeon, he felt he was doing something useful.

"I see you found your way back," Ryker said when Adam reported to duty.

"Yes, Sir."

"How's the arm?"

"Better, Sir."

"Let me see." Ryker took hold of Adam's hand and squeezed.

Unleashing fiery pain, Adam flinched. "What're we going to do with you, Private?" Ryker shook his head. "Not much good in the trenches. You're liable to get yourself finished off next time."

"I'm not planning on it, Sir. I'm wondering if you need help with your horses and mules," Adam stumbled. He'd thought about it all the way here.

Ryker stepped back. "What makes you think I need another …" But then he hesitated. "It just so happens we've lost a man. Unfortunate accident. You know horses, then?"

Adam nodded. "It's what I did at home."

"All right. Report to Sergeant Livingston in the morning. I'll send him a message."

"Thank you, Sir," Adam said, but Ryker had already walked off.

Tip was responsible for driving Miss Millie and Giselle wherever they wanted to go. All across the town, the war was leaving its marks. Flags and posters hung on every corner, where men marched, their uniforms dirty and shredded.

The worst were the men sitting or limping along, arms and legs missing, black eye patches and scars marring their faces. They looked stony, as if even breathing required too much effort.

Compared to them he was lucky, Tip mused, as he guided the horse carriage back to the plantation. His back felt a lot better, though he could no longer bend easily because of the scars that ran like cordwood down his spine.

He noticed that Giselle sat much closer than she needed to. When had that started? Sure enough, a hand planted itself on his forearm.

"Ain't it a beautiful day," she said.

He nodded. She was right, of course. It was beautiful, the air filled with the song of cardinals and the knock-knock of assorted woodpeckers. He loved summer, the country still lush despite the raging battles, his new home better than the Billings.

Master King was a jovial fellow with a round belly who laughed a lot just like his daughter. He wasn't around much, but even the overseers acted more civil. Tip had never known such freedom to wander about and even sit idle while he waited for Miss Millie and Giselle to get ready.

He sniffed. His sense of smell was coming back. After the

beating he hadn't been able to taste or smell much of anything, but now he clearly made out the rich scents of purple passionflowers and lavender.

Yet he couldn't enjoy it. He was still a slave, still had no rights. He missed Mama Rose and the life he'd known before the war.

"You want to take a walk later?" Giselle asked as they passed by the vegetable garden.

Right in the middle of the patch, Master King held up a shriveled vine. "Look at these tomatoes. They're ruined."

"So sorry, Master." The gardener, a slave with a shorn head and not much older than Tip, stood with his head low. "I only pick cotton before. Don't know much about gardens."

Ignoring Giselle's tugging hand, Tip stopped the wagon and clambered into the garden. "It's the hornworm. Eat the leaves and fruit if you let it. Need to pick them off early, plant dill and basil around." He bent with effort and picked a fat caterpillar off a vine to inspect it. It was as green as the vines. "Buggers always hungry." He dropped it and squished it under his boot. "Eggplant and peppers eaten too."

"Tipper, right?" Master King squinted above his glasses. "How do you know?"

"I keep Master Billings garden." Tip took in the weeds between the disorderly rows of vegetables, the stunted bush beans and withered onion stalks. "Need water," he mumbled.

"You know about produce."

"Yessir, I know all about it."

King nodded slowly. "All right, from now on you'll help Eli. On second thought, Eli will help you."

"What about Miss Millie?"

"I'll talk to Millie about another driver. You can start right now. See if you can save some of these tomato plants."

Tip smiled.

Tip rinsed the soil from his forearms and grabbed a towel.

"You never tell me you know gardens." Giselle bit her lip.

"What?" He hadn't even noticed her approach.

"When you learn that?"

He shrugged. "Spent ten years in the garden before Master sell me."

"I miss you driving us. Miss Millie too."

Tip kept silent. For the first time in years he was... content. Today he'd felt a bit like coming home. As soon as Master King had disappeared, he'd taken off his shoes and marched back and forth between the rows of vegetables and berries to inspect the damage. He made lists in his head of what to do first. Oh, how good the soil felt between his toes. Nature's rules were simple and reliable, the earth welcoming him. There was no cruelty, no hidden thought of revenge, no expectations.

"I want to write a letter," he said into the stillness that settled uncomfortably between them.

"You have a sweetheart somewhere?" Giselle sounded pouty. "What her name?"

Tip shook his head. There was Elda, but who knew what had happened to her. Master was bound to give her a baby or sell her off. Maybe she'd married one of the other slaves, the stable boy or one of the field hands. No, his former dreams were done with.

"My mama, Mama Rose. I want to let her know where I am. And my friend, Adam. He live on a farm nearby."

There was the hand again, patting his arm. Tip closed his eyes. Why couldn't he just enjoy her touch? She'd saved his life, he was sure of that. It'd be easy to move forward. The signs were there.

Toward the end of the row, of slave huts stood a slightly larger one. Tip hadn't been inside but had heard of the woman who lived there. It was late afternoon on Sunday and Millie had disappeared with Giselle, who was helping her dress for dinner.

Tip knocked.

"Come in." The voice was ancient as the world.

Tip stepped into the gloom. Near the hearth sat an old woman, much older than Jonas, older than anyone Tip had ever seen. Her face was covered in so many wrinkles that she looked shriveled, like a forgotten potato after a long winter. Her hair was long and white. Supposedly, she'd been Master King's nanny years ago. The other slaves took care of her, dropping off meals and taking care of her laundry.

Behind her on a shelf stood five or six books, something Tip had only seen in Master Billings house.

"What you want?" The old woman looked at him with rheumy eyes, yet he felt as if she could read his mind. "You the new Negro helping Miss Millie and now the gardener."

Tip nodded.

"But you not happy. I see it in your face. Tell me boy, what you want."

"I want to send a letter to my…Mama Rose…and my friend, Adam."

"Where they live?"

"Greeneville, at the Billings plantation. Adam live on a little farm."

"You know his last name?"

Tip nodded again.

"Sit, boy." The old woman straightened slowly. "My body too old for this life," she muttered while rummaging through a wooden box in the corner. Tip watched in awe as the woman fell back into her seat, her wrinkly fingers holding a quill, paper and ink.

"What you want to say?"

Tip looked around. In his head he'd written a hundred letters. Now that he sat here he knew not what to say. If he concentrated he'd be able to write himself. But he was unsure of so many words, the lessons long ago. Worse, the beatings left him fuzzy brained, unable to concentrate. Giselle said it'd pass, but he was impatient and angry with his feeble body.

"How about you tell her you all right, being a driver for Miss Millie and working the garden?"

"Sure," Tip said, relief flooding him.

The scraping of the pen mixed with the crackling of the fire. "You want to talk about Giselle?"

"Eh, what?"

"You sweet with Giselle?"

Tip felt his cheeks grow hot. "No, I…."

"Giselle my granddaughter. She a good girl with a good heart."

Tip felt dumbfounded. Had they talked about him? Made plans to hook him?

After finishing a similar note to Adam, the quill sank to the paper. The old woman's eyes zoomed in, making Tip feel naked.

"You not ready, boy. You want to run. I see it."

With sudden fierceness, the old woman gripped his hand and pulled it close to her chest. Tip felt her forefinger scrape along his palm.

"Hmmm," the woman said, "hmmm."

"What is it? What you see?" Tip yanked his hand back.

"Boy, you be careful. You danger written in there. There's death, too and…" The woman closed her eyes and sighed. "Better go soon. Giselle find other husband."

Tip nodded, but then he straightened. He was tired of being told what to do. "You teach me to read and write first? I already know the letters."

The old woman leaned back, her wrinkly lids almost hiding her eyes. "Boy, you push your luck."

Tip kept waiting. He knew it was risky. Negroes were forbidden to read and write. Mama Rose had always said that smart people were powerful. He was done cowering. He was going to ask for what he wanted. In the silence he heard kids playing outside, their high voices happy and careless.

"Come after dinner. I teach you."

Tip nodded. "What I pay?"

The old woman shook her head. "No pay, boy. Go now."

Lying awake half the night, Tip thought of what he'd heard. The letters had been sent with the house boy who'd promised to add them to Master King's outgoing post.

The old woman was crazy, of course. She knew nothing of him. And what was that about danger and death? For the first time in many months, he felt halfway safe. All he had to do now was stay and do his work.

"Brought you some sweets." Giselle smiled down at Tip, holding a plate with a cloth cover. A week had passed. It was evening, almost dark, and most of the house slaves lingered outside their cabins. He sat on a log by himself, his mind filled with the adventures of Pip, the reading lesson from earlier. He felt just as alone, but the way the main character hoped for a better future gave him courage.

Tip patted the space next to him. "Sit by me."

Giselle's smile grew wider as she slumped next to him. "Miss Millie say to share." She removed the cover to reveal a piece of peach pie, the aroma going up Tip's nose. He sucked in the heavenly scent, taking him back to Mama Rose's kitchen.

"What wrong?" Giselle asked.

"Nothing. My Mama a great cook. She famous for miles."

"Where is she?"

"Billings plantation in Greeneville." His voice grew heavy.

"Don't know if I ever see her again. You always live with Millie?"

To his surprise, Giselle shoved the pie into his hand and ran off.

Tip caught up to Giselle in the peach orchard. "What wrong? Tell me."

Giselle gulped air, wiping her face. Supporting her elbow, he led her to a stack of empty crates. "Sit."

Giselle threw him a thankful glance. "I live with other family." Her eyes looked black in the dusk, her cheeks damp with tears. "Master come to my hut. Every night he come. Even when I was with child. Missus angry with me. I try to send him away many times. He cruel. I had a little girl. They sold her to a slave trader. I never sees her again." A sob escaped her. "She four now."

Tip patted her hand. "They sold you, too."

Giselle nodded. "Missus made sure, though I lucky to have Grandmother."

Fresh heat seethed up Tip's chest. It was like that everywhere. Mothers were raped by their Masters, stripped of their children until they had nothing left to give—until their souls were gone. At least Mama Rose would get his letter and know he was alive.

"Tip, wait." Giselle waved as she ran to catch up with Tip, who was carrying a basket of produce to the kitchen.

Over the last month, the garden had been transformed. Orderly beds, bean stalks eager to reach the sky, a new herb patch with parsley, chives, basil, dill and thyme. Marigolds and other edible flowers ringed the outside to fend off deer. Master King had given Tip free reign and allowed him to buy vegetables and herbs from neighboring plantations and in town.

"Look, look." Giselle held up two letters.

Tip's heart squeezed with excitement.

"Can you read them?"

Tip slowly nodded. He'd been making such progress reading from Great Expectations that the old woman was mumbling praise. But every night she warned him to keep their meetings secret. It wasn't exactly easy when Giselle was poking her nose into his business every minute.

"Dear Mama Rose,
I work at Master King's plantation near Kingsport. I take care of

Master's garden. Do not worry about me. I'm fine.
    Your son,
    Tip"

Even before he finished he realized that this was the letter the old woman had written. He turned the paper back and forth. *Un...deliver...able* was stamped on the front, the same writing on the letter to Adam. The mail had travelled all the way to Greeneville and been returned.

Something was terribly wrong. What was going on with his mama? With Adam? His stomach cramped painfully as he imagined Mama Rose dead and Adam's farm gone. Maybe Master Billings had made good on his promise. Maybe the Adam's family was destitute and spread to the winds.

"What it say?" Giselle asked.

"Nothing. Neither of the letters was delivered."

Saying it out loud was worse. Something had happened to Mama Rose. The old woman had been right when she'd mentioned *death.* He shuddered, his eyes flowing over. He furiously wiped his face and stomped off.

"What you going to do?" Giselle called after him.

He shrugged. There was only one thing he wanted now.

CHAPTER TWENTY-SIX

"All ordered to march by nine o'clock," somebody yelled into the barn. Adam was cleaning hoofs and shoeing a honey-colored gelding. By the time he finished, the camp was buzzing, men breaking down tents, collecting gear, and filling latrines. The air was thick with smoke from extinguished cook fires.

In the heat of late June, a heavy dust cloud hovered above them, the air rippling and shimmering and so gritty, Adam tasted it between his teeth. He'd been fighting for two years, but he'd never get used to it. Yes, he was a lot tougher, but the heat, icy winters, the meager rations, and the constant moving from camp to camp had taken its toll. If he allowed himself to think, he felt like he was in hell most of the time.

For most of 1862 they'd battled around Cumberland Gap, a hilly, heavily wooded pass near the junction of Kentucky, Virginia and Tennessee. The Rebs wanted that spot bad, trying to push north into Kentucky. In the fall they'd succeeded driving the 2nd Tennessee into retreat. Adam's regiment had traveled to Ohio, then Tennessee and back to Kentucky in the spring...where he'd started. It was like being on a merry-go-round he'd once seen described in a newspaper, moving in a circle from place to place, setting up camp, taking down camp, marching into numbness.

Worse were the flood of injured and dead soldiers, bringing with them the smells of blood, metallic and foul in the air, clouds of swirling flies eager to land on open sores, and an unending stream of hopelessness. He often felt sick now. The longing for his home, Ma, and Sara was like an open wound that refused to heal.

Some days it was so bad, he hardly knew how to get through each hour. The cries of the dying soldiers drilled into his mind like rusty screws, and the hollow looks of his friends, Marty, Thomas and Wes haunted him. Marty hardly joked these days, and Wes was altogether mute.

Only now, from the middle of the bloody war, did he recognize the gladness that had filled his heart once. He remembered watching his father step behind Ma for a quick squeeze, the way her eyes filled with mirth in response, their meals around the table, Pa's description of what he planned for the farm, the smell of warm bread, the way the logs settled in the stove and filled the cabin with warmth…all that had been home. Instead of appreciating his life, he'd been filled with longing for his own horse, more time alone, and a myriad of insignificant nonsense. His memories blazed bright against the dull gray backdrop of the war.

And yet he realized he was lucky not having to fight like Wes, Marty and Thomas. Taking care of the never-ending stream of horses was infinitely easier. After one of the skirmishes, Doc Kline, the single veterinary surgeon in charge of more than a thousand horses, handed him a tattered copy of 'A Treatise on Veterinary Medicine,' a treasure he protected with his life.

"Here, Blythe, make yourself useful." Kline's leather apron had sparkled dark red with blood, his arms crimson to his elbows. So Adam went to work next to Kline, cutting, sawing, digging for bullets, handing tools and wiping the doc's brow.

When others in camp smoked, slept, wrote diaries, shot the breeze and were bored to their skulls, he studied the book on horse ailments until his eyes blurred in the dim light.

Word got around quickly he was "good" at dealing with injured animals, sickly ones, and dispirited ones. They had shoe boils, saddle sores, bullet wounds, torn shoes, rain rot, infections from bug bites and lately, malnutrition.

The worst was Glanders, causing lesions in lungs and skin, a highly infectious disease considered deadly. Adam quickly learned that even the slightest suspicion was cause to separate and shoot a horse, a necessary precaution to protect the rest.

He still never got used to it.

Feed ran out constantly. A single warhorse required fourteen pounds of hay and twelve pounds of grain a day. During breaks

Adam hurried through camp, reminding soldiers to forage for hay and grain while they were out. At times they resorted to pasturage, though this caused some horses to lame or founder. Horses feeding on acorns developed colic and bloody diarrhea. He didn't understand the reasoning but told every man in the cavalry to stay clear of oaks.

Despite the horror and cruelty, he loved them all, and somehow they felt it. When he failed, they were shot. And so he tried all his tricks, learning new ones along the way.

When his right hand finally healed, he remained with the horses and mules. Ryker had requested him back, but somebody higher up he'd never met had intervened. So, he'd stayed, even missing most of the battle action because he was too valuable to be on the front.

But his mind never stood still as he waited for news from home. Some word about Tip, about Ma and Sara. The last letter he'd received had arrived seven months ago. Since then, nothing. He'd written every other week, addressing his letters to Allister Porter, who was supposed to give them to Ma. Had something happened to Allister? Adam couldn't figure out why Ma didn't write back. Were the letters being intercepted? Had they somehow forgotten to address them to Adam Blythe? It couldn't be.

Fresh worry crept up in him, an ache in his heart that never quite went away.

Once the majority of camp had gone, Adam, his helpers and the ambulances followed with injured soldiers and ailing horses, the feeble ones all reminding him of Charlie. That he wanted to go home. In a way he wanted to heal them to make up for Charlie.

But as the war escalated and battles followed battles, as men died and got maimed, fewer and fewer soldiers were allowed furlough. He'd been lucky to get a month off with his arm. Nowadays, *light* injuries were not considered reason for leave at all.

He coaxed the Chestnut out of his box. The horse had been hit in the chest with shrapnel, and now his skin was dotted with bright pink scars. "It's all right," Adam soothed. "We're going to move camp." The Chestnut was weary, the whites of his eyes showing. The constant gunfire and artillery messed with their nerves.

Adam continued talking and rubbing the horse's forehead until it followed. If he failed, the Chestnut would be shot. The

Army had no patience for skittish horses.

The path was easy enough to see, deep ruts, torn earth, where the artillery had been dragged across. Adam sighed. When would it ever be finished? Early on, Marty and Thomas had spoken of going home by Christmas, the war being over any day. Nobody spoke like that anymore. With every week and every month the war dug itself deeper into the country, tearing it apart like ice breaking a rock.

Adam visited the boys at night, often sitting next to Wes who was still moody and mostly quiet. To his shock, Wes's uncle was still in the Army. Adam had run into him once on his way to Wes's tent, the man's eyes full of hatred.

"How you doing?" he asked Wes after they'd settled down for a visit in the new camp near Lexington.

Wes shrugged. "No better or worse."

"I know what you mean. Haven't heard from Ma in months. It's driving me crazy."

Wes shrugged, the history of his family as murky as Adam's.

"You think this war will ever end?"

Wes stared into nothing. "Don't know what I'd do either way."

"What do you mean? You don't want to go home?"

"Nothing there for me."

"What about your uncle?"

Wes's eyes flittered across the tent. "He'll get me again one of these days."

"Can't we go to Ryker?"

Wes's cheeks flushed. "And say what?"

Adam wanted to add more. Wanted to calm his friend and tell him they'd find a way. Except he wasn't at all sure how to help— Jon Westfield was not only still alive and unhurt, he was a lurker. "Never mind. I better head back," he said aloud.

"You be careful too. He doesn't forget."

"I'll be fine."

"Blythe?" one of the stall boys hollered when Adam returned to their new makeshift corral where they kept the sickest horses.

"You've got a letter," the boy said. "Looks like it's been on the road a while." The paper was smudged and stained, his name barely legible. But that wasn't what made Adam's heart pound. The writing was neither in his mother's nor his sister's hand. Somebody else had written, somebody with bad news. His fingers shook as he tore open the paper, his eyes trying to focus on the slanting script.

April 18, 1863
Adam,

Your Ma is in a bad way because of your sister. She didn't want you to know but I think you should. A little while ago Nathan Billings regained his memory. It was coming back a bit at a time and one day he showed up at our farm, demanding to see you. Of course, we said you were gone and we didn't know where you were. But he remembered seeing you in uniform so he squeezed some more information out of your mother. He told us he'd get revenge and that he'd see you hanged. But that wasn't the worst part. Not too long after, Sara went to town to pick up supplies. I was busy with Grandfather mending fences and...I shouldn't have let her go alone.

She didn't return as expected, and we finally found her in the woods, a half-mile from our farm. She'd been trying to walk home, her dress torn. She was talking funny, and we finally got it out of her that she'd been attacked by Nathan. He'd seen her at the store and followed before forcing himself on her. Grandfather and I went to see him and demand an explanation. Nathan said he loved Sara, but he was acting all crazy, worse than he ever had. He's drinking even more now that he's regained his memory. He said we couldn't say anything or he'd tell the sheriff about you and they'd put out a search warrant.

You better stay far away from here. It's not safe.
Allister

P.S. I heard a rumor that Tip was shot during his attempt to flee from Rawley's farm. Sorry, I know he was your friend.

Adam's cheeks swam—snot clogged his throat. Sara had been violated. Her face floated in front of him—her bright blue eyes, the little dimples when she laughed and made fun of him. Nathan Billings had defiled her.

Adam dragged himself into a corner to throw up. The terrible cruelty of it all hit him as if he'd been punched in the stomach. He was stuck in this ridiculous war that killed men and horses by the thousands while all the people he held dear were being tortured at home.

His thoughts traveled to Tip and he felt himself begin to shake. Tip's death was the Billings's fault, too. All Tip had done was take care of his garden and his mother. Now he was gone.

Adam thought of Mama Rose, the way her eyes had looked dead. Tip's death was going to kill her. He sank into the straw and curled into a ball, rubbing his hands over and over. He had to find a way to get home.

He was going to kill Nathan Billings—this time for good.

"You can't go, not without furlough," Wes said, his voice heavy with emotion. In the early morning, Adam had snuck across camp. He had to talk to somebody before he went crazy. Wes wouldn't tell. He had secrets of his own.

Adam had hardly been able to speak and they'd scrambled off to the outer edges where dozens of corrals held hundreds of horses.

"I'm going to get him," Adam said. "If it's the last thing I do." A sob escaped him, but he didn't care, not now, not even in Wes's presence. Wes awkwardly patted his shoulder.

"You'll find a way. Maybe you'll need another injury to join Company Q," he said, trying to be funny. Company Q was their nickname for the sick list.

"They won't let me leave, not unless it's really bad."

"I could go with you," Wes said. "Sounds to me like you could use the help."

Adam shook his head. "It's my fight. It's dangerous, and you could get killed."

It was Wes's turn to shrug. "Ha, nobody even cares I'm alive."

At that moment Adam realized how much Wes meant to him. Wes had become his family. He produced a smile. "Don't say that. For one, I'm glad."

Wes grimaced back. "What what're you going to do?"

CHAPTER TWENTY-SEVEN

"Blythe, report to me in fifteen minutes." Ryker, red-faced, his boots crusted with mud, materialized next to Adam.

"Sir, I am supposed to feed the animals."

"Not anymore, Blythe, orders from Brigadier General Shackelford. Rebs are on the run, need every man. Must be prepared to light out at a moment's notice."

"Yes, Sir," Adam said, his mind reeling. He could hardly breathe with the anger and worry about home. The letter lay in his pocket like a poisonous snake and he was waiting for a chance.

A chance of what?

The first days after the letter he'd almost done it. Almost packed his knapsack, almost snuck out. But every time the moment passed. And he'd stayed. Now it was July. Hard to believe he'd been gone from home almost two years.

There were the boys he'd disappoint. There was Wes he'd never see again. There was Ma telling him he'd entered a contract with the Army.

Last time he'd run, it was to avoid the noose. This time he'd be running from his responsibility. And so he stayed. And marched, set up camp, fought a little, marched again, set up camp, and so on. He'd stopped counting engagements. All they did was zigzag around Kentucky and Tennessee like lost sheep. With soap and water as scarce as hen's teeth, he developed a healthy amount of camp itch, the skin on his underarms and legs red and infected. Now they wanted him to get into yet another skirmish.

And despite all this trekking, they were lucky. Words about Gettysburg had traveled to them, a three-day battle with terrifying results. It was rumored more than 50,000 men lay dead, the ground soaked red, trees and brush burned, the earth upturned and covered with bodies. Supposedly, the Feds were ahead, but at what price?

He hated the war, which led nowhere and did nothing but wear them down and destroy the country. His uniform hung in tatters, stained and loose. Just like the boys, he'd lost weight. Of course, that hadn't stopped him from growing almost a foot and sprouting hair all over his chin.

With a sigh he pulled together his mess kit, haversack, tent half and musket. He patted the chestnut's nose and mumbled good-byes, wondering who'd take care of the horses from now on. Chances were good they'd die while he was gone. Nothing he touched mattered. Everything had a way of falling apart.

"Glad to have you with me," Wes said as they lined up in rows of two. It was late afternoon, the wind blowing superheated air across the fields.

Adam spit grimly, trying to rid himself of the grit between his teeth. Despite the dust that covered everything, invaded his eyes and nose and made it hard to see, the ground was a mud hole, reminding him of the hog pen at home. He inspected his boots covered to his ankles in muck.

Home, no, he couldn't think about that right now. Not now that he *wanted* to live.

They traveled all day and made camp at night, the woods around them dark and silent. The word was that General Morgan was raiding from Tennessee to northern Ohio, spreading fear and panic among citizens and federal forces alike. General Shackelford had vowed to stop Morgan at all cost, sending Union forces in pursuit.

Men coughed here and there, but otherwise Adam only heard the breathing of the boys near him and the shrill whine of buzzing mosquitoes. The constant itching from their bites drove him crazy, his neck and hands covered with welts. Only the smoke of their cook fires brought some relief. Of course, with the Rebs close, fires were out of the question and so he gritted his teeth, wishing himself far away, wishing for some distraction.

The next day they did the same and the day after that, the land covered under dense forests, falling and rising in unending waves. Every time the ground climbed steadily, the exhaustion bathed him in sweat, his butt and thigh muscles on fire. He'd been glad to have a horse, but they often had to dismount when crossing treacherous terrain.

Nobody had told them where they were headed or what was going to happen, but he could tell they were traveling north toward Indiana.

Around midnight, they took a short break, chewing a bit of hardtack and some deer jerky they'd foraged the week before. Adam's mouth was dry with thirst, his canteen long empty.

One week turned to two as they chased Captain Morgan all over Kentucky and Ohio. They found plenty of signs, broken down wagons, rutted paths, torn trees and burned farms. A week prior they captured some thousand Rebs in a two-day skirmish at Buffington Island.

But their commander, Shackelford, wasn't happy. General Morgan continued burning bridges, raiding farms and stores and generally spreading unrest.

Their own forces swelled to more than three thousand men. Adam felt insignificant in the sea of grim faces.

In the early morning hours of July 26, they were ordered to form a line of battle when the men in front suddenly stopped and whispers about rebel forces ran up the ranks. They'd traveled north and east deep into Ohio, but close to the Ohio River because it was said that Morgan wanted to double back south. So far he hadn't done so.

Adam wondered how far back in the line he was. It was still pitch black, and no fires were allowed. As he waited for further news, the damp air soaked his hair and he began to shiver. He'd never expected to be so tired all the time. And dirty. And hungry. It seemed most of his time was spent trying to ignore his misery, not to mention the guilt that forever accompanied him like the grim reaper.

He had to remain focused. Trying to keep his mind blank, he walked a few steps to relieve himself.

He was just buttoning his pants when another whisper ran up the rank. *Spread out and advance slowly. The Rebel camp is straight ahead. Not a sound.*

Adam gripped his musket and, sensing Wes next to him,

scurried forward in a crouch.

Shouts broke out ahead. It was still dark except for a few torches between the trees. The screams and cries grew, horses neighed and people scattered. As far as Adam knew, Wes was still next to him as he charged downhill toward the racket.

Out of nowhere, a horse reared up not three feet from his head. Adam swung sideways to avoid the lethal hooves. The horse whinnied, momentarily confused with all the movement around it. Adam heard the rider grunt and shout a command, disappearing between the lines. As the air filled with the stench of manure, the faintest gray appeared on the horizon, not enough to shed light on the horse and the identity of its rider.

Shots rang out. At first a few, then growing into a roar. Adam ducked low next to Wes and Marty. The whir of bullets filled his ears like hornets, his nose stung from the acrid smoke. He aimed, shot and loaded, aimed, shot and loaded, a mindless body, a tiny wheel in the insane war machine clicking away toward a climax. There was no way to tell if he hit anyone, let alone Johnny Rebs, the air so fogged with gun smoke, it was as if he were sitting in the middle of a smoky fire.

Drums pounded, the sign to move forward. Head low, Adam scurried along, more feeling than seeing the men next to him.

"Adam." Wes's terror-filled voice reached his ears through the racket of the gunfire.

Adam turned and saw Wes fall on his knees next to Marty. Adam ran back to them. To heck with the fight.

Marty lay on his back. His great moustache drooped, his face pale. Red spread across his middle with such speed that his entire jacket seemed to turn crimson in seconds.

Carefully loosening a few buttons, Adam felt his fingers turn warm with Marty's blood. Despair gripped him, and by the time he looked up, Marty's eyes stared unseeing.

"He's dead, isn't he," Wes said quietly. Adam nodded.

"Damn Rebs. I'm going to kill them." Wes jumped up and stopped. "What the…"

Adam wiped his face and glanced across the field. Clouds of smoke wafted across the bodies of men and horses. The fighting had ceased. In the distance Rebs were being corralled, hands held high.

Adam scowled. Another victory—one tiny skirmish among thousands. What did it matter? Marty was dead. He wiped his face, hardly aware that his hands were sticky with blood.

"You soldier, get a move on," somebody yelled. "Morgan escaped again. We're lighting out in pursuit."

Nodding numbly, Adam raced toward his horse. It was just as well. His legs were so tired, he could hardly keep his knees from collapsing, his muscles seizing up in painful cramps.

From what he could tell, the officer upfront who'd ordered him to follow was a major. They rode past the battlefield, men collecting arms and moving the injured. Fleetingly, Adam thought of Wes who'd charged into the fight when it was already over.

Poor Wes. His uncle, the creep, was probably still among them, and Wes was undoubtedly afraid of being caught alone.

"Who's the officer?" Adam asked some soldier as they slowed down, crossing a ravine to climb another hill. It was like this everywhere. Down one hill, up another.

"Major George Rue."

The arm signal to halt was given and Adam reigned in his mount.

Ahead, a handful of Rebs crouched between horses that looked like they'd fall over any minute.

"I surrender," one of the Rebs, wearing the insignia of a general, said to a militiaman in his own group. Adam knew both sides employed thousands of private volunteers as militia to help with the war. They weren't regular Army or Infantry, but just as lethal.

"We surrender, too," several officers in gray uniforms yelled.

"I'll pardon you," the militiaman said.

"Not so fast." Major Rue slid off his horse. Adam followed suit and marched toward the men, gun at the ready.

"General Morgan, you're under arrest," Rue said. "Take him, boys."

Adam charged forward as several of his fellow men took Morgan and his officers between them.

"I protest!" Morgan's pointy beard quivered. "I've been pardoned."

"We shall see. Right now, you're going to prison," Rue said, a note of satisfaction in his voice. Despite Morgan's fancier outfit, he looked as filthy as Adam and his company.

One of the men patted Adam on the back. "We caught ourselves a big fish."

Adam nodded. He didn't care.

Marty was dead.

"Where've you been?" Wes asked when Adam rode back into camp.

"Caught Morgan."

"You better stick with horses, Blythe," Ryker said, marching up to them. His uniform was stained with blood, but his eyes burned as fierce as ever.

"It's true, we caught General Morgan."

"You were there?" Ryker whistled. "Finally we caught the son of a gun."

"Looks like we're heading back south soon. Better take care of these mounts, Blythe. Captured a load of them though most look ready to shoot.

"Yes, Sir," Adam said, patting his horse's rump, a reddish-brown gelding with white markings on its forehead. The memory of Charlie, the horse he'd rescued from Rawley's farm, flashed by. Strange that Allister hadn't mentioned him. But then it had been such a terrible letter to write about what happened to Sara.

"And Blythe... I shall make a favorable report. Good work today."

"Eh, Sir," Adam said at Ryker's back. "You heard, Marty..."

Ryker shook his head. "A shame, good man that one."

Wes, standing next to Adam, sniffed and turned away. "I'm going to fix me some of that desecrated vegetable."

"Good idea." Adam patted Wes on the back, thankful for having a buddy who didn't need a lot of words. "Have you seen Thomas?"

"He ran off after Marty..." Wes cleared his throat. "You think you'll get a medal?" He asked as they scouted for a suitable spot to set up camp. The ground was so uneven, they mostly slept face up or down, wedged between tree stumps and rocks or worse, in the mud.

"What for?" Adam snapped back, glancing at the narrow valley below where houses and farms dotted the hills. *Salineville* they called it. Everywhere he could see, Union soldiers milled, inspecting Reb provisions and ammunitions. Horses were being corralled along makeshift ropes. To his left, men assembled wounded cavalrymen. Here and there horses lay dead among the mingling soldiers. Flies swirled in clouds.

"If I might have a word, Sir?" Adam said that evening when they'd settled in camp.

"Make it fast," Ryker said.

"I'm wondering..."

"Be quick, Blythe. Got to get some order into this place."

"Sir, I'm wondering if I can get furlough to visit my kin. It's...kind of an emergency."

Ryker stepped closer, his ruddy face right in front of Adam's. "Blythe, save yourself the conniption fit. My orders are clear. No furlough at this time. We've got work to do. Heading south, back to Tennessee, to root out more Rebs."

Adam lowered his head.

Ryker's voice softened. "What can possibly be that important?"

"My sister... she's in a bad way." Adam faltered.

"Tell me."

Adam looked up surprised. It was the first time Ryker had shown interest. "Sir, I..." Adam closed his mouth. In order to explain Nathan Billings's motive, he'd have to go way back. It was a secret he couldn't share. "Never mind," he said aloud.

Swiveling around, he headed back to the spot where Wes was fixing a meal in a tin cup.

He'd never leave, but even if he did, he'd be hanged before he could ever help his family.

CHAPTER TWENTY-EIGHT

Tip squatted low. Compared to running from Rawley's farm, this time had been easy. Too easy. Surely, something was going to happen. He knew if he'd get caught again he'd die. He didn't have it in him to return from that place on the edge when he'd about entered heaven. Not now. Not since the letter he'd sent to Mama Rose had been returned last summer. This time he wouldn't bother. He'd welcome death.

But here he was...still in one piece despite the cords on his back and the stiffness in his left arm. All he wanted to do now was get away from it all. Not think about Mama Rose, or Adam, or Elda.

Over the past fifteen months he'd collected intelligence from several slaves and kept his eyes open in town. He knew Kingsport was close to Virginia and if he went straight north, he'd soon be in Kentucky.

He opened his pack inside of which he carried the tattered copy of Great Expectations. He'd talked the old woman into loaning him the book, reading every night by the light of a candle stub, dreaming about getting away. Despite its recent publication, the copy was missing its cover, the pages brittle and yellowed as if it had been pulled from the flames.

Unlike Dickens's make belief story, Tip's life contained no secret benefactors. Whatever he, Tip, wanted, he had to do himself. So here he was, alone and on the run once more.

The crude map he'd drawn from hearsay was stuck between

the pages, showing the state line and the direction he was supposed to travel. It was early in the day and he'd spent an uncomfortable night in a thicket. His bundle was filled with several days' worth of bread, grains and jerky. All he had to do now was not get caught.

A shiver ran down his back. He'd learned his lesson and stayed away from any farms and most of the roads, but you never knew. Fate was a strange beast.

He often walked late into the night to avoid being seen. Freedom was what he needed now. He could not stand one more minute of being somebody's property. Not even on Master King's plantation, where life was much easier. If he got caught now, he'd be sold or maybe put to death. He didn't care. At least he'd tried to go after his dream, no matter how comfortable he'd had it, and no matter how much Giselle wanted him to stay.

They'd argued. That evening after he'd received the returned letters, he'd told Giselle it was no use. He had to go. He had to try to find happiness somehow, somewhere. It wasn't at the King plantation. Not with her.

"Then I want to come with you," Giselle had said, her eyes large and glistening.

Tip shook his head. "You happy with Miss Millie. They catch us, you get sold or worse."

"What will I do?"

"Forget about me. Forget I was ever here."

Giselle turned away, sobbing. Tip looked after her, unable to say anything or follow her. His former self would've gone to talk to her and explain. Now he didn't care. His heart was a block of pond ice. *You cold-hearted bastard.*

He'd contemplated returning to Greeneville to see for himself why Mama Rose hadn't written, and why Adam's letter had been returned. In the end, he could not. The risks were too high and he couldn't face the fact Mama Rose was dead.

A moan escaped him, startling a blue bird. It squawked loudly and flew off. He hurried on. No more thinking back. He had to move forward, ponder his plans. He wanted to reach Ohio, far enough north to escape the slave states. He'd heard Master King talk to one of his guests about huge factories employing whites and coloreds alike. They'd all laughed incredulously as if the notion of black men working independently were some joke.

He'd see about that. He was going up there and earn money.

Live free.

Somewhere beyond the brush, he heard movement. Marching feet, lots of them. He threw himself into a clump of honey suckle.

"You think we'll go home soon?" a tired voice sounded to his left.

"Nah, war isn't rightly over. Who knows how much longer," someone else said.

Tip peered past the undergrowth. Just a few feet ahead, men moved along the narrow trail. He'd almost run into them. Five or six men in the gray of the Confederates were marching past, guns on shoulders, their faces strained under beards. Soldiers.

How could he have missed it? Where there were five, there could be hundreds. He may have landed smack in the middle of some battle. Though there was no indication the soldiers were particularly careful or quiet.

Tip ever-so-slowly curled his legs to his chest until he was hidden beneath the vines. Men trampled all around him, horses snorting among the long hum of voices that sounded drained and depleted.

The trek seemed to go on for hours, and by the time Tip emerged, his limbs were stiff with cold. He hugged himself, massaged his freezing feet and calves to be able to move. The soldiers had left a clear swath to travel on. Tip followed. From what he could tell they were moving north and west. Sort of the way he wanted to go.

As long as he followed slowly, he should be all right.

"You there, get up."

Tip rose from heavy sleep. After nine days on the run, he'd finally collapsed, his body demanding rest.

Tip blinked as he tried to focus on the face hovering above him. "What?"

"You on the run, boy?" The man's eyes were blue pools in the mist of the early morning.

Instantly awake, Tip's gaze darted between the man and the dangers lurking behind him. This is what he'd wanted to avoid. He'd tried so hard to be careful, yet here he was on the ground with some slave trader or informant hanging over him.

He listened for the yapping of dogs. Nothing. The air was still.

"Can – you – speak?" the man said slowly.

Tip opened his mouth, but his throat was closed up with nerves, his body ready to pounce, his chest heaving.

"You better come with me."

Tip shook his head. Rawley's nail was long gone, but if he jumped quickly, he could throw the man on his back. *He may have a weapon. I got to risk it. I ain't going back.*

Tip scrambled to get his legs under him and tensed. The man looked to be in his fifties with narrow shoulders and a pale face that was hard to read. From what Tip could tell, he had no gun. It wouldn't be hard to knock him down and run.

The clatter of several horses grew steadily louder. So the man was part of a search team.

To his surprise, the man put a forefinger to his lips. "Come quick, before they see us."

Through the leaves of a Green Mountain Boxwood, Tip watched three riders draw steadily closer. Each carried a rifle. Last night when Tip had gone to sleep he'd thought he was far from any path.

A hand landed on his forearm. The man's head jerked toward the undergrowth, urging Tip to follow.

Tip scrambled after him.

A hundred yards into the woods, the man collapsed onto an upturned log. "You know what you're doing?"

Tip said nothing. It was time to leave before the man came to his senses. Without another word he walked off.

"You won't last another hour out there," the man called after him.

Tip abruptly turned. "What you mean?"

"I mean there's a big hunt going on. Several slaves from a nearby farm escaped. They've got dogs and riders combing the forest. You'll simply be a bonus to them."

Ever so slowly, Tip approached the man who was still catching his breath. Now that the sun was up, Tip could tell he was sick by the way his face shone white as goat's milk.

"You one of them?"

With a chuckle the man shook his head. "My name is Dale Hubbard. I'm a *conductor*."

The way the man said it, it had to mean something. Tip wracked his brain. He'd heard of people helping coloreds escape to the north.

"The Underground Railroad," Dale said. "You've heard of us?"

Tip nodded. "Can you help me?"

"You must do as I say."

"Yessir."

"Follow me. Not a word."

CHAPTER TWENTY-NINE

November 1863

"You see him?" Adam asked as he slipped into the tent.

"Who?" Wes inspected a sliver of hardtack, dusted it off and took a careful bite. If it wasn't infested with weevils, hardtack was known to break teeth.

"Your uncle. Wasn't twenty feet from here." The realization that Jon Westfield continued lurking in the shadows, ready to slip a knife between his ribs, made Adam shiver.

Wes squinted briefly and resumed chewing. To the naked eye, he looked like always, but Adam noticed the tensing in his shoulders and heard his breath catch.

"Doing what?" It sounded gruff.

"What if he's spying on you...us? Looking for a chance..." The memory of seeing Wes with his uncle in the woods brought heat to Adam's cheeks. He abruptly bent over his canteen and shook it. When Wes remained silent, Adam took a careful glance at his friend.

In the gloom of the tent flap, Wes's eyes glittered.

Intense sorrow swept through Adam, yet he knew that saying as much was the wrong move. "I'll kill the son of a bitch," he muttered. When Wes didn't answer, he crawled back outside.

How much longer, he thought as he slumped down next to the campfire, trying to suck up a bit of warmth through his damp uniform. The afternoon had brought a cold wind. He took a whetstone to sharpen his knife. How could he have ever thought that joining the Army was a way out? It was laughable. A few months ago, he'd turned eighteen, and while he still hadn't grown a serious beard, he knew he'd changed a lot. He was on his third pair of boots, courtesy of a dead Marty, and taller than most of the men. The face he'd recently seen in one of the looking glasses that Wes had swiped from a fallen Reb, was that of a man. He hardly recognized himself, his eyes burning within the shadows of their sockets, filled with what he'd faced for more than two years.

They'd turned into animals, all of them, Rebs and Yankees alike. General Grant had won in Vicksburg and they'd defeated General Lee in Gettysburg, but what did it really mean? The Rebs didn't stop and so the North continued as well. After chasing Rebs to Virginia, they'd returned to Tennessee, somewhere near Rogersville. Around and around they went, leaving destruction and death in their path.

He'd caught himself smiling grimly when watching a Reb bleed out. He was getting immune to the limbs piling up beneath the surgeon's table, the deafening sounds of artillery and the cries of fallen soldiers. Marty had been an exception, maybe because he'd been a friend, one of the boys in his tent. In the end nothing mattered, but the stupid meandering, insane war.

"You've got to help me," Thomas said quietly. Adam hadn't even noticed he was there. "I've got the Tennessee Trots. Don't rightly know where to turn with all the latrine visits."

Adam nodded. All around him boys were dying of diarrhea or dysentery, a miserable drawn-out death. Thomas who'd been thin when he joined, looked like a walking skeleton, his Adam's Apple bobbing furiously up and down beneath the folds of his neck.

"Saw some blackberry vines in the ravine," he said. "Let's make you some tea." A lifetime ago Ma had made tea from blackberry leaves to treat his lose bowels. If nothing else, it'd put some liquid into his friend.

As Thomas produced a weak nod and leaned back against a tree stump, Adam headed to the edge of camp. He nodded at the private on picket duty and climbed downhill. The ground fell sharply, impossible for camping. Nobody wanted to lie on a slope with your head two feet above your feet.

They were no more than fifty miles from Greeneville and yet he was stuck. What he would give for a few days of furlough. Of course, Wes was right. If he left, he'd not be able to return. And who knew what awaited him at home. Last time he'd run, he'd lost everything he held dear. If he disappeared now, he'd lose Wes, too.

The blackberry vines tore at his coat and bloodied his fingers, but he barely felt them. What was a little blood after the rivers he'd seen? At least the frost hadn't arrived yet. He'd have to borrow a few canteens to heat water. Thomas needed lots of fluids. Stuffing the leaves into his pockets, he climbed through the brambles.

"You still alive, I see." Like an apparition, Jon Westfield stepped from a tree, chewing a blade of grass. "Thought God Almighty would take care of it for me."

Adam's stomach lurched. "No such luck." He threw a glance around him and realized with a pang that they were alone.

Wes's uncle had gone from bad to worse, his uniform a pile of rags, his features gaunt with a yellowish sheen on his cheekbones. Liver, Adam thought automatically. Wes had told him in a rare unguarded moment how his father and uncle had drunk their weight, going on binges that only ended when all the money was gone. For a while they'd operated a still, producing the vilest 'shine' in eastern Tennessee.

"What you gonna do now?" Westfield grinned, the gaps in his teeth wider than Adam remembered.

Something cold ran down his spine. The man's eyes glittered with evil, small and hard as pieces of coal. The realization he might die this afternoon at the hands of some lowlife drunkard made Adam gasp.

"None of your business." Adam fought to keep his voice strong. No way he'd let the man see his fear. He almost wanted to chuckle because all of a sudden he was afraid, something he'd forgotten how to feel in the infinite horror of the war. His stomach roiled, and despite his fatigue he felt a surge of adrenalin.

He glanced around quickly, looking for a way out, uphill to safety where his friends were. Heck, anyone would do. Wes's uncle had picked his time wisely, following when he knew there wouldn't be any witnesses. They were in the middle of a ravine covered in seven-foot brambles, impossible to see from the top of the hill. Nobody in their right mind climbed down here into the thorns.

A blade gleamed in the low light of the afternoon. Adam grabbed for his knife and inwardly cursed. He'd thrown his knife down while sharpening and the new 1863 Springfield rifle he'd received after Morgan's capture lay in front of his tent. They weren't supposed to go anywhere without it, yet here he was without his gun *and* his knife.

"Getting sloppy," Westfield cackled. He jumped forward and swiped at Adam's chest. "Not so cocky now, boy."

Adam kept his eye on the knife that flew back and forth between Westfield's hands.

"Cause me nothing but trouble. Corporal always checking on me. I know it's your doing."

"You won't get away with it."

"Watch me. Plenty of soldiers die or disappear. You deserted, simple as that. Nobody cares. Not even your buddy, Ryker."

Westfield was probably right. Their regiment had shrunken, been reorganized and shrunken again. Soon the country would be empty of men.

"Wouldn't count on it," Adam said, jumping to his right. Too late. Sharp pain ran up to his neck as the knife sliced through the opening in his jacket. He sucked air, feeling the familiar warmth of blood flowing beneath his shirt. How deep was the cut? Pay attention.

Why had he made it this far to get slaughtered? There had to be another purpose. Something he'd survived for all this time.

And there, in the middle of all this mess, he heard his father's voice. *Make sure you do the right thing. A man must live a lifetime with his deeds.*

He was so surprised he hardly heard Westfield say, "You're mine now."

Westfield jumped forward, the knife cutting the air upward in a vicious jab. Adam was quicker. He thought of bending down to pick up rocks, but the ground was covered in grasses and brambles. He'd need time to free any rock. Nor were there any sticks, nothing between him and crazy Westfield, the molester.

"Why don't you find your horizontal refreshment somewhere else instead of attacking defenseless boys? Don't you have any shame? He's your nephew."

"Some sweet piece of meat."

"Swine."

The blade answered, making contact with Adam's forearm. Adam jumped back, risking a glance at his hand. Westfield was carving him up a cut at a time.

He couldn't let it happen. Not now. His father's message

nagged. What did it mean? Surely not sparing Westfield. No, he had to go on and find out, think it through to understand what his father was talking about.

Screams erupted uphill. Somewhere in the back of his mind, Adam registered horse gallop. Many horses. Westfield paused—the knife glinted red. They were too low on the slope to see what was happening.

"Hold the position," somebody shouted.

"Attack...take cover..." Even from a distance Adam recognized Ryker's voice now filled with a mixture of panic and anger.

Adam threw another glance at Westfield who stood, undecided. The coward. He was going to wait it out down here.

Without another thought, Adam raced toward camp. He'd rather take a bullet than die from Westfield's knife.

Blackberry thorns tore at his coat and face as he scrambled uphill. In the racket above he couldn't tell if Westfield was following, and he didn't want to waste precious seconds to look back. His thighs burned with fatigue as he forced his body uphill. Faster. The air grew thin as he gasped for breath. Not much farther.

Shots rang out. Lots of them. He was still thirty yards away from the edge of camp when he noticed movement to his right.

As if in slow motion, hundreds of Rebs rode side-by-side in a wall of gray terror. Around him, shells exploded as the air fogged with acrid smoke.

Get to your gun. You must get your gun. The next moment he tripped and landed headfirst in somebody's campsite. A man lay face down, his back soaked dark. Adam crawled over him to grab the dead soldier's rifle.

Adam took aim at the wall of Rebs and fired. He managed a second round before the boys around him shouted surrender, threw down their weapons and lifted their arms. There had to be more than a thousand enemies.

Adam turned on his back and looked at the sky where gun smoke mixed with the white of the clouds. His arm and chest ached from Westfield's cuts.

It was over.

"Let's go." The Reb, not much older than Adam waved a gun.

Adam walked toward the line of Union soldiers. Somewhere ahead he thought he saw Wes. They were corralled into a horse enclosure, hundreds of them. Resigned to his fate, Adam squeezed through the men.

Wes leaned against a post, his eyes worried. "Where've you been?" he said. "I thought they shot you dead."

Adam shrugged. How could he tell Wes about his uncle? "Took a walk to get blackberry leaves for Thomas."

Wes abruptly hurried forward. "You're bleeding."

Adam jerked away his arm. "It's nothing. Leaves may help Thomas's flux." Adam looked up. "Where is he?"

Wes scratched his nose, but he kept looking at Adam's hand. "Don't rightly know. He wasn't there when the Rebs came. Don't see Ryker either. A lot of them got away."

New worry rose up in Adam. Thomas was too weak to run and had probably been at the latrines. What if they'd shot him? What if he'd collapsed and needed help?

"We've got to find him."

"I'll ask around."

Just then Adam saw Thomas escorted by two Rebs enter the group. He hunched over as if his insides were tearing him apart.

Adam pushed his way through the crowd. "Over here."

A look of relief washed over Thomas's face. "Thought you'd gotten yourself shot."

"Not a chance." Adam stuffed a couple of blackberry leaves in Thomas's hands. "Got you some leaves."

"How are we going to fix that?" Wes threw a longing glance toward their campsite. "We left all our gear."

"We'll find a way." Adam nodded toward Thomas who stared at the leaves in his fist. Inwardly Adam wanted to scream. He'd escaped Westfield only to fall into the hands of the Rebs.

"If you follow orders, you'll be spared," somebody yelled with a southern drawl. "We'll march in the morning."

Adam looked around. Dusk was setting and right about now they'd fix dinner. Even if it wasn't much, they had lost even that and he felt an intense longing for the familiarity of his evening routine. The boys mumbling softly as they fixed their rations, the scraping of quill on paper, the scraping of wet stones on knives. Resigned, he pushed his way through the crowd to the edge where Rebs stood shoulder to shoulder, rifles at the ready.

"Sir, may I get some water for my sick friend?" Adam addressed a Reb in a mismatched uniform, his boots as torn as his own. He looked no older than fifteen. "He's got the runs. He needs to have water."

The boy hesitated, looking uncertain, but then his neighbor, some rough-looking fellow with a beard covering most of his face, answered for him.

"Orders are you stay in the bull pit. Can't let you gallivant around."

Adam turned. It'd be a long night.

CHAPTER THIRTY

"I'm not staying," Adam whispered. It had to be after midnight and though he was bone-tired, sleep wouldn't come. He sat back to back with Wes to give his weary bones a reprieve. "We've got to find a way out before they march us to prison."

"What about Thomas?"

Adam had thought about that. "He's coming with us."

"He'll slow us down."

"He's coming."

"Fine."

A voice nearby could be heard. "I'm going with you. No sense to wait around to be strung up or shot."

"Me, too...me, too." Voices reverberated through the rows. "Let's do it soon."

Adam cringed. He'd hoped to creep away, grab a horse and disappear. There had to be three or four hundred prisoners. The more men, the more noise they'd make.

Out of nowhere a song rose into the night...

"In the prison cell I sit, thinking Mother, dear, of you, And our bright and happy home so far away, And the tears, they fill my eyes 'spite of all that I can do, Tho' I try to cheer my comrades and be gay..."

More men joined until they all belted at the top of their lungs.

"Tramp, tramp, tramp, the boys are marching, Cheer up, comrades, they will come. And beneath the starry flag we shall breathe the air again, of the free land in our own beloved home."

The noise swelled into the sky like a tidal wave, and in the darkness Adam smiled.

"In the battle front we stood, when their fiercest charge they made. And they swept us off a hundred men or more, but before we reached their lines, they were beaten back dismayed, and we heard the cry of vict'ry o'er and o'er.

Tramp, tramp, tramp, the boys are marching. Cheer up, comrades, they will come. And beneath the starry flag we shall breathe the air again, of the free land in our own beloved home.

"Time to go," somebody whispered after the last notes died away.

Adam patted Wes on the back. "Let's take him between us."

Thomas moaned. Adam bent low, trying not to breathe the stench emanating from Thomas's backside.

"We're making a run for it."

"Now?"

Adam grabbed Thomas and tugged to no avail. Despite his frailty, Thomas felt like an oversized sack of corn. Around them, men stirred, the air charged with renewed energy.

"Come on," Adam urged, trying to convince Thomas to stand. He angled his shoulder toward Thomas's armpit for leverage and pushed him upright.

"Let me be," Thomas whispered. "I'll slow you down."

"You're going," Wes said as the crowd began to shove into them. With a grunt, Thomas straightened.

Murmurs traveled among the men, "...now...now...hurry. Forward," they whispered. Adam felt Thomas's body lean into him. He set his feet, determined to keep his friend upright.

A shot rang out. The Rebs were awake. One by one, torches sprang up in a semi-circle.

Adam glanced around to see what was going on. He was taller than most now, but before he could make up his mind, the pressure from behind increased. Men pushed and shoved, all intent on watching. Feet shuffled, the breaths of hundreds of lungs loud in the night.

They came to a stop not twenty yards from the enclosure. Adam cranked his neck to catch a glimpse of the other side, where two Rebs pointed rifles at a man. He was on his knees and even without seeing his face, Adam knew it was Wes's uncle Jon Westfield.

"Stinking Yankee, caught him sneaking around the Yank camp," one Reb, clad in a yellowish uniform, said with a thick

Kentucky accent.

"How about we teach him a lesson," the other said. "Make an example."

A thick laugh followed. "Get the colonel. I'll keep him safe."

As the other man ran off, Westfield swiveled his head.

"What's that Reb butternut doing?" Wes asked. A few inches shorter than Adam, he was stuck behind a couple of taller soldiers.

Adam shrugged, his escape from Westfield's knife replaying in his mind, the crazy glint in the man's eyes, the blade cutting into his flesh. His forearm and chest still burned, but he had no way of checking how bad the cuts were, and besides, they had lost all their medical supplies to the Rebs.

From the corner of his eye, Adam saw a commotion. Just as Westfield flung himself into the darkness, a shot rang out. Westfield crumpled to the ground.

"What happened?" Wes asked.

Adam blinked. Even from a distance and in the semidarkness he knew Jon Westfield was dead as a wagon wheel. "Your uncle…he's gone."

Wes elbowed his way past the two taller men. "The son of a bitch is actually dead." His voice was heavy with sadness and relief.

Adam placed a hand on his friend's shoulder. He said nothing, but the words in his head might as well have been aloud. *You don't have to be afraid any longer.*

The men now stood shoulder-to-shoulder, everyone pushing forward to learn more, curious what would happen next.

Thomas half leaned, half stood, his eyes clouded. He groaned, oblivious to the shooting and the charged air around them.

Adam remembered the blackberry leaves and stuck one in Thomas's mouth. "Chew."

Thomas spit out the leaf. "I'm thirsty."

Wes caught the mashed up leaf and stuffed it back in Thomas's mouth. "We'll find water. Blythe says chew. It's an order."

Without warning, Adam was catapulted forward, the shoving so great, he almost lost his footing. All he could do was pull Thomas along and hope Wes was following.

The pressure behind them intensified, the shoulder blades of the man in front painfully digging into his chest wound.

And like too much water breaks a dam, the crowd of Yankee

prisoners broke through the enclosure in a mad dash.

Rumors of a death camp in Andersonville had circulated for months. Obviously people weren't going to wait out the morning or see more of their fellow men shot.

"Left, push left," Adam cried, dragging Thomas with him. The darkness was liquid with movement. They stumbled across the trampled remains of the horse enclosure when a volley of shots rang out, followed by screams. The sounds came from their right and slightly behind. Torches flickered, not close enough to expose them. Not yet, anyway.

"Hurry."

They stomped across deserted fire pits, tents and gear. Right now it was completely dark, clouds racing past, the air filled with the smell of rain. Most of the area was heavily wooded, a perfect hiding place…if they made it.

Thomas leaned on Adam, his breathing harsh and his weight growing with every step. Why didn't Wes help? Adam had no air left to utter a word.

Others had the same idea, and soon the area swarmed with moving shapes. It was impossible to tell who was who.

Adam frantically tried to remember the camp's layout. This morning he'd tethered his horse on a pasture behind the woods, intent to supplement the meager hay and grain rations. It was a risk, but he refused to watch a horse starve. Not after Charlie…

As they trudged on, Thomas began to wheeze. Behind them, more shots were fired. Men squealed and cried as the faint shine of torches danced between trees. The escape had been stopped.

The hair on Adam's neck rose as he pictured a bullet finding him. It would be quick, no more than a flash, a matter of fate.

Not now, he thought.

He urged himself to concentrate, glad infantry life had taught him to feel his way through a terrain.

They struggled on when a twig snapped. He froze, pressing a hand on Thomas's chest to signal him to stop. He listened again. Above them the trees whispered.

Nothing.

If anyone found his horse first, they'd have to continue on foot. With Thomas they'd be caught at first light.

Ahead, the darkness lifted the tiniest bit: a pasture or at least some meadow illuminated by a sliver of moon. Adam whistled low.

A whinny answered. His horse. After Charlie, he'd never named a horse again.

"This way." They stumbled toward the sound until Adam felt the horse's short hair under his fingers. "Good boy." He ran his fingers along the soft nose, along the jaw and gripped the reins.

After helping Thomas mount, they slipped across the open field into another patch of woods.

"Where do you want to go?" Wes asked. They'd slept in the mow of an abandoned hay barn, the roof half collapsed, the farmhouse burned to the ground. The hay was long gone, raided to feed the thousands of Union and Confederate horses.

"Don't know." Adam stared unseeing through the opening of the barn. In the early morning light, his stomach rumbled painfully. They'd found a creek and gotten some water, but they had no gear, no cups, nothing to make fires with, no bedroll, and certainly no guns.

Thomas looked worse this morning. He'd dragged himself off twice already to hide in the brush.

"Ryker said we should assemble in Knoxville if we get separated," Wes offered, chewing a piece of straw he'd found in some crevice.

"We've got to find help for Thomas," Adam said. Anxiety nagged him, a constant tingling as if a thousand ants were crawling on his skin.

Here was his chance to disappear. For all the Army knew he was dead or captured by the Rebs. Even if they'd look in Greeneville, with his fake name they'd never find him. As far as he was concerned, he'd done plenty for the Army.

A man has got to live with his actions.

"...you listening?" Wes straightened.

"What?" Adam looked up, becoming aware of Thomas's groans as he curled his spindly legs into the fetal position.

"We better go, find us some food."

They half dragged, half carried Thomas to the horse and marched off.

"I reckon Knoxville is southwest," Wes said, squinting at the weak sun above them. Adam shivered, not from the cold but from the realization that he was stuck between two choices, each of them with unknown consequences, and each of them unacceptable.

If he stayed with Wes and Thomas they'd either get shot or—if they were lucky—rejoin the Union in Knoxville. If he left, he'd lose his only friend and break his contract. He'd have to live with the knowledge that he was a deserter. And Thomas would certainly die—if he wasn't already beyond help.

For once in your life you've got to do what you signed up for. No more running. Even if you die now, at least you've done what you promised. Just this once.

"You're lucky," Wes said, taking in Adam's frown.

"About what?"

"You had all that, your kin, a home...love."

"I lost it all."

"But you had it." Wes's eyes were glazed. "The memory of it fills your heart. It's..." he was obviously searching for the right word, "a precious thing, a gift you'll carry with you forever."

Adam watched his friend, whose slumped shoulders seemed to carry the weight of the war. He opened his mouth to argue...and closed it. With a pang, he realized Wes was right. Wes, the fellow from some unknown village in Tennessee, Wes, the boy who'd lied about his name and talked too much or not at all. There had been a time when he'd felt smarter than Wes. Obviously, he'd been the stupid one.

"What about you?" he said gruffly. "Surely, you've got something pleasant to remember."

Wes gazed into the distance. "Pop drank away his pay, and Mother worked extra to feed us."

"You got any brothers or sisters?"

"Had a baby brother. Born too early." Wes's voice labored as if somebody were sitting on his chest. "Pop knocked Mother around a lot. He had the devil in him when he drank. Mother was with child when he kicked her. Hard. I was five.

"The baby came early and died. Mother never recovered. She passed the following spring."

Adam's heart ached as he imagined a little Wes watching his mother die.

"Pop went downhill from there, and that's how I ended up with my uncle."

Who molested you. "Is your father dead?" Adam said aloud.

"Don't rightly know."

Adam searched for something to say, some way to take away

the hurt. He knew he couldn't, and so he said nothing. It explained Wes's aversion for liquor. When Marty and Thomas offered a share of looted whiskey, he'd always declined. A bitter laugh bubbled up in Adam. What a rotten life Wes had had. First his parents, then his uncle…and to top it all off…the war.

Adam bit his lips. Despite it all, Wes had made him see something he'd been blind to. You could acknowledge your loss and sadness, but you didn't have to let it consume you. You could choose to move on.

He straightened and rummaged in the horse's saddlebag.

"Let's fix worm castles," he said, holding up a package of forgotten hardtack.

Wes's eyes lit up.

CHAPTER THIRTY-ONE

Tip slouched brooding in the parlor of a two-story farmhouse with whitewashed trim and a broad veranda. The room was tidy and sparse. Afraid of dirtying the scrubbed wooden floor, Tip occupied one of the four straight-backed chairs. A woman in her fifties, equally pale as her husband, was fixing a meal on the kitchen stove. The smells of cooked oats and honey filled Tip's nose until he had to swallow repeatedly.

Without a word, the woman handed him a mug with water, followed by a bowl of oats.

"Thank you, missus," Tip said.

The woman showed the hint of a smile, but then she shook her head and put a finger on her lips.

The oats tasted heavenly, and for a moment Tip was transported to his mother's kitchen. He closed his eyes, the honeyed oats filling his senses. Warmth spread along his throat and down into his stomach. Out of nowhere, the memory of Elda, the house slave returned. He'd walked with her one Sunday at dusk, and they'd stopped at the little creek near the slave quarters. His hand had grazed hers and he'd finally taken her small fingers into his. Her eyes were the color of walnut, a warm brown, her skin soft as the peaches he'd picked. They'd looked at each other, but words had failed him, his mind as mushy as a rotten pumpkin. Oh, how he wished to be back there right now, telling Elda that he loved her—that he wanted to spend the rest of his life looking at her lovely face.

Dale reappeared in the kitchen, rifle in hand. Tip wiped his eyes and realized he'd scraped clean the dish without knowing it.

"We'll wait till dark." Despite his outward calmness Tip sensed fear in the man's face. "I'll take you to a station. There'll be two or three other passengers."

Dale stepped to the fireplace and slid aside a panel next to the lone bookshelf. "For now you'll wait in here. Water is in the jug." Tip took in the outline of a straw mat and a bucket inside the hold. There was no window, not even a candle.

What if this was a trap? He'd be stuck inside with no place to go. He tried to recollect the stories about the Underground Railroad, mere rumors where he'd been. Twice he'd heard Negroes whisper about whites and free coloreds helping slaves hide and escape to the north, a complicated network of routes and stations created by abolitionists and church people.

Tip thought of his dead mother and reminded himself he had no place to go. Did it really matter if he died? Might as well see what happened.

Stooping low, he slipped into the hole and curled up on the mat.

A dancing light woke him.

"Time to go." Dale stood in the opening, an oil lamp in his hand. "The wife wants you to have this." He held up a dark coat. "It was our son's."

When Tip opened his mouth to thank him, Dale waved a hand. "No need."

Tip pulled on the coat. Though a little tight in the chest, it felt gloriously warm. He grabbed his bundle and followed the conductor outside where a wagon was stacked with hay. "All the way in, and not a word from now on." Dale's gaze fell on Tip's pack. "What do you have in there?"

"Nothing much…a shirt and a book."

"A book?" New fear showed on Dale's face. "You read?"

"Yessir."

"You know what they do to Negroes who read books?"

Tip straightened. He wasn't about to part with his most prized possession.

With a sigh Dale waved him on and Tip worked his way into the fragrant pile. Time seemed to retract as he listened for sounds.

The creaking of the wheels, the snorts of the horse, the faint swish of the trees overhead took him back to the last trip to Rawley's farm. For the first time ever, he felt the tiniest flicker of something light and airy, a lifting of sorts, as if his soul had seen a bird soar into the sky. It reminded him of something long ago, the last time he'd seen Adam in the grain shack...his friend.

But now his life was in the hands of a man who looked too sick to be outside, not to mention steer a wagon into the chilly night. Once again he had no control—a white man taking over. All his life he'd depended on others, been ordered around. Would he even know what to do if he reached freedom?

A tiny voice whispered in his head. *You'll know. You've always known... because no human is supposed to be owned by another.*

How could you ever understand what drove a man? Some like Rawley were filled with venom and hatred, ready to torture and kill. Then others like the conductor and his wife risked their lives to help an unknown slave boy. He'd never understand either one. Tip dozed off.

Elda stood in the door wearing a sunflower yellow dress, her skin dark and glistening as if she'd stepped from the river. She smiled at him, her eyes filled with longing. "Will you marry me?" she said, her voice soft and pleading. Then her face morphed into Giselle's. "I'm waiting for you." Giselle's face transformed again into the old woman who'd written the letters for him. "It is too late. Death is following you."

Tip awoke. Panic choked him as he spit out bits of hay. It was completely dark, the air closing in around him. He remembered the sounds from earlier, the gentle creaking of the wheels, the horse's clip clop.

Now there was silence. No creaking, no footsteps, not even rustling or a whiff of wind. Nothing. A vacuum as if he'd stepped in-between worlds.

Something was wrong.

Tip couldn't take it anymore. The silence was squeezing his insides. He'd once thought all white people hated Negroes until he met Adam and his Pa. Adam had fought for him. And Adam's Pa had lost his life trying to do the right thing, fighting for freedom.

But after Rawley, something had changed. He'd lost all trust in human decency. Even Milly had not respected him. To her he was a play toy, not a human being with his own wants and dreams.

No. Few men were that generous.

Adam one of them, but a whole lot of good it had done. Adam was gone, probably dead.

His thoughts drifted to his mother. The need to learn what had happened to her twisted like a knife in his gut.

Even if he lived, he would have to start over with new people far away from home. *You could've stayed with Giselle. She was the only one who wanted you.* He sighed, the sound loud in his ears, making him aware of the silence once more.

Tired of waiting, he crawled out of the hay wagon. The quarter moon carved a hard crescent into the sky. He shivered as the icy air crept beneath his coat.

Tip peeked around the wagon, which stood in front of a low barn. He couldn't tell what was beyond except for the faintest shimmer from a narrow window.

As he stepped around the corner, a shadow rushed him, accompanied by barks. Tip froze. He'd heard terrible stories about slaves being torn to pieces by tracking dogs. Any second he expected to feel teeth slicing into his legs.

Another shadow rose from behind the post as the dog hurried away. "Who's there?"

"Tip," Tip croaked. The dog had not moved.

"Come inside. Quick."

Tip stumbled past the animal up the porch steps where he came face to face with the dark shape.

"Dale let you sleep," the man said.

The front door opened with ghostly fingers, the glimmer of light reflecting on the man's rifle. Tip shivered. He was again at the mercy of strangers, though this one's voice lacked all menace.

He gritted his teeth and stepped through the door.

"Ah, here is the third passenger." Dale waved him inside. In the corner near the fireplace of what looked like another formal parlor sat two coloreds, a man and a woman. They had the downtrodden demeanor of slaves being hunted, their heads low and their eyes wandering nervously around the room. Tip knew the look too well. It was what he would surely see in the mirror.

No more. He'd not cower any longer. No sir, from now on he was going to stand proud, and if things didn't turn out, he'd die knowing he'd been a man. Not a colored or a white, but a man with wants and feelings who mourned his mother and a good friend. A light spread within him then, giving him strength and purpose. He was no longer a kid picking peaches for rich folks. He was going to find his way past the darkness.

He lowered himself next to the two slaves and took in the room. Aside from the pasty man, two more whites sat in chairs, rifles leaning against their legs.

Tip imagined taking one and shooting the men. Nobody knew Adam had taught him how to use a rifle, just as nobody knew he could read and write. He smiled to himself.

"You've got to reach the Ohio by morning," Dale said to the two fellows. In the low light of the candles, his forehead glistened with sweat. "Boat is arranged."

"What about the patrols?" One of the other men asked, his jaw hidden behind a tangle of gray beard and long sideburns.

"It matters none," said the third. In the gloom it was hard to tell his age, but judging by his voice he wasn't much older than Tip. "They can't stay here. Too risky."

"I've got only one fresh horse," said the bearded man. "It won't be enough."

"Then they walk," the younger man said.

"You'd think our jobs were done by now. Lincoln's proclamation has done us a lot of good." The bearded man scratched his sideburn.

"It will. One day soon, you'll see." Dale nodded as if to reassure him.

The young conductor consulted a pocket watch and straightened. "Time to go. I'm heading home."

Within minutes, Tip squeezed himself next to the colored couple, the wagon open with a thin layer of straw. There was no hiding now. Neither of them spoke, the woman between them shivering in the cold air, their fear as palpable as if they'd screamed. Their names were Newman and Ann Parks, and they'd been married less than a year. Tip slowly chewed a piece of bread the men had given him. It wasn't enough to calm his stomach, but it served as a distraction.

"Shhh." The sound made him look up. It was just as dark, yet he felt the presence of something evil, something hovering nearby.

He could tell the other two slaves were equally alert.

"Somebody is coming," the wagon driver said. "Get out

quickly."

Tip scrambled from the cart and helped Ann, who was clumsy and slow.

"I distract them," said Newman and melted into the shadows. Tip tucked the woman's elbow under his and led her into a thicket. At least that's what it appeared to be in the darkness.

On the path a torch approached, illuminating the simple horse cart they'd just left.

"Evening, Sir. We're looking for a couple of runaway slaves, a man and a woman, early twenties." The voice sounded scratchy as if the man had a permanent sore throat. "Rumor has it, they've got some help from these abolitionists." Tip glanced at the quivering shape next to him. All he wanted was to bolt…away from these men who'd drag him south again. *You no longer fear them.*

"Hope you catch'em," the wagon driver said. Tip recognized the man with the gray beard. "Heading home to my wife."

"You won't mind us inspecting your wagon then?" The man attempted to sound jovial, but a cold edge remained.

"Go ahead. I've got nothing to hide."

Tip lowered his gaze as two riders slowly advanced on the cart. They were no more than twelve feet away.

"Nothing here, boss," one of them said. Somewhere ahead something splashed. "You hear that?"

"Go," the slave trader said. "You better not be involved. We'll track you down."

The wagon driver mumbled something and urged on his horse. "Good luck." It was hard to tell if he meant it for Tip and his companions or the slave catchers.

The torches flickered toward the splashing sound. The horse gallop faded, and the forest grew quiet. Ann still trembled, so Tip put a hand on her shoulder.

"We go north, catch the boat," he whispered. "You know the way?"

"No."

Somewhere in the distance a shot rang out. Then another, followed by a man's cry of agony.

"They catch my husband," Ann cried. "Oh, Newman."

"Shhh." Tip gripped Ann's forearm and pulled her upright. "Nothing we can do." He threw another glance at the trail where the horse cart had vanished. "We head the way we came first. Dey won't expect dat."

Instead of an answer, Ann leaned on his arm. Tip picked his way back, trying to be quiet, trying not to twist his ankle. Why had the husband run ahead instead of taking the woman with him? Whether Newman had led them away from her or tried to save himself, he, Tip, was stuck with an extra burden. It was hard enough taking care of himself.

Every few steps he stopped to listen, his heart hammering in his throat, his breath like one of those steam locomotives he'd seen in Kingsport at the depot.

The noise behind them had died, but that was less than reassuring. The only reason they hadn't been found was that the slave catchers didn't have dogs.

"I need to rest," Ann said quietly. "I'm with child."

Tip swallowed a curse. How had he missed the woman's bulging middle? Now he was responsible for a baby, too?

"Over here, lean against the tree," he said, his last thought that he couldn't afford to fall asleep.

Something bright glittered behind Tip's eyelids. With a start he remembered last night as his heart began to stomp around in his chest with foreboding. Alarmed, he opened his eyes, only to close them again. A ray of sun blinded him. He carefully turned to his side and tried again.

Ann wasn't there. He sat up slowly, growing aware that his pants and coat were soaked. He got up and stepped behind a tree to relieve himself. His stomach churned with hunger, his mouth was dry. He remembered the splashing from last night, but he couldn't even remember where he'd come from, nor did he have any idea how far they'd traveled.

"You awake?" Ann clambered to his side, rubbing her arms. In the sharp light she was stick thin except for her belly protruding among the rags. How could he have missed that last night? She looked like she'd give birth any moment.

"How far you along?" Tip asked, taking in the traces of tears on her cheeks.

She shrugged. "Eight months."

"Can you walk?"

"I'm ready."

Tip scanned the sky, where white puffs raced along. At least he could tell north today.

To his frustration they had to stop every hour, the woman panting and rubbing the sides of her belly and her back. Without her he'd be miles ahead.

"You have kin up north?" she asked as they sat on a log for yet another break.

"No family, just freedom." Despite being angry with their slow progress, he produced a smile.

"I have a sister in Cincinnati. My babies all gone."

"How many you have?"

"Three, two is dead, one sold."

Tip stared at the woman next to him. Ann couldn't be older than twenty. She'd had three children and was pregnant with a forth when he hadn't even laid with a woman once. Sure, he could've done it with Giselle. She'd been willing, but it had felt wrong. His heart swelled when he thought of Elda, her shy smile and the way she'd squeezed his fingers.

You are a fool. Elda is long gone and you die a virgin.

"You got a girl somewhere?" Ann said as if she'd heard him. He shook his head, too afraid what would happen if he let somebody look into the abyss of his heart.

Straightening he held out a hand. "We better go."

CHAPTER THIRTY-TWO

Every place Adam and the boys passed showed signs of war. Burned buildings, abandoned fields and broken fences, the earth rutted and torn.

Thomas was getting worse by the hour, and they had to make sure he didn't slide off the horse. Three times they stopped to get water and let Thomas go into the bushes.

Adam caught Wes's expression as Thomas dragged himself away. "You think he'll die?"

"He's weak. Have seen too many men like it…"

When Wes didn't continue, Adam abruptly jumped to his feet. He wasn't going to give up. "I've got an idea."

It was clear from the way Wes shook his head that he didn't put much stock in Adam's comment.

They took the route south and Adam soon recognized the path he'd taken long ago. Snippets of memory urged him on. Chances were the woman was gone by now. Maybe the Rebs had caught her. Maybe she'd died alone. In the afternoon they came across a cornfield. Compared to many others they'd seen, the stalks had been cut.

Adam breathed deeply as he took in the modest farmhouse surrounded by conifers, a ribbon of bluish smoke rapidly spreading in the sharp wind.

"Rebs or Yanks?" Wes asked.

Adam suppressed a grin. "Union."

"How do you—"

"You stay with Thomas." Ignoring Wes's curious stare, he hurried toward the farmstead. He felt naked without any way to protect himself. What if the woman's husband was back ready to shoot him? A hundred years had passed since he'd been here.

And this time there'd be no Marty or Thomas to rescue him. Marty was long dead and Thomas wouldn't make it much longer, either.

Maybe it was best to take a couple of things and leave. He zigzagged to the barn. As his eyes adjusted to the gloom, he listened for the cluck-cluck of chickens. Hadn't the woman served him the most glorious omelet? Just the thought of sitting down like a normal person at a clean table with plates and a fork made him tremble. He sucked in a breath, aware he'd stopped moving.

Something rustled in the corner where a partition had been wire-fenced. Six or seven hens looked at him curiously and resumed their scratching.

"Hey, mister, you're not going to steal our chickens. Might as well turn around and leave now."

Adam slowly rotated. In front of him stood a girl of maybe seventeen, her coveralls coated with a blanket of dust, an ancient musket pointed at him.

"No, I was just—"

"Ma, come quick. Got another one of those Yankee soldiers."

The entrance to the barn darkened.

"Give me the gun." A woman with broad shoulders in equally dirty coveralls approached and…froze. "I'll be darn." She stepped closer still, her eyes squinting at Adam as if she were nearsighted. Then she clucked. "The boy who was going to visit his uncle in Lexington."

Adam kept gazing at the barrel. "You going to shoot me? Make it quick. I've seen enough suffering to fill up a hundred lifetimes. Losing this one doesn't make a lick of difference."

"You leave him be," Wes shouted, hurling himself at the woman who shrieked and dropped the gun. Quick as a flash, Wes grabbed it. "Now you listen, folks. Me and my partner here are just going to take a couple of things and we'll be on our way."

The girl who had the same blond hair threw a protective arm across her mother's shoulders. Adam's heart ached. This is what Sara would've done.

"Leave them be," he heard himself say. "She's helped me

186

before. I'm not going to harm them." He stepped toward Wes and yanked away the musket.

"You crazy?" Wes swiped at the gun.

Adam ignored him and handed over the musket, butt first. "I'm rightly sorry to have disturbed your day."

The girl gripped the gun and swung it around, only to have her mother push the barrel to the floor. "It's all right, Lillian. This here young man is an old friend."

Adam blinked.

Adam awoke from a daze. He'd slept more deeply than he had in years. The haymow was warm and smelled nice. After taking a bath in a tin tub while the women washed his clothes, he felt like a new man. Almost.

A long time ago he'd been anxious to head north and sign up for the Army. Yet, no matter how far he'd run, he knew now that the only place he wanted to go was home. The woman had been right all along. Why hadn't he listened? *You were a kid then.*

Thomas groaned in his sleep. He'd been cleaned up and the woman had fed him broth and tea. He hadn't run to the outhouse for a few hours.

Outside, a few sunrays crawled across the horizon. Adam climbed down to find the pump.

"Morning." Lillian emerged from the barn, a basket of eggs dangling from her arm. Now that she wasn't angry or scared, her green eyes sparkled.

"You hungry?"

Adam nodded.

"Tell your friends Ma will have breakfast ready in a few minutes."

"Sure." He wanted to say something smart, something witty, but his mind felt like mush. What was the matter with him?

By the time they went inside, the table was loaded with delicacies. Cold venison, fried eggs, oatmeal, honey, butter and fresh bread.

"I've gone to heaven," Wes exclaimed as he plunked down on the bench. Adam agreed though he couldn't quite draw his eyes away from the girl. Every time he did, his gaze wandered back. Once or twice she'd caught him looking at her and smiled.

Now he felt a deep heat rise up his neck into his cheeks.

Clearing his throat, he asked the woman, "How come I didn't see Lillian last time?"

"Hid her away," the woman said. "Too dangerous to have a young girl out with all them straying men looking for trouble."

Nathan Billings appeared in Adam's vision, lurking in the bushes to wait for Sara.

"What happened to your husband?"

"Don't rightly know." The woman's eyes grew glazed as she jumped up. "Who wants seconds? Better eat while it's hot."

"You need help with that?" Adam hurried to Lillian's side to grab hold of a log.

"Firewood's low."

"Let me do it." He pointed at the ax lying on a tree stump.

"You think girls can't split wood?"

"Sure, but I want to help. You've been very kind to take us in."

Lillian threw him a curious glance. "How old are you?"

Adam stretched himself a bit, though it wasn't necessary. He was easily a foot taller than the girl. "Eighteen."

Amazing. Three birthdays had passed while he'd been a soldier, each of them a nonevent. At first he'd kept quiet because he'd lied about his age. Okay, he'd used the trick with the paper in his shoe, but he was pretty sure Marty and Thomas, even Ryker had known he was way younger than he'd pretended. To their credit, they'd all kept to themselves. The second and third birthday he'd been in skirmishes or marching and nobody cared about some birthday when they hardly had enough food or dodged Reb bullets.

"Ma says you came by near about two and a half years ago? How come you went into the Army so young?"

"It's a long story." For the first time since he'd left Greeneville he wanted to tell somebody. No, not somebody, he wanted to tell *this* girl.

Lillian abruptly turned away. "Never mind." Obviously she had taken his answer as a rejection.

"No, no, I mean I'll tell you some time if you want to hear it."

To his surprise she faced him and nodded earnestly. "We could go for a walk after my chores."

The familiar heat rose to his cheeks and he bent over quickly to grab the axe. "Sure thing."

"You going sweet on the girl?" Wes called from the roof as soon as Lillian disappeared into the house.

"Mind your own business."

"That's what I'm doing," Wes said good-naturedly. "Misses has me fixing shingles."

Adam kept his head low, swinging the axe. He couldn't quite understand it himself. His body churned and felt strangely alive. A sense of breathlessness followed him throughout the day. Even more strangely, he caught himself smiling over nothing at all.

The last time he'd seen girls his age was at the dance with Sara and Allister. He'd been so mad then, he'd ignored any friendly faces brave enough to come near.

He was no longer mad. Certainly not at the things he'd been furious about then. So what if he hadn't gone to become a veterinary surgeon. He could've stayed with his mother and sister and kept them safe. *Nathan Billings would've had you killed.*

It was too late anyway. If the war had taught him one thing, it was to take nothing for granted. Life could change on a whim, in a fraction of a second, with a wrong step, a misplaced word, or a cough in the night. Bullets found men in the unlikeliest places. There was no rhyme or reason, just sheer luck of the draw.

"That's quite enough for the time-being." The woman stood, her hands on her hips, watching him.

Adam wiped a hand across his sweaty forehead. To his surprise, the heap of logs piled several feet high. "No bother. I'll stack it up now."

"If I may have a word."

Adam stopped in midair, shocked at the harsh tone. He lowered his axe and stepped closer, taking in the new lines on the woman's face, the gray strands in her blond braid. Life had been hard for everyone. An urgent longing for his mother gripped him and he felt his throat tighten.

The woman didn't noticed, her lips pressed thin. "Lillian is quite impressionable," she said. "I've kept her safe for these mad years. I don't want any funny business."

Adam felt his cheeks burn. "I've got no ill intentions."

"I may be a woman, but I've been living like a man for years. So don't underestimate me." She turned and disappeared into the house.

Adam hurried to the pump to wash, in truth to cool himself

off. So the mother had noticed something, too. It wasn't in his head alone. The girl liked him. He grinned. Something new and amazing was happening. Something he couldn't quite grasp except that it made his stomach lurch and his head cloudy.

For the next three days, Adam took up walking the fields with Lillian. He carried a musket each time, never forgetting the feeling of utter helplessness when he'd encountered Westfield and the Reb Army. And every day he dreaded the end of their time alone. He caught himself wanting to take her hand. Every time he froze.

They just walked side-by-side, Adam telling her about his home, his father's death and the fight over Tip. He left out nothing, feeling vulnerable and wonderful at the same time.

"What about the war?" Lillian asked as they made their way back to the house. "Was it terrible?"

Adam nodded. He couldn't really put it in words. No, he'd never talk about the bloodshed, the rage and fear that tore at his heart and blackened his soul. The fight with Nathan Billings had been nothing compared to what Adam had seen people do. He preferred to keep the door closed to hide the darkest of his memories.

As they approached the farmhouse, he noticed Wes sitting on the tree stump waiting for him. His face was serious, the way he looked when he'd made a decision. Adam's insides cringed. He knew what was coming.

"You're leaving." Lillian gripped his hand. She'd seen it, too.

Adam nodded, his attention on the girl's palm, calloused from too much work. "We're still in the Army. We've got to finish what we started."

Lillian nodded, her eyes bright. Then she tore her hand from his grasp and disappeared around the barn.

"We've got to talk," Wes said as Adam drew near.

"I know."

"Then you know we need to leave... now that Thomas is well enough to travel. They expect us back in Knoxville."

Adam threw him a nasty glance and headed for the barn. Ryker didn't even know they had escaped...or survived.

"Lillian?" he called out.

"What?" Lillian sat on a straw bale, quickly rubbing her face with her forearm. A piece of hay stuck to her cheek.

"Easy," Adam said softly as he picked the blade off her face.

The feel of her skin under his fingertips made him shiver. "I'll come back to you."

"You say that now. Look at what happened to Pa..."

"He may be back one day," Adam said.

Her eyes found his and Adam forgot his shyness, forgot his fear of offending her. He gently cupped her face and kissed her. He'd never really kissed before, but it felt good. No, it felt right—the most natural thing in the world. Their embrace tightened, and in the silence of their touching bodies, the pounding of Wes's hammer on the roof faded.

He smelled her hair, something fruity like peach jam, and the soap on her neck. Every cell in his body jingled and rattled, his mind fuzzy yet aware of every breath, the folds of her shirt pressing against his chest, her boots rubbing his. He stuck his nose in her hair, drank in that peculiar peachy smell, and asked himself whether this was what coming home meant.

No, it wasn't that. It was something different, like a walk on a high wire or a jump into an unknown canyon. Nothing mattered but this girl, this person in his arms that made his insides burn with longing before he'd even left.

"Lillian?" The mother's voice had an edge. "Where are you?"

Lillian pulled away. "I must go," she whispered. "Mother will be cross." She gave him a quick squeeze and hurried off.

Adam stood unmoving, the feeling of the girl in his arms so fresh, he felt her body's impression on him like a touch. So that was what Sara had experienced with Allister all those years ago. He shook his head. What a fool he was. Fighting a war and never even knowing how good it was to have a girl.

The door to the barn sprang open. "By Jiminy, you still in here?" Wes said.

Adam abruptly turned to face him and yelled, "we'll leave in the morning," before marching past Wes into the house and hoping to catch Lillian's attention one more time. The feeling of warmth switched to fury. Anger broiled inside him, anger so hot, he wanted to hit somebody. At last he'd found love. At least that's what he thought it was. And what did he have to do? Leave to reenter the war. Why couldn't he hold on to anything he enjoyed?

Ignoring Wes's curious glances, Adam waited for a chance to see Lillian alone again, but no matter how he tried, she stayed close to her mother all evening, refusing to meet his eye, refusing to speak to him.

"Be safe," the mother said the following morning. It was barely dusk and they'd had an early breakfast, each of them carrying a bundle of provisions.

"I can't thank you enough," Adam said. He squeezed the woman's hand. "I'll write to you." He really meant it for Lillian, but couldn't make himself speak to her directly. Not in front of everyone when his emotions stood written all over his face and had a way to creep into his voice. Lillian stood half hidden behind her mother, her head low.

Thomas hugged the woman. "You saved my life," he breathed, tears in his eyes.

She patted his arm. "Just promise me to be careful."

Adam swallowed away the lump in his throat and headed down the lane. It was the hardest thing he'd done since running away from home.

CHAPTER THIRTY-THREE

By the time Tip and Ann reached the Ohio border, he had lost all sense of time. Despite the frigid November wind, the weather had held up well enough for him to tell directions. But he was so weak, his legs stumbled on their own. Ann was worse, and he half carried, half dragged her along. Her cheekbones stood out sharply against her forehead, her lips chafed and her eyes clouded.

"We here," he panted as they dropped to the ground on the banks.

The river looked huge, several hundred feet of gray mass, ready to swallow them. He had never learned to swim, and seeing the sheer immensity of the swollen water made him quiver.

All this time he'd dreamed of reaching the Ohio. The rumors and murmurs at the plantations had always ended there. Reach the river. Beyond lies freedom. Beyond lies a new life without fear.

But here he stood. It was a miracle, really, they'd made it this far. The arranged boat was long gone, and he had no idea how to find a new one. Without a sturdy boat there was no way to cross the expanse. Ann would never make it even if he'd been able to swim.

All a smart slave catcher needed to do was roam along the river. And there they were…ready for pickup. Just the thought of returning to King's plantation or any other slave owner made him sick. He realized he'd rather die here and now.

He was so weak he hardly had energy to straighten his legs, not to mention search up and down the river for a possible place to cross, some caring soul who'd take pity on them and risk their life to help.

The thought of reaching the river had kept him going. They hadn't eaten since the bread at the farmhouse, the land void of food, lying cold and fallow with the approaching winter. He found himself staring, the gray waves hypnotic, lulling him away from his thoughts.

Yet, his body revolted, demanded to be heard. His innards cramped. There was a metallic taste in his mouth as if his stomach were trying to eat itself.

As the light faded across the river, he forced himself to stand. Ann half leaned, half lay against a piece of driftwood, a huge log, the mighty river had spewed out like a toothpick. Once in a while she moaned.

"I go find food."

"Don't leave me. Not now…"

"We got to eat."

"The baby is coming."

Tip dropped to his knees. "Why didn't you tell me?"

"I ain't sure, sometimes it false. But my water break."

Tip leaned closer. Ann's dress was soaked underneath.

He looked around helplessly. He'd never even been with a woman, and now he had to deliver a baby? He threw a glance at the sky as if he expected some miracle. Mama Rose had taught him about God and he'd prayed in the past.

Since Rawley, he no longer asked God for help. God had forgotten him, Ann, and her baby…and all the Negroes trying to escape and failing. There was nothing but cold ground, the whoosh of the river, and a darkening sky. They didn't even have a blanket.

"How long?"

"Two hours maybe three."

Tip straightened again. "I be back. Don't move."

Instead of answering Ann cried out. Contractions distorted her famished body.

"Please God, if you hear me, show me the way," Tip muttered as he stumbled along the banks.

He had to save Ann's baby…the only one she'd be able to raise herself.

With every step, Tip grew more desperate. He was out of time. If he didn't find help now, they'd die—all three of them. How could he let an innocent baby die? It hadn't done anything to deserve such a short life. Nor did Ann.

Fighting his way through thick underbrush, he came upon a log cabin. It stood at the edge of a forest, a small garden and a couple of sheds next to it. Everything looked old yet well kept, bringing back memories of Adam and his homestead.

Tip's eyes blurred. He'd never see Adam again. Well, of course, Adam was likely dead. He'd probably been caught by the Billings and sentenced to hang for the murder of Nathan.

His head drooped. His boots were falling apart, the soles ripped away from the tops, soaking his feet. Not that it mattered much. Not when your stomach kept you awake and you wanted nothing more than to lie down and give up.

But something kept him going. Something that reared its head every time he was ready to die. He couldn't give up. Ann was having a baby, and he was the only one to save it. He realized there was nothing he wanted to do more.

Hiding behind a clump of blackberry bushes, he forced himself to scan the buildings. Somebody was inside because a thin ribbon of smoke meandered from the chimney.

This was his last move. If he was wrong, he'd seal their fate. He took a couple steps toward the tiny porch that barely allowed for a bench.

"Hold it right there, mister." A woman shot from the front door, pointing a rifle at him.

"I'm sorry," Tip blurted. "I need help for Ann...the baby. I don't know what to do."

"We don't want no trouble, so you better go." The woman waved her gun.

"No trouble, just a bite to eat and maybe a blanket for the baby?"

"What baby?"

"My friend, she having a baby right this minute. I don't know nothing about delivering."

Something softened in the woman's demeanor. Her eyes widened and she tilted her head to the side. "Where's she, your woman?"

Tip wanted to scream. She isn't my woman, just somebody I picked up on the way. "By the river, not far," he said instead.

"You better tell the truth. I've got no patience with this war tearing us all to pieces." When Tip didn't answer, she yelled over her shoulder. "Tilly, better come and get the buggy. This man's wife is having a baby."

A second woman about the same age, and by the looks of it a sister, hurried out the front door, wrapping a shawl around her.

Tip blinked several times, the excitement and lack of food making him woozy to the point that his sight turned fuzzy around the edges like looking through a fogged up window. He leaned back in the cart, directing Tilly toward the Ohio while her sister sat in the back, loosely training a rifle on his heart.

Ann lay on her side, her eyes closed. Her breath came in spurts. The two women forgot they were afraid of Tip and, clucking their teeth, bustled around Ann.

Louis Parks was born in the early evening, an angry bundle of wrinkles with a voice worthy of a Baptist minister. As Baby Louis and his mother slept, Tip ate dinner with the two sisters, Helen and Tilly.

Corn, potatoes, gravy, rolls and smoked ham piled high on Tip's plate. He had trouble looking away, afraid it may be an illusion and disappear.

"There's more," Tilly said. "Sis always cooks for ten, even if her kin is long gone."

"What were you thinking, running off with your wife pregnant like that?" Helen's voice was full of scorn.

"Ann's husband caught by slave traders. I was nearby and help her."

"Oh." Helen looked at him as if she saw him for the first time. "You've fallen on hard times. I can see that. The whole country is a terrible mess. Men die in the war, more men die at home."

"Where're you heading?" Tilly asked.

"Cincinnati," Tip said. Where had that come from? It was as good a place as any. "We miss our boat. The River, it's so big."

Tilly laughed, a strange sound coming deep from her throat. "The mighty Ohio is like a border. It stops people from going either direction."

Helen, who hadn't joined her sister's mirth, nodded slowly. I may know somebody who can help. You assist us around the house while your friend is healing, and I'll see what I can do.

CHAPTER THIRTY-FOUR

Tip's palms cramped painfully as he held on to the boat's edges. It wasn't really a boat, more an oversized bathtub with hardly a bow or stern.

Ann was doing worse. She clutched baby Louis to her chest as if she wanted to squeeze the air from him. Louis answered with a wail.

"If you want to make it, keep that babe quiet, Missy." The boat's owner, James, dressed in a long black coat and rubber boots, was rowing, the oars digging deep without splashing.

How they were supposed to see anything in the pitch black was anybody's guess.

"It all right," Tip whispered, surprised he hadn't lost his voice from fright.

All he wanted was for it to be over. He couldn't swim, and the idea that they were out here in the rushing waters of the mighty Ohio was enough to make his skin crawl. He'd heard nightmare stories of boats being shot at and capsizing, men, women and children being swept away in the river's liquid grave.

Why hadn't he stayed with Giselle? She'd wanted to get married, of that he was sure. Instead he'd run into the unknown. Look where it had got him. He was helpless, at the mercy of strangers. The Underground Railroad was a bizarre organization. Nobody knew more than one or two people. Some were conductors, others sympathizers. It didn't particularly make him feel safe, running and hiding in endless basements, attics, lofts and secret rooms with false walls.

They stayed with the sisters for two months until Ann was strong enough to travel. Tilly and Helen had turned out to be kind hosts who helped with advice and food. Though they'd never married or had children, they'd been a wealth of information, cutting up sheets to make diapers and blankets and resizing a dress and coat to fit Ann's delicate frame.

Tip had been anxious to move on. Master King was surely looking for him, and despite Lincoln's best efforts, the rich continued to own slaves in the south. And there were the slave hunters who'd shot Ann's husband. One never knew when they'd show up.

During the day he stayed indoors, helping around the house. At night, after cutting wood, repairing fences or whatever else the sisters needed, he roamed the area—not far, that would be foolish—but just enough to give himself the impression of freedom. Even in his worst time he'd been able to breathe fresh air during the day. He'd felt stifled, and the inactivity made him jumpy. He'd thickened around the waist, and his arms and legs felt strong again, the sisters generously digging into their stores to feed them all.

After a month, the sisters had introduced him and Ann to James, another member of the Underground Railroad. Since he was one of few who owned a boat, and one small enough not to cause suspicion, he was in high demand, and the wait was long.

Tip never saw any other slaves or anyone involved with the railroad and he suspected the sisters had extended their stay to take care of Ann and Louis. They fussed over the little one, carrying him around night and day as if they were aunties.

Tip had been more than thankful, but he was glad overhearing James urge the sisters to send them away. It was a matter of time before somebody saw them. Tip never lost that gut-wrenching feeling of anxiety he'd experienced on the run and enthusiastically agreed to moving on.

Now they were on the open water, Tip ready to throw up and Ann not doing any better. He felt her bony shoulders poke his side. The birth had left her underweight and fragile, with hardly enough milk to keep Louis quiet.

"Shhh," James hissed when they heard something splashing. Ferries, paddleboats, barges, Army vessels and pleasure boats crisscrossed the Ohio, and they had to avoid running into one.

Tip heard it too, but he had no idea how far away anything was. The air was thick as tar and so damp, it was like breathing water. He shivered despite the coat, his cheeks and nose numb with cold. How long had they been out here?

Please let me arrive on hard ground again. He patted Ann's hand, her fingers bony icicles.

It seemed like hours before they reached the shore. Somehow in the sea of blackness, James had done the impossible. Ahead and to his left flickered a light.

No, it didn't flicker. It swung back and forth as if to welcome him.

Before he had a chance to say thank you, the man and his boat melted away and Tip was face-to-face with another man.

"Welcome to Ohio." The voice was soft and calm, accompanied by the shine of a dim lantern. To his surprise the boy in front of him was colored and no older than fourteen.

Tip's knees gave as he crawled up the slope, dragging Ann with him. He managed to straighten. Solid ground welcomed him back. He stomped his feet a couple of times before taking Ann's arm.

"Come with me," the boy said.

Tip had expected to be excited, even happy. He'd made it to Ohio. He was free. Yet, he felt nothing but exhaustion, his mind restless and fuzzy from lack of sleep.

To distract himself, he focused on Ann. "Let me carry Louis for a bit."

Ann handed the baby over without a sound, and together they stumbled after the boy.

The barn he showed them was equipped with a dozen cots, some occupied with sleeping forms under ragged blankets.

Tip situated baby Louis next to Ann, covered them, and collapsed onto the next bed. He was chilled to the bone from the damp cold and curled into a fetal position.

It was over.

The running and hiding had ended at last. He was no longer a slave, though he had no idea what it meant. All his life he'd belonged to somebody else. The Billings, Rawley and the Kings. He'd even belonged to Mama Rose. Now he was independent.

And alone.

You have Ann. He sighed. What was it about him that attracted women? Ever since they'd stayed with the sisters, Ann had showered him with affection, touching him whenever possible, her eyes dark and sweet. Once when the baby slept she'd stepped to his bed, pulling up her gown a bit to invite him to her.

He'd put a hand on hers and shaken his head. I can't he wanted to say. But it'd been in his expression and Ann had turned away. Since then she'd been less obvious, but he knew she was waiting for him to change his mind. She probably hoped they'd become a family.

Something rattled in his chest, a mix of sob and sigh. Elda's face swam into his vision, but it was so faint he couldn't tell anymore what she looked like. Strange how he didn't remember her face, but the feel of her hand in his, the calluses on her palm, the oval nails that shone pale as milk coffee. Most of all he remembered how he'd wanted to wrap her in his arms to protect her from the world. She'd made him feel strong…invincible.

Forget her. She dead or married.

Until now all he'd wanted was to escape. Get across the Ohio River. Get away from the slave owners and assorted traders, the cruel men who thought owning another human being was their right. Now that he had arrived he was no wiser. He felt empty as a drained bucket. Without his mama and a place to call home, he was nothing but a drifting leaf in the wind.

He turned on his back, knees bent, and stared at the sloped ceiling. Maybe it was best if he went along with Ann to her kin in Cincinnati and settled there. He'd have a place again, somewhere to belong with people to love.

It was early morning before Tip fell asleep.

"Where you heading?" The boy with the soft voice appeared with a notepaper next to Tip's cot. It was hard to tell the time, the light in the barn still dim.

Tip glanced at the paper and recognized a list of names—surely other runaways—next to locations like Calgary, New York and Detroit.

"Cincinnati," Tip heard himself say. He didn't need to look to his right to see Ann's reaction. She gasped and a small giggle escaped her. Maybe it was the best thing to do. At least he had a new destination.

"Let me see when the next train travels north," the boy said.

"You going with me," Ann said once the boy had left. "My sis happy I bring you."

Tip only nodded, equally envious and leery of her excitement. Ann was heading to a place where she had family, to build a new life. His heart was stuck in the past. Everyone who was left down south was trying to catch him, no matter that Lincoln had declared Negroes freemen. The war kept grinding on, the South trying to hold on to its old ways.

He abruptly straightened. "I get food."

CHAPTER THIRTY-FIVE

Screams and whistles echoed across camp. Like a wave they rose and fell from tent to tent.

"We're done," Thomas yelled, running toward Adam and waving his arms like a windmill.

Adam stopped sharpening his knife as Wes's face appeared in the tent opening. "What is he talking about?"

"Service is over." Thomas stopped and doubled over to catch his breath. "Remember, we signed up for three years? We will be mustered out." He paused and looked at Adam. "Unless you want to reenlist."

For a moment Adam was quiet. Then he smiled. "Not a chance."

As Wes whooped and did a dance around the fire, the shouts of *hooray* traveled down the camp rows. Adam glanced at his friends, the boys who'd been with him for three years. In many ways, they knew him better than his own family.

When he'd signed up he'd never expected to live another month, let alone three long years. Everyone back then had expected the war to be over within the year. Yet, here it was October 1864 and they still fought.

He'd been lucky to be stationed in Knoxville for most of his last year. Arriving in late November, they'd witnessed the last stages of the siege on Knoxville under General Burnside. Of course that hadn't lasted. The Rebs under General Longstreet had launched an attack in ice and snow, slipping and sliding into telegraph wires and hidden ditches, they were unable to escape from, and picked off by the hundreds in a horribly one-sided battle.

Afterwards he and Wes had helped carry the dead Rebs on blankets into no-man's-land for pickup. Longstreet left, effectively ending the siege and leaving the Union in charge of Knoxville. They'd escorted Burnside to Kentucky, returning to Tennessee and then Knoxville in April. General Morgan had been killed last month in—of all places—Greeneville, Adam's hometown. Even a canny and famous man like him had not outrun the war.

After leaving Lillian, Adam hadn't cared to continue at all. He'd wanted to be near her, his body aching with longing. The next minute he felt guilty for not yearning for his mother more. And yet, he knew he had to see her first, and find out more about Sara.

Unless he'd hide from Nathan until eternity, he'd either go to prison or hang. The war had kept him away from the people he loved, his family who needed him badly. He wasn't any good to them even now. Not with Nathan Billings lurking in the shadows, waiting for him.

He thought of Tip, long dead. He missed his friend, the hole in his chest fresh as ever.

"What are you going to do?" Wes stood nearby, his face hard to read.

Adam shrugged. "Can't stay here, so I guess I'm going home." He glanced at Wes, surprised at his own words. He was going to face whatever fate dished out. He realized he was ready. And for the first time in months, he grinned.

"I wonder," Wes slapped at a gnat, "if you need company?"

"You aren't heading home?"

"What home would that be?"

Adam hesitated. Taking Wes with him would be comforting, a friend he could rely on. But Nathan was waiting and Wes would be in danger. *Any* friend of his would be at risk.

His brows darkened. "May not be such a good idea." He regretted it as soon as he said it. Wes's face fell as sadness made his shoulders drop.

Adam thought back at the first time he'd seen Wes, how he'd smiled and chattered his ears full. Not much was left of the old Wes, his features drawn and thin, lines carved around the edges of his mouth. He hardly smiled these days and spoke even less. All of a sudden, Adam had a fierce need to protect his friend.

"Never mind." Wes turned and headed for their tent.

"Wait," Adam tried, "I don't know what's going to happen to me. It's danger—"

"You don't have to explain."

"But   I   want   to."

"Well, don't." Wes disappeared inside the tent, leaving Adam standing there.

Thomas hurried up the path, a broad grin on his face. "Time for a new life, old chap." He good-naturedly cuffed Adam on the shoulder. "I'm heading home after dropping off my stuff."

"It's been good knowing you," Adam said.

"Likewise, Blythe." He paused, his gaze intense. "If you ever need help...or a place to stay. My home in Jefferson City is always open to you. I'll never forget what you did for me."

Adam smiled. "I appreciate it. You take care of yourself."

Thomas winked before heading down the path. He was still as thin as ever, his legs bowed, but the bounce in his step had returned. "Stay out of trouble," he called before disappearing in the quartermaster's tent.

All around them men were collecting gear, taking down drying laundry and heading in the direction of the officer quarters to muster out. Wes had not reappeared, so Adam crawled into the tent to collect his rifle, blanket and mess kit.

Wes sat staring at the tent flap as if he could see what was on the other side.

"If you want to come along, I've got to tell you something," Adam said, his voice strange in his ears. And then he realized that saying just that had lifted a humongous burden from his shoulders, the lie he'd lived while being in the Army.

Wes still had his back to Adam. It was better that way. Easier to talk when nobody was looking.

"I changed my name because I nearly killed a wealthy landowner before I joined. First I thought the evil peacock died, but then I saw him when I visited after my arm injury. He didn't recognize me, and I found out he'd lost his memory."

Wes turned abruptly. "But that's great. He won't know you did anything."

"He got his memory back and is waiting for me. And while he's been waiting he...raped my sister." Adam's voice broke. He'd never said the words out loud.

"So you see, I'm a wanted man and they may hang me as soon as I show my nose."

"You need a reliable friend to help you," Wes said, a new glimmer of hope in his eyes.

"You don't understand. My friends are vulnerable, just as I am. You don't know Nathan Billings. He's crazy, especially when he drinks."

"I'm not afraid."

Adam felt his face soften into a slow grin. Suddenly he felt relieved, almost elated. He slapped Wes on the back. "You are a corn-eating son of a bitch," he laughed.

"Why are you still here?" Ryker hovered in the entrance. "What's so funny, chaps?"

"Nothing, Sir," Adam said. "We're just glad we're done."

"So am I." Ryker's ruddy face showed the hint of a smile. "Time to hand in your gear, boys. And then you better hightail it home." He hesitated and saluted. "It's been an honor serving with you, Brown. And you, Westfield." He gruffly wiped a sleeve across his face and marched off.

"We will, Sir," Adam shouted after him. Only then did he realize that Ryker had used their real names.

How long had he known?

All the way to Greeneville, Wes asked more questions while Adam told him about Tip, Ma and Sara.

The war had pushed them this way and that, seemingly at random or the Union seeing fit. And yet, here he was in one piece, or nearly so, walking home with Wes by his side. The urge to provoke fate had faded and been replaced by the will not only to live, but to make good what he'd run from more than three years ago.

"I know them already," Wes said as Porter's farm came into view. Adam's voice didn't quite work. It was early afternoon and a weak October sun illuminated the glorious fall colors of northern Tennessee. "Is that it?" Wes asked.

Adam nodded, his steps slowing. The faint pounding of metal on metal came from the kitchen window. He wanted to delay the inevitable, seeing his sister's suffering and his worn mother.

How could he have wasted three years in a war? For Tip's sake, to stop slavery? He wasn't so sure. He'd run like a chicken from the axe, saving his own hide, abandoning Ma and Sara when they'd most needed him.

He abruptly turned and rushed into the barn. "Charlie?" He glanced around, the barn's partitions empty except for a pile of hay and straw.

"What are you looking for?" Wes said behind his back.

"My horse, he…I rescued him from a slave owner. The Army must've taken him."

"You know we all needed things," Wes said in a small voice.

Adam nodded, remembering the quivering mass of skin and bones at Rawley's farm and how he'd taken Charlie home. He turned abruptly and wiped his face. In a way, Charlie had reminded him of Tip, as if by taking care of Charlie he could've protected his old friend.

"Let's meet your kin." Wes awkwardly patted his arm.

They hadn't quite reached the porch when the door flew open and his mother rushed into his arms. "Adam!"

"Ma." Adam rested his head on top of his mother's. She seemed to have shrunken.

"You're so tall…and thin," she said, tears bright in her eyes. "And you have a beard."

He smiled, his insides a turmoil of relief, joy and sadness. Suddenly remembering Wes, he leaned back. "Ma, this here is Wes, my comrade from the war. He's with me now."

His mother gripped Wes's forearm and shook it. "So pleased to meet you."

Wes pulled back slightly, looking a bit worried. "Thanks, Mrs. Brown. Pleasure is all mine."

"Oh, come on in," Adam's mother cried as she pulled both of them by the hand.

Adam took in the scrubbed floors, the old table and cupboards. The house was as he remembered it and the air left his lungs like a deflated balloon.

"Sit, sit, you must be exhausted." Ma busied herself on the stove, poured water and cut bread.

"Ma, where is Sara?"

The knife halted in midair.

"Allister wrote to me." Adam's voice quivered. "I know what happened."

His mother slowly turned, her face drawn as if all the pain had collected there. "She's not here."

"Where is she then?" Adam could feel something dark brewing in the air, washing over him like an approaching tornado.

Ma hadn't moved, so Adam jumped up and grabbed his mother by the shoulders. To his shock and surprise she slowly crumpled into his arms. A silent tremor went through her, yet still she couldn't speak.

Adam's stomach began to ache, a deep hollow throbbing that spread to his throat. "Is she dead?"

Ma stiffened and got hold of herself. "No, no. She's with Nathan Billings. She...they got married a month ago."

"What?"

Just as relief had swept through Adam a minute ago, a wave of fury now took hold. "How could you let him do it? She was supposed to marry Allister. Live here with you."

His mother sighed, a deep heavy sound like an old bellow. Then she slowly sank onto the bench. "I couldn't do anything. Sara had waited for you. She wanted you in the wedding... And after Nathan remembered what had happened, he threatened to track you down and have you exposed and hanged for attacking him. I...Sara was afraid he'd get you killed."

Adam's legs felt as if he'd been walking for weeks. It was all his fault. Ever since Pa died, everything had gone wrong. They'd lost the farm, Tip was dead, and Sara was in the fangs of a madman.

"Where are Allister and Mr. Porter?" he managed after a while. He wanted to ask about Charlie but didn't have the strength.

"Prepping the fields for winter. Allister is beside himself."

Straightening with effort, his mother placed mugs and slices of bread on the table, her movements mechanical. Wes bowed a polite thank you.

Adam was no longer hungry. He rushed to Ma's side, repeating himself. "But she was supposed to marry Allister."

His mother nodded—a single tear perched on her eyelashes. The quietness of it was worse than if she'd screamed and hollered.

CHAPTER THIRTY-SIX

During the winter, Adam and Wes helped Mr. Porter and Allister with chores, tending winter crops, repairing fences and farm equipment. But no matter how hard Adam worked, Sara's face kept appearing in his vision. Twice he'd approached the Billings's estate, twice he'd turned around. Christmas came and went without a word from Sara. Ma sent a packet with homemade jam and bread and a note from them all. Still, there was silence.

By March Adam was convinced that something awful had happened. In his dream, he saw Sara floating dead in the river, her skin bloated and icy. One night he went so far as to visit the local cemetery to look for fresh markers.

When he returned home in the early morning, Wes was waiting for him in the kitchen.

"You about done with your gallivanting?" he asked.

"I'm not *gallivanting*."

"Then what the dickens are you afraid of? It's your sister, isn't it?

Adam grunted, his throat too tight for words.

"Why don't you go and visit her?"

Adam's gaze met Wes's. "Nathan won't let me."

"Why not? You're her brother." When Adam didn't answer, Wes jumped from the bench and pounded Adam in the shoulder. "You and me, we survived so much." He cleared his throat. "What's one more asswipe after all those Rebs?" He stretched himself tall. "Of course, I'm going with you."

A grin crept on Adam's face.

"At last," Wes said dryly. "I thought that mug of yours had frozen right along with the pond."

As soon as they'd eaten, Adam hurried out the door, Wes struggling to keep up. The words of Mr. Porter kept echoing through his mind. *Be careful. Don't trust Nathan, especially now that he has his prize.*

Every time the memory of Lillian crept into his head, he pushed it away. His sister had sacrificed her life for him. He couldn't imagine what it had to be like to live in a sick place like the Billings plantation surrounded by stuck-up cruel men.

He had to see for himself, make sure she was all right. Why had he waited this long?

"You want to talk about it?" Wes asked, scrambling up beside him. "You said it was dangerous."

"It is."

"Then let's give him a piece of our mind."

Adam watched his legs stride out as if they had a mind of their own. Here he'd hidden, lied, fought and almost died a hundred times and where was he going? The very place he'd escaped from. But not going...impossible. A long time ago he'd left for the wrong reasons. Now he was going back for the right one.

He felt Wes's presence on his left.

"What's wrong with Nathan Billings?"

"I can't talk now."

"Fine."

Adam hurried on until the Billings's massive two-story mansion came into view. Now that he saw it, he had no idea how to go about seeing Sara without alerting the entire Billings clan.

He thought of Mama Rose. Maybe he could sneak in the back and ask her to find Sara. It was worth a shot. He ran around back and carefully looked for any movement. A light rain drizzled, soft drops falling from a gloomy sky. Spring was on its way.

To his surprise, the kitchen was empty. A single pot bubbled on the stove and Adam motioned Wes to come inside. Maybe Mama Rose had gone to get supplies. When nobody appeared after a few minutes, Adam tiptoed to the double swing doors that led into the mansion. He'd never gone beyond. It was hard to imagine his sister living here now.

The hallway was deserted, and Adam, with Wes following closely behind, found himself staring at several doors. Which one was he supposed to take to find Sara? Where was Mama Rose? And where were all the other servants?

A new sense of doom took over, a creeping sensation that started at the base of his stomach and made its way up his spine.

"You reckon we should've brought guns?" Wes whispered. "They might blow us to hell if they see us."

Adam ignored him and carefully twisted the knob on the door in front of him, only to stare into a pantry filled with dishes, table clothes, and candles.

He quickly moved to the next door. Before he could step aside, it swung his way and banged into his forehead. "Damn."

His vision blurred as he stared at a servant girl who looked vaguely familiar.

"Elda?"

"Who are you?" The girl said, her eyes large and full of fright.

"I'm Adam, Tip's old friend."

"Oh, Adam," she breathed, quickly closing the door behind her. "What you doing here? You can't stay. Hurry before Master sees you."

"I came to visit Sara. Where is Mama Rose?"

Elda shook her head. "Mama Rose in bad way. She no longer cook."

"What happened?"

The girl began to tremble, whether from being afraid of running into her master or from remembering Tip, Adam didn't know. "Please leave."

"Listen," Adam said, taking hold of Elda's bony forearm. "I'm not going to hurt you, but I'm not leaving until I see Sara."

"Miss Sara in her room most of the time." Elda threw a suspicious glance at Wes. "Who he?"

"He's with me."

"Better go."

"Where *is* her room?" he murmured between clenched teeth.

"Second floor left wing, the last door on the right."

Instead of an answer he placed a forefinger on his lips and headed through the door Elda had come from, shutting out her warning cries.

Wes nodded encouragingly though his expression reminded

Adam of the morning before a battle. Adam scanned the foyer, a huge rectangular space covered in carpets, gold and brocade curtains and a man-sized fireplace. The effect of the opulence was stifling, and worse than that, there lay a hush over the house—a kind of sick quiet, as if the place were cursed.

On each side, a staircase wound its way to the second floor. Adam climbed the one on the left, Wes on his heels.

The doors looked identical except the last one had a key stuck in the lock. Adam knocked a couple of times, but heard nothing, just this strange quiet that made the blood rushing through his ears sound like thunder.

He tried the doorknob. Locked. Ever so quietly he turned the key and opened the door. The room was nearly dark, the large bed dominating to his left.

"Sara?"

Nothing. He stepped into the room, gesturing for Wes to close the door.

"It's me, Adam."

A movement came from the bed. "Adam?"

Adam rushed forward as his stomach plunged to a new low.

Sara struggled to sit, her voice much softer than he remembered. "Is it really you?"

"It's me. I'm here now," he said, taking in his sister's haggard face, the new lines on her forehead, chastising himself for waiting so long. Her eyes were worse. They'd always shown some sort of mischief, a twinkle of something, a joy for life. The color was still remarkable, a deep blue no sky could compete with. But the light had gone from them.

"Oh, Sara, what happened to you?"

Sara stared past him. "Who is your friend?"

"Wes, one of the boys from the Army."

Sara extended an arm. "Where are my manners? I'm sorry, I haven't been feeling well. Hello, Wes."

To Adam's surprise Wes bowed formally as if they were at a fancy dinner. "Glad to finally meet you."

Adam scanned the darkened room, the heavy curtains and marble fireplace. "No wonder you're sick," he said dryly. "You need fresh air." He rushed to the window and tugged at the stuffy curtains, glad for something to do. The additional light made Sara look worse. Her eyes were sunken and her skin had a bluish tinge instead of the healthy glow he remembered.

"Why did you do it?" he said, taking her hands again.

"What do you mean?"

The words stuck in Adam's throat. Impossible to say Nathan's name out loud. "Marry that monster."

"I couldn't bear the thought he'd do something to you," she stammered, her eyes filling with tears. "Please don't be mad with me."

Adam laughed, the sound harsh in his throat. "Mad with you? Ha!" He bent lower to embrace her as a new tremor came over her. "I could never be mad at you," he whispered. "I'm just so furious at these people destroying our family. I've got to find a way to get you out of here."

"You can't," Sara whispered. "Promise me you'll go away quietly."

"If it isn't the lost soldier." Nathan Billings stood in the open door as his gaze flicked back and forth between Adam and Wes. "Brought reinforcements, I see." His eyes blazed with contempt. "Not that it'll do you any good. Now I've got you for trespassing."

"Please don't, Nathan," Sara urged from the bed, her arms flailing. "I beg you, leave him alone."

"Why should I?" Nathan walked nonchalantly to Sara's bed. "The law is on my side. I can shoot him myself, and that mangy sidekick as well."

"Say the word," Wes said quietly.

Adam shook his head, but his eyes remained glued to Nathan's face. "We're leaving." He walked to the door, his arms raised. "I had to see her. She's my sister, surely you understand that. Please take care of her."

To Adam's surprise, Nathan backed down. "Sure will." He placed a possessive hand on Sara's shoulder. "I'm taking real good care of her." He smiled, his expression a shade of crazy.

Adam turned away and rushed down the hall, his insides hurting so badly he wanted to tear himself apart. Sara was legally married, and there was nothing he could do. He was too late.

"I wanted to punch'em," Wes said as they hurried toward Porter's farm. The air was heavy with the promise of more rain. "I can't believe you didn't do anything."

The fury in Adam boiled over. "What would you have me do? Smack him in the nose, shoot him? I'd be hanged."

"There's got to be something we can do."

"I'm fresh out of ideas." Adam stomped off, leaving Wes running after him once more.

"It wouldn't hurt you to share your thoughts once in a while. Maybe, just maybe, we could come up with a plan *together*," Wes yelled at Adam's back.

Adam abruptly turned. "Who are you to tell me to share? You of all people who never say a word about *your* family. All these years, and I don't even know your first name."

"I'm not the one who's losing his sister to a vile zealot."

"And you're not the one who lost his father and his farm and whatever future you'd ever thought possible," Adam shouted. "To hell with this life. I should've died in the war." As soon as he'd said it, he knew he'd gone too far.

Wes was pale, the evening light gray on his skin. Drizzle turned into a downpour but he didn't seem to notice, water dripping down his nose and chin.

"You've got that right," he mumbled before he abruptly turned and marched the way they'd come.

Adam spit a couple times as if he could somehow expel the anger raging inside him. Damn war, damn Billings and now damn Wes, too.

Adam's feet stopped, the drip-drip of rain hitting leaves and grasses, a sad sound that made him feel even more desolate. He was lost but somehow, somehow he had to find a way. Wes was right. They had to rescue Sara.

He raced after Wes.

CHAPTER THIRTY-SEVEN

Adam awoke, his neck and forehead soaked in sweat. It was dark. How long had he slept? What time was it? All he could hear was Wes's even snore next to him. All he felt was an uncertain pressure in his middle, an unpleasant foreboding. For a moment he envied Wes's ability to sleep wherever and whenever. Even during the war he'd been able to nap through cold, hunger and gun smoke.

In the end, he was glad he'd followed Wes. At first they'd walked silently, but then Adam had punched Wes in the arm and jokingly asked if he intended to hire on at the Billings. A slow grin had spread on Wes's face and they soon returned to Porter's farm. They hadn't survived three years of hell to break their friendship now.

Adam's thoughts wandered to Sara. Maybe Nathan Billings was forcing himself on her right this minute. A stifled sound escaped Adam and he sat up, his throat tight with dread for his sister. She already looked sick and would soon die unless he found a way.

A sigh escaped him, a lonely sound in the darkness. He could appeal to Janet Billings. He didn't really know her, but she was a woman. If nothing else, maybe she could be persuaded to offer Sara a shoulder to cry on, some sort of female companionship. It was a start.

Adam pulled on shirt, pants and socks and tiptoed to the door without a sound. In the quarter moon, Wes lay on his side, a small crumpled figure like a child. Adam swallowed, suddenly aware how much he cared for Wes. He was his only friend now and whatever ailed Wes, he would see to it that he'd make it better.

The rain had stopped, but the air was cold and damp. White clouds puffed from Adam's mouth as he made his way to the barn.

After they returned last October, Allister had called to him.

"Look who's here to see you," he said, waving Adam inside the barn.

And there in the box, munching on a pile of fresh hay, stood Charlie.

Adam's throat had tightened as he rushed into the stall.

The stallion had filled out, his coat shiny and his mane dark and long. He stood proudly, the way Adam remembered him from his first visit.

"Hey, old friend," he croaked, "I thought they'd taken you away."

Allister chuckled. "We hid him most of the time. Too good a horse to lose. I worked with him every day until he learned to trust again. He's a fine horse. He's yours, of course."

Adam looked up, the edges of Allister's hair blurry. What had he ever been mad about? Allister was a good man, better than most he'd met in the war. "I won't forget it," he managed.

With a grin, Allister turned to leave. "Better give that horse some loving. He missed you."

Adam didn't need to be asked twice, babbling to Charlie about the war and his life, Sara, Lillian and Wes. Scars crisscrossed the stallion's fur, but he whinnied and nuzzled Adam the way he had the first time they'd met.

Now Adam lit a lantern and rummaged for a saddle as the horse eyed him with interest.

"Let's go for a ride." He patted Charlie on the rump. "Just you and me."

He guided Charlie into the woods and across the fields to the Billings plantation. Lights burned in the upstairs windows, except for Sara's room, dark and ominous in its blackness.

Hopefully one of these rooms belonged to Janet Billings. He had no idea how to find her, until he remembered Elda.

He dismounted and quietly walked Charlie down the backside of the property. Slave row was deserted.

From what he could tell, most slaves had left. As the war tipped in favor of the Union, regaining territories in the south, the pressure on landowners to release their slaves grew. Many slaves simply melted away.

Adam tied Charlie to a pole and knocked on Mama Rose's door.

"Elda?"

For a moment nothing happened. He knocked again. "It's Adam, open up."

"Go home." Elda's scared voice could be heard. "You get me in trouble."

"I just have a question. I promise I'll not do anything crazy."

In the shine of a lantern the door creaked open a few inches, revealing a slight form. Elda's hair stood in all directions, her eyes frightened pools in the shadows. "I just need to know where Janet Billings sleeps. I'm going to ask her to help Sara." He'd beg her if he had to.

"Right staircase, second to last door on the left. The last one belong to old Master Billings." She hesitated. "Don't tell them I talk to you."

He glanced over Elda's shoulder toward the still form on the cot. "How is she?"

"Same, never says anything."

When Elda moved backwards, he took a few tentative steps, his gaze never leaving the bed. "What's wrong with her?"

"Mama Rose don't move no more. I worry she die soon."

Mama Rose lay on her back, her lids half open as if she couldn't decide whether to sleep or be awake. There was something final about her features, her eyes unseeing.

"Master say the stroke hit her hard."

Adam bent to touch her hand, her skin the texture of aged paper. "I'm glad you're taking care of her." Adam's heart grew heavy with the memory of Tip, their walks in the woods, Tip harvesting in his garden, his teeth flashing in the dusk. "Tip would've been proud of you."

"I miss him." Elda's voice cracked. "Some days I not know how to go through with it."

"I understand how you feel." Adam straightened and awkwardly patted her shoulder. "You have no idea."

"You better hurry," Elda said with a sniffle. "Missus always go to bed at midnight."

Adam snuck to the backdoor of the kitchen. He was back in

the war, sneaking around enemy territory. The slightest sound could get him killed.

The door wasn't locked. He slinked past the deserted stoves and counters into the hall, then the foyer. Everything was quiet. Oil lamps threw dancing shadows across the flight of steps as Adam made his way upstairs. He was tempted to check on Sara. Just for a minute. Instead he headed for Janet Billings's room. Strangely, he was no longer afraid.

To his relief, a light shone underneath the door. He was about to knock when he heard voices on the other side.

"...you're still reading them," Jack Billings shouted.

"I...I'm sorry, I don't know what you're talking about." Misses Billing's voice was soft...pleading.

"These atrocious love letters. You're still pining for him, I never thought..."

"You knew?"

"There isn't much I don't know." Jack Billings's voice, filled with rage and sadness, seemed to reach through the door.

"It's nothing."

"It's everything. You and I, our marriage, it's shameful."

"But nobody knows." Janet Billings's voice faltered.

"Nobody knows what?"

"About Nathan..."

Adam took his ear from the door. This was horrible stuff, embarrassing details about some love affair. What was Misses Billings talking about?

He needed to leave. The sounds of Jack Billings's jeering voice made him lean in again.

"I know, and people do suspect. There is talk, especially lately. The way Nathan acts, his cruelty. He's an embarrassment. No wonder."

"Please, Jack."

"You—"

Sharp pain shot through Adam's neck as he felt a blade dig into his skin. The voices on the other side faded, replaced by the awareness of a terrible presence.

"Look what I found lurking in my own house," Nathan said. Compared to his father, his voice was quiet, but the icy edge was worse than any yelling. Unlike Adam, who'd grown taller but thinner, Nathan had put on weight. The vest across his stomach stretched tightly.

Nathan pushed open the door to his mother's room and shoved Adam forward. "Look who I found trespassing."

"What are you doing here?" Misses Billings leaned against a mountain of pillows, almost cowering from her husband's huge frame at the end of the bed. Her bony shoulders trembled, the cap on her head like a lopsided creampuff. She wore a ruffled nightdress and wool jacket. Her hands nervously fluttered to her face and back down to the bedcover. Papers that looked like letters covered the sheets and expensive rug.

Jack Billings, his cheeks inflamed, swayed and teetered toward Adam. He'd obviously been drinking, the room heavy with the scent of whiskey. "Adam Brown?" he mumbled as if he had trouble recalling how he knew Adam.

"Mother, what's going on here?" Nathan rushed to his mother's side. "Why don't you leave her alone?" he hissed at his father.

"It's about time you learn your mother is a whore." Mr. Billings's voice was granite.

"Mother, what is he talking about? What happened?"

By the way Nathan formed his words carefully, Adam knew he was drunk too.

"Please Jack, let's keep him out of it," Misses Billings said.

"Oh, your *dear* son. It's time for him to know. Right this minute. You tell him or I will." Jack's voice trembled with fury as he took a step toward the bed again. He'd obviously forgotten about Adam.

"Leave Mother alone," Nathan said.

"Before your mother married me, she was seeing another man and you're not—"

"What're you talking about?" Something aggressive had crept into Nathan's voice.

"You're not my son."

Nathan gripped his mother's bony hand. "Mother?"

"I meant to tell you," Janet cried. "It was just...I was frightened, and your father...I mean Jack..."

For a moment the room turned quiet. Logs settled in the fireplace. Adam took a careful step backwards. They'd obviously forgotten he was here. It was time to go. This was getting out of hand.

At that moment Nathan screamed, "Liar!" and jumped on Jack Billings. Both men grunted and fell to the ground.

The old Billings huffed for air. "You're an abomination, God's punishment."

"I'll kill you," Nathan cried though he seemed in no position to make a move. Jack Billings had pinned Nathan's arms to the sides and sat on his legs.

"Stop it this instant," Janet Billings sobbed.

As she crawled out of bed, Adam rushed forward. "Please Mrs. Billings, leave them be."

The struggle on the floor continued, both men groaning with effort. Nathan worked free his right hand and groped in his pocket.

Adam watched the two men. He was no stranger to seeing fights. They were part of camp life and a way to break up a boring afternoon. Usually, it was best to let them work out their anger.

Misses Billings pushed Adam aside and threw herself between the men.

"I beg you, Jack. Leave him—"

A shot rang out... a feeble cry.

Adam watched in horror as Misses Billings slowly crumpled to the ground. Her hand plopped lifelessly next to Nathan as her nightgown turned crimson with alarming speed.

A high-pitched scream echoed through the room. "*You* murdered her," Nathan cried, throwing the gun he'd held at his father's head. It missed and clattered to the ground. "You were never good enough for her." He was panting, shrill sounds like a whistle.

"Look at you." Jack Billings's voice was full of revulsion as he took in his wife's still body. For a moment it looked as if he'd bent down, but then he straightened with effort, steadying himself on the bedpost. "You just shot your own mother. Even now you're blind. Blind to your mother having a child with another man."

"What are you talking about? What lies are you telling?"

"Your mother deceived me, and you're not my son," Jack said quietly. "It's time you leave my house."

"Liar. Anything to dirty my mother's good name."

"You don't believe me? Read the letters." He pointed at the papers covering the bed and carpet. "I gave her everything, but even now she is heartsick, longing for her lost love."

Nathan picked up a note and half-heartedly began to read.

"I'm going to send for the sheriff," Jack Billings said as he glanced at Adam. "Time to turn in this intruder and straighten out this mess."

He turned back to Nathan. "I want you out of my house by morning."

The letter sailed toward Adam as Nathan lunged at his father. "Never."

They hit the floor hard, rolling back and forth. Nathan tried to get the upper hand. But Jack Billings was strong, and despite his age he had no trouble holding Nathan down.

Adam's eyes lodged on the paper at his feet. He picked it up and was about to read it when he heard Jack Billings gasp.

"You're no son of mine or you'd at least put up a decent fight." And frighteningly, he began to laugh. Then he rose, pulling himself up a second time. "Get out of my sight."

He turned away and Adam watched in horror as Nathan attacked from behind, viciously slicing at Jack Billings's throat. The old Billings swayed, his arm shot up to inspect the damage.

Too late.

Blood poured from his wound in great spurts. He gurgled and collapsed to the ground, his eyes turning cloudy.

Jack Billings was dead.

CHAPTER THIRTY-EIGHT

As Nathan crawled to his mother's body, Adam tried to figure out what to do. His breath was a windstorm. If Nathan was capable of killing his own parents, there was no telling what he would do with an old enemy.

Two people lay dead in the room, and Nathan was now the sole heir of the vast Billings estate. Adam knew he had to leave, but what would happen to Sara, alone here with a madman?

He stepped backwards to put distance between himself and Nathan when his boot got tangled in Jack Billings's coat. Nathan, who'd embraced his mother, noticed his movement, their eyes meeting across the room.

"Damn spy," Nathan cried, ignoring the snot and tears on his face. His sob turned into giggles as he jumped up and moved toward Adam. "It's perfect. You've hated us all along. Now you came to kill my parents and I caught you in the act. Naturally," he halted, taking a deep breath, "I had to put you down." Coming from Nathan's crazed mouth, it sounded as if Adam were a rabid dog.

Adam glanced around the room in search of a weapon. He wasn't afraid of Nathan, not anymore. All he felt was a cold loathing for this maniac who'd never done anything but fulfill his own whims, who lived like a king while the rest of the country starved and suffered. The gun lay near Jack's lifeless body, no doubt empty of ammunition. The blade, Nathan had retrieved from his father, glinted—the same knife he'd used on Tip.

Without warning Nathan lunged forward. Adam stumbled against the wall. Glass exploded, and the pungent smell of kerosene filled the room. Nathan pounced, the movement so sudden and close, Adam felt the air move across his throat.

Adam slid sideways, trying to get hold of Nathan's arm. But the knife kept coming. Sharp pain shot through Adam's arm, momentarily taking him to the battlefield long ago.

Whether the growing madness was giving Nathan strength or Adam was exhausted from three years of war, Nathan was gaining. Adam knew it. He launched a kick at Nathan's knee… and missed.

Get out of here, the voice in his head commented. He scrambled sideways when he spotted the poker near the fireplace. Ten feet. A matter of seconds under normal circumstances.

Nathan's pale eyes gleamed feverishly as he hissed, "Dirty bastard. It's all your fault." Despite his formal dinner jacket, he moved like a dancer, the knife in his hand slicing the air.

That's when Adam noticed the rising heat and the smell of something burning. He risked a quick glance past Nathan's shoulders. Flames spread across the floor as the cotton sheets on Janet Billings's bed disappeared in a sea of dancing light.

Seemingly oblivious to the fire, Nathan launched another attack. Adam jumped away from the swinging blade, getting closer and closer to the window. His right hand ached and felt sticky, but he had no time to look down to inspect the damage.

He yanked at the curtains and pulled one down, catching the unwieldy fabric just as Nathan struck.

Like their fight in the grain shack a hundred years ago, Nathan moved silently. Unlike last time, his eyes sparkled with insanity, his lips drawn back exposing his teeth like a wild animal.

He's going to kill you. Fighting down rising panic, Adam pushed the bunched-up fabric between them. Nathan kept coming, slicing and writhing as if he were possessed. The blade caught Adam's arm, and intense pain raced up his shoulder.

Time slowed. Blood kept dripping from his right arm as the heat and smoke billowed near the bed. He couldn't move, and a paralyzing feeling of fate came over him. He'd run off three years ago to avoid being hanged because of Nathan Billings. Maybe he'd been meant to die back then. Maybe Sara would have been safe. *Sara.*

A shout reached his ears, breaking into his thoughts. He never knew if it was his or Nathan's. Something glinted. Nathan's knife hacked toward Adam's face. Adam jumped sideways, took hold of Nathan's forearm and twisted, the way he'd learned in combat. It was enough. The knife disappeared among the curtain folds.

I just need a second, he thought, trying to bend away from the heavy cloth while wrapping Nathan into it. Sara needs you. *You DID NOT survive three years of war only to be killed by Nathan Billings.*

Out of nowhere, iron fingers found his throat. Adam gasped, desperately shoving at the hand with his left, his right out of commission. He kicked, his foot making contact with Nathan's shin, confirmed by a muffled shriek.

Fabric ripped, and from the corner of his eye Adam saw a flash of something bright. The curtain on the other side of the window burst into flames. Smoke rose from the floor and bed as the roar of the fire grew louder. Pulling free, Adam kicked again, but his foot came up empty. Nathan shoved aside the curtain and scrambled away from the heat.

For a second he feigned retreat. Too late did Adam see the knife half covered by the curtain and Nathan gripping it once more.

Adam was getting desperate, his throat raw with smoke, his eyes tearing. The old mansion was made of dry seasoned wood and burned like tinder. Already he could hardly see the crumpled bodies and the door, his only escape. Nathan didn't seem to notice, his eyes glittering evil.

He had to keep Nathan at bay, avoid the flames, and inch his way toward the fireplace. He stepped backwards and tripped over a footstool. In vain, he tried to stay upright, arms flailing as Nathan jumped at him. They crashed to the ground. Adam landed heavily on the tiled inset. Nathan's grimace was inches away, his breath nauseating with liquor.

Before Adam had a chance to push him away, the knife stabbed at his chest, only stopped by a brass button on his coat. He grabbed Nathan's throat with his left hand and squeezed hard, but the knife immediately followed Adam's arm, slashing at his wrist.

The poker. You need the poker.

But his mind was powerless to urge on his body. The previous months and years had taken their toll. With effort, he lifted his right arm to grope behind him, exposing his chest and arm once more.

Pain seared through his shoulder and the poker slid from his blood-slick hand. Nathan's hate filled face grew hazy.

A cry rang out, a high-pitched cry. The knife stopped. In wonder Adam watched the poker smash onto Nathan's back a second time. Above him stood Sara in her nightgown, her cheeks red, her eyes determined.

As Nathan sagged forward, Adam crawled from beneath his grip.

"Let's get out of here," Sara cried.

"Am I glad to see you." Adam coughed but managed a grin. Hardly able to breathe, he tried to pull himself upright, the smoke so thick now, he could no longer see the door.

Sara half-dragged him toward the exit, toward Jack Billings's body, away from the crazy eyes and the scorching heat. "Come on, no time to waste."

Already the hallway was engulfed in smoke, flames licking the banister and taking hold of the oil paintings and wooden carvings.

A cry rang out behind them. Adam turned just in time to see Nathan Billings, terror in his eyes, his elegant coat and pants aflame, charging at Sara. Adam wanted to stop him, wanted to throw himself in front of his sister, but she was faster.

As if in slow motion, he saw her duck to avoid the brunt of Nathan's charge as the madman draped across the balcony and in one horrifying movement... disappeared.

A scream rang out and then all was still except for the fire's roar growing louder. Adam peeked over the railing. Nathan was lying below on his stomach, his burning body feeding the carpets and floors below. By the way his neck bent, it had to be broken.

The last thing Adam saw was Sara leaning across the bannister, her fist still holding the poker. Then he passed out.

"Adam, wake up!" Sara's face floated in and out of Adam's vision.

How much time had passed?

"We must go."

He saw the panic in her eyes. "I can't carry you."

Behind them something crashed to the ground. Adam forced his vision to focus on the flower pattern of her nightgown. Rosebuds in red and pink, green leaves...

"Adam, come on." Sara's voice was sharp as she half-slapped his cheek. "I'll help you get up."

He felt her arm grip around his back and managed to straighten. Black smoke roiled toward them from the staircase.

"We need to crawl," he said. They dropped back down and shuffled along the floor, which felt hot to the touch. Behind them Janet's room was completely engulfed. Soon the entire second story would be gone.

Find a way, his mind urged. You only have a couple of minutes, before the house is consumed. On the balcony behind them another oil lamp exploded. Sara couldn't die. Not now that she'd escaped Nathan.

"Do you have any water?" he asked.

"My wash basin."

"Let's go." They crawled farther down the hall toward Sara's room. "Put on some clothes and soak them. Get a wet cloth and put it over your face."

They pushed their way in, the fire seemingly on their heels. Behind them, the staircase exploded in flames. They were trapped.

"We've got to climb out the window," Sara said. Without waiting for an answer, she yanked down two curtains and tied them together.

When she opened the window, the fire, fed by more oxygen, roared like a heard of angry lions, charged into the room. "Hurry," she shouted, her face lit by the dancing flames, behind her blackness. "Help me."

Adam shoved the four-poster bed toward the windows.

"We need a rope," he said as a new coughing fit overtook him. His lungs ached with every breath now.

Sara shook her head. "No time."

"You first, then. I'll be right behind you."

She climbed across the sill, the last thing he saw were the dancing flames reflecting on her face. The entrance to Sara's room caved in with a loud whoosh singeing Adam's hair. He pressed himself against the window frame, watching Sara slide down the curtain.

Adam looked at his right palm, dark with congealed blood. In the smoke and gloom it was hard to tell what he was looking at, his fingers stiff and nearly numb. He coughed again. The heat was so intense, he felt as if the fire was melting his lungs.

The flames nipped at the bed, cotton sheets incinerated as if they'd been soaked in kerosene. He climbed across the windowsill when he noticed the curtain knot on the bed. The fire was advancing fast now. If the knot broke, he'd fall thirty feet and break his neck.

He gulped air and rushed back to the bed, tugging at the knot, swearing at his right hand that didn't belong to him. The flames lapped at the bed, the heat rising through the soles of his boots. He dove to the window and climbed across, his last view at the bed now engulfed in flames.

He held on with his left hand, immediately aware that his right wouldn't hold him. He tried to squeeze the fabric under his arm, but the material was too slippery. Losing his hold, he grasped the curtain with his left hand and slid once again.

He knew he was too slow. Above him, flames shot into the night sky. The curtain would burn in seconds. He loosened his grip and started slipping when he felt the whole thing go. With a yelp he fell.

He slammed into the ground and tried to roll sideways—his battered body refused. Burning bits of fabric floated toward him. *Move, you idiot.* He tried crawling away from the fiery heat, but his legs and arms no longer belonged to him, his skull about to burst from a pounding headache.

The air turned black.

"No time for a nap."

Wes's voice seemed disembodied, like some ghost visiting from another life. He had to be dreaming.

"Adam?"

When Adam opened his eyes, he found himself fifty yards away from the fierce heat.

"Wes?" Adam had never felt this relieved. "Where's Sara?"

Wes, a neckerchief across his nose, appeared out of the gloom. His forehead, speckled black, glistened with sweat.

"Sara is right here. She fell and turned her ankle, but she's all right." Wes pointed toward a figure sitting on the lawn. "I reckoned you went back. Could've asked me along."

Adam blinked, hoping his limbs would obey him one last time. "We better leave." He had to get Sara away from this place.

"Sara can't walk far," Wes said as if he'd heard him.

Adam sat up and heaved, trying to suck air into his lungs. "Get Charlie," he panted, "by the slave huts." Take a wagon, he wanted to say, but no words came out. Instead he crawled toward

Sara, who sat on the ground shivering.

"Let's go home." He tried a smile though he could tell his face wasn't cooperating.

Sara, who'd been staring at the fire roaring a hundred feet into the air, nodded and took his hand into hers.

Wes returned with Charlie pulling an open cart, the kind used to transport supplies. For a brief moment Adam remembered Tip being hauled away by Jack Billings and the sheriff. It had been a lifetime ago.

"We have to get Mama Rose," he said aloud as he forced his throbbing limbs into action. He'd been unable to protect Tip, so he'd at least help his Mama and Elda. Wes helped him lift Sara into the cart and grabbed the reins. So close to the fire, Charlie was skittish. He rolled his eyes and whinnied, pulling hard. "Shhh." Adam rubbed his nose with his good hand.

"Who's Mama Rose?"

"My friend Tip's mother."

They headed back to the slave quarters where Elda rushed to meet them. "What happen?" she squeaked. "The house, Master Billings?"

"No time," Adam said. "We're taking Mama Rose with us. You can come, too."

"But old Master Billings and Missus."

"They're dead," Adam said, the finality of it hitting him like an icy rain. He'd expected to be happy, but all he could feel was dread and sadness.

The thin light of dawn broke over the fields as they approached Porter's farm. Nobody spoke, Adam too exhausted, the two women too sick.

Whatever Wes was thinking remained securely hidden behind his forehead.

CHAPTER THIRTY-NINE

Adam collapsed into deep sleep and didn't get up until the following evening. The three women moved in, Sara upstairs with her mother, Mama Rose and Elda in the storage room off the kitchen. It was hard to tell if Mama Rose knew what was going on, or if she was even aware of being in a different place.

She stared at the ceiling, the right side of her face off-center and paralyzed. She'd lost a lot of weight, her frame frail now, her clothes in folds draped around her body.

At dinner, Adam was able to recount the story of visiting Janet Billings and becoming witness to their family tragedy of forbidden love. His mother had bound his hand and arm—his chest just a scratch thanks to the button.

That night, despite being exhausted, sleep wouldn't come. Every time he closed his eyes he saw Nathan Billings charging him, his mouth twisting with hate, the bloodied bodies of Janet and Jack Billings, the letters incinerating above the bed, red hot flakes raining down. His nose seemed permanently filled with smoke and the horrific stench of burned flesh.

It was hard to imagine that all the Billings were dead. For the past three and a half years, Adam had lived in fear and worry, always knowing that Nathan would get his way, that wealth conquered all.

Now Nathan was gone, but the scars he'd left ran deep. Tip was dead. Sara appeared kind of hollow, her movements jerky and her smile—if she smiled at all—a mask. Their farm had crumbled

228

and Ma was a permanent guest at the Porter's.

Where did that leave him? He wasn't sure how he could restart, where he fit in, what his role was supposed to be. He couldn't possibly stay with Allister and old Mr. Porter. The little farmhouse was bursting at the seams. But where was he supposed to go? All he knew was that he couldn't rejoin the war—now in its fourth year—a war that continued to mutilate and destroy.

He thought of his dream of becoming a veterinary surgeon. It was a joke to think he'd ever do something like that. Maybe he could rebuild his old farmstead. But he had little more than a hundred dollars, not nearly enough to buy lumber and supplies. Maybe he could cut trees like his dad had done. He also had Wes, his friend who'd saved his life and Sara's. Adam grimaced in the dark, peering at the sleeping form on the floor.

It was after midnight before he drifted off.

A loud knock reached Adam's consciousness. By the light outside it had to be early morning. Somebody was shouting downstairs, Wes's bedroll empty. A second later, the door flew open.

"Come down quick," Wes said, catching his breath. He looked worried, but before he could say anymore, he was shoved out of the way.

"What is it?" Adam said, rubbing his eyes. His right palm ached beneath the bandages.

"Get up," Sheriff Tate's voice was deep and hard. "You're being arrested for the murder and arson of the Billings family.

Adam stared in disbelief as rough hands grabbed him from his bed, barely able to put on shoes. What was the man talking about?

"Let's go, Judge Dowell is waiting," Tate barked.

"I haven't done anything," Adam cried, taking in his mother's frightened face. Sara looked shocked.

"It's a mistake," his mother said.

"No mistake, Ma'am." Sheriff Tate puffed out his chest. "Now let me through." He headed outside, pulling Adam with him.

"In there," Tate said, giving Adam a rough shove. The holding cell, surrounded by the usual bars, had a bucket in the corner and a two-foot wide cot with a moth-eaten blanket.

Adam curled up on the bed. His hand throbbed with every move. His fingers had swollen to the size of sausages, and just like last time when he'd been shot in the arm, he couldn't move them. He wondered if Nathan had severed the tendons and he'd never use his hand again. He was sure there was some kind of poison brewing in it. And without his mother who knew how to treat all kinds of wounds and diseases, he was liable to lose his hand.

But then, did it really matter?

He'd come a long way, had gone off to war and survived, had made it out alive after Nathan's attack, and where did he land? In jail. The thought of fate catching up with him returned. It had all been meant to be. If he'd turned himself in, he could've easily avoided three years of hardship, of pain and seeing his friends die. *You wouldn't have met Lillian.*

Fragments of scenes returned. Lillian in the barn collecting eggs, the first time he'd seen her. The flaxen braid dangling between her shoulder blades. The way she stood proudly, her clear green eyes twinkling.

A sigh escaped his chest. He closed his eyes, trying to conjure up the memory of their kiss, the way her lips felt on his. He'd trembled all over, hardly able to still his hands on her back. He knew it had been the same for her. Even with this…everything had been worth it.

The clinking of keys woke him. "Come along," Tate said, impatiently waving at Adam.

To his surprise, the courtroom was filled to its last seat with spectators. More were crowding in the aisles so that Sheriff Tate, pulling Adam with him, had to barrel his way through.

As soon as Adam was placed at the defendant's table, Tate secured him to the chair with handcuffs and Judge Dowell entered the courtroom.

"All rise," the clerk shouted. Adam stood half bent and locked to his chair.

"Sit," Dowell said, arranging his robe around his ample middle. For a moment he scanned the room, clearing his throat several times. At last his gaze fell on Adam, who stared back in bewilderment. The cart ride to town had done nothing to clear his confusion.

"The day before yesterday," Dowell began, "some of our most honorable citizens died." Immediately, the crowd began to shout so that Judge Dowell smacked his gavel. "Silence, or I'll have all of you removed." His eyes glittered fiercely, leaving little doubt he meant it.

"This is a hearing to establish a crime was committed and to determine whether a trial should be held. Mr. Miller, as the prosecuting attorney, you may begin."

At the opposite wall, a man straightened his collar and stood. "Thank you, Judge." Miller walked five steps and turned to face the courtroom, visibly enjoying the attention of the crowd.

"In the early morning of March 31, 1865, a fire broke out at the Billings plantation. The fire was deliberately set to cover up the gruesome murder of Jack and Janet Billings and their son, Nathan Billings. The prosecution maintains that Adam Brown, sitting over there," Miller glared at Adam, "snuck into the Billings home and killed the three people mentioned, set the fire to cover his crimes and reclaim his sister, Sara, the spouse of Nathan Billings. He then proceeded to take Mama Rose and Elda, the Billings remaining servant and deposit them at the Porter's farm, where he's currently residing." Miller paused for effect. "We, the people, demand that Adam Brown stand trial for first-degree murder."

"What makes you think Adam Brown was at the scene of the crime?" Dowell asked.

"He was seen by Mr. Flint, the Billings's next door neighbor, and by Elda, the Billings's servant girl. As to his motives, it is well known he's been feuding with the Billings for years, especially after he assisted Tipper, Mama Rose's son, and at the time, a Billings slave, in running away. Subsequently his family was sentenced to pay a $1,000 fine. It is further known that he was adamantly opposed to the marriage of Sara to Nathan Billings. And while we concede that he fought in the Union Army, he may have lost all decency in the process."

"Let's leave the speculation out of it, Mr. Miller," Dowell said.

"Sir, in my nineteen years serving as prosecuting attorney, I've never seen a clearer case." Miller smiled as if he could already taste victory. "I therefore ask the court to set this case for trial as soon as possible."

Adam stared at Judge Dowell who seemed to process what Miller had suggested when a commotion behind him made him turn. In the far back he saw his mother pushing her way through the gawking crowd, Sara and Wes in tow. "Let me through," she said quietly, but her words, sharp and clear, reached him like an embrace. Only then did the impending horror finally sink in.

He'd been sitting numbly listening to Miller and the judge, a spectator at somebody else's trial. His mother's voice had changed that, and he became acutely aware of the terrible situation he was in. After his history with Nathan Billings, nobody would believe him. He was sure Nathan had talked about being attacked in the grain shack, especially when he was drunk. All the Billings's neighbors and friends were wealthy and would see to it that somebody was blamed and held accountable.

With the Billings dead, he had no witnesses. A dread like he'd never known took hold of him then. He bent over, suddenly sick to his stomach, clasping his knees so tight, his knuckles turned white. He'd be hanged just as Nathan had threatened so long ago. After all he'd gone through, his father's death, the fights with Nathan, losing Tip, the war and Sara's rape, he'd walk straight into a noose.

The deaths of Jack and Janet Billings had been Nathan's doing. If he, Adam, hadn't intervened, Nathan would've been left a very rich man. He would've made up some story about his parents and walked away. A strange flutter bubbled up in Adam. He giggled, yet he felt as if he were being strangled by it. Fate was cruel. Nathan had won in the end.

"Does the defendant wish to make a statement?" Judge Dowell stared at him curiously.

Adam rose slowly, his handcuffed wrist forcing him to stand crooked.

"Sir, your Honor, I am innocent. Despite what it looks like here, I was merely witness to a family tragedy." He closed his mouth abruptly, remembering Nathan's sneer change into terror as he realized he was on fire, remembering Sara smashing the poker across Nathan's back. Nathan would've been able to put out the fire, had it not been for Adam fighting him. *His hatred for you was stronger than his fear of burning.*

"Go on," Dowell said.

"I went to speak with Mrs. Billings about Sara. And—"

Dowell raised an arm to cut him off. "Save that for the court. I think we have sufficient evidence for a trial. We shall reconvene in three days, starting at nine o'clock. Court dismissed."

As Dowell disappeared in his chambers, Miller joined the crowd gathering around him, talking loudly about justice.

Adam sagged back into his chair and didn't listen. He'd

reached the end.

CHAPTER FORTY

The early April wind and drizzle matched Adam's mood. He'd spent five nights in his cell, and though his mother and Sara visited every day, and they repeatedly discussed the events of the evening in question, none of them had any ideas what to do.

They had no money to hire a lawyer, so Adam was on his own. All he could hope for was to tell his side of the story and for the jury to believe him. It was a long shot, but he'd at least try.

"Time to go." Sheriff Tate rattled the keys. Adam nodded. They'd allowed his mother to treat his shoulder and hand. His fingers still felt numb, but the deep grinding pain had been replaced by a dull ache. He washed in a bucket of water and dressed in a new shirt and pants he recognized as his father's. Wes had dropped them off, taking his singed clothes with him to wash.

The courtroom was filled to the last seat, the aisles stuffed with more spectators. Adam saw old neighbors, Wilkes, the Billings's former overseer, Selma from the general store, Mr. Porter and Allister. Wes, his mother, and Sara sat in the first row right behind the defendant's table. Despite the cold outside it was hot and sticky in here. Adam, immediately drenched beneath his shirt, tried to ignore the shreds of conversation that discussed his certain hanging, the fights with Nathan Billings, and helping Tip.

As soon as Judge Dowell appeared, the voices died down. The quiet grew deep, as if the entire community were holding its breath.

"Adam Brown, you're here to stand trial for the murder of the Billings family, Janet, Jack and Nathan Billings. How do you plead?"

"Not guilty," Adam said, struggling to keep his voice steady.

"Mr. Miller, you may begin."

Adam stared unseeing as the prosecutor recounted the fire and Adam's presence at the Billings mansion, driving off with Sara, Mama Rose and Elda. Miller then proceeded to call his first witness, Mr. Flint.

"When did you first become aware of the fire?"

"Don't rightly know," Flint said, twisting a gray felt hat in his hands. "The wife thought she saw something ungodly bright and sent me out to investigate. When I stepped outside I knew something large was burning, with all the heat and smoke almost choking me a half mile away."

"So you don't know the time."

"No, Sir, I just hurried over to see if there was something I could do."

"And you saw what?"

"I saw him." Flint nodded in Adam's direction. "Adam was crawling on a cart and next to him I saw several women folk, the old cook was one and Elda, the girl who stayed with the Billings when all the other slaves left. I mean—"

"Who else did you see?"

"Another young man was leading the horse. He had red hair, but I didn't recognized him."

"Is he here in the courtroom today?"

"He's sitting right over there." Flint pointed at Wes.

"What do you think he was doing at the Billings place?"

Flint shrugged. "Don't rightly know, sir."

"Did the defendant have any weapons?"

"None I could see."

"No further questions," Miller said.

Dowell nodded at Adam. "Do you have questions for the witness?"

Adam awoke from the trance that had taken hold ever since he'd sat down. He eyed Flint who he'd never seen before and shook his head.

"Let it show that the defendant has no questions," Dowell said.

Flint was dismissed and Elda called to the stand. She trembled as she sat down, her eyes moving wildly across the room, avoiding

Adam's corner. After swearing in Elda, Miller had the girl tell about Adam's recent visit, finding him in the hallway behind the kitchen on his way to Sara's room.

"And the second time?"

"He...he come to my door...my house."

"What time was that?"

"I don't know, late. Missus Janet always goes to sleep by midnight so I told Adam to hurry."

"You told him where her room was?"

"Yessir."

"Did you see any guns or other weapons?"

"No, he said he was going to talk to Missus about Sara."

"Why?"

"Because...Sara is...was locked up all the time. Young Master hard on Miss Sara. She cry all the time."

"Why would she cry?" Miller chuckled. "She married into a rich family, lived in a big home."

"Sara not happy," Elda whispered.

"Sounds to me like she was thankless," somebody in the audience mumbled.

Adam felt a deep ache in his stomach, reminding him of the helpless fury he'd felt when Nathan was alive. They made it sound as if Sara had been spoiled when it was well known that Nathan Billings had a history of violence.

Tell them that he hit her, Adam urged with his eyes. But Elda cowered in her chair, hardly able to speak while Miller gloated above her.

"No further questions," Miller said, nodding at the judge.

"Mr. Brown, would you like to ask the witness any questions?" Dowell said.

Adam pushed back his chair and stood. He cleared his throat. "I would, your Honor."

Elda looked at him, her eyes a mix of guilt and fear as if she suspected him to have committed the murders.

"Did you ever see Nathan Billings hit Sara?" Adam asked.

"Your Honor, this is hardly relevant," Miller interjected.

Dowell waved a hand as if Miller were an annoying fly. "I'll allow it."

"Yessir, many times. You see, young Master drink a lot, he often angry."

"Did he ever hit you?"

Elda's eyes grew large. "Yessir."

"Did he ever force himself on you?"

Shouts echoed through the courtroom and Miller jumped up. "Your Honor, this line of questioning is confusing the issue." Shaking his head in mock disbelief, he glared at Adam.

"Indeed, where is this going?" Dowell said.

"Sir, I'm trying to establish that Nathan Billings wasn't just angry, he was cruel and violent."

"I'll allow it," Dowell said. "Elda, answer the question."

Elda covered her face with both hands and leaned forward. "Master sometimes come to my hut."

A murmuring went through the spectators.

"When was the last time?"

"I ain't sure, maybe two weeks ago."

"*After* Nathan was married?"

Elda nodded, her eyes glued to Adam's face, her cheeks burning with shame.

Miller stood up again. "I really don't see what the relevance is. If anything, it presents more motive for Mr. Brown here."

"I agree with you, Mr. Miller, but Adam chooses his own questions," Dowell said.

Sweat dripped down Adam's temple. He couldn't breathe, the air stale in his lungs. He'd intended to show how dishonorable Nathan was. Instead he'd made himself look guiltier. His stomach clenched with helplessness. He had no idea how to continue.

"No more questions," he managed.

Miller jumped into action once more. "Your Honor, we call Samuel Westfield to the stand."

Adam heard commotion behind him as Wes made his way to the witness stand. He was sworn in and sat down, his gaze on Adam. Adam gave the tiniest nod. He'd finally learned Wes's true first name.

"Please tell the court what you saw," Miller said.

"Sir, I arrived during the fire. Hardly made my way to the house and helped 'em get home on the cart."

"Where were the Billings?" Miller asked.

Wes shrugged. "Don't rightly know. I think they were already dead."

"Did you not ask the defendant...Adam about them?"

"There was no time. The house was about to explode. But I know Adam would never kill those rich folks. He and I…we've seen more killing than…"

"Your Honor, the witness is speculating."

Dowell cleared his throat. "Mr. Westfield, please stick to the facts. The jury will disregard this last remark."

"Adam is no killer," Wes repeated.

"Thank you, Mr. Westfield." Miller turned to his paper. "No further questions."

"Would you like to ask the witness?" Dowell asked, his eyes peering over his glasses at Adam.

Ignoring Wes's pleading look, Adam shook his head. Wes couldn't help him. Not now. Nobody could. He'd been alone with the Billings. Everything he said could be twisted into a lie.

"I'd like to give an accounting of the events the evening of the fire," he said.

"Fine." Dowell nodded toward the spot by his bench. "Take the witness stand, Mr. Brown."

Adam headed to the chair, trying to ignore the crowd, the men and women in the jury box, the judge and Miller. As he was sworn in, the room grew quiet except for the creaking of radiator pipes and the rushing of blood in his ears.

"I went to see Mrs. Billings to ask her help with Sara," he began. When he got to the part of Jack Billings talking to his wife about the love letters, Nathan being an illegitimate child and the gunfight between Nathan and Jack Billings, the crowd gasped.

"Silence," Dowell yelled, wielding his gavel.

"I know Nathan and I fought," Adam said, "but his clothes caught on fire. He didn't want to stop and put out the flames and when he attacked me on the balcony, he fell to his death. It was a terrible accident." His gaze met Sara's who was shaking her head. No need to involve her.

By the time Adam finished his story, the room erupted in whispers. Even Judge Dowell didn't interrupt.

"That's all I have to say."

"Mr. Miller, do you have any questions for the defendant?"

Shuffling a couple papers, Miller stood.

"Mr. Brown, you mean to tell me that Nathan Billings shot his own mother?"

"I believe it was an accident. He meant to kill Mr. Billings or maybe frighten him. He did stab him in the end."

"Why didn't you stop them?"

"I couldn't—"

"Sounds pretty farfetched to me. And that bit about the letters and love affair. You mean to tell us that one of the most respected families in the county, if not in the state, acted in such a dishonorable way? Of course, all the evidence conveniently was destroyed in the fire." Miller paused. "From what I can tell you're trying to defile a good family's name after you cold-bloodedly murdered them. I've never seen a more despicable crime."

Adam shook his head. "It's the truth," he shouted as the noise in the courtroom grew to a new dimension.

Judge Dowell smacked his gavel. "Silence."

"Mr. Miller," he said, once the spectators quieted, "do you have any more questions for Mr. Brown?"

"No, Sir."

"Adam, do you have anything else to say before we send the jury to deliberate?"

Adam stood with effort, his legs weak as if all the energy had drained from his body. "I'm innocent and what I said here today is true."

The gavel struck. "Very well, we shall reconvene tomorrow morning at nine o'clock to hear the jury's verdict."

As the courtroom emptied, shreds of words reached Adam's ears. "He's going to the gallows...what a horrible crime...shame on him."

He felt a hand on his shoulder. "It'll be all right," Ma whispered though he could tell in her eyes she didn't believe her own words. He lowered his head, defeated, and patted her forearm. "I'm sorry, Ma."

"Nothing to be sorry for," Wes said, his voice thick with anger. Adam knew him well and he could tell that Wes was about to explode. "I've got to go think."

Adam paced in his cell. It was Sunday and all he could think was that he'd be dead by next week. A few years ago he'd had so many plans. He'd helped Pa work the farm and dreamed about going to veterinary school. He'd gone off to war hoping to die and he'd returned wanting to live. And all for what? He grimaced. At least he'd tried to do the right thing. Been on the right side of the law, help President Lincoln free the slaves. Even if it was too late for Tip, he'd done his share.

And yet. Their farm was in ruins and he was about to be hanged.

"Good job," he mumbled. "You sure did it this time."

"You say something?" Sheriff Tate looked up from his plate of fried chicken. Ordinarily Adam would've been starving, his last meal a bowl of cooked oats for breakfast. But his stomach felt as if he'd eaten rocks, his throat tight with unshed tears.

"Nothing."

"We're here to see Adam." His mother's voice sounded strong, though he detected the tremble beneath. It reminded him of when she'd first heard the news about Pa's death. Sara's face showed all her emotions, her eyes filled with tears, the clear blue of a spring sky covered in rain clouds, her beautiful mouth trembling.

"Take your time, Mrs. Brown," Tate said.

Sara slipped a tied cloth bag through the bars. "We brought you dinner."

Adam grabbed her hand and held it. He couldn't speak, his throat so thick he was choking.

"You're free now," he whispered finally.

"Thanks to you," Sara said. Her eyes found his. "Why didn't you tell them it was me?"

"You saved my life…and you sure didn't kill him either."

"But—"

"No buts. Enough that one of us sits in here."

"There's still hope," Ma said as she sank onto the bench to sort through her basket.

"Where is Wes?" Adam asked. Secretly he was disappointed Wes wouldn't spend a few last minutes with his friend.

"He mumbled something about a trip and left right after the trial."

Adam frowned. Maybe Wes couldn't take it and had disappeared for good.

"He *is* a bit strange," Sara said. "Sweet though."

"He had it pretty hard growing up," Adam said. "No real family at all, so he's sort of learning what it is like. Not that we are a good example." He scowled.

"All I see is that Wes is a wonderful friend," his mother said. That last bit put Adam over the edge. Tears rolled down his cheeks and wrenched his body in silent shudders. He couldn't move and he couldn't speak, Ma and Sara hugging him through the bars.

"I messed it all up," he finally managed.

"You saved my life," Sara cried into his chest.

I just made it harder.

"I forgave you a long time ago," she whispered. "It's time you forgive yourself."

He stared at her, realizing his actions had been governed by his love for Sara and Ma. Even the hate he'd felt for Nathan Billings was gone. In some way he felt sorry for Nathan, who'd been despised by his stepfather and had never known his real father.

"Promise me you'll help Wes…when this is over." Adam glanced at the barred window as if he could see Wes somewhere beyond. "He has no other place."

"It isn't over yet," his mother said. "I will not accept defeat until it is over."

"Promise me," Adam cried.

His mother sighed. "Sara and I will take him in. I know Mr. Porter is glad for the help."

Adam turned his back and dropped on the bed.

He had less than seven days left to live.

CHAPTER FORTY-ONE

If anything, Monday morning's courtroom was even more packed. Everyone fell silent as Adam was marched to the defendant's table. In their eyes, he was as good as dead. A triple murderer and arsonist who'd slandered a good family's name to defend himself.

Dowell looked somber when he plunked into his seat. Miller looked as if he'd already won, his face smug, trying to appear grave.

"Mr. Miller, do you have a last statement?"

"Your Honor, if I may," Miller said. "I'd like to say that I'm sure that justice will prevail today. A terrible crime was committed, taking from our community one of our most esteemed families. Just yesterday we laid to rest those who could not help themselves... whose innocent lives were lost."

"Hear, hear," several voices shouted.

Miller smiled. "All we can do now is bring judgment to the person responsible for this unmentionable bloodshed, so that he may burn in hell for eternity."

Whistles and clapping erupted in the crowd. Adam sat frozen, his arms and legs cold and unfeeling as if his head were the only thing left alive. Yet, he couldn't think, his mind filled with cotton, his ears ringing.

"Mr. Brown, do you have anything more to say?" Dowell leaned forward, peering over his glasses.

"No," Adam whispered. He cleared his throat. "Nothing," he shouted.

"Very well, then." Dowell tilted toward the jury box. "Have

you reached the verdict?"

A tall man, Adam remembered seeing once in the general store, stood. "We have, your Honor. We find the defendant guilty on all charges."

Adam heard a suppressed sob behind him and he knew it was from his mother. She'd been brave and held onto the belief that the truth would come out.

But instead of shock he felt a terrible fury taking hold. His body tensed. Sweat poured from his armpits. He wanted to shout and hit somebody. For a brief moment he thought of running. They'd shoot him, of course, but that was better than being hanged. Still, he owed his mother and Sara a good-bye.

New shouts broke out in the back of the courtroom. "Let me through," somebody yelled. "Step aside."

Adam blinked in disbelief as he recognized Wes shoving his way through the crowd. His eyes flashed and his hair stood in all directions.

"Your Honor," Wes yelled. "I've got another witness."

Judge Dowell who'd been talking to the court's clerk looked up. "Mr. Westfield, you are disturbing my courtroom."

"Sir, everyone calls me Wes."

Adam swallowed. What was Wes up to?

"And what business is it of yours to appear now? The verdict has been made."

Chuckles rang out behind Adam while Miller shook his head, mumbling something like imbecile and idiot.

"Sir, I believe when it comes to truth, it is never too late," Wes said.

"Wise words, young man." Dowell paused as his gaze wandered around the courtroom that held a collective breath. "This is highly unusual...but..." His eyes lodged on Adam and swiveled back to Wes. "What is it you want to tell us?"

"Sir, I brought a witness who is willing to testify and who will confirm Adam's story." Wes turned and waved at a man standing behind him. In his fifties, he was no taller than Wes and except for his wide shoulders looked almost elfin. "This is Colonel Edgar Tuttle who'd like to say a few words."

"I hate for the court to waste any more time," Miller intercepted.

"As far as I know I'm still in charge," Judge Dowell said. "The war tried to teach us that a man's life has little meaning. I beg to differ. A few minutes won't hurt when it comes to condemning a man. Why don't you come forward, Colonel?"

Tuttle nodded and seated himself on the witness stand.

Deep lines furrowed his face, camouflaging a four-inch scar across his right cheek. His eyes were light blue, almost watery. Despite his small stature and thinning gray hair, his authority was unmistaken.

"As Mr. Westfield said, I'm Edgar Tuttle. I was a Colonel in the Union, but that is of little consequence for what I'm about to say." He leaned back a moment as if to gather his thoughts.

"Many years ago I was acquainted with Mrs. Janet Billings. Back then her name was Barnes. She and I were in love." A small smile crept on Tuttle's face as if he were reliving his memories while the courtroom exhaled a collective sigh. "I wanted to marry her, and she wanted to marry me. Foolish young people we were. Her parents didn't approve. They thought I wasn't good enough. I'd joined the cavalry and was rising in rank fast, but Janet's parents were wealthy. They had other plans."

Adam listened in awe at the man in front of him. What was he up to?

"Sir, I hope you're getting to the point here soon." Judge Dowell inspected his golden pocket watch. "It's almost lunchtime."

Tuttle nodded, but didn't seem upset. "Janet wanted to run away with me, but I had enlisted and could not take care of her the way she deserved. I begged her to wait for me until I had made something of myself. Tuttle took out an embroidered handkerchief and wiped his forehead.

"But her parents had found a perfect match—Mr. Jack Billings. Janet...she didn't want to marry...she was heartbroken. About two months before her wedding she came to visit. Janet was distraught. She said she'd never love another man and that she wanted only me. I was upset too, but I had committed to serve. One thing led to another...It was wrong, I know." Tuttle looked up, his eyes unseeing. "She was expecting by the time she married Jack Billings."

The courtroom exploded in shouts and Dowell smacked his gavel as if he wanted to take apart his desk.

Tuttle continued. "I saw her one final time when she came to tell me about the baby. I asked her to marry me on the spot, but

Janet was scared that her parents would find out about her pregnancy. She married Jack Billings. We'd written often, but she never answered my last letter. It was the last correspondence we had."

"So what you're telling us is that Adam Brown spoke the truth about the letters. And that Nathan Billings was indeed your son and not the son of Jack Billings."

"That's right," Tuttle said. "I wouldn't have come. I wanted to put it all behind me forever, especially hearing about Nathan's terrible actions. But when I heard that a man, a fellow soldier, was accused of lying when I knew it was the truth…Well I came. I know Janet Billings kept my letters. I met her once years later at a ball, and she told me. She was very afraid her husband would find them one day. I was mad at her at the time, thinking that she should've told Nathan about me. But we all do things, we have secrets that are difficult to explain."

"This is hardly evidence," Miller shouted, ignoring the ruckus behind him.

"But this is." Tuttle rummaged in his pocket and held up a wrinkled paper. This is the letter I wrote her once I found out that she was carrying my child."

"Why don't you read it out loud, Colonel Tuttle?" Judge Dowell struck his gavel. But there was no need. The crowd quieted to catch every word.

Dearest Janet,

I'm deeply moved about your news. You're with child and I cannot bear the thought that somebody else will raise our child. I want others to know, I want to marry you. Please cancel your wedding, and I promise we shall be together very soon. I'll ask for leave as soon as I hear from you. Let us make arrangements so that I can love you the way you deserve to be loved. Write to me soon.

Yours always,
Edgar Tuttle, Corporal

"I'm curious, though," Dowell said into the lingering silence. "How did you come about a letter that you'd written to Janet so many years ago?"

Tuttle nodded. "Mr. Westfield found it in Adam's pocket, the only way it survived the fire." As the courtroom exploded in shouts and the jurors looked at each other, Adam stared at Tuttle and then Wes. He must've put the letter in his pocket during the fight.

"May I see it?"

Tuttle handed over the paper. Judge Dowell tapped his chin with a forefinger while he read. At last he looked up. "Sir, have put an impossible spin on our verdict this morning. I must recluse myself now to think about our next steps." He smacked the gavel. "We shall reconvene shortly."

As Dowell disappeared into his chambers, Adam turned to make eye contact with Wes.

"How'd you do it?"

Wes shrugged. "I was lucky, rode Charlie to Knoxville and asked at the fort. They had records, and Tuttle had recently returned from the war and retired nearby. At first he didn't want to go, but I told him you'd die unless he shared his story. He was quite moved seeing the letter." Wes frowned. "I hope I'm not too late."

Adam's mother dabbed her eyes. "You did more than any of us could've expected. I'll always be grateful no matter what happens."

Despite the late lunch hour, none of the bystanders left, everyone too curious what the Judge would decide. When Dowell finally showed up, his face gave nothing away. Without introduction he addressed the jury.

"Because of what came to light this morning, I'm going to ask you to return to deliberation. It is obvious that Adam spoke the truth about the Billings's fight. Nathan Billings was not the son of Jack Billings. He was likely distraught about learning this news." Dowell gazed across his spectacles. "While we can only speculate what happened inside the Billings estate during the fire, we do have testimony from a young man. And the parts that we could confirm with the help of Colonel Tuttle are true." Dowell paused. "Furthermore, Adam served three years in the Army. And while we may disagree which side is right, we can agree that a soldier is bound by his values. By the truth." Dowell gazed at Adam and then to the jury. "I will send for refreshment momentarily."

One by one, the jurors left the room. Everyone else remained as if they were afraid of missing a crucial piece of information.

"What now?" Sara asked, her eyes puffy from earlier.

"We wait." Wes waved at Tuttle, who joined them. "I can't tell you how thankful I am." Ma gripped Tuttle's right hand. "Regardless of what happens."

Tuttle bowed and squeezed onto the bench next to her. "Pleased to make your acquaintance, Mrs. Brown." He nodded at Adam. "I hope justice will prevail."

"I'm sure it wasn't easy to revisit all this," Adam's mother said.

"It was a long time ago." Tuttle smiled, his eyes not following. "Much has happened to all of us. It made me realize one thing. My love for Janet was one of the happiest times of my life. I'll always be grateful for that."

To Adam's surprise, his mother's cheeks reddened. "I hope you're going to join us for dinner and—"

The door to the jury room opened and, one-by-one, the jurors filed in.

"Have you reached the verdict?" Dowell said.

The same man stood. "We have, your Honor."

Adam held his breath. This was it.

"We find the defendant, Adam Brown, not guilty on all charges."

The gavel cracked. "Case dismissed."

For a brief moment the courtroom remained silent. Then followed an explosion of hollers and screams in the first row. Adam sat staring at Judge Dowell who looked relieved.

He wanted to feel relief too, yet he just sat, words and scenes tumbling through his mind.

The room turned blurry and a tremble ran through him.

He was free.

He'd be able to help Sara and his mother.

Wes climbed over the banister and slapped him on the back. "I think this calls for a pint. My throat is truly parched."

Without a word Adam got up and hugged him tight. "You saved my life. Again," he whispered. "I'll never forget it."

When he pulled back, Wes's eyes were shiny. "You're a pain in the ass, but you're my best friend." He paused as a tinge of red crept into his cheeks. "I reckon it was fair after what you did."

"How so?"

"My uncle... you saved my bacon. I'll never forget that."

They looked at each other and Wes began to grin, then broke

into a chuckle. A gurgle broke through Adam's throat, followed by a roar. Pretty soon they just stood there, bending at the waist, slapping each other on the back, tears running down their faces.

When Adam came up for breath, his mother, Sara and Tuttle surrounded him, followed by Allister and Mr. Porter and assorted neighbors. Some of the same people who'd wanted his head a few hours earlier now told him they'd known all along he was innocent.

"You're free to go," Sheriff Tate said. "I do need a word with Sara, though."

Wiping his face, Adam put a protective arm around her shoulder. "What about?"

"Mr. Bird has asked for a meeting." Tate waved at a man waiting a few feet away. He wasn't much over five feet tall and wore golden spectacles and an immaculate shirt and vest.

"Who's Mr. Bird?" Wes mumbled aggressively as if he were ready to take on the next opponent.

"No need to get angry, Wes," Tate said. "Mr. Bird is a solicitor."

"What does he want?" Adam asked, anticipating another disaster.

Bird hustled closer, his expression serious and businesslike. "I've got to discuss a matter of high importance with Mrs. Billings," he said, his voice high yet indignant.

"Nothing you say that can't be shared with my kin," Sara said.

Bird squinted in disapproval. "Fine then, I do suggest though that we go somewhere more private. My office, perhaps?"

They all looked at each other. "You lead the way, Mr. Bird," Adam's mother said.

Bird rummaged through a stack of papers on his desk and pulled out a folder. "Ah yes, here it is." He peeked at Sara before continuing. "Mrs. Billings. I'm the executor of Mr. Jack Billings's estate. Since you were married to Nathan, you are the only surviving family member and therefore the only heir."

"What are you saying?" Adam asked.

"I'm saying, Mr. Brown, that your sister is a very rich woman." Bird consulted his document. "It appears that Mr. Billings owned vast tracks of land, several saw mills, and a tobacco plantation in southern Tennessee along with assorted accounts. And though the main house burned with all its possessions, Jack was a careful man who believed in insurance." He bent forward. "I've taken the liberty of contacting the insurance company on your behalf. They're prepared to send imbursement of $100,000 in tomorrow's post. I shall deposit it in your account at First Tennessee Bank."

Everyone gasped, but Bird went on.

"Now I'll need some signatures so that we can complete the property transfer. I trust you'll continue to retain my services to manage your affairs?"

Sara nodded. "I...yes, thank you." With a shaky hand she took Bird's ink pen and signed her name.

"Congratulations, Mrs. Billings." Bird bowed. "Just send word when you want to discuss building another home. I know the most excellent architect."

Sara rose and held out a hand. "Thank you, Mr. Bird. I'll be in touch."

Adam followed his sister, whose world had just turned a hundred eighty degrees. As they entered the street, screams erupted up and down the sidewalk.

A boy hurried past, waving his arms. "General Lee has surrendered. The war is over. The Union won!"

Wes hollered and slapped Adam on the back. "It's about rotten time," he shouted.

They exchanged a quiet nod, an acknowledgement of shared fate, of friendship and redemption.

As a weak April sun crept from behind the clouds, a melody rose from Adam's throat past his lips into the world. He whistled *An Old Oaken Bucket*, the tune Wes had hummed when they'd first met.

In the evening, after an excellent meal of roasted chicken, fried potatoes, baked rolls with butter and his mother's famous apple pie, they sat around the fire. Relief was written on their faces. Relief about Adam's fate, but most of all about the war being finished at last.

"I'd like to discuss my plans," Sara said. She straightened and looked at everyone. "I'm now in the position to buy things. Lots of things. But I need help. I don't know what to do, so I want us all to decide together."

"We must repay Mr. Porter." Adam's mother glanced at

Colonel Tuttle, whose pipe filled the air with fragrant puffs of smoke.

"I will do that tomorrow, with interest," Sara said, smiling at Allister. "What do you want?" Sara asked Adam.

"Help you build a house, I guess. Or start a new farm, a bigger one with lots of cattle."

Sara eyed him curiously. "I thought you had other plans."

Adam shrugged, glancing at Wes, who sat quietly in back, his gaze withdrawn as if he weren't there.

"Something wrong?" Adam whispered.

Wes shook his head. "I better be going tomorrow," he said, avoiding Adam's eyes.

"What're you talking about?"

"I mean now that you're with your kin and you're...rich, I don't want to intrude any longer." Wes blinked, his eyes glittering.

"And where exactly are you going?" Adam said.

Wes shrugged.

"I really need a manager," Sara interrupted. "I thought of you, Wes. I can't imagine not having you around."

Wes looked up, his mouth working, a slow smile spreading across his face. "You serious?"

Sara nodded and her blue eyes flashed the way Adam remembered from years ago. "Please stay with us. You aren't just Adam's best friend, you're part of our family."

That last word unleashed something as Wes suddenly bent low, hiding his face. Only his shoulders shook. Adam looked at his mother and Sara, and patted Wes on the head.

"You're one of us now," he whispered quietly.

Wes finally looked up, wiping a sleeve across his eyes. He wore the biggest smile Adam had ever seen.

CHAPTER FORTY-TWO

Tip slowed. Any moment he'd see the Billings's main house. Though he'd taken the train most of the way, he was exhausted, the late April air announcing rain.

President Lincoln's assassination had shaken him to the core. Still, the war was finished—the South had lost and according to the law, he was a free man. But one never knew. He had no papers that confirmed he was a freeman. He'd heard of lynching and attacks on coloreds. Slave traders still roamed the country, even in the north.

He'd made peace with the fact that Mama Rose and Adam were gone, but there was still Elda. Chances were she was long married. But maybe he'd find where she'd gone or where his mama lay buried. Somebody had to know and he wanted to see her, speak to her one last time. Learn about his mother's death.

The bag Tip carried dropped to the ground. He stood rigid, staring at the charcoaled remains of the largest mansion in Greeneville. It was all gone, the porch he'd labored on reduced to a few charcoaled remains, the house dissolved. Five chimneys lay in crumbled heaps. The kitchen where Mama Rose had created her famous dishes was hidden under rubble.

Unsure what to do, Tip turned back toward town. He pulled a handkerchief from his pocket and wiped his face. Everything he'd called home was no more. The only person he'd ever loved was gone. Maybe Elda had perished in the fire.

He meandered through town bustling with wagons and merchants. Women carried baskets filled with goods from the mercantile, men nodded their hats at each other. For a moment Tip contemplated going into the store to ask about the fire.

Instead he continued past the shop, down the hill past the bank and the lawyer's office. Deep down, he was still afraid to enter a business. Visions of Rawley returned, the vein on his temple pulsing with rage. In his heart, Tip knew Rawley would go under, if he hadn't already. He took a deep breath, realizing he'd never again suffer from the hands of another.

His feet carried him into the woods, across the low rising hill down toward Adam's farm. Maybe somebody else lived there, somebody who knew what had happened to Adam and his family.

His steps slowed again. In the distance he made out the remnants of a farmhouse, the chimney the only thing intact. He hurried closer, hoping deep down that he'd somehow confused the place. But no, there was the overgrown vegetable patch, the chicken coop in shambles and the old barn half collapsed. Adam's home was no more.

Tip made his way into the barn and sank to his knees.

The world he'd known had disappeared. The war had taken it all. And though he was free now without a master to tell him what was right, he was a prisoner of his past.

He couldn't breathe. Thoughts of Giselle and Ann returned. He could've stayed with either one, gotten married and raised a family.

But no, he'd run off thinking that something better was waiting for him. Ann had finally succeeded in luring him to her bed a few times in hopes his heart would warm to her.

He'd wanted it to, but no matter how he tried, it was no use. He'd worked alongside Ann's uncles in the beer factories of Cincinnati for nearly fifteen months, bought little gifts for baby Louis and paid his share for meals. In the end, he couldn't move on to a new life with Ann, his soul unable to rest, an abyss of sorrow for an existence that was no longer.

City life was stifling. At night, the streets filled with thousands of dwellers whose shared quarters drove them to socialize outside. The air was filled with the smoke of factories and the stench of too many humans. Tip longed for his garden, his bare feet touching the fresh soil, the aroma of fruits and berries, the joy of seeing things grow, even the composting smells of rotting leaves.

A long time ago he'd told Adam he was going to have a farm.

He'd loved gardening and the feel of fresh air on his face. All he did was walk the narrow streets that reeked of garbage and work inside factory walls and dank cellars.

When Ann finally gave him an ultimatum to get married or leave, he'd taken his meager savings and said his good-byes. And one way or another, his feet always traveled south. Though he was independent as they said, he had nothing now, nothing to look forward to. No friends. No place. No home. The freedom he had so longed for meant little without somebody to share it with.

He kneeled and picked up a small wooden cage, its door open. Memories of Adam fixing the Robin's wing returned. Adam had not only accepted him as a human being, but a friend. He thought of the way Adam's eyes turned dreamy when he talked about becoming a veterinary surgeon. Adam's dreams were as dead as his own.

A sob rose in the stillness. He realized he didn't know where to turn or for that matter why to bother. He was a piece of driftwood on the Ohio River.

He'd tried the impossible. Make the past return. *You're a fool,* Tipper. You were a slave. Owned by others like furniture. To do with and discard as they pleased.

But he'd had his Mama and Elda. Now he had nobody and no home.

He chuckled, thinking of Pip in Dickens' 'Great Expectations' walking through the mist where Satis house used to stand. Here he was back home just like Pip, but Elda was gone just like Biddy was married to Joe. Unlike Pip, who'd met Estella for a happy ending, he was alone.

"You're a fool," he said into the stillness. "Life ain't no book."

By the time he rose, it was dusk and a cool wind tore at this coat. It was too dark to read, his last candle long gone.

Tomorrow he'd make a plan, find work some place. Or should he volunteer for the Army? He'd heard about great victories, black regiments had accomplished. He spit. The papers had made it sound as if this was highly unusual. As if coloreds couldn't fight just as well or better than whites. He spit again. Even in the north there were prejudices. Many people didn't care for coloreds just like in the south.

At least the German immigrants in the beer industry had been accepting. They'd worked side-by-side twelve hours a day. One man's sweat was as good as the next. No, he wouldn't join any army.

He'd leave this area forever. Go back north to Cincinnati where he felt safer, where many coloreds had created homes among the German immigrants. He'd work hard and start a family. Get his own place, a decent home with two or three rooms and a yard to grow a garden.

He sauntered into the corner and dug under a pile of moldy straw. A grim smile played on his face. Maybe he'd look for Giselle on the way. Other than Ann, she was the only other person he'd cherished who wasn't dead.

Adam saddled Charlie. "A nice ride will do you good."

Mist lay like milk over the land. It was his favorite time of morning, the spring air crisp and still, the day full of possibilities. He breathed deeply as he led the stallion away from Porter's farm and let him gallop across the meadows, marveling at Charlie's speed, his powerful strides. All he did was bend forward and feel the strength as the wind filled his ears and nose, his body responding to the up and down of the saddle.

It was time to leave the Porter's. Now that Sara was free she would marry Allister. For him there was only one place, Pa's farm. It was the one spot he felt truly at home and almost at peace. He gently guided Charlie through the woods and familiar fields.

The old ache tugged at him as he approached the burned-down ruins. He remembered how Tip had been here looking for help, the bloody pulp of his back, the swollen-shut eye.

With Wes's assistance he'd build a new place, a bit larger maybe, but nothing outrageous. He'd use the rock from the old fireplace to build a new one and move the new house farther down the hill to overlook the pond.

Deep in thought, he dismounted and wandered along the deserted ground. He'd grow wheat and corn, maybe a bit of tobacco. It'd make him feel closer to Pa.

A rustling from the barn made him stop. He threw a glance at Charlie fifty yards away. His rifle was secured to the saddle. There were vagabonds everywhere, men who'd lost their homes, bandits and slave catchers. After four years of war, the country was stirred up and dangerous like a muddy river with lethal currents.

There…another sound. He abruptly turned and broke into a

run toward Charlie. He'd feel much better if he had a weapon. The back of his neck began to tingle as he reached for his rifle and swung around.

A black man stood in the remnants of the barn entrance, his gaze a mixture of sadness and mild curiosity, an inch-wide scar on his cheek.

"Top of the morning," the man said as he brushed remnants of straw from his shirt. He looked well dressed, wearing dark pants, a vest, and a floppy hat.

"Morning to you," Adam said. He carefully moved closer, one eye on the man, the other on the barn. Maybe there were others ready to attack.

The man also took a few steps. "You from these parts?"

"As a matter of fact I..." Adam's throat tightened. He knew this man, he knew the way he stood, his head tilting left just the slightest, the scar across the right eyebrow. "Tip," he croaked.

Tip froze, his eyes wide. He opened his mouth and yet nothing came out. He swallowed and tried again. "It cannot be," he cried. "God has taken me into a dream to meet my old friend again."

The next seconds were a blur as the friends embraced.

"I thought you were dead." Tears spilled down Adam's cheeks. Almost four years had passed, sending him away on a life-and-death ride. Nothing was the same and yet, everything was. In that moment it was as if no time had gone by, his old friend was back.

"I thought *you* was dead." Tip wiped his eyes and attempted a smile. "Where you live now?"

"With Mr. Porter. It's a long story, but I'm going to rebuild this place. Pa would've wanted me to, and Ma needs a place to grow old."

A shadow crept over Tip's face. "Whatever happened to the Billings? The house gone." Tip went on. "I come to visit, see what happen to Mama Rose. I send her a letter and it get returned."

"Everyone died."

Fresh tears appeared in Tip's eyes. Adam slapped himself on the mouth. "I'm such an idiot. I mean all the Billings are dead, Mr. Billings, Janet and Nathan." He meant to say he'd witnessed everything, but the memory of Janet Billings's bedroom still made him cringe. With all the senseless killing of the war, this seemed to have been the most senseless and tragic of all. "Your Mama is staying with us," he hurried, "...and Elda. Mama Rose isn't well, so—"

"My mama alive, and Elda with her?" cried Tip.

Adam nodded, taking in his old friend's expression of wonder. "She had a stroke and doesn't get out much anymore." Then Adam smiled and the smile grew until his eyes began to tear again. A chuckle bubbled from his middle and he slapped Tip on the back. "I thought I'd never see you again."

Not that long ago he'd lost everything, or so he thought. He'd wanted to die and then he wanted to live again. He'd lost his family and found them again. He'd lost his best friend, and now here he was, a grown man—no longer a slave but a free man standing proud. Somehow, through all the suffering he, Adam Brown, had taken a tiny part in helping to make it happen. It had all been worth it.

Tip rode behind Adam as they approached the Porter's farm. On the front porch, an old woman sat bundled in blankets, her head drooped forward in sleep, her mouth open.

Tip slid off the horse and quietly walked toward the house just as the front door opened. A young woman in a red and white-checkered dress appeared, carrying a tray with a pitcher and two glasses. She was about to put down the tray when her eyes lodged on the visitor.

A hand went to her mouth as she swayed, and Tip worried she might fall and break the dishes.

"Elda?"

"Tip."

Tip flew up the stairs and embraced the girl who'd grown into a woman. A woman he didn't know at all. "I thought I lost you."

Elda shook her head, her face pressed against his chest, her tears soaking his shirt. Tip marveled at the small body in his arms, his chin easily resting on her head. His heart pounded, and a wave of heat swept through him. It was the comfortable warmth of logs burning in a woodstove in the middle of winter, a heat he wanted to bathe in forever.

"You get my lemonade?" a feeble voice said behind them.

Elda abruptly leaned back, a teary smile on her face. "I have something else you really love," she said with a trembling voice.

"Oh, child, what an old woman need?"

Tip turned and dropped to his knees next to the chair as Mama Rose's gaze tried to focus on his face. With shock he noticed the wrinkles furrowing her skin like deep ruts in a field. Her left arm lay uselessly on her lap. "Mama, it's me, Tip. Your son."

"Mama Rose not see too well on her left," Elda said. "Move over a bit."

Tip slumped across his mother's lap, so that his face was right in front of her.

"Tipper?" Her good hand lifted to pat his cheek. "I gone to paradise to see my boy."

"No, Mama, I am right here." Tip leaned into the warmth, the touch he'd longed for, the home he'd missed. "I ain't ever leave you again."

CHAPTER FORTY-THREE

Thanksgiving 1865—Seven Months Later
Sara shouted over the din, "Time to eat!"

One-by-one, people assembled around the huge dining table, the air heavy with the aroma of roasted turkey, leg of lamb, potatoes, beans, fresh bread and apple pie. Wes clapped Allister on the back. His eyes flashed a smile. The race was on. Both of them shared the reputation of making huge amounts of food disappear in record time.

They had developed an easy friendship, exchanging strategies about farming and raising livestock. For the time being, Wes stayed with Allister and Sara to help them get a grip on the vast holdings Sara had inherited.

Sometimes when Sara felt unobserved, a shadow traveled across her features as if an old wound hadn't quite healed. After her inheritance, Allister and Sara had married and bought a large piece of land near Adam's old farm. The new house was about done, and they'd gathered to celebrate Adam's visit.

"I thought he'd be here by now." Adam's mother wiped her hands on her apron. She lived with Sara and Allister and kept a tight rein on the vegetable garden.

"He said afternoon." Tip's one palm lay protectively on Elda's middle, the other on his mama's shoulder.

Tip and Elda had married within a month of Tip's return, and Elda was four months pregnant. Mama Rose had had a miraculous recovery. At least that's what the doctor had proclaimed after her speech returned. She walked with a cane and dragged her left foot, but she was mobile and a force in the kitchen. Adam had put Tip in charge of rebuilding his family's farm with two houses, one for Adam and one for Tip and his kin.

Everywhere you looked, fields, paths and forests carried deep ruts like knife wounds. Fathers, cousins, uncles, brothers and nephews had returned home, reuniting families and mourning the dead. Everyone had lost someone and everyone had injuries, some obvious like the wounds on Tip's face, some deeply buried. With the war, the country had lost its moral compass and yet, Lincoln had made it possible to regain their pride. Tip and his mama were free now. All coloreds were free.

After Lincoln's assassination in April and the end of the war, the sense of loss and confusion was slowly fading. Stomachs and larders were empty, fields lay bare, and there was no time to sit idle. They had to regroup and move forward. The American spirit was reawakening, albeit slowly and reluctantly. People were ready to mend the scars of the earth and the scars in their hearts.

"Where is that boy?" Adam's mother said for the tenth time, a worry frown above her nose. She nodded at Mama Rose who was watching over the stove. "We better eat. No sense waiting."

Old Mr. Porter bowed his head. "Let's pray." He'd gained a few more wrinkles, but his eyes shone as young as ever. He wasn't busy enough these days, he often said, though they all knew he was happy to leave the hard work to their newly hired farmhands.

The door flew open and banged against the opposite wall. "Sorry we're late." Adam strode into the house, bringing a wind gust with him. "I brought a guest," he yelled much too loud. "My fiancé."

The girl next to him wore her hair in a braid and took in the welcoming room, the smiling faces and laden table. "I'm Lillian, glad to make your acquaintance."

"Well done," Allister cried.

Wes whistled and Tip jumped up and bear-hugged Adam before bowing politely toward the girl.

"Come sit with me." Sara took Lillian by the elbow. "Just ignore these idiots and tell me about your travels. You must be hungry and tired."

Adam embraced his mother, noticing with relief that her eyes had a new sparkle. "You look well."

She patted his cheek, wind-burned from a long trip. "How is veterinary school?"

Adam beamed. He looked around the room at his friends who had become his family, Ma, Sara and his love. They'd survived terrible hardships, all of them. And yet here they were, together, stronger than before—united.

Pa would've been proud.

THE END

AUTHOR NOTES

The U.S. Civil War (April 1861 – April 1865) was the bloodiest war in American history, a conflict that pinned brother against brother and split thousands of families. More than 600,000 men died as a result of battles, starvation and disease. Much has been written about the largest and bloodiest battles and the leading men who fought and died. As usual I wanted to show a lesser-known angle, that of a young man and his best friend, one of over three million 'common' soldiers and the parallel ordeal of a slave fighting for his freedom. While all main characters are fictional—to me they are, of course, quite real—the battle scenes and war-related leaders are based on history.

Historical Battles Depicted in this Novel
Though Adam fought in many skirmishes, he participated in four noteworthy Civil War battles:

The Battle of Barboursville, Kentucky (today Barbourville) on September 19, 1861, was tiny yet significant because it presented the first decisive win by the Confederate Army and shook the somewhat complacent and self-confident North into action.

The Battle of Mill Springs on January 19, 1862 marked the first larger Union victory, stopping Confederate Brig. General Felix Zollicoffer from taking a stronghold in Kentucky. Unbeknownst to Zollicoffer, Union Brig. General George H. Thomas had requested and received additional enforcements and drove the Confederate Army back into Tennessee. Zollicoffer was killed.

The Battle of Salineville, Ohio on July 26, 1863 was part of Morgan's Raid and one of the northern most skirmishes in the war. Starting in Kentucky, Confederate Captain John Hunt Morgan carved a swath of destruction through Kentucky, Indiana and Ohio. Intent on drawing attention away from the Confederate movements in southern Kentucky, Morgan survived the battle, a decisive victory for the Union, but was caught a few miles away.

The Battle of Rogersville, Tennessee on November 6, 1863 was a surprise attack orchestrated by Confederate Brig. General William Jones against an unsuspecting Union force occupying Rogersville.

FROM THE AUTHOR

Thank you for reading EVERYTHING WE LOSE: A Civil War Novel of Hope, Courage and Redemption. My sincere hope is that you derived as much entertainment from reading this story as I enjoyed in creating it. If you have a few moments, please feel free to add your review of the book at your favorite online site for feedback (Amazon, Apple iTunes Store, Barnes & Noble, Kobo, Goodreads, etc.). Also, if you would like to connect with previous or upcoming books, please visit my website for information and to sign up for e-news: http://www.annetteoppenlander.com.

All the best, Annette

Contact Me

I always appreciate hearing from readers. Please contact me via the following social media channels:

Website: www.annetteoppenlander.com
Facebook: www.facebook.com/annetteoppenlanderauthor
Twitter: @aoppenlander
Pinterest: @annoppenlander

ABOUT THE AUTHOR

Annette Oppenlander is an award-winning writer, literary coach and educator. As a bestselling historical novelist, Oppenlander is known for her authentic characters and stories based on true events, coming alive in well-researched settings. Having lived in Germany the first half of her life and the second half in various parts in the U.S., Oppenlander inspires readers by illuminating story questions as relevant today as they were in the past. Oppenlander's bestselling true WWII story, Surviving the Fatherland, was a winner in the 2017 National Indie Excellence Awards and a finalist in the 2017 Kindle Book Awards. Her historical time-travel trilogy, Escape from the Past, takes readers to the German Middle Ages and the Wild West. Uniquely, Oppenlander weaves actual historical figures and events into her plots, giving readers a flavor of true history while enjoying a good story. Oppenlander shares her knowledge through writing workshops at colleges, libraries and schools. She also offers vivid presentations and author visits. The mother of fraternal twins and a son, she recently moved with her husband and old mutt, Mocha, to Solingen, Germany.

"Nearly every place holds some kind of secret, something that makes history come alive. When we scrutinize people and places closely, history is no longer a date or number, it turns into a story."

If you enjoyed EVERYTHING WE LOSE, you may also like my #1 bestselling novel, SURVIVING THE FATHERLAND: A True Coming-of-age Love Story Set in WWII Germany. Winner of the 2017 National Indie Excellence and Finalist in the 2017 Kindle Book Awards, this novel took fifteen years to complete and is based on my parents growing up as war children in WWII Germany.

SURVIVING THE FATHERLAND

A True Coming-of-age Love Story Set in WWII Germany

CHAPTER ONE

Lilly: May 1940

For me the war began, not with Hitler's invasion of Poland, but with my father's lie. I was seven at the time, a skinny thing with pigtails and bony knees, dressed in my mother's lumpy hand-knitted sweaters, a girl who loved her father more than anything.

It was May of 1940, my favorite time of year when the air is filled with the smell of cut grass and lilacs, promising excursions to town and the cafes in the hilly land I called home.

Like any other weekend, my father came home that Friday carrying a heavy briefcase of folders. Only this time, he flung his case in the corner of the hallway like it was a bag of garbage. You have to understand. My father is a neat freak, a man who keeps himself and everything he touches in absolute order. And so even at seven—even before he said those fateful words—I knew something was different.

My father had been named after the German emperor, Wilhelm, and Mutti called him Willi, but to me he was always Vati.

Ignoring me, he hurried into the kitchen, his eyes bright with excitement. "I've been drafted."

At the sink, Mutti abruptly dropped her sponge and stared at him. Her mouth opened, then closed without a sound.

I didn't understand what he was talking about. I didn't understand the meaning of a lie, yet I felt it even then. Like others detect an oncoming thunderstorm, pressure builds behind my forehead, a heaviness in my bones. There is something in the way the liar moves, his limbs hang stiffly on the body as if his soul cringes. His look at me is fleeting and there is something artificial in his voice.

At that moment I knew Vati was hiding something from us.

"They want me there Monday. I'll be a captain." His voice trembled as he sank into a chair, still wearing his coat and hat.

"But that's in three days." Mutti picked up Burkhart, my little brother who was a just a toddler and had begun to whine. "It's fine," she soothed as she paced the length of the kitchen, the click-click of her heels like an accusation.

I frowned and moved closer to my father. Since my brother's birth, Mutti had been spending every minute with the baby. No matter how well I behaved, how I did what she asked, I rarely succeeded drawing her eyes away from my brother. It annoyed me to no end that I couldn't stop myself from trying.

"Vati, where are you going?" I asked, secure in the knowledge that my little brother wouldn't draw away his attention.

My father's cheeks glowed with excitement. As if he hadn't heard me, he rushed back into the hallway and knelt in front of the wardrobe. I followed.

One door gaped open, revealing a gray military uniform. He was rummaging below.

"What are you looking for?"

"Just a minute." He emerged with a pair of shiny black boots.

He knelt at my level and to this day I remember smelling the cologne he used every morning, a mix of spice and citrus.

"I am packing."

"Where are you going?" Vati had never been away, not even for one night. In fact, he and Mutti had strict routines, and these were dictated by the clock. We ate every night at six thirty sharp. Even on Sundays. Breakfast was at seven in the morning. Clothes never ever lay on the floor, each item brushed and aired and returned to its spot in the closet. Life was laid out in rules, washing hands before dinner, carrying a clean handkerchief at all times and always, always looking spotless when leaving the house.

He smoothed the pants of his uniform. "I'll be helping out in the war."

"Will you be back for my birthday?" My birthday was on June fourth and I worried about our customary visits to town. In the window of *Wiesner*, our local toy store, I'd discovered a *Schildkröt* doll. Her name was Inge and I wanted her badly. Vati said she looked just like me, with blond hair and this pretty red-checkered dress with a white apron and white patent shoes you could take off.

As Vati lifted me in the air and turned in a circle, I shrieked in surprise and delight. I was flying.

"They want me after all! With all my experience, they should be glad."

Mutti put Burkhart on the floor and leaned in the doorframe to the kitchen, her arms folded across her chest. "I wish you didn't have to go."

"It's not so bad, Luise." Vati gripped her shoulders as if he wanted to infuse his excitement into her. "I'll be back soon. We're so much stronger than last time."

"All I see is Hitler sending more men into battle. Do you at least know where you're going?"

Vati shrugged. "Probably France or Scandinavia."

"Will you be back soon?" I tried again.

He patted my head and returned to his chair at the head of the table. "I'll be home before you've found time to miss me." As he began to whistle, something nagged my insides like a tiny clawing animal.

A screeching wail erupted. Sharp and metallic, it cut through doors and walls and echoed through the streets. No matter that the siren blasted every day, it made me shiver.

I watched my mother freeze, her eyes filled with something I would soon learn to recognize as fear. The siren continued—up, down, up, down. Another wail erupted. This time it sounded like the foghorn of a ship, signaling the end of the alarm.

Relieved that the horrible noise was over, I climbed on my father's lap, running a forefinger across the bluish stubble of his jaw. "Vati?"

"Not now, Lieselotte, we are talking," Mutti said.

I looked up in alarm. Mutti had said Lieselotte when everyone called me Lilly, a sure sign she was mad. I slid back off, keeping my hand on Vati's arm.

Mutti tucked a strand of pale hair behind her ear and slumped into a chair. "I hate these air raid sirens."

Vati didn't look up from the newspaper. "It's just a test... a precaution."

Mutti abruptly straightened. "I should work on dinner. You *do* remember that my brother is visiting tonight?" Two red spots that didn't quite match her lipstick glowed on her cheeks. "Lilly, there's honey all over this table. Wash out the dishrag and wipe this down."

"Yes, Mutti." I clumsily scrubbed the surface, glancing back and forth between my parents. Vati's eyes, usually a watery blue, sparkled like an early morning sky.

"Don't you see that this is important?" he said, letting the paper sink once more. "We're fighting against England and France, even Scandinavia! Our country needs us."

"You mean they need you."

"Everyone has a role to play."

"They didn't ask me if I wanted to play a role." Mutti's voice was shrill as she set a pot on the stove and began to peel potatoes. "I'll be stuck with two children to take care of."

"That's exactly what the Führer wants you to do. Girls are meant to be mothers and take care of our families. We take care of the rest."

"Like your war?"

Hearing my parents argue made my insides turn knotty. I wanted them to stop, yet I finished cleaning and said nothing. All I did was return to Vati's chair as their arguments continued flying like knives above my head.

"We have to make sacrifices," Vati said. "You're a strong woman. Besides, isn't the government taking care of things? Every family receives rations, even for clothes. They're thinking of everything."

"These ration cards are so cumbersome. And the sirens drive me crazy."

Vati got up and patted Mutti's back. "Don't worry, everything will work out fine.

During dinner, I continued watching my parents. Heavy silence lingered except for my brother's babble and the scraping of spoons across porcelain bowls.

I didn't taste much of the soup. My eyes were drawn to the stony faces on either side as I recalled the events of the afternoon, wondering if I had done something to make them angry. In that stillness of the kitchen, I sensed that my life was about to change. Something dreadful lingered like a wolf lying in wait behind a bush ready to pounce. You didn't see it or hear it, yet you knew it was there.

"Tim says that women who wear lipstick are whores," I said, my gaze lingering on my mother's mouth where the remnants of lipstick clung to her lower lip.

"Who is Tim?" Mutti snapped.

"A boy in my class. His older brother is in the Hitler youth and they say girls should not paint their faces and listen to the men—"

"Young girls like yourself are pretty just the way they are," Vati said.

I was sure Tim had talked about all women and though I burned to know what a whore was, I decided to keep my mouth shut. My teacher's probing eyes appeared in my vision, and I remembered my earlier mission.

"Vati, will you read with me tonight?" I was a terrible reader, hated it, especially when I had to read aloud in class and Herr Poll slammed his ruler on my desk when I got stuck.

Mutti's mouth pressed together in a straight line as she headed for the window to pull down the blackout shutters. "Not tonight," she said. "Clear the table while I cover the other windows and change your brother. Then you get ready for bed."

Vati jumped up and disappeared in the living room. "We'll do it another time," he said before he closed the door.

As I watched Mutti carry Burkhart to bed, I felt as transparent as the air around me. But not in a comfortable way—more like a sore throat that sticks around and reminds you off and on that you're still sick.

After stacking our dishes in the sink, I followed my father, who was studying a file of papers.

"Vati?"

"What is it, Lilly?"

I hesitated. Was this a good time to ask about *Inge*, the doll? Vati was acting so strange. Even now his face had a damp shine to it as if he'd run to catch the streetcar.

"Nothing," I said. *Gute Nacht, Vati.*"

"Sweet dreams."

Disappointed, I quietly closed the door, stopping halfway to my bedroom. No sounds came from the kitchen.

I was about to climb into bed when the doorbell rang. I froze. Something bad was going to happen. Was the war coming to get Vati?

But when I heard voices in the corridor I recognized Mutti's brother, August, my favorite uncle. He always brought me gifts, a chocolate éclair, a flower from his garden or a bowl of sweet cherries.

I breathed again, growing aware of my icy feet on the linoleum.

By the sounds they'd gone into the living room, a perfect opportunity to see my uncle and find out more about Vati's plans. If I pretended my stomach ached, maybe, just maybe I could visit for a while. I bent over my brother who was lying on his back, his mouth relaxed in sleep, blonde curls framing his face. In that moment I envied him. It wouldn't be the last time.

On the other side of the wall, Vati shouted. Alarmed, I tiptoed into the hallway and peeked through the living room door. Uncle August, his legs stretched long in front of him, lounged on the sofa next to a young woman I didn't recognize, while Mutti sat on an armchair by the window.

"I don't believe this. How can you be so enthusiastic?" August's voice rose as he spoke, at the same time patting the young woman's knee. "Don't you remember the last war? You of all people."

"Nonsense," Vati said from somewhere beyond the door. "This war will be over quickly. Our weapons are superior. I mean, Poland practically fell in a day and France and Scandinavia aren't far behind."

August shook his head, his eyes squinting. "I don't understand how you turn your back on your family." His voice was filled with disgust. "Aren't you worried about leaving your wife and children? This damn thing gives me the creeps. The SS and Gestapo are watching our every step. Just the other day—"

"Shhh," the woman next to him said. "August, please be careful. What if somebody listens?"

"I'm not turning my back," Vati shouted. "We've got to do

our duty. Besides, the Führer is taking care of everyone."

August threw a glance at Mutti. "Since when can we trust the government?"

Mutti leaned forward. "The apartment below is vacant. When Willi leaves, I won't even have a neighbor to talk to," she choked, her eyes glistening. "You want me to ask Herr Baum? He's older than Methuselah and can barely walk, let alone help if things get worse."

I cringed. I liked the old man next door, especially his knobby hands that were brown and gnarled like miniature tree trunks. He always listened when I spoke as if what I said were important.

"I'm convinced this war will be over before the year is up." Vati sounded irritated, and there was that darkness again, that fakeness in his voice. "I, for my part, am proud to help out."

August jumped up so suddenly, I nearly banged my head against the doorframe. "Well, I'm not." His eyes narrowed. "I thought your job at the city was highly important. Strange they let their top civil engineer walk off like that."

The silence that followed reminded me of dinner when my parents hadn't spoken, yet I could hear their anger as clearly as if they'd screamed at each other. I no longer wanted to go inside, yet I couldn't leave, my legs as rigid as Herr Poll's ruler.

"Either way," August continued, "all I wanted was to introduce my fiancée, Annelise. I'm sorry I came."

Mutti stood up, wiping her eyes. "Please August, don't go yet. I'm sure it'll all work out."

"That's right," Vati said, sounding calm again. "Let's drink to your engagement. I'll get a bottle of wine from the cellar."

I rushed to my bedroom and curled up tightly the way I did during thunderstorms. It took me another hour to get to sleep, my mind firmly on the image of Vati handing me the doll, Inge, for my birthday.

CHAPTER TWO

Günter: May 1940

"Attention! Feet together, arms down, hands at your pant seams. Look straight. Stand still," the boy shouted. He was no more than sixteen, and the khaki uniform hung in folds around his narrow chest. The hair around his ears, shaved to the skin, left a tuft of blonde on top like a bird's nest.

He paced up and down in front of us, a row of eleven year-old boys, his eyes narrowed into angry slits. "Men," he yelled, "you are the future soldiers of Germany. You don't fight to die, but to win." He yanked open a book. "I quote. Nothing is more important than your courage. Only the strong person, carried by belief and the fighting desire of your own blood, will be master during danger." The book snapped shut. "I expect absolute obedience."

I stood next to my best friend, Helmut, at the sports stadium where the local Hitler youth met for drill. We'd lined up in rows of three deep in the middle of the grass-covered field. Another boy with red and blue patches on his shirt appeared in front of us.

"Tuck in your shirt, pull up your socks," he said, pointing at Helmut. "Look at the filth on your shoes. This is no way to dress. Show some pride."

From the corner of my eye, I watched Helmut adjust his shirt and rub his shoes. Helmut sometimes forgets about these things. Thankfully my own socks stretched to just below my knees. Still, I held my breath as the boy passed by. Earlier today we'd bought a uniform: black shorts and beige shirt, neckerchief with leather knot, armband, and the best part, a brand-new knife. Mother had grumbled about spending so much money.

"But Mutter, all boys have to go," I'd argued after we left the store. "They told us at school. It's our duty." I didn't tell her how excited I'd been about my new outfit. Most of the time I get the hand-me-downs from my older brother, Hans.

"What're they going to do with you?" she'd said, her voice stern with irritation.

"Make fires and camp." I didn't tell Mother that I couldn't wait trying out my new knife and going on adventures with a bunch of boys.

Now I waited in a line and couldn't move a muscle. Stupid.

"Attention! Turn left, march! One, two, one, two, follow me." Birdsnest headed down the field while the other youth observed, waiting for us to trip and fall out of line. We marched back and forth, left and right, crisscrossing the field. What a bore.

The air smelled of early summer and warmth. Dandelions and forget-me-nots dotted the grass like a colorful carpet. Imitating my classmates, I fought the urge to look around, keeping my head straight toward the horizon as if I could see what was coming a mile away.

A man in a brown uniform with a red armband watched from the sidelines. Distracted for a moment, I stepped on the heels of the fellow in front.

"Ouch," the boy yelled. "Watch yourself, idiot."

"You're the idiot. Why did you stop?" I said.

Birdsnest materialized in front of us. "What's going on here?"

"He stepped on me," the other boy said.

My cheeks felt hot. "He suddenly stopped."

"Name."

"What?"

"Your *name*."

"Günter Schmidt."

"Listen to me, Günter." Birdsnest's eyes narrowed. "Quit playing around. You're training to become a soldier. On the ground. Give me twenty pushups, quick."

"Yes, sir." I hurriedly dropped to the grass and hid my face because my head had turned into a super-heated balloon ready to fly away.

Out of breath I returned to the row, swallowing the choice words choking me. The marching continued, followed by singing:

"Our flag flies in front of us;
To the future we trek man for man,
We march for Hitler through night and adversity
With the youth's flag for freedom and bread.
Our flag flies in front of us,
Our flag is the new era,
Our flag leads us into eternity,
Yes, the flag is more than death.

Birdsnest continued reading from his book about becoming heroes, but my thoughts, sped up by the gnawing in my stomach, wandered to the dinner waiting at home. On dismissal, Birdsnest gave me a nasty look before reminding us to practice marching and standing to attention. He never mentioned camping or making fires. *Boring.* We weren't allowed to use our knives either. Worse, we'd have to go again Saturday.

By the time I arrived at my house, it was late and I was in a rotten mood. Helmut is much more of a talker, but he was grumpy, too, and we'd walked home in silence.

I lived on the first floor of an apartment house on *Weinsbergtalstrasse,* one of a row of identical three-story homes. Recently built of brick and stucco, they were considered modern, each house painted the same pale green except for an occasional flower box in a white-framed window. I loved our new water closet. You pulled on the chain, which I was strictly forbidden to play with, and the water released from a tank under the ceiling, flushing everything away. Helmut still had an outhouse.

Entering our flat, I tossed my cap in the corner and headed to the kitchen. "I'm hom—"

The words stuck in my throat because the table, set for five, was untouched, the room deserted. A sense of unease crept up inside me, quickly forgotten because of the delicious smell emanating from the cast-iron pot. I lifted the lid and let out a sigh: bean soup with ham and smoked sausage. I glanced at the clock, seven-thirty. No wonder I was starving.

We never ate later than six. Something was wrong.

Reluctantly, I turned away from the soup and tiptoed down the hallway. Voices came from my parents' bedroom.

Stopping at the threshold, I knocked. "*Vater?*"

"Come in."

I cracked open the door. "Are we going to eat?"

Mother sat hunched over on the bed, my father kneeling in front of her. I wanted to enter, but something in their expressions held me back.

My father straightened with effort. "I'm leaving tomorrow."

"What do you mean?" I looked back and forth between my parents.

"I've been drafted."

I stared at him as his words echoed through my head. "But you said they needed you in the factory. You said you had more work than you could handle, making those fancy swords for the officers."

"That's what I thought." My father's voice remained steady but his jaws were tight.

"Can't you tell them you're too busy?"

My father sighed and put an arm on my shoulder, his expression serious. Despite being short, he could carry a hundred kilo sack of grain as if it were a small child. He wasn't the hugging type, but tonight he held on to me.

"That's not how it works."

"Where will you go?"

"Don't know. Maybe to Scandinavia."

Wiping her eyes, Mother stood up. "Why don't you get your brothers and eat? We'll pack and be in soon. And take off those clothes."

During the night, despite being tired, I tossed and turned. I'd burned my tongue on the soup at dinner, and my stomach was making weird noises. By the sound of it, my older brother, Hans, wasn't sleeping either.

While the radio proclaimed victories daily, news of fallen soldiers had begun to arrive, and announcements appeared in the newspaper. A square black cross was printed above each obituary and Mother grumbled and shook her head, reading the names and ages of the dead. I envisioned my father stumbling blindly toward a sea of barbwire, his head and eyes wrapped in bandages, his arms stretched in front.

Time stood still in the early morning hours as I wondered if my father would return with limbs missing or not at all. I imagined the obituary in the paper: Artur Schmidt, died in battle. I considered asking Hans what he thought would happen, but before I could, a soft snore came from the other bed.

I turned on my back and stared into the darkness. The apartment was silent, but not the silence of peaceful sleep, rather an artificial stillness of cries muffled by pillows and of thoughts that whirled without end. I turned again, facing the wall, my last thought of my father waving to me with a rifle.

In the morning I awoke with a start. My brother's bed was a pile of sheets and blankets. Remembering last night, I sighed. Soft murmurs drifted in from the kitchen—my father's voice. I wanted to stay in bed and listen, and at the same time I wanted to be near him.

With a sigh, I jumped out of bed.

"Günter, you sleepy head." My father opened his arms. "Give me a hug."

I buried my face in the folds of my father's shirt. "Are you leaving now?" My father smelled of shaving soap, reminding me of his ritual, the razor, a single sharp blade, swiped back and forth across a leather strap to sharpen it further, the soft foamy soap and the thick brush made of badger hair, my father disappearing under a layer of white bubbles before taking the knife to scrape away the stubble.

"It's time."

Everybody crowded in. I sobbed, my throat tight and achy.

My father grabbed me and Hans by the arm. "You two need to take care of your mother and Siegfried."

I swallowed hard, the lump in my throat threatening to expand to my eyes. I knew that Hans was upset by the way his shoulders trembled. My baby brother, Siegfried, was only three and had no idea what was going on.

"I don't want to hear of any mischief. Do what you're told."

"Yes, *Vater*," I said. "When will you come back?"

"As soon as they let me."

"Promise?"

"I'll write." My father moved toward Mother. "I'll see you soon, Grete," he whispered.

Wiping his eyes with the back of his hand, he turned. For a moment he looked around the living room, the leather sofa, his favorite chair in the corner, the walnut table and matching sideboard.

A bright morning sun beamed into the room, throwing patterns on the wood. A starling trilled high of summer and new beginnings. With a final nod, my father hurried to the door—and was gone.

Mother dabbed her eyes where fresh tears kept arriving. "You heard what your father said. We better talk about your new responsibilities."

"Can't we do it after school?" My legs were heavy from lack of sleep.

Mother resolutely picked up pen and paper. "Who wants to help with laundry?"

"That's girl's work," Hans said. "Besides, I'm too old for that."

"Not me," I said.

"Enough." Mother smacked a fist on the table. And though she was a short woman and even at eleven I was taller than her, I bowed my head. "You heard what your father said. Günter, you'll help with laundry. Hans, you'll do the ovens. I also need someone to clean the hallway stairs and sweep the sidewalk." I tuned out.

Life was going to be one big chore.

End of Preview

Made in the USA
Monee, IL
02 November 2020